Bitterroot

BITTERROOT

—An American Epic—

Kent Gramm

RESOURCE *Publications* · Eugene, Oregon

BITTERROOT
An American Epic

Resource Publications
An Imprint of Wipf and Stock Publishers
199 W. 8th Ave., Suite 3
Eugene, OR 97401

www.wipfandstock.com

PAPERBACK ISBN: 978-1-6667-4782-9
HARDCOVER ISBN: 978-1-6667-4783-6
EBOOK ISBN: 978-1-6667-4784-3

VERSION NUMBER 102622

for Camelia

Contents

Preface: An American Epic

In 1877, seven hundred Nez Perce women, men, children, and their elderly led the United States Army and Cavalry on a thousand mile odyssey, fighting four major battles and numerous skirmishes. These American Indian people did not want war: they were a peaceful nation, who neither tortured nor scalped their enemies, and even nursed soldiers who fell within their lines. But at the core, this was a war of the quintessential American issue: race. It was also a conflict of cultures and religions. It involved soldiers who had fought in the Civil War; legendary figures like Calamity Jane and Yellowstone Kelly; and ordinary people like Joseph, Looking Glass, and White Necklace.

Every epic has a hero, and this hero was as formidable as Achilles, as resourceful as Penelope and Ulysses, as dutiful as Aeneas, as doomed as Hector, and as haunted as Evangeline. This hero could be as wise as Mentor or as impetuous as Hotspur, was young and old, "Half Man Half Woman," a warrior and a Dreamer. The hero of this story was the Nez Perce, *Nimiipuu*: "We The People."

This narrative reflects to some extent the language and notions current in 1877. It is therefore probable that some words and stereotypes will give offence; nevertheless, the intent throughout is to honor those who were caught up in the events of this American epic.

I

War

Looking Glass is dead. His body lies frozen on the bare ground, the mirror on his chest reflecting a gray Montana sky. Across the war chief's open eyes blow grains of dry October snow.

Many of the chiefs are dead. The old warrior Toohoolhoolzote has not been buried: his lined and weathered face beholds the Ghost Road; the body lies stiff and twisted. Ollokot, another leader in war, brother of the Dreamer chief Joseph—Thunder-Rising-To-Greater-Mountain-Heights—the fighting brother, is dead too, shot down by half a dozen soldiers. Now Joseph—*Hinmatooyalahtqit*—holds his rifle in a strong right hand. He stands in a hollow facing Two Moons, Red Elk, and other leaders of The People.

In front of them on higher ground, the remaining young braves watch and fire from dugout holes: careful, deadly, conserving their last ammunition. Across the gullied, draw-crossed ground, a semicircle of prone troopers of the Seventh Cavalry and all their infantry supports lays down a steady fire, a *crack crack* of carbines and Sharps rifles. Many soldiers are dead too, rows of them dragged to the rear, lying unburied.

In sight of them the One Arm General, Oliver Otis Howard, gnaws a hard crust of Army beef. He asks, "You think Joseph has had enough?"

Colonel Nelson Miles tells Howard, "For three days they've fought us with more desperation and more skill than I thought possible—before you arrived—threw back our charge—slaughtered my men like trained soldiers. They won't give up now until they've tried to rush us and break through."

"What? Rush us? Joseph has more sense. I know the man."

"We'll see," said Miles.

1

And back across the whitened scrap of high plains battlefield, Joseph speaks in a low voice, "Hear me, my chiefs!"

*

The way it's told in Stevensville, you see exactly how the war began. At first We The People—which is what the Nimiipuu call themselves—were a rumor, lots of rumors, coming through the Bitterroots at Lolo Pass, brought by travelers and whoever had heard one thing or another from some settler in Wallowa Valley across in Oregon and Idaho, the place the Nez Perce called home—how "the Indians" had balked at going on a reservation and killed a lot of innocent farmers, the numbers increasing with distance, told different ways depending on how badly the teller thought you'd scare. They had done murder, a few taking the choice out of the hands of the many.

It seems there's always two of everything. The Nez Perce divided in the days of Old Joseph, Joseph's father. As a younger man "Old" Joseph and many others had converted to Christianity. A Presbyterian missionary must have preached a powerful Gospel, or else a vivid fire and brimstone hell, or both; and these new Christians signed a treaty giving up the largest portions of their land. You have to understand that signing treaties meant two different things to Native People and whites in two respects. First, a mark on a sheet of paper kept by whites meant ownership to them, a concept neither understood nor credited by Native People, who saw the paper as a thing reminding whites of a word given—and the word not anything like ownership, but permission. You couldn't give away land like a knife because it wasn't yours to give. You belonged there; you can't give away where you belong. Or if you do, you're saying you no longer exist. Native Americans quicker on the up-take soon realized there were consequences to that paper—it always meant that whites moved in and stayed.

The second thing was that when white men signed promising something, like keeping off land that "Indians" hadn't given permission to settle, the whites broke the promise. So a treaty means you give away half your land and then white men take it all. Old Joseph caught on and wouldn't sign a second treaty, the one of 1863 that took ninety-five percent of all the rest of the Nimiipuu land.

Only the whites called them Nez Perce back then; it wasn't the Nation's name. Worse than that, it was French. And then still more, it was inaccurate. Few if any Nez Perce ever pierced their noses. Whites named Old Joseph, too, giving him a Bible name when he was baptized.

It should be remembered that the United States wanted a treaty in 1863 because of gold. The stuff had been discovered on Old Joseph's land—the chief was called "Old" Joseph because by then he had a son, Joseph, whom we know now simply as Chief Joseph. Gold means death—death to those who have it, death at the hands of those who want it. So Old Joseph, who was not a theologian, saw Christianity in practical terms. Christians crave gold, steal land, kill Indians, and sell whiskey. He concluded, on second thought, not to take the Christian heaven on speculation, given what the Christian earth was like. The spirit-land of his fathers was plenty good enough. And you could see the path to it, sparkling in the night sky; and the whites could never take that, no matter what kind of treaty Christians made up.

So Old Joseph and the other non-Christian Nez Perce became "Non-treaty Indians." When Old Joseph lay dying, he held his son's hand and asked him to promise—no treaty necessary, just his word—that he would never sell his father's grave. And Joseph was the best of sons: he never sold. It's almost wrong to call him Joseph, that son—all things considered—a white name from a Bible whose self-proclaimed representatives would pursue him and his people to grief. After the war, the reservation's doctor would report, "Chief Joseph has died of a broken heart." Died on the cold high desert Colville scrub, as different from his heartland—the green and steepled Wallowa Valley—as the moon is different from sweet, storied old Eden.

Young Joseph was tall and strong, and carried himself like a free man; he bore himself as if the word Dignity were about to be invented, and Nobility about to be defined. His real name meant something like Thunder Ascending To Ever Greater Mountain Heights—distant thunder rising in the mountains.

Two Civil War soldiers enter Nez Perce history at this point: General Oliver Otis Howard and Colonel John Gibbon—who was Otis Howard's better by a long shot, considered in strictly military terms. Some have said the same as far as character went, too; though as for that, there is another side to tell.

Howard was John Gibbon's superior, commissioned earlier. He graduated West Point a few years before Gibbon, and although the younger man caught up to Howard by the Civil War's end—both commanding a corps—Howard retained a general's rank after the great Grand Army of the Republic marched down Pennsylvania Avenue, peace won, the Rebels made to feel the rule of law, the Union of the States restored, slaves freed, Lincoln laid in a nation's grief to rest—and all the boys went home. Gibbon had made the Iron Brigade—the best fighting unit of the Civil War. He trained and commanded it with intelligence and courage, and governed his volunteers with fairness and respect. He rose to division command by Gettysburg; his division took the brunt of Pickett's Charge and shattered it.

If Gibbon's Iron Brigade was the Union's best brigade, Howard's Eleventh Corps was the Union's worst corps—perhaps no fault of theirs. Stonewall Jackson surprised those boys at Chancellorsville through Howard's negligence. He later blamed his soldiers. He was a teetotaler, and half his corps were beer-drinking German immigrants. They didn't get along. At Gettysburg his corps was ripped again—his fault again—but as is the way of this world, Howard was given the Congressional Medal of Honor for that battle—for leaving one of his brigades on Cemetery Hill, which turned out to be a very good place to have left reserves, seeing as his corps—misplaced, mishandled, and unled—would need a line to fall back on. He was sent with his disgraced Eleventh Corps out West—that is, to Tennessee, where U.S. Grant would make a decent soldier of the man.

"The Christian Soldier" he was called, not intended as a compliment. Some wondered if the contradiction in the term was meant as part of the insult. But probably the phrase meant he didn't swear or smoke or drink or dance or gamble, and he said "Thank you" when an orderly handed him his horse's reins. But somehow Stonewall Jackson, who had fit the same description except for "Thank you," did not receive that compliment. Perhaps the Yankee nation was an honest one and saw the rubbing terms for what they were. No matter how they sized him up, Howard kept the rank of general after the war, got appointed head of the Freedman's Bureau looking to the welfare of former slaves, and founded Howard University to give young Blacks somewhere to get themselves a higher education. Officers who served with him called him honorable, a gentleman in uniform; and significantly, Joseph considered him a friend. When Joseph later made that speech to Congress—"Let me be free," or some might put it, *Let my people go!*—who had brought him there? Howard. But who began that Nez Perce War—or who, some might say, set up the feelings for war, or failed to do his job—which was to talk the non-treaty bands onto the reserve?

The U.S. government had ordered Howard west to the Department of Washington, Oregon, and Idaho, instructing him to get the Indians under control. He called the chiefs together, and some hot young men came too—made hotter by Howard. "You've got to show them the rifle," Howard told his officers before the meeting. This was not the first meeting. Howard remembered a meeting in November when Joseph had taken charge. That would not happen again. Joseph had brought all the history then. Now Howard had enough history. Now was now. But Now is Now, and this is the history Joseph brought, November 1876, the hundredth year of American independence, year of the election swindle, year of Custer:

Before the memory they told of it, thousands of years as white men figure, The People lived along the salmon rivers, their houses made of mats and leaves and stone; they fished the silver streams of salmon once as heavy in the water as mayflies in the warming wind; filled baskets with hills of blackberries and sprinkled them on cakes of ground and pounded Camas Root. They shaped and strung tough bows of smooth horn to hunt deer in those hilly forests and bighorn sheep on mountains pushing up to the clouds. Only Shoshone people to the South would bring fighting. The People lived in peace with Cayuse, Umatilla, Salish, and Palouse, who shared the prairies and the woods with them. But then came white man's time, the early years of the 1700s: the first horses, brought by Shoshones who had walked the plains, and now The People herded them, bred them with the Palouse ponies, becoming rich in herds—bred the best horses, the spotted ponies, tough and beautiful—the strong, fast Appaloosa, spirited and quick, smart horses good for climbing hills, crossing streams, and moving through close-grown balsams and firs. The People took these horses and explored, found out for themselves that beyond the Bitterroots an endless sunny grassland flowed toward morning, and it was covered with buffalo— herds as far as you could see. They traded, robes for dried salmon, with the Absaroka—Crow—who showed them tipis of buffalo hide, travois of poles and skin, gave them meat of grass-fed bison. The Crow saw their horses. The spotted ponies would be good hunters, good buffalo hunters. And so The People began to travel almost yearly east for buffalo summers, sometimes living on the prairies the whole year, drying hides and meat, growing their strong ponies on good grass, learning war on horseback from the Crows' enemies—the Lakota, the Cheyenne—learning, but always returning to the green spruce.

And then in late summer, 1805, the first white men, starving, seven of them, weak, exhausted, helpless: the American Corps of Discovery, Lewis and Clark. The People welcomed them, fed them salmon, buffalo, cakes, and fruit. For three weeks the whites recovered their strength, taught English words to The People, together laughed, gave and received love, believed peace and promised peace from their hearts. (Seventy-two years later, shortly after this war, a son of William Clark died with the Nez Perce survivors transported to the punishing heat of Oklahoma Territory.) The explorers always spoke respectfully and affectionately of the Nez Perce, whose hasty name some French trappers had used for them; and The People remembered. For seventy-two years no whites were killed on Nez Perce land, though by then some thirty of The People had been killed by whites, an unknown number of women raped. But those first whites had come helplessly and The People took them in, revived them, built them canoes, and guided them half way to the Pacific Ocean; welcomed them when they came back through heading East, where they would write of numberless buffalo, game of all kinds, rivers running with salmon, hills and mountains rolling with beaver pelts, strange species, manageable savages, and the Ocean—an American dream. The People benefited, it appeared, as whites began to travel through the mountains on their way to settle Oregon: cotton and wool replacing native skins for clothes and blankets, steel knives and copper kettles, smooth saddles; and of course the rifle came. The early price was smallpox. European germs had decimated Native People on this continent: rivers of other nations died. Now came the Nez Perce's turn. One-third of them were killed in fifty years. Then the missionaries came. Christianity made two out of one—two peoples of The People, "not peace but a sword," the one true religion at last, several of them: Catholic, Presbyterian, with Baptists, Methodists, and more to come.

Old Joseph was the second to convert, a distinction he became less proud of with the passage of white man's time. Measles came, then gold, and before long eighteen thousand Americans were panning for nuggets, selling jeans and grub and liquor and women right there on Nez Perce land, and The People numbered only a few thousand by now. In 1863, white immigrants wanted a new treaty. At Fort Lapwai, Nez Perce chiefs met agents of the Government, who singled out a chief named Lawyer—fitly named, it proved—to speak for all The People. The Nez Perce never recognized the concept of one chief above of all the rest. Other chiefs held more authority than Lawyer, which was exactly why the whites chose him. Lawyer was a Christian, every bit as Christian as the agents were, and sold the Nez Perce land to them, reducing what the whites thought the Nez Perce owned to one-tenth. The Christian chiefs all signed; the rest walked out, Old Joseph among them. A catalogue of warriors left the meeting, who had been peacemakers: Old Joseph, Old Looking Glass, Big Thunder, Toohoolhoolzote, White Bird, Red Owl, Eagle From the Light. Their five bands were called "Nontreaty." Old Joseph ripped his copy of the "thief treaty" into scrap, and for good measure he did the same to his white man's Bible. A few years later, a Dreamer again, he died.

The Dreamers followed the old ways but with the differences that, while like the Christians they awaited a Spirit-restored salvation, it would be a kingdom without a king, white soldiers gone, things as they used to be. Two dreamers with two dreams, the Nez Perce and the European, and one Mother Earth who loved them both torn between them. Young Joseph, who had been baptized as an infant, made his filial promise, Dreamer to

Dreamer, but saw no visions or illusions. Joseph would lead The People in all things but war; his brother Ollokot would lead in war.

Now U.S. Grant, Howard's old commander, was President of the United States—"The Great White Chief," the agents said in redskin baby talk. Grant understood that The People held to no concept of majority: those who did not sign the Lawyer treaty did not feel bound to honor it. They walked away; no vote committed them. The treaty was not of those people, by those people, for those people, so Grant signed an order protecting half the earlier reserve. Half was better than a tenth. But two years later the President rescinded the order. The pressures were too great now. European Americans also brought a history: poverty, religious wars, Napoleon, despots, crowding, failed democratic revolutions, a sick Old World to get as far away from as they could. Four million spindly children breathing Eastern coal smoke could grow up out West. The Nez Perce must move, about a thousand of them. And so General Howard was sent to read them the law. The law was power; the law was theirs who wielded it. A dream that is no use must perish from the earth.

In that same year a white man named Larry Ott killed Eagle Robe, a Nez Perce man, or so the Nez Perce said—though Ott denied the charge and was acquitted by a white jury. A man named Benedict killed another Nez Perce, and now The People were angry. But Joseph knew the meaning of revenge: it meant the whites would send soldiers in. The young men grumbled, saying, "Let them come." Then Howard called his meeting of the chiefs. Joseph, Rising Thunder, was thirty-six that November. Witnesses wrote of him, "A man in his full vigor, six feet tall, well formed and muscular, his forehead broad, his face is handsome and his musical voice is full of sympathy. His expression is calm and sedate, but when moved he is magnetic. He is alert and argues with dexterity and intellectual force." Howard read Lawyer's treaty and said that it would be enforced—on all of them.

"When this treaty was made we divided. The treaty was the cause of it. From that time we have been separated. We still remain so. The treaty is not ours." Joseph looked calmly at his chiefs and the officers. "The treaty was not signed by our chiefs, but by a man called Lawyer. We do not accept his authority. It is a treaty of men who have no authority over us." He addressed Howard. "Lawyer could not sell General Howard's house; he could not sell our land."

Howard said, "I have my orders. They are to enforce that treaty. I am a soldier and I must obey my orders."

"I am a free man," said Rising Thunder, "and I speak as one free man to another." Howard became silent. Joseph continued, "The land I have so great affection for I will not sell. If I did, where would I be? I do not sell my wife or my children. A free man does not sell anything he loves. Are Americans free? Do Americans sell their wives or their children, or their land? Are you and I the same?"

Howard cleared his throat. "Land is not everything. Land is not wives and children. The land is not your life."

"You do not know the land or yourself. The Earth and my body are the same. The Earth and myself are of one mind."

"All this land is just as much ours as yours."

"And no more."

"This discussion is of no consequence. I have my orders and you have yours."

"If I thought that you were sent by the Creator, then I might think you have the right to order me or to dispose of me. Do not misunderstand me, but understand fully when I speak of my affection for the land. I never said the land was mine to do with as I choose. The One who has the right of it is the One who has created it. Only that One can dispose of the land—not I, not you. I claim the right to live upon the land where I was placed, and I accord to you the right to live upon the land where you were placed. I grew up here. I look upon this land with great pleasure: it was finished with great beauty, and nothing can improve it. It is clothed with fruitfulness. In it are riches given to me by my ancestors. I have always loved this land, and I am thankful that it was given to me."

"Thankful to whom? Thankful to what?" Joseph would not answer Howard's question, so Howard spoke again: "I will use force if I must."

Here Joseph looked hard but calmly into Howard's eyes. "We are not to be trampled upon. Do not trample upon us, or try to take our rights from us. Right to this land was ours before the whites came."

"Well, we are here now."

"Yes, but so are we."

Howard glared at Joseph but said quietly, "I hope we can resolve the Ott matter. Perhaps a resolution could be useful."

"Do you expect to trade? Do you think we will sell our land if the white murderers are punished?"

"Peace is better than war."

"Yes, peace is better than war."

"I wish to show good faith; I wish to create good feelings."

"Our young men are angry for war."

"I know."

"What will you do?"

"I will bring the accused to court."

"A white man's court? We understand white justice."

"And what is your justice? I understand the red man's justice. I know what you would do."

"You are wrong. I have thought long and conclude to let the guilty man escape, let him enjoy good health, and not to take a life for the one he took. I want no payment for the deed he committed. I pronounce this sentence: he should live. I spoke to him. I told him that I have great affection for the land where he shed one of my people's blood. I saw that all the settlers took his part. I told them that there is no law, white or Indian, in favor of murder. We have seen one of our bodies lying dead on the land. We cannot leave this land."

"So we are back to that. Joseph, I commend your mercy. It is a Christian act. But you are dreaming empty dreams if you believe that you will not have to leave. The sole issue now is peace or war. I shall give to you the one you choose."

Others spoke, but Howard had determined to close the conference and leave it to the chiefs to understand they had no choice. In his report, Howard wrote "pernicious doctrines" of the Dreamers encouraged the Nez Perce still to believe that they could hold their land. He proposed if worse should come to worst, nontreaty leaders be put under arrest and sent away to Indian Country; that is, Oklahoma. "I will give them until April."

Chief Toohoolhoolzote, one of the old men, steel hair, deep voice, stubborn, tried to tell Howard that there was no sense to an Indian signing away land—no one owned the land—and that ancestral land was sacred to them. But the General wouldn't be lectured: "Enough of this! You have said again and again the Earth is your mother, the Earth is your mother. I have heard enough that the Earth is your mother. Let us get to practicalities!"

At the Nez Perce campfires, some young men who had silently listened to Howard now spoke. "The whites think they can speak to us however they please. And they told the son of Eagle Robe that nothing would be done."

*

Shore Crossing had been a tall, good-looking boy of fourteen summers when he gave his word to White Necklace. His father, Eagle Robe, had staked out land along the Salmon River many years ago—the River gave the boy his name—and now the family cultivated there the dark fertile soil along the stream and hunted game in stands of shimmering birch that grew around the meadows. White Necklace, daughter of a man in White Bird's band called Bowstring—she was the older daughter, the beautiful one, whose mother loved therefore to adorn her with her own jewelry—she had given her word to the older boy, older by one summer; and when The People traveled to buffalo country, the two young ones would be together riding, talking, walking, whenever they could.

They loved the Place of Ground Squirrels—or the Big Hole—where The People camped after crossing the mountains. Everyone was always happy when they spent the days there, singing and dancing at night, grazing their winter-worn horses on the thick grass that grew beside the stream. Summer was beginning, The People had time and leisure with their friends; families would raise their tepees next to families they loved and hadn't seen since last summer or the year before. Then after the hunts far out across the running prairie grass, The People returned to Big Hole, raising racks of dried buffalo meat and scraping thick, new robes and supple hides. The Big Hole was beautiful, the hollow of Mother's hand, ranges on three sides, and in the spring you could still see snow on the high peaks. In August, days could be very warm, but cool air came from the mountains, and across the creek dense pines along the hillsides made a clean aroma. Though no-one lives who could know for certain, it was said that here Shore Crossing and White Necklace married in his eighteenth year.

The young man was a warrior now; he meant to be as great as his father-in-law. He had ridden with the Crow men against a Cheyenne raiding party, had counted coup in the way of the Lakota; but home along the Salmon he was smart at farming with his father, would make good in providing for his beautiful White Necklace and the children they would have together.

Early in the previous winter, the man who called himself Ott, Larry Ott, a prospector fifty years of age, had come to Eagle Robe asking for a place to set his winter camp. He wanted running water, a place to fish, some cottonwoods to lash together for a lean-to, a few old birches for firewood. In the Nez Perce way, Eagle Robe welcomed him and sent him Camas Root that his wife had shaped into cakes, dried fish, and meat—good winter provisions for a miner on his own.

This autumn Ott returned, re-occupied his lean-to, making it more sturdy with young birches, walling it around like a one-room house, and in the early summer he came to Eagle Robe, asking for a small plot of ground to make a little garden for himself. Eagle Robe had nodded him permission but when he told his son the young man grew hard-eyed and silent. He began to walk away but turned in quiet rage. "You should not have let him have the land, Father!"

"He does no harm, Son. And he is alone among all The People in this valley. All of us have more land than we need along the river; no family is jealous or in need. The Great Spirit has given everything to us. We are not like white people; I will not act toward him like a white man. Maybe this Ott will learn our ways." But Shore Crossing glared quietly. "My Son, it troubles me that you do not show our People's heart. You have not been so in the past." Shore Crossing nodded to his father but would not speak.

In the spring before, the first warm days, the young husband and wife had walked far from the river into the trees. Larry Ott had come upon them in the birches. He was carrying his pistol in his belt, a knife, and a hunting carbine. He watched a moment until White Necklace saw him and screamed; Shore Crossing jumped up facing Ott but the white man's carbine pointed at the woman. "You back away," Ott said grinning. "Farther." He dropped the gun and pulled his pistol. "Wasn't loaded, just in case you got ideas." Leveling his pistol at White Necklace, he unhitched his belt, and kept the pistol held against her head, looking at Shore Crossing while he did it.

Afterward, still leveling the pistol, he said to the stone-faced young man, "You made the right decision, young fella. A little pleasure for a lonesome old man ain't worth your life and hers. I know you won't come and get me later. That ain't the Nez Perce way. Anyhow, kill a white man and the U.S. Army takes it all."

When The People returned that autumn, Ott came again to Eagle Robe, requesting a little land to fence off for an orchard and a vineyard. This time the son stood by, and broke in saying, "No." Eagle Robe was outraged that his son had interrupted his elder, but would not show this feeling to the white man. He said nothing. Again his son said, "No." Ott nodded, smiled and left. The young man cried to his wife that night, "Whose child will it be?" and she answered, "No child will come to birth." It was five winters before she would be ready again for a child.

That next summer The People did not travel across the mountains to Crow country, and one high-sun day Eagle Robe heard axe head on wood along the river. He set out on foot, unarmed, and found Ott hitching his horse to a sled he had piled with rails. "You have no permission to cut my trees for rails!" Eagle Robe said loudly. "You may take the firewood that you need, but no more."

Ott later said the old Indian stood in his way and even shook his thin blanket in the horse's face. "What would you have done?" Ott asked the men called by a judge to look into the miner's confession. They found no cause for trial.

Eagle Robe's wife heard the gunshots and ran to find her son. She told him why his father had gone into the woods. He cried the mourning wail, and when he went, he brought his wife. Eagle Robe lay dying of a gunshot to the chest. The old green shirt he wore was soaked dark with his blood. His mouth dripped blood when White Necklace lifted his head. Shore Crossing wiped his father's mouth with cloth ripped from the bottom of his shirt. Eagle Robe looked at his son while his head was held steadily and gently in the loving daughter's hands. "I know you, my son. I know you act with your heart. Think of my daughter, your wife, who holds me now. Think of your own spirit!" His words came with coughed blood. "Do not bother this white man for what he has done to me! Let him live his life!" Eagle Robe gasped for breath but his son said nothing through the hot tears that streaked his face.

So the young woman pleaded fiercely, eyes on Shore Crossing: "He will do as you say, Father! He will not harm the white man." The fire in her eyes told Shore Crossing, "I will do it for you."

Calming himself, the young man laid a hand against Eagle Robe's face, then looked at White Necklace and his eyes told her "No."

"See them!" cried the old man weakly. "My old friends come for me! They are here! You must see them! There stands Crow Blanket, and Curlew, and Sun Faded." He closed his eyes. "They have come to take me to the Beautiful Place."

Nothing was done. They went to Joseph, and Joseph rose up and went to the settlement, and he went to the soldiers. All the Nez Perce people heard of it, and the whites. But nothing was done. The civil authorities had not seen fit to bring Ott to trial, an officer at Lapwai told Joseph. "This murder brings shame upon all my people, shame to all the warriors. This murder brings hatred. All we ask of you is justice."

"I hope," answered the officer, "that you will control your young men."

"It is more to be hoped," retorted Joseph, "that you will control your old men!" For his insolent behavior, as it was reported, Joseph was now looked upon by the settlers and Army as a troublemaker. As for Ott, he left his little claim on the Salmon River and opened up another claim much closer to the settlement. Later, he wrote his adventures. Did he really say to Shore Crossing, "You made the right decision"? "Hell, yes I did, and meant it, too. I commended him. The Nez Perce were good Indians. That squaw was the best Indian I ever had."

*

The Commission of November produced a report December 1, '76. General Howard had had some time to think about the way Joseph had dominated him. He told an Army doctor's wife, "It is my usual manner, rising from the kindest motives, and from my wish to behave as a gentleman even to the weakest and the most ignorant human being." Or in Ollokot's words, "They treat us like dogs."

Howard's Commission wrote, "For in the interest of the Indian, to change his habits of life and render him speedily self-supporting, there is required patient, constant perseverance to instruct him, correct him, reprove him. They are grown-up children." The Nez Perce read the Commission's report. "You have no right to compare us, grown men, to children," said Toohoohoolzote. "Children do not think for themselves. Grown men do think for themselves. The government at Washington cannot think for us. It is you who take orders."

He said this when the new Commission met in May. An Army doctor's wife, young Emily Fitzgerald, watched the massive tent go up on the parade ground of the fort. She wrote, "About a hundred Indians squat in and all around the tent, dressed in the most gorgeous get-ups you can imagine. The General and his aides and officers, the Indian agent too, are in the tent with them, outnumbered ten to one. Outside, the gathering is ringed with crowds of squaws and papooses."

Toohoohoolzote, the old chief, told Howard, "I have heard about a bargain, a trade between some Indians and the white men concerning land, but I belong to the land out of which I came. The Earth is my mother."

Howard, there to show the gun this time, not get lectured by the chiefs, stopped Toohoohoolzote, saying, "Twenty times now I have heard that the Earth is your mother. I do not want to hear this any more. I don't want to offend your religion, but you must now talk of practical things. We shall come to business at once!"

Chief Joseph had stood silently while his elder spoke. Now he asked Howard, "What is our business, General Howard?"

"Whether you'll come onto the reservation yourselves or whether I shall force you there."

"I am a chief!" Toohoohoolzote barked. "Who can tell me what to do in my country?"

"I am that man!" Howard rose from his chair shouting. "You will come to the reservation or my soldiers will put you there, or shoot you down!"

Chief Toohoohoolzote shouted back, pointing at the one-armed general, "I am a man! I will not go! I will not leave my own land, the land where I grew up!"

Howard calmed and quieted his voice. "Then you do not propose to comply with my orders?"

"So long as Earth helps me. I want to be left alone. You are making small the law of the Earth."

Howard smiled pleasantly. "Our old friend does not seem to understand that the only question here is, Will you come peaceably onto the reservation, or do you want to be put there by force?"

"I never gave the chiefs authority to sell away my lands! Let others do what they like, but I will not leave my land."

Howard called a soldier up, and pointing to the old chief said, "Take him to the guardhouse." All the sitting Indians arose but Joseph waved them still.

"General Howard, we will speak no further now."

Howard showed no fear, and said, "It is agreed. We shall speak again tomorrow—without angry words." But Howard wrote of Toohoohoolzote, he was a "thicknecked, obstinate, and ugly savage of the worst type;" or as a witness by the name of Bow and Arrow Case phrased it, "Chief Toohoohoolzote was arrested for speaking his mind."

The old chief was held in the guardhouse for eight days, the duration of the Council. "I have been to many councils," Joseph said, "and am none the wiser." Now Howard had to deal with Joseph. He listened to the other chiefs one at a time. He promised education, settled farms and independence from the government, at last suggesting churches and becoming full Americans. And somehow Joseph sized him up. "Tell General Howard I know his heart," Joseph would say the last long day of the war—but what was Howard's heart? Joseph said that he declined the offer of churches. To Howard's now stony face he explained, "Churches bring fighting." The General returned to practicalities, the question "our old friend" had failed to comprehend.

"Will you go peacefully or not? I have seen much war and I would rather have peace between your people and my soldiers, but I stand for the President of the United States and do his will. I have my orders. There is no spirit, good or bad, that will hinder me."

(A few days ago White Bird had begun to rise and go to the parade grounds of the fort before the bugler sounded reveille. The soldiers coming out, sleep in their eyes, would see the old chief standing like a ghost in the muted silver of the early dawn, wrapped in his blanket, motionless, watching as they formed their line for roll call, snapped to attention; watched them march in unison, evolve from line of battle into column; he watched them drill by company and squad. He heard the orders, saw them crisply bring their rifles to right shoulder shift, ground arms, present arms. One afternoon he challenged officers to a friendly horse race, old man on his old pony against the proud young men riding the strongest, best trained horses the U.S. Army and Cavalry could bring to the field. He found not one of them could match his Appaloosa running, doubling back, pivoting, turning, lasting; nor could the young men hold their seats as well as he, the old buffalo hunter. A strange old Indian, amusing.)

"You have your choice," said Howard, but Joseph answered,

"There is no choice."

"Your people will comply? All the Nez Perce will move to their reservation in peace?"

"I know you wish peace, and I know your terms for peace. My people will all be killed if we fight your soldiers. There is no end to the soldiers, but we are few now. We do not wish to leave our land, but I will not have my people dead upon the land. We have spoken, with sad hearts. Looking Glass and White Bird and the chiefs have all spoken. We will do as you ask."

The next day Howard and his soldiers rode with Joseph, White Bird, and Looking Glass up the Lapwai Valley to the Reservation. The treaty Nez Perce farms were small and neat and fenced, but no good land remained. The following day they rode up Clearwater Valley, where Joseph and the nontreaty People were to farm. "Here," said Howard to the chiefs, "you will have real houses."

Looking Glass said he was glad for peace, and Joseph said that he would build a good frame house. The three chiefs looked straight ahead and rode slowly to the fort. By now three hundred infantry and cavalry from Fort Lewiston had arrived to back up Howard's force, and on the 15th Howard concluded the Council. He gave his final order: "Be on the reservation thirty days from now."

Startled, Joseph could not find words at first, then bluntly objected, "We cannot move in thirty days!"

"You shall."

"Our large herds are up the canyons and our cattle are scattered on grazing land from here to the mountains. The rivers are full and strong at this time of year and we cannot cross with our herds. Let us wait until fall, when the Snake River will run low. We need time to hunt our stock and gather in supplies for winter."

"Here is your answer. I will tolerate no more delays. If you let the time run over one day, I shall conclude you want to fight, and I shall send soldiers to drive you here. All your cattle and your horses will fall to white men. You have my final order."

*

As June began, The People came together near the ancient lake now called Lolo Lake, surrounded by the sacred grounds called Split Rocks—all five nontreaty bands: Joseph's band, the Wallowas, led by Ollokot in war and Joseph in peace; White Bird's band, the old war chief a man who knew his war; the band of Looking Glass, a man of middle age whose name had been his father's among the whites–Flint Necklace to The People–known for his ability in war, all too well known among Shoshoni enemies; the old chief Toohoolhoolzote, who had been released by Howard from the fort's guard house; and fifth, a small group of Palouse, cousins of the Nez Perce, led by Husis Kute. One hundred warriors, just as many men too old for war, four hundred women, and the children of the bands. The other war chiefs of the bands—White Bull, Red Elk—and the young men of The People all rode the stony circle around the camps—a ceremony played before the older chiefs, the women, children, old men—rode a grand procession around the outside boundary wearing beaded buckskin from the big plains and boasting, one and all, of what they did to Shoshoni invaders—drawing blood with hatchet or knife, or counting coup in the Lakota way: being brave enough to strike a live enemy with the coup stick, even though the Nez Perce's short horn bows were powerful and made for shooting from a turning horse. The Nez Perce took no scalps, but they did wear the paint of southern tribes and raised the yipping war cry of the Cheyenne. Whites said it sounded like the Rebel Yell they'd heard during the War except more clipped and rapid, a one-note staccato, not quite the rising Southern banshee wail, but like the Yell in the corkscrew effect it made up soldiers' spines. These warriors praised themselves as if without their words, their deeds would die away across the reservation's line and not exist in that new small world of little farms where there could be no war forever—preserving war in stories, in memory, where names like Many Coups and Left-Hand Knife could still mean something. The young brave Shore Crossing and his friends rode the circle boasting until an old man called Red Grizzly Bear shouted up to them as they passed beside: "Who said that these could ride and speak of war, these women-men whose fathers have been killed by whites and lie together in their graves? Are sons too cowardly to take revenge permitted now to ride with braves?"

That evening, standing apart from women, children, and the aged, chiefs and warriors asked if this must be the last time they would talk as free men. Would they never draw paint across their faces again, would the children of their children never sing the war chant, and would there be no more buffalo hide except what the white trader sold to them? What of the long sky in buffalo country, where you could see the Ghost Road all the way from sun falling to sun rising—had they seen it for the last time?

"We will see it when we set our moccasins upon it, and turn our horses' heads to the Spirit Land," said Joseph staring at sparks rising from the last campfire.

"I am not an old man," shouted Shore Crossing.

Then Ollokot, Joseph's brother, turned on Shore Crossing. "You breathe fire to the white man but you buy his fire water! We are not old men either."

"Like old men, you do nothing!"

Ollokot pointed to the tipis. "You have a wife. You should not be foolish like the single young men."

"We are all wives!" shouted the young man.

Toohoohoolzote, still a powerful chieftain at his age, struck Shore Crossing hard enough to send the unsteady warrior onto his back. "You reek of white man's liquor! Go home and sleep!"

Shore Crossing's friends walked beside him from the fire into crowds of women watching and out into the night that lay around the camp like days unseen. One said to him, "Ha! Shore Crossing, ha! Now we will call you Hard Struck!"

"Or No Revenge," said another.

Shore Crossing's cousin, Red Moccasin Tops, said quietly, "They laugh at our family."

"No-one will laugh tomorrow," said Shore Crossing.

At the fire, Joseph looked at his brother and his chiefs. Their faces shone orange and grave. "My chiefs, my brothers, we are the last of The People. The People always were free—free under these lights of the sky, free on our land, free wherever we chose to go. This is the fire of our people."

"It might be good to die fighting," said White Bird.

"Better than to live as the dead on the Americans' reservation," said Ollokot.

"It is shame not to live as men," said White Bird.

"It is never good to die," said Joseph, "unless you are old and have no family. For myself, death is all right. I have seen the spirit world. Our fathers and our mothers are waiting for us. But how would my wife and children live? Who would feed them? Who would teach them? Only the white man. He would teach them his religion."

"No chief is for war," said Toohoohoolzote. "Only the young men. They know nothing."

"What will your young men do?" Looking Glass asked quietly. "Can you control your young men?"

"As well as I can control the wind and the fire."

"Let them go and die," said White Bird. "Better than to become old men like us next month. Let them go and be killed."

"No!" said Looking Glass. "They would not die alone. If they find trouble, the whites will send their stinking soldiers to kill us all."

"My young men are not murderers," White Bird answered. "There will be no trouble tonight."

Shore Crossing stood over his wife, reaching for his rifle. "You understand," he said.

"I understand!" she retorted. "You have hated yourself enough. But you have drunk too much. You will be killed!" She stood and said angrily, "Our child will have no father!" The husband placed one hand on her stomach, holding the rifle with the other. "I hardly feel a child. But if he is a boy, let him know the father who blessed him was a man. And if she is a girl, let her know her father loved her as he loved you, with all my life. I would not have you bound to shame, to a husband who was no man."

"Why didn't you go before the child came? Why?"

"You know. We would have been the last."

"We are the last."

He let the rifle fall and bent to hold her close; he pressed her face against his. "You see, I am not so drunk that I do not know who I love, or that I do not know what I must do."

"I will ride along with you, and hold your horses."

"My young cousin Swan Necklace will hold them."

"That is no name for a warrior, a man!"

"He will earn a better one."

"I will come!"

"The child!" He laid his hand on her again and said, "Our only child."

Joseph looked up at the great figures in the sky. The high swath of the Ghost Road sparkled and ran far behind the mountains. He drew a deep breath, inhaling the last smoke of the orange embers. "This is the last night of peace, too. On the reservation it will not be peace, only stillness, and nothing to do."

"We will become Americans," said Looking Glass.

"When stars become Americans, then I will become an American."

"The stars are white, Joseph," said Looking Glass.

"A few are red. There is room for them, too, in the sky."

"But not in America," said White Bird. "Soon enough the whites will find a reason to kill us all."

"Then let them," said Looking Glass. "Let them kill me in my good house made of wood painted white. Let them. Another dead, drunken Indian."

"I will kill the man who kills you," Red Elk said.

"If you are still alive to do it."

"I am tired," said Joseph. "If staying on my feet could change tomorrow, I would stay. Let the young men stay out; let the old men find their warm buffalo hides and lie down."

While riding toward the Salmon settlements, Red Moccasin Tops repeated with rising rage what Yellow Wolf, a brave twenty-one summers old, had witnessed at Howard's peace council. "Yellow Wolf tells no lies. The old men trust him because he is against fighting white soldiers. He was with them in the tent. He heard, himself, and he saw with his own eyes: the one-armed soldier, Howard, showed the rifle, talking war at a council of peace! We show him now what happens when white men show us the rifle at peace councils!"

Shore Crossing rode without speaking, his wife in his eyes.

"You do not want to turn back?" Red Mocassin Tops asked. "You think of your home."

"I do not want to turn back. You have drunk too much."

The boy, Swan Necklace, riding behind the two, touched heels into his trotting horse. "Howard put old Toohoolzote in jail!"

Smiling grandly, Shore Crossing said, "You also drink too much before hard work. His name is Toohoohoolzote."

"What kind of name is that? It means nothing!"

"Like white men's names," Shore Crossing said. "Ott. What does Ott mean?"

"Howard. What does Howard mean?" asked the other man, "Nothing! White men's names mean nothing! They are nothing!"

"It will not be like killing an Indian, Shoshoni or Cheyenne."

"Have you killed white men?" Swan Necklace asked.

"Many," Shore Crossing answered, looking at Red Moccasin Tops.

"A hundred," said the other.

"I am no fool! You have never killed a white man. No Nez Perce has killed a white man. I know what killing this white man will bring. War comes now."

"We are fighting war already," said Shore Crossing. "It is a war where white men kill and red men die. It is a war where white men take and Indian People give. Now both sides will fight. We will see how the whites like it!"

"What will Joseph say! All the chiefs say No war."

"The chiefs are old men," said Red Moccasin Tops.

"We always do what the chiefs say!" said Swan Necklace. "The chiefs decide for all The People."

"You are a good Indian, brother—boy brother."

"We decide," said Shore Crossing. "Old men are more weak than wise. We decide, no matter what the old men say."

"I have heard that Joseph loves white people," Swan Necklace said.

Shore Crossing reached to grip the boy's bare arm. "Who says that? Who?"

"I heard it. Boys were talking."

"Boys know nothing."

"Boys know nothing, old men know nothing. Only you two know!"

"After tonight," his brother said, "you will be a young warrior too. You will understand."

"Rising Thunder does not love the whites, and he does not hate the whites. He loves our people and our land. Tonight we force him to do what is in his heart. The whites will see justice tonight, and we will all die before following white men's orders. We show them the rifle!"

But Ott's new house farther down the Salmon was dark, his saddle horse was gone, and no stock stood watching in his pen. No dog barked warning. Shore Crossing raised the latch and kicked the door, and all three Nez Perce stood in the white man's house. Shore Crossing tore the curtain away from the window, then raised his rifle butt and stove it through the glass. Red Moccasin saw plates and glasses standing on a shelf and swept them down with his rifle barrel. Swan Necklace threw the pieces around. Then Shore Crossing saw the full glass lantern on the table. "Find his fire! His matches!" The boy looked to the mantel on the ashy hearth—a box of long matches rested there. "Go out," said Shore Crossing. "Get out of here!" He threw the chimney from the lantern, lighted the wick, bent down to touch the fallen curtain, then threw the lantern at the stack of firewood in the corner. It boiled into flames and the man picked up his rifle and walked outside. "This is not all!" shouted Shore Crossing. "This was not the only white thief and murderer!" They ran to the horses tied up at the corral fence.

"The trader," said Red Moccasin, as flames grew inside the broken window.

Farther up the Salmon, above the farms and ranches planted close beside the water, William Collins had built his general store. His quickest money came from selling whiskey to the Native Americans who rode out from the reservation, but as if his profits weren't enough without a little extra made from enterprise, he watered down the hootch he sold to them. "You make them laughing drunk and it don't matter what cheap bellywash they're pouring down their thirsty gullets." When squaws came in for flour or calico he never gave them change. "Gratuities" he called the dirty money, his fee for talking pidgin Indian. He'd shot a crippled Nez Perce who came begging—"He was a thief," he told the white jury. "I caught him skulking around behind the store one time too often." It had happened seven years ago: what began this night was a war of memory. The three braves rode in the starry night, the constellations as fixed and unresisted as the warriors' rage, revolving slowly in the ancient sky above, lighting them along the muted silver river.

A man with the promising name of Samuel Benedict farmed above the river east of Billy Collins's store, but he never had a good thing to say about or to the Nez Perce—called them lazy savages and heathens. He had once accosted unsuccessfully a young Nez Perce woman named Hears Children, betrothed to the young man who rode beside Shore Crossing now.

They found Benedict sleeping in his barn, his house dark to fool them because the settlers were more suspicious than the Army of the Nez Perce gathering at Lolo Lake. Red Moccasin Tops went into the barn looking for horses and found Benedict camped out on straw and blankets. The man rose slowly, reaching for his revolver, but the brave was on him with his knife. "Come in and look!" he shouted, and the other two came in. Swan Necklace looked down at the white man lying open-eyed, his chest and throat all blood.

"What is that smell?"

His brother answered, "White man's blood."

The boy doubled over and vomited. "It stinks," said Shore Crossing; "but it is good. We must have more!" The Nez Perce say the smell of fresh blood turns wrath into crazyness.

The neighboring farm was worked by a man the Nez Perce knew as Speaks Bad Language, a German by the name of Juergen Elfers. He had a wife, a baby, and two boys. The woman always acted terrified when in the settlement she saw a male Indian, no matter what age. Tonight, as the three Nez Perce rode toward his big barn on their way east, Elfers saw them from his doorway. He went inside to fetch his wife and two men sleeping there tonight, Robert Bland and Henry Beckrodge, neighbors who'd come to stay awhile and help the frightened Germans protect themselves in case of an outbreak. They got up and walked out in their long johns holding carbines to make a show of force.

"They show us the rifle," muttered Shore Crossing, diverting his horse from the river trail toward the house, and the other two followed.

"We have rifle!" shouted one of the farmers, and seconds later the German fired his, the bullet shot straight up at the stars. All three men leveled their guns at the braves, but Red Moccasin Tops leaped from his horse, stood with his rifle steadied on a corral post and fired. One of the men in pale long johns slammed back against the house and pitched forward as the other two got off shots that buzzed high over Shore Crossing's head. He aimed his rifle from horseback and put his bullet into the German's stomach. The other man hesitated, as if wanting to run inside the house, and the second bullet from Red Moccasin found his head. No sound came from inside, no screams—but Swan Necklace saw two boys in nightshirts running, stumbling, from behind the house toward the trees.

"Two boys!" Swan Necklace shouted, pointing.

The two men looked and saw them, but Shore Crossing jumped down from his horse. "Hold our ponies!" Shore Crossing and his cousin walked to the three shot men and stood a minute looking down at them. Red Moccasin Tops knelt over Elfers and pulled a big revolver from the German's belt. He stood and cocked it, aiming at the gut-shot man in bloody long johns writhing on the ground—fired the gun and missed, again aimed the big pistol and shot again, hitting the man. Even where he stood holding all three horses' leads, Swan Necklace smelled the blood. He heard a baby's cry quickly muffled inside the house. Red Moccasin Tops stood a moment looking into the doorway, then handed the revolver to his cousin.

When he came back out a little later, Swan Necklace cried, "What did you do?"

His brother smiled, "Brother, I did not kill a baby. I did not touch the woman. She is well. Let us drag the dead bodies to the river and throw them in."

"No." said Shore Crossing. "Not now. Too many shots. Let's take their horses and hurry!"

The two men ran to the corral, picked up bridles hanging on the posts, and led out three horses. "Mount the fresh ones!" Shore Crossing shouted. The three leaped up, holding their own ponies' leads, and kicked the horses to a gallop. In a few moments they topped a hill overlooking the store and farm of William Collins.

The man himself was running, leading a horse toward the corral. He dropped the reins when he saw the three braves riding down from the hill, and dashed toward his house. Shouting a war whoop, Shore Crossing urged his horse and raised his rifle, firing at full run. Collins spun, sprawled to the ground crying out, and just then four rifles opened up from the store windows. Another two shots were fired from windows in the house, and Red Moccasin Tops' horse went down. The brave rolled, throwing his rifle, and was up running to Swan Necklace. "Give me this horse and ride your own to camp! Get the young men. Tell them we have killed white men!"

More shots cracked from the buildings. Shore Crossing had turned his horse and all three now rode hard for the woods. Shore Crossing shouted to Swan Necklace, "Tell the old men that we have war!"

Joseph and his brother Ollokot had gone with Wetatonmi, Ollokot's wife; Joseph's older daughter, Sound of Running Feet; Half Moon; and Welweyas, who was called Half Man Half Woman—to butcher beef to dry and take with them to the reservation. Joseph's wife was soon to give birth, so stayed in camp on Camus Prairie near Lolo Lake with the five bands, only a day's journey from where Howard had ordered them to go. Butchering done, Joseph's small party started for the camp with twelve pack horses loaded with all their hasty beef. Nearing camp, they saw a rider coming on a streaming run, and Welweyas, who felt things about to happen, cried out, "It is the Army riding fast on hooves of death!" The brothers with two minds as one kicked up their horses, riding out ahead to meet the story that could have only one end.

Ollokot shouted, "Welweyas is never mistaken!"

Joseph rode grim-faced. They saw it was Two Moons, a man of Joseph's band who had not agreed with the angry young men. He pulled up his horse and shouted, "War has started! Three young men mad for fighting killed white men!"

"Who are they?" Ollokot asked sharply. "Whose band?"

"It doesn't matter now," said Joseph. "I know that they were not our men."

"I want to know."

"The three are White Bird's men."

Joseph said again, "It doesn't matter now."

"Maybe it does," said Ollokot. "When did it happen?"

"Three days ago."

"It is probably too late," said Joseph, "but I will talk to Howard."

"Can you do it?" Ollokot asked.

"They are criminals. It is either those three who will die at the white man's hands, or all The People. There is no choice."

"I will go with you," said Ollokot.

"No brother; the soldiers hate you more than they hate me. And I think Howard does not much like war." The three men rode back and told the others to continue forward slowly, while they rode faster to the camps.

It was not long before the men saw many riders coming their way, but they came slowly. Soon they saw chiefs at the head, followed by pack horses bearing tipi covers, lodge poles, blankets, and a herd stretched out behind. "Looking Glass," said Two Moons.

"Looking Glass!" cried Joseph. "Why is he coming this way? The reservation is behind him!" Once again the brothers urged their tired horses to a gallop.

Looking Glass, tall and grim and angry, sat upright like a rifle, leading his band. Forty warriors followed him, then the rest of his people, ponies trotting. Looking Glass halted and raised his hand to Joseph, Ollokot, and Two Moons.

"What does this mean?" cried Joseph.

"It means that White Bird did not control his young fools and the soldiers will come out against whoever stops in camp."

"They will come for you, too," said Ollokot.

"I am taking my families back to our land, away from trouble. I will have no war. I am not going to have my people killed."

"We must go onto the reservation in any case," said Joseph. "I will try to make Howard understand that only a few young men want war."

"Joseph, your first wife will have her baby soon. Get her out, get your whole band out and as far away from here as you can go. Maybe war will not follow you."

"Is that what you think?" Joseph asked.

"No," said Looking Glass. He nodded, turned his horse, and waved his people on.

Before the two started forward, Ollokot laid his hand on Joseph's pony. "We can't go on," he said. "We can't leave the others, my wife, to ride alone." Joseph sat watching as Looking Glass's band passed. Ollokot said "Three."

"Red Grizzly. Four. Four of his young men are not here. Go back with the women. I will ride ahead. I can reach our camp before morning."

*

That night General Howard finished talking with the settlers from Lapwai, four farmers and two of their sons, who had come to ask the Army's help. They walked from his small office out to the parade grounds. "This isn't war, not yet, not if we don't make a war. I am confident that Joseph doesn't want war. If I know my red man, Joseph will be here tomorrow or the next day, offering to bring in those three drunken young wretches."

"If he isn't one of the drunken wretches himself," said one of the men. "My son here says a witness told him Joseph himself committed one of the killings."

"It is a substantiated fact," asserted another.

"You may find that witness and send him to me," the general said. "I happen to know that Joseph does not drink. He is a man I can understand. The tale that Joseph murdered one of those men with his own hands is nothing but a rumor, a foolish and incendiary rumor. Joseph himself will be here within two days, proof that he has no blood on his hands. And if I know him, he will ask for more time. I shall not give it to him. The Nez Perce will be on the reservation, one way or another, and the cowardly braves who did this will be hanged according to the laws of the United States, I assure you. This is a crime, not a war." Reaching the open gate of the stockade, they heard the pounding of two riders coming fast.

*

When Joseph reached the Camus Meadow camp, morning light had just begun to thin the darkness, the Ghost Road's sparkle fading like camp-fire smoke. He saw the tipis laid out small and sparse, ghostly gray and too few. Riding to his tipi, he dismounted. As Joseph hobbled him the horse softly whinnied, and quickly Yellow Wolf, Joseph's nephew, pushed back the opening and stepped outside. "Thunder Rising in the Mountain," the young man said, continuing, "many are gathered here."

"How is Springtime?"

"Your wife is well. No child yet."

Joseph entered and by the light of several coals he saw his wife. She lay sleeping on her side, head resting on his folded old soft blanket. She was covered by a buffalo robe up to her shoulder. Seven men and Yellow Wolf sat along the tipi's heavy skin walls. Joseph knelt and touched Springtime softly on her forehead, not waking her, and then sat down.

Red Elk sat across from him. "It is good that you are here. We must go somewhere today, but we do not know where. You have heard what has happened?"

"I have heard."

"Some are saying now that we must fight."

"What do you say, you who are here?"

Red Elk spoke again, "It is only our band left here. Looking Glass and the other bands have gone. Our best warriors, Rainbow, Five Wounds, and others, are still in buffalo country. How can we fight? We have only twenty strong men."

"Have more young men gone off to find trouble?"

"Only one of ours."

"I am glad."

"You know that we have two, maybe three men, who can't be counted on."

"I know."

"So twenty men."

"Tomorrow I will go to General Howard. Maybe we can settle everything."

Yellow Wolf spoke. "Uncle, forgive my speaking up," Joseph nodded. "The other young men who have gone are crazy, they are out of their minds, but—"

"Others have gone?"

"Yes."

"How many?"

"I do not know. From all the bands, ten, twelve, maybe a few more."

"When?"

A voice broke in from the neighboring tipi. "You poor men are talking about nothing! It is too late! My son has just returned from killing more whites."

Joseph rushed outside, the other men following. Wounded Head stepped out from his tipi and Joseph asked, "What more has happened. Tell me!"

"The young men killed several white men, five or six, and a woman, two white children—"

"No!" cried Joseph. "My people!"

"—and the young men raped two women."

"They are not Nez Perce!"

"Yes they are, Thunder Rising in the Mountains."

"*The Army coming, riding horses of death,*" Joseph repeated, looking down at the ash of a cooking fire. "Should we pack now, not wait for light?" Joseph asked loudly.

"It is enough light," Red Elk said. "We should start. Morning is coming fast."

*

The Chamberlin and Norton families had thrown some valuables into a wagon when Lewis Day rode down to Cottonwood with news that up at Salmon River Indians had gone on the warpath. Cottonwood was a little settlement: a hotel, way station, general store, and stables all at once—a large, two-story building made of cottonwood lumber, with its stables, sizeable corral, other outbuildings, all surrounded by a few ranch houses. Lew Day had torn into the barroom where everyone was sitting, shouting, "Better load your rifles and get ready, the Nez Perces are in war paint two or three miles behind me!" He told them of the four men killed a couple days ago, and then this afternoon: "You know that Billy Collins ran a store up by the river, always sold cheap whiskey to the Indians up there? Shot a Nez Perce robbing him a while back—no love lost between him and the Indians. I was in his store this forenoon, and he asked my help in loading up his wagon full of whiskey barrels, tools, and gold dust—everything of cash value he could carry. Asked him why and he said, 'You just stay here 'til night and you'll find out. Give my respects to our native friends.' He was a funny man, Collins. He told me straight out, 'You take anything you want, the redskins will clean everything out anyway.' God's truth, he told me I could. No reason to hurry so I stood a minute in the store looking things over, what was left, and I hear war whoops, and they're on him before he even gets to the bridge in front of the store. I made to run for my horse but a half dozen braves are riding up to the store and there's no chance for me. I stand in the door thinking they'll shoot me like a dog and I see them jump Billy's wagon, cut his throat, and drag him down—and these six braves just push me aside and barge into the store, ignore me like I wasn't there. They didn't take nothing, just smashed and shattered and they took a bag of gold dust—legal tender—and poured it outside on the ground. All this while I'm standing by and inching toward my horse. They lit fire in the building, just brushed past me going to the loaded wagon. I led my horse quiet around behind the store and then took off for the woods. I get there and look back and all of them are breaking barrels, drinking streams of whiskey and I expect they're all a few miles back drunk as all hell, and you know what that means—you get out quick!"

The people inside ran all directions getting their things. Joe Moore, minding the bar, dashed out to hitch the team, and Ben Norton ran to saddle up while his wife and son packed fast. Lewis Day did not stand and wait this time but swung up to his saddle, heading for Cottonwood Hill behind the hotel. He didn't get far. The Nez Perce had fanned along the road and sent two braves ahead, and one of those shot Day as he was riding up the hillside, the bullet creasing him along his back, around a rib. The strike of the shot threw Day forward on his horse's neck and almost off, but he kept his seat and spurred around to the building's back door.

Mrs. Norton pulled him in and called for her husband. The two of them and Jennie Norton's cousin, eighteen-year-old Lynn Bowers, cleaned his wound and tied a cloth around the man. The two Nez Perce rode back the mile or so to bring the others at a gallop.

John Chamberlin, his wife Nancy, and their two little girls—one just an infant—climbed into the wagon with Jenny, Lynn, and ten-year-old Hill Norton, lifting Lew Day up with them, while Joe Moore and Ben Norton rode beside on saddled horses. Under a full moon they made about four miles, but with five miles to go before the settlement of Grange, the drunk Nez Perce overtook the party. Joe Moore and Norton halted and began to fire while Chamberlin whipped up the team—but no more than seconds later Moore's and Norton's horses and both the team had been shot down. Moore's hip was shattered by a bullet but he managed to crawl under the wagon with Ben Norton. The rest stayed low in the box, Chamberlin looking up and shooting as fast as he could while the Indians kept their distance, circling, weaving on their ponies, riding in and shooting, riding away to drink from barrels they had packed on Bill Collins's two horses. Both families jumped out and crawled under the wagon. Day had been hit again and became feverish, both he and Moore crying out for water. When Ben Norton climbed for the jug of water, he fell back to the ground shot through the chest. A moment later Jenny Norton cried, "My God, I'm shot!" A bullet had gone through both legs. She gripped the wagon wheel in front of her and made no sounds.

John Chamberlin had all that he could take. "Come on!" he said to his wife. "We'll get out in the sagebrush and make for Grange!" Ben Norton said they mustn't throw away their lives like that; but when clouds covered the moon Chamberlin scrambled out, pulled the little girl, and Nancy obeyed, carrying the infant. The Indians were off with the whiskey and the Chamberlins ran out into the brush, but there wasn't much brush. As an old man, Hill Norton still could hear Nancy Chamberlin and the young girls screaming in his dreams.

Ben Norton, choking, whispered to his son and niece to try to go another way and double back toward Grange. Though growing weak and dizzy, Jenny screamed out, "No, they'll be killed too!"

"Jenny," Norton whispered, "It's a sure thing we'll all die here!" Lynn Bowers slipped out of her heavy skirt and the two crawled out and ran for it, splitting up, trying to stay low and aiming for brush. All night Hill Norton crouched and crawled, staying quiet when the moon was out, crawling out when it was darker. More than once Nez Perce ponies passed close enough to touch, once stepping over him. He heard nothing from his cousin, out somewhere half-undressed.

As morning light came, the boy heard hoofbeats coming toward him. He was in tall grass now, knew he must be a mile or two from Grange—too far to jump up and run. The horses slowed down to a walk; he heard a carbine jacked. He looked up, then clambered to his feet clapping and hoarsely crying, "It's Mister Fenn, it's Mister Fenn!" Frank Fenn, a settler, knew the Norton boy—had been the schoolhouse teacher. Now he pulled him up behind and started at a gallop for the settlement.

Fenn found five men gathered trying to figure out the rumors, got two of them agreed to go with him, and the three men were soon galloping west on the stage road. They found the woman, Jenny Norton, still alive, but Benjamin was dead. Breathing, not much more, Day and Moore lay underneath the wagon with the Nortons. The three unhitched the wagon from its horses, rolled it out and backed two of their saddle horses to the traces—then heard the shooting of awakened Nez Perce. They got the living loaded in the wagon, but not the dead. Poor Jenny sobbed and suffered but they left her husband lying in the road.

If the road to Grange had been uphill they never would have made it, but the road declined toward the settlement. Fenn rode the near horse, another man the off, and they used with energy the halter ropes as whips; and still the road seemed endless. The Indians had come almost to shooting distance when up from Grange a dozen white men riding hell for leather came in sight around a bend, rushed past them drawing rifles and revolvers. It wasn't U.S. Cavalry but just as warlike: settlers rounded up by the other men that Fenn had found.

The Nez Perce, with their pounding heads splitting, slowed, reversed direction, and the settlers pulled up their blowing horses. They got Ben Norton's body and a sad, bleeding procession started toward Grange Hall.

Ten of the men, including Fenn, rode through the sagebrush around the place where it had happened. Several hundred yards up from the road they found John Chamberlin covered in blood and dead. His girl lay dead on his arm. They found the infant girl alive, curled up and silent. She'd bit through her tongue or it had been cut half off.

They searched for many days, but they never found the mother, Nancy Chamberlin. Ben Norton, Johnny Chamberlin, and three-year-old Hattie Chamberlin are buried in the town of Mount Idaho. Hattie, it is said, lies on her father's arm.

General Howard called for cavalry—two companies from Lewiston— and got his Seventh Infantry supplied with pack mules, ammunition, and enough to live on for a twenty-day campaign. More reports had come in, not just of the Norton Party but of six other white men killed—reports that were true—and also of one woman captured, two children wounded, two women, Helen Walsh and Elizabeth Osborn, raped by drunken Nez Perce warriors. And one more report came in: A woman named Nancy Chamberlin had been knifed to death—the drunken Indian who thrust that knife being Joseph himself. This last report the General did not believe; furthermore, there was no body, but sixty years later, when a motion came to Congress for a monument to Joseph placed at his graveside, the Congressional Record, noting the measure's failure, cited Joseph's murder of a white woman, Mrs. Chamberlin. To the colonel of the Seventh Infantry, General Howard said,

"After all, you scratch them deep enough and the Nez Perce are Indians, no better than the rest."

Writing to his superiors, Howard said although he had been forced to war, "We shall make short work of it." He would disarm them and drive the non-treaties onto the reservation, arresting the ringleader, Chief Joseph.

*

Among the Nez Perce, women owned the goods—the lodge, furnishings, nearly everything not of war—and were free to trade or sell any of it as they chose; therefore women did the packing and the loading—but not this time. Joseph and the men helped take down the tepees, loaded travois, in addition to rounding up and bringing in the herd. By mid-morning all the killings, drinking, thefts, woundings, and the two rapes had been told. Red Elk and Ollokot rode at the front leading the warriors, trotting their ponies as The People of Joseph's band moved out. Chief Joseph rode back with his wife, the women, the children, and the old men. Regularly he rode out to the youths who drove the herd. "Your brother," Red Elk said to Ollokot, "did everything that could be done. And now it is up to us. It is now the warriors' work, and I wish that it would not be so."

Ollokot nodded, grunting softly. "Yes. White Bird it was who failed."

"He is a great warrior, White Bird, even though the cold snows of seventy winters lie upon his head. He brought up his young men as warriors, and warriors they must be. It would be good to have them with us now."

"We will have them."

"But he has taken all his band back home to the canyon in the hills."

"The soldiers will attack all non-treaty bands, White Bird's too. We will all join together or die."

"I am glad if you are right."

"It is right for him to join us, for his best young man is the one who started all this trouble."

"Shore Crossing. I have heard that in winter every day he swims the Salmon River, across and back again, to keep strong."

"Yes, but many of White Bird's men do that."

"Every day?"

"Maybe not every day. And no other man can hold two unbroken horses without being dragged or getting his shoulders torn."

"He will be a great war chief one day."

Lean Elk's face took on a blank stare. Ollokot laughed. "After you die! And I die—and after Looking Glass and Rainbow and Five Wounds die."

"Maybe it will not be long."

"We need Looking Glass."

"He will not come. He hates White Bird for letting this happen. He has taken his people away and he will keep them away."

"He will come if we all agree to do as he says."

"It is not The People's way to give authority to one man."

"Looking Glass is arrogant but he is wise and knows the soldiers. It will be his war if he comes together with us. His to win or lose."

"The whites think your brother is the sole war chief."

"'Let them think I am the war chief,' my brother says. 'Then the whites will think they can easily defeat us.'"

II

White Bird Canyon

Shore Crossing held his wife while she upbraided him: "You shouldn't have been drinking, Dearest Heart! Not only whites but all The People soon will blame everything on drunken braves instead of where the blame belongs."

"My head feels as if an axe were in it."

"Oh! You—how could you drink so much?"

"Others drank more."

"Heart, you know I wanted justice against white criminals. Why the women? Why the child? Why—"

"I touched no woman!"

"I know, My Heart. But why didn't you stop them? You of all men, who had to watch—"

"They were many!"

"No, never too many for you! You can humble three men, and they listen to you!"

"I was too drunk. I was too sick drunk."

"You great elk of a man. You are the greatest young warrior of all The People, but a small cup of white man's whisky makes you a sick child. Oh, my husband!"

"It was right to go raiding against those white men."

"Yes it was. But the whites do not think of war as we do. They will not raid us and then stop, as Indian People do. For them, war will never end, until we or they are all dead!"

"No, Howard's soldiers will not follow us forever. If we cross the Bitter-root Mountains, they will turn back. Our People will live free in Montana, in buffalo country."

"Whites are whites."

"They have no quarrel with us in Montana."

"The United States Army will follow us."

"Then let us defeat them."

"We should have simply gone to Montana."

"You know the big chiefs would not go unless war made them act."

"Joseph would have brought you to General Howard for peace."

"Let him try. But now it is too late for that. Joseph is good for talking to the whites, but now the time has come for war chiefs to decide things, not Joseph. They know all of us young fighters will be needed."

"You most of all."

"I will protect my people. I will protect you."

*

Howard had called out two companies of cavalry under Captain David Perry, one hundred men; a good dozen civilian volunteers; and a few treaty, Christian, Nez Perce scouts. Perry commanded Company F himself. His second in command, Lieutenant Edward Theller, had like Perry served with the First Cavalry a dozen years and knew Indian war. Company H was commanded by Captain Joel Trimble, a veteran not only of a dozen years in the West, but of the Civil War; he had fought at Gettysburg. He was one of Grant's soldiers at Cold Harbor, and was in on the kill at Five Forks. His first lieutenant, Bill Parnell, an Irishman, had fought for years in Europe, and been one of the Six Hundred in that bloody charge at Balaclava. These four men knew war but most of their men did not. The U.S. Cavalry, except for some hard-used and well-led units like Custer's Seventh Regiment, was full of men who drifted in from all parts of the poor, desperate corners of the white world: recent immigrants from Germany, Italy, and Ireland; young eastern factory workers sick of dullness and foul air; farm boys from Ohio, hardy enough but not killers; Confederate refugees from an exhausted South; grand and petty criminals, and drunks who could not hold a job; and a few hard-bitten sergeants as brutally ignorant in their way as Eastern tycoons and congressmen. Many troopers couldn't ride well, let alone shoot; combine the two—shooting from the saddle—and you had nothing but fireworks. Cavalry horses were good enough for steady work, but few of them were trained like Indian ponies to stand still with rifles firing and bullets slitting the air. The usual tactics called for the men to dismount, one in four holding horses, but that one sometimes held more than he could handle, so in battle many troopers lost their mounts—their rearing, frantic horses plunging off in unknown directions. A soldier packed a Springfield carbine, breech-loading but single shot—a good short-barreled weapon needing to be taken down and cleaned with regularity—new repeating lever-action carbines trickling in over time—and a Colt .45 revolver. He wore cotton long johns, a blue light wool uniform, trousers and jacket or blouse, black hat, leather boots and gauntlets. His outfit consisted of a tin canteen, shelter tent, a cloth haversack for personals—Bible, cards, comb, toothbrush, photographs, utensils, letters, dime novel—and of course his saddlebags and tack, holster and leather carbine sling. The infantry outnumbered cavalry and got places the same way as always—walked—the good old Army mule carrying the beans and bacon, blankets, shelter tent, ammunition—all the burdens warring flesh inherits. The Indian Fighting Army, though not well trained, was well-equipped and ultimately numerous. General Howard regarded Perry's prospects of quick and easy success with "the serene confidence of a Christian holding four aces."

*

Years later, Yellow Wolf remembered why the Nez Perce had no more than sixty braves to make their stand at White Bird Canyon. Half again as many had gone up ahead with hundreds of The People and their stock. When these were safely off, most of the men turned back to join the warriors—but on their way they stopped to inspect a general store on White Bird Creek. The store had stocked a generous supply of whisky, and the men went out of action for a good twenty-four hours. It took a while for Native People to get a grasp on what the white man meant by war. One of the braves that hit the store told Yellow Wolf that when the owner took to horse with his small boy up behind, he followed with intent to kill the man. His arrow missed the man and hit the boy's upper arm. The boy cried out; at that the warrior pulled off and turned away. The pitiful cry, the warrior said, had hurt his feelings, so he let the two ride on. Unknown to him, it was a girl and not a boy.

The man commanding all United States armed forces, William Tecumseh Sherman—a man who offered gentle terms to the last sizeable Confederate army in the Civil War—said two things memorable: one was, "War is all hell;" the other was something like, "The only good Indians I have ever seen were dead."

Old Chief Toohoolhoolzote talked war with White Bird, Ollokot, Red Elk and other Nez Perce fighting men. Five bands were now together in White Bird's country. "The soldiers must come down the canyon road," he said. "The scouts count two Long Knives for each warrior."

"Sixty," Red Elk murmured. "No more today, half our young men drunk. It is bad until our buffalo hunters come back, until Looking Glass makes up his mind."

"He will fight, but not until he is forced to," said Ollokot.

"The same for all of us," the old chief reminded them.

Red Elk spoke again: "Together we have five carbines and eleven old muzzle loaders, with few cartridges."

"We must take their carbines."

"No need, if we defeat them here," said White Bird. "Maybe then they will leave us alone."

"Does the mother grizzly leave her cubs far off on the hillside?" Red Elk asked. "These white men will not leave us alone, ever. We must take as many carbines as we can get."

"But we have to fight them first—without carbines," Ollokot put in.

"We must ride in close to them and use our bows," said chief White Bird.

"We can outride them," said Red Elk. "Our women will bring each warrior one, two fresh horses in the battle. The Long Knives will have ridden fifty miles, all day and night, to come here."

"Then we come from flanks and behind once they pass the high ground on each side," said White Bird. "The Whites fear nothing more than flank attacks."

"If they scare," said Ollokot, "we can run them, stay with them, shoot from horseback. Then we will take many carbines, and shoot many soldiers."

"If they do not scare?" Red Elk asked.

"Then we will fall back, farther up the canyon," said Ollokot, "and try again."

"They will scare," said White Bird. "I will send Shore Crossing and my young men to ride behind the soldiers after you stop them. He will scare them."

"They will think that Indians are everywhere," said Toohoolhoolzote.

"They will think we have three hundred men," White Bird added. "They will run all directions."

"If all goes well," said Red Elk. "If all goes well."

The old chief who had watched the soldiers said, "I have told you of how they fight and move together. We must break their discipline. My young men will fight together, not like single crazy Indians. When we break up their line, they will not know what to do."

*

Trimble left his company and cantered forward past the walking column of F Company, pulling up beside Perry. "What are my orders, Captain? It looks like we'll hit the mouth of the canyon about an hour from now." The hilly, green landscape showed a fold up ahead.

"As we approach, you'll bring your company up in column alongside mine. We'll stay on this wagon road through the mouth, which is narrow, but then deploy in line, you on my left. The scouts saw their tipis about a mile in along a creek. We'll charge the village at a trot until the last two hundred yards."

"Expect they'll put sharpshooters in the rocks along the heights as we come in."

"We'll kick it up as we go in. I've never seen a red that could use a rifle at any distance. If they come in with bow and arrow, we'll pick them off."

"Might be expecting us, Captain, before we pay our respects to the village."

"We'll charge through them straight ahead, and keep going."

"Once the canyon widens they could hit our flank."

"They're just a bunch of god damned Indians, all due respect. Raiders, probably drunk on all the firewater they've stolen. Nez Perce are not fighters like the Modocs. We'll make short work of them."

"Yes, Sir. I hope so, Sir, tired as the men and horses are."

"No worse than you and me, but I admit that three hours sleep in forty-eight is not enough. You get cautious when you're tired, Trimble."

"Not a bit. My column will come ahead when you give the word, Sir!" Trimble turned aside and rested his horse while Company F passed. The troopers rode with heads down, half asleep, tin cups, plodding hooves, and blowing horses wearing a comfortable cacophony into the warm morning. He turned in beside Parnell at the head of his company. "Our men look better, William!" Trimble said.

"Better they are, Captain. It's leadership, I don't mind saying."

"We're to double on their column through the pass and then deploy on Perry's left to charge the village."

"Very well, Sir."

"Captain Perry expects little trouble."

"Nor do I. The Nez Perce ain't—"

"Fighters."

"Not exactly British regulars. Or Russians, for that matter."

"And damn well not the Army of Northern Virginia, the likes of which you never saw, Parnell."

"Yes, Sir."

"We'll cut through them all right, Lieutenant."

*

Isabel Benedict was walking in a nightmare that morning. Three days ago Nez Perce in war paint rode up to the store she and her husband ran, and shot dead August Bacon, their employee, when he opened the door with a rifle in his hands. Samuel told her to take the baby and their son Frankie out the back and hide, which she did, crouching all day in the creek screened by reeds, listening to Indians get drunk, break windows, buck and dash like circus riders, finally galloping off at sunset. Returning to the house, she found August Bacon lying unmolested where he fell, but no trace of her husband. Afraid to call for him, she waited with the dead body until nearly dawn. The young braves had not left a scrap of food. She picked up the baby Julia, took little Frankie's hand, and in darkness went back to the creek. Two days and nights they followed it up through White Bird Canyon, hiding by day. Last night, dizzy with fatigue, hunger, and thirst, they hid in rocks along the wagon road going up toward White Bird Pass while the Indians had ridden slowly through, hundreds of them, passing so close she heard the dappled horses huffing and papooses mewling; close enough to hear the scrape of travois poles. Her baby was near death, too weak to cry, and when the Indians at last were gone, Frankie took a little shoe from Julia's foot and crept down to the creek. He filled it, brought it back so carefully, knelt beside his sister holding it to her lips. But she couldn't hold a drop down, too exhausted and insensible to swallow moisture in her mouth. Lying in the rocks, they heard more horses as the morning rose.

Lifting her head, Isabel saw the double column of men in blue and staggered to her feet. Halting for a moment, Perry ordered up some water, bacon, and hardtack crackers for the three. "I begged them," she wrote later, "send a man with me to Cows Prairie Settlement, but the Captain said they couldn't. It would take ten men or more to keep us safe, and he could spare none just then, for they expected to fight the Indians that passed us last night. He was going to drive and capture them all day and half the next, so we should stay put there, and they would return for us in two days. But they were back within an hour, and in a hurry too, with seemingly the whole Nez Perce nation at their heels. They came—at first just a few, and then the way was lined with flying soldiers. Riderless horses bounded past with turned saddles, reins flowing, close enough for us to hear the poor beasts' hard-drawn breathings and feel the flecks of foam thrown from their nostrils."

The routed soldiers gave no thought to the woman and her children until a volunteer civilian from Grangeville dismounted shouting, "Stop, someone, for God's sake! We can't leave this woman and her baby!" He stood with arms raised in the road, and two soldiers slowed enough for him to lift the baby and the boy into their arms, then caught a riderless cavalry mount and boosted Mrs. Benedict into the saddle. He mounted, told her to let her horse run, and dashed away at a clattering gallop. The woman, glad her children would be safe, held on the best she could, but not long: the saddle turned and she pitched off, again on foot and helpless. Now no soldier stopped for her and as the last plunged wide-eyed past she cried out, pressing arms across her breast in a storm of warriors.

*

Joseph had heard the last words of the chiefs, before the soldiers were seen up at the head of White Bird Pass. He'd ridden up with two men of his band and now he insisted, "We have never killed soldiers. No chief who loves his people may begin war unless he has tried everything to save peace. I will ride to them in truce and offer peace, offer to give them all the young men who have crimes."

"Not my young men," said Toohoolhoolzote.

Joseph turned toward White Bird. "You know the whites are grizzlies and we are deer."

"I know. Go talk to them. We will wait."

Joseph clipped his Appaloosa with his heels and cantered up the canyon with two warriors.

"We can use the time," White Bird said quietly.

"They will shoot him like a dog," Toohoolhoolzote cried out.

"Worse things could happen," said White Bird.

Ollokot kicked his horse and Red Elk followed him, running their ponies after Joseph. "Joseph!" called his brother. "Do you know what you are doing?"

As Ollokot drew up beside him, Joseph said, "I know only what I must do."

"But you have a baby two days old!"

"I know. That is why I must try for peace."

"The soldiers will shoot us."

"I will hold up a white cloth."

"Yellow Wolf will hold another. Do you trust the soldiers?"

"No more than you do. But the soldiers do not shoot well from horseback and we will have time to turn back if they do not accept a truce."

As they approached the narrow passage from the canyon, four riders came in sight—two Christian Nez Perce scouts and two white volunteers.

"I know one of those white men," said Yellow Wolf. "The big white hat, sombrero—his name is Chapman. The whites call him Squaw Man for his Nez Perce wife. He and my father lived as friends one year in the same house. He will not shoot us."

Joseph's other warrior, Mean Person, laughed and shouted, "Why does he ride rifle raised?" They saw a burst of smoke and then heard the rifle crack, and a bullet zipped near enough to hear plainly.

Ollokot lifted his carbine, a repeater, to his shoulder. The four white men stopped, turned their horses, and rode back toward the pass. They recognized the tall warrior on the big white horse.

An *Ooh! Ooh!* of a brave rose from the left far up the canyon.

"Soldiers coming now!" cried Yellow Wolf. "It is the call of Going Alone!"

"Be steady," Joseph said. "We have a little time."

Ollokot said evenly, "Now we go to war."

Yellow Wolf and Mean Person were stripped for war and painted, but the chiefs were not. The two young men rode behind Ollokot and Red Elk up to the left. Joseph turned back to the tipis, riding fast.

His older wife was not yet ready to move as quickly as the younger women, so all of Joseph's family were here. He bent into the semi-darkness of the tipi. His wife sat holding their infant daughter. Joseph lifted the baby girl to his face, then knelt and touched his wife's cheek with his. She took the stout horn bow lying beside her and raised it to Joseph.

"The best buffalo bow," he said, taking it in his hands. "It has never drawn blood from a man—until today."

A young woman, Snows Resting, stood quietly holding a quiver full of arrows. Joseph took the quiver and embraced her briefly. "I will come behind you with two fresh horses," she said.

"No, No! Stay here and watch the child and mother."

"Sound of Running Feet is here and she is old enough."

Joseph nodded, turned, and held out a hand to his older daughter. Sound of Running Feet took his hand and said, "You must not be killed, Father! May your guardian spirit go with you now!"

*

Captain Trimble trotted forward leading his column of twos beside the walking column of Company F. Beside him trotted Lieutenant Parnell chucking his small sorrel up to keep the pace. "Parnell," the Captain asked, "how soon do you figure Joseph's sharpshooters will take us in their sights?"

"That's just the beauty of it, Captain. Show me the redskin that knows how to use a rifle sight and I'll show you a monkey that can read the Revelation of John. They'll pepper us and run away."

"And wait for us to evolve out of column into line of battle? I think not, Parnell."

They now had ridden even with the leading pair of Company F, Perry and Theller. "We won't give them the chance to attack us strung out in column, Captain," Perry said. "The pass is narrow, but we'll deploy immediately where it widens. I've sent a couple scouts and volunteers ahead to make sure Joseph isn't massed in front of us. After we get through, take your company right in two detachments. I'll put the scouts and volunteers to left of my company to secure that flank."

"What of the right flank, sir?"

"You will be tight against a ridge, I think, while my left will be in the air. We'll do it differently if what I have been told is wrong."

"Yes, Sir," Trimble said, and settled into his thoughts.

*

A short time later, as the double column entered the narrow upper pass, Joseph caught up to his brother. Slowing to a quick trot, he rode with Ollokot, Toohoolhoolzote, Red Elk, Two Moons, Yellow Wolf—most of them fathers of families like Joseph. "I will go with some of White Bird's young men to threaten them in front when they come out," said Ollokot. "We will ride at them and ride back, like Indians."

Two Moons, his face painted with two white circles at the eyes, allowed himself to smile a little. But then he became almost sad. "So the elder men, thirty, forty winters, who cannot ride like young men any more, must make the real attacks. Get on their flank and shoot along their line. You will have to stay where you are, not run back freely. We will stay like white men, but fight like Nez Perce, two by two. You women!" he called. "What do you want to do?"

Snows Resting and two other women rode forward, leaving their extra horses back with twelve other women mounted and holding strings of two or three horses. "We will wait until the soldiers run," she said, "and then come fast behind you men."

"Will you run in when there is shooting?"

"We will not run in."

"Good. You must not come into the shooting. The People can survive with few men, but not without the women. The soldiers will shoot at you. White men do not value life."

"We will not run in." She smiled at Joseph, whose furrowed face portrayed his disbelief, then turned back with the other two women.

White Necklace watched her husband ride ahead with eight other young men. Shore Crossing rode taller than the others, his broad shoulders making him out as the best target, she knew. She could not keep up with the men, but she would wait close by to nurse anyone shot by the soldiers. The group turned to the right down a small defile, and rode behind the hill where older men of White Bird's and the small bands were waiting. Now they rested their ponies. Shore Crossing walked back to White Necklace, handsome as the sun on mountains, love shining from his face even as his eyes were lit with eagerness for battle. He stood tall beside her on her small pony, his shoulder at her hips; he laid his powerful hand on her knee. "I will protect you, my wife. No white man will ever hurt you again."

"I am not afraid for myself any more. If I were your Wyakin I would stay as close to you as the wind."

He reached up and stroked her cheek, and she placed her hand on his. Then he turned and walked toward the men. She watched his long strides and then her eyes misted, and she turned her head away.

*

"Hold up, there!" shouted Captain Perry. "Halt!" The word sounded several times down the line behind him. Up the narrow road trace ahead and out into the widening canyon, his Indian scouts and two volunteers rode toward a party of Nez Perce warriors. He could not see paint on their faces at that distance, but two of the braves were stripped for battle. Trimble said, "They've been expecting us, Captain."

"Yes. I had allowed myself to hope they weren't when they didn't shoot at us back up there. Deploy your company, Captain. Keep contact with me and extend to that slope. Send one squad up ahead as skirmishers."

"Yes, Sir!" Trimble turned to Parnell. "Take 'em off."

"Sir!" Parnell saluted, turning his horse. "Company, deploy, line of battle! By the right flank, march!" He pointed at the bugler, who raised his instrument and blew the staccato notes for the advance.

"Trimble!" Perry shouted, twenty yards to the left. "Send your bugler over here! My god damn bugler lost his god damn bugle!"

Trimble smiled but Parnell said, "Damnation!" waving the soldier over to F Company.

"We'll just have to holler louder, Lieutenant!" Trimble shouted, still grinning.

Parnell didn't like it but kicked his horse to lead the right flank into position. He snarled at Sergeant Scott, "Get a squad up front!" and passed him, still cursing. Captain Perry rode to his left flank, catching up to Theller.

"Lieutenant, take a dozen men and some volunteers up there." He pointed at the slope of a broad hill. "I'll direct the company. Secure the left. I'll send the scouts and the rest of the civilians to your front and left as skirmishers." The crack of a rife down in the valley brought his attention to Chapman's party. He saw the five Nez Perce turn back, then split, while the two scouts and the settlers made several rapid shots from horseback. They turned and galloped back toward Perry's line. "Slow it down," the Captain muttered. "Don't waste your horseflesh, you damn fools." He turned to Company H's bugler: "Slow advance, walk."

The line of cavalry started forward, strung out from the right flank, brushing the slope on the left, a scattering of skirmishers trotting in the open country. Perry saw four of the warriors go to his right and vanish in low ground; the lone rider continued along White Bird Creek, and then rode out of sight around the bend in the stream masked by several hills. The rider must be headed to the village Perry's scouts reported, maybe giving the alarm. These peaceful Nez Perce did not know enough to set out pickets, after all. Except that two braves—but now as the rider disappeared, a crowd of galloping braves came out around the herd.

Perry reacted instantly—raised his hand, reined his horse: "Companies Halt! Dismount!" Behind him bugle notes, piercing, sounded and repeated, turning to the left and right flanks. The men, except the skirmishers up front and Theller's flankers, dismounted and grouped their horses. "Holders, retire!" Perry shouted. One man for every four led horses to the rear. Perry now rode toward his left, saying to the men, "Hold fire until ordered. Let them come to us. Let them wear their horses out."

At first low, the thundering of hooves came to the men and some believed they felt the ground shaking. The warriors came on, a thousand yards, eight hundred, seven hundred—now they heard war whoops—high yipping, howling—a sound that chilled the spine and made the stomach turn. The men lifted cartridges from their belts with slippery fingers, loaded them with shaking hands.

"Steady," said the sergeants and lieutenants evenly, repeating calmly but with a certain catch and crispness in their voices, "Steady." The men held their carbines angled down, sweat running from their wrists.

"Ready!" Perry called. The order was repeated along the line. Perry watched the skirmish squads ride wide right and left of the charging braves—looked like thirty, maybe fifty. Four hundred yards—a little far, but how long will the men hold out? "Fire at will!"

Men in front of him pulled their triggers before the last word left his mouth; the whole line firing then, sheets and rolls of thick smoke roiling out into the air. Reloading hastily, the men fired randomly, a steady cracking fire. Seated above the line, Perry saw the warriors, none of them felled, turning their ponies, breaking into a milling spread of darting figures. Some shot forward raising bows and taunting, then galloping away as others dashed up, a confusing, hideous display.

"A shooting gallery!" Perry shouted—but still too far. His men loaded and then fired without aiming. "Forward! Let's give them hell!" He looked back to the bugler—perhaps the man hadn't heard him or seen his arm wave forward—saw the man buckling in his saddle, surprise and pain shooting across his face, then falling. A jolt of understanding filled the captain's body. Looking at the hill to the left, he saw a group of mounted warriors, one dismounted, lowering his rifle. "Too far!" was Perry's thought, then, "Oh my God, we're flanked!"

Theller's flankers up ahead were throwing themselves from their horses, attacked by other warriors. Perry looked quickly to the right. Up on the slope beyond the bare right flank the old chief White Bird with five older men had left their horses and crawled behind rocks.

Among them, they had nearly all The People's good rifles. A seasoned hunter named Fire Body said to White Bird, "See the one who holds the bugle!"

White Bird answered, "Shoot him and the soldiers cannot hear the orders!"

"It is a long way, too far, but I will make a good shot!" He steadied the old rifle on the rock in front of him and looked hard, then pulled the trigger. The rifle's stock hit him at the bang, but his tough old shoulder barely moved.

"Your shot has knocked him down!" White Bird told him. "It will be trouble for them." He shouted toward the other men, "Start shooting!" One by one and carefully, the other warriors chose their targets and pulled triggers.

Fire Body called to White Bird, "We can stay here until the sun goes down! The soldiers will not hit us!"

"We did not come to stay!" The old chief now clambered back up the rocky slope to where he could be seen by Shore Crossing, waiting with his braves and women holding horses, and pointed in the direction of the troopers' rear.

When the young men weaving back and forth in front of the soldiers rode back, they made a wide arc ending near the squads of soldiers and civilians Lieutenant Teller had brought to secure the command's left flank. As these warriors neared, the whites dismounted and prepared to shoot from any cover they could find. The braves, some riding close with bow and arrow—shooting from around beneath their horses' necks—kept up their hit and run tactics for a short while, but then they left their ponies standing, rawhide halter ropes dangling to the ground, and began working forward two by two.

Joseph, Ollokot, and Toohoolhoolzote, together with Two Moons and Yellow Wolf, dismounted with these young men. The older warriors ran into the swale down along the creek, spread out, and rose to fire arrows at the volunteers. One man with Joseph, Hawk Heart, had a gun and saw a white man running close. "Stand still!" he shouted. "Stand still so I can shoot you!"

The white man froze, then ran with twice the speed and kept running out of sight.

Ollokot's repeating rifle cracked, and a settler named Herman Faxon felt a shock along his side. "I'm hit!" he cried. "Oh God, I'm killed!" He too ran back as fast as he could to their horses.

"Indians were everywhere," a citizen wrote afterwards. The arrows of the young men found one or two targets, and suddenly the volunteers were running, all of them, their Nez Perce scouts running too, not caring to be left alone with these most unappreciative cousins.

Two Moons ran up behind Joseph and Hawk Heart, shouting, "Come! Soldiers and scouts on that hill up there! They will not be scared so easily!" The warriors ran ahead. Down behind them the women watched, holding the horses.

Out on the trooper's right, Parnell saw old White Bird up the hill, his back turned, waving and then pointing. "I know what they're up to!" He called to a Corporal Dietz: "They'll ride around behind us! Damn Perry!

Did he think that all we'd have to do is form a line and charge? Corporal, take the right squads and refuse this line!"

The corporal ran back from the line shouting, "Refuse that flank!" But as the German hurtled past Parnell he fell to the ground, writhing with a bullet in his lower back.

Parnell dashed to the last man on the right, pulled him by his collar, pointed rearward, then ran to the next man, heard the dull chunk of a bullet, didn't stop to see the man fall; the next man turned his head, saw Parnell, and followed his gesture, falling back.

Now the next several men understood, began stepping rearward, and Parnell walked behind them pointing where to stand. "The red bastards are riding around behind us," he shouted. "Keep your heads!"

But some men farther down the line thought it was retreat and began to make for the horses. "Stop them, Sergeant!" Parnell screamed above the firing. "I'll shoot the first man runs!" He drew his .45 but just then heard war whoops coming down the slope to his right rear. Taking aim, he fired at the warrior in the lead, a tall young brave on a white horse, missed, fired again, but in that moment had to dive away from the big stallion.

The warrior Shore Crossing rode among the soldiers dashing for their horses. Leaping from his pony he hit the ground swinging his iron-headed axe into the face of a big trooper, whose body fell backward. Whooping, the big warrior, naked but for moccasins and breechcloth, painted on the chest and face, ran to a soldier frozen in terror. Like a man dreaming of falling, the trooper suddenly jerked, held his rifle with both hands to ward away the heavy hatchet. Shore Crossing's axe head struck the man's neck—a leaping spurt of blood spattering the warrior's livid face and painted chest. Now other warriors ran among the troopers raising war clubs and shooting arrows from their short bows.

Soldiers fired off rounds and ran, one bullet striking Bow and Arrow Case between the hip bone and ribs and passing through his body. The young warrior clutched his side and fell crumbling like a mountain lion speared through the belly—but as he lay grimacing on the ground two women lifted him under his arms and with a third carried him away from the fighting.Brandishing his pistol, Parnell herded men up toward a small ridge while the left and center of the company fell back walking. Trimble shouted hoarsely, "Keep your heads, you sons of bitches! Keep your heads! Walk!"

But then White Bird's men on the hill began to run down toward them, snapping arrows in a flurry, troopers struck, dropping rifles, clutching shafts in wondering pain. Trimble shouted now, "Make for the horses! Run, men!"

Out in front of Perry's troopers the skirmish squad had taken shelter in a small, rocky gully. Joseph, Yellow Wolf, and other running men jumped down into the rocks. Young Yellow Wolf sensed something, turned to see a trooper aiming his carbine at him, ducked, dodged, and ran into another soldier facing him, thumbing a cartridge into the chamber. The warrior swung his bow, striking the man pointlessly across his head, then grasped the trooper's rifle and tried to wrench it from him but could not. The trooper fell backward but still clutched the gun until Two Moons behind Yellow Wolf shot an arrow into the man's chest.

Now Two Moons strung his bow, facing a soldier aiming a pistol down at him, firing, missing, aiming again, but Yellow Wolf got the wounded trooper's rifle, fired, and struck the soldier's abdomen. The two resumed their hunting, one first, the other following with arrow strung. In this stony gully Joseph and his brother moved more cautiously, Joseph first, bow ready, with Ollokot's repeater a half dozen paces behind him.

Not ten minutes did the fighting last among the rocks. The witness, Yellow Wolf, in later years said not one trooper left that place alive. The Nez Perce scouts were not trusted to carry rifles, and these men tried to leave the field as soon as their detachments were attacked, but three of them were captured running from Theller's volunteers. Several younger men surrounded them and led them back at arrow point a hundred yards to Two Moons and some older men.

The scouts lamented loudly, crying, holding up both hands and begging for their lives. "These poor Christian Indians!" said Two Moons. "They must be crying about what they are doing to their own people! Let them go home." And Two Moons and his friends ran on to the attack.

Four Blankets, a younger warrior, said to the three, "If you help the soldiers any more and we catch you, we will whip you. We will cut hazel switches and we'll beat you good!" The Christians caught their horses and galloped for their lives.

A short while later, Four Blankets rode toward the main line of the soldiers, passing near the skirmish squad on Perry's left. He heard a shout, "Moositsa, danger!" (Moositsa was his Nez Perce name.) He saw no one but pulled his halter, leaning back a little, and a bullet passed under his stomach, cutting through his raised thigh.

Shore Crossing and his young men now ran back to their ponies, but White Necklace and two other women held fresh horses there for them. The warriors leaped onto the ponies' backs and as he snatched the halter, Shore Crossing caught a soldier's rifle thrown up to him by his wife. "You have been running too close," he said to her, smiling. He kicked the pony and the young men rode back toward the ragged line that Trimble and Perry were trying to hold together.

The men from the two companies intermingled, loading, firing frantically as now twenty braves rode toward them, shearing off and firing from behind their ponies under their necks. "The redskins all have rifles!" one man shouted.

"Came well-armed, the bastards!" yelled another.

Other soldiers thought the Nez Perce were running wild horses at them, not seeing the braves riding down around their horses' bodies. Some braves could throw themselves a step in front of their slowing ponies, make a rifle shot with one foot on solid ground, then spring back onto the pony's back.

Parnell shouted to First Sergeant McCarthy. "Hold your men together while I fetch these men up there behind us! I'll come back with them!" He ran up toward the rear where some troopers from the shattered right had dodged in among a scattering of rocks. On the far left, Perry saw Parnell and other troopers running for the rear and yelled, "My God! We'll all be killed! Fall back! Get all the horses!"

But running back, they found their waiting horses twisting, dragging rein, plunging and rearing, slipping from the grasps of panicked holders, who mounted up themselves while gripping only one or two wide-eyed mounts, or letting go. There was no order now as soldiers ran to catch their horses, galloped up the pass, or rallied with the shouting officers. Lieutenant Theller's volunteers had bolted, and now Perry caught sight of him. "Theller! Take command of those men!" He pointed toward a few troopers making their way on foot toward the rear. "Stop them! Rally them!"

Theller would have run past Perry had not the Captain grasped his sleeve and lifted his revolver. "Rally those men you son of a bitch or I'll blow your brains out!"

"Yes, Sir!" Theller shouted. "I'll rally them, Sir!" Drawing his revolver he ran after them, yelling, "Stop, you sons of bitches, stop! I'll blow the brains of any man who runs! Rally!"

Soon he had a group of eight or nine men who had thrown away their rifles turned and facing Shore Crossing and other braves riding in among the backwards-walking line of Perry and Trimble. Surrounded by their own frantic mounts, Theller's men fired revolvers at the galloping warriors. When a burly black horse ran near Theller, the lieutenant threw his pistol down and ran after it.

Shore Crossing saw the running officer, leapt from his pony and in twenty steps had almost caught the terrified man. Theller grabbed the saddle horn and vaulted up as the horse broke into a run. Fastest of all the

Nez Perce, Shore Crossing kept pace with the white-eyed stallion, grasped the leather ammunition belt on the lieutenant's back, and pulled him flailing like a salmon from his horse. The two rolled apart in dust and rocks, and as the warrior sprang back up and drew his knife a shot from horseback tore through Teller's back, exploding out his chest with bits of bone. The man ran several steps, his head back like a gutted fish, and pitched face down onto the hard ground.

"Two by two we fight," shouted Strong Eagle, the brave who shot the officer. "The Nez Perce way!"

Behind him Red Moccasin Tops raised his rifle and sang out a war cry.

"I would have eaten him alive," said Red Sunrise.

"Plenty of soldiers left to eat!" Strong Eagle shouted.

Rock to rock, older Nez Perce warriors shot their arrows at close range at the confused and formless crowd of Perry's and Trimble's troopers. The soldiers fell back, turning, running in squads, firing while men behind them ran, then running as the first men fired, but Joseph and his older friends were soon in among them. Two Moons picked up a rifle, threw it to Joseph, then ran on, stopping to fire until out of ammunition. Joseph looked for soldiers lying dead and saw Snows Resting dash ahead to a soldier getting up on all fours. She unclasped his cartridge belt even as the soldier fumbled for his pistol, ran with the ammunition back to Joseph, who said, "Wife!"

"Go after them! They're running!" Joseph looped the belt across his shoulder and started up the slope.

"That way!" shouted Two Moons, waving toward the soldier's horses crowding up the wagon road. Some troopers were managing to catch loose mounts. "Cut them off from their horses!"

Some cavalry mounts had been carelessly saddled, and when men tried to mount the wheeling horses the saddles turned, spilling men onto the ground. The older warriors stood taking careful aim and shot them flat, while whooping younger braves galloped past them chasing soldiers who had mounted dashing horses.

Talking many years after, a warrior known as Wounded Head recalled the part he played at White Bird Canyon. Days before, at Camas Prairie, some Nez Perce men had told him white soldiers were making war. Refusing to ride off with them (they were the young men who would strike Norton's party), he nonetheless thought he should buy a gun. He had good horses, so he traded one of them for a repeating carbine. He and his wife had been nursing their sick little boy for days. When he came back inside their tipi with the gun, his wife exclaimed, "'You are an awful man, buying a gun to go to war! Look at our child sick in bed! What is wrong with you?'" "'I did not buy this rifle for war! I bought it for summer, hunting buffalo. I will not kill men.' I did not want to go with the five bands; I wanted to stay where we were in hopes the Army wouldn't bother us. But Red Cloud, my old war mate, came and told us we must go or else be slaughtered in our tipi by the soldiers. There was a war by then, and Red Cloud said we had no choice but to go with our People. Some days later, when we camped in White Bird Canyon, warriors came with barrels full of good whisky—good whisky, that the white men drank, not whisky sold to Indians. I got drunk that night. Next morning I was not inside our lodge. I must have lain out in the bushes through the night. Some women found me there and told my wife. 'What are you doing here?' She cried so loud it hurt my head. 'The men have gone up the canyon to the fighting.' 'Is our child no longer sick?' I asked, but all she did was go and get my horse, wake me up again. 'Your best horse, Last Time on Earth.' She called me by my old name, and at that time it did not make me happy. 'Where is your rifle?' She asked. Someone had taken it to the fighting. I jumped on my horse, riding away fast with her scolding me behind. I came to an old man walking and asked if he had a gun. He had an old time pistol with its last ball and powder cap in place. He gave it to me and I rode on toward the sound of fighting. Our warriors were chasing the soldiers up the canyon. I came on dead and wounded white men. I saw one soldier lying on the ground moving so I rode to him but he was well. He asked no questions, just pointed a rifle at me but I shot first and he fell over backwards and did not move. My bullet hit him between the eyebrows. I took his new rifle and left the old man's empty pistol lying on his breast, a present for him. The whisky made me too late for the good fighting. The young warriors were chasing soldiers through the pass. Where I was in the valley, women went from soldier to soldier, getting what they could off them—rifles, bullets, gold, pistols, leather belts to carry bullets, good Army shirts and trousers. There was no scalping like the Sioux, no cutting up bodies. Two of our younger men were catching soldier horses to bring to our herd. I joined them. We came to two soldiers hiding, who made to shoot at us when we came close. We left them dead. By then the fight was far away, too far to catch, so I turned back, riding to the wagon road. Some Nez Perce women called to me, said, 'Look at what is coming!' I looked. A white woman was running, trying to escape from us, going down the hillside. I rode to her. She crouched and crossed her arms across her breasts, crying that I should not kill her. I motioned her to get up behind me on the horse, pulled her up. I had stripped for war. I rode back to the women, asking if they wanted to take care of her. No, they answered; she was mine, and I should take her home to be a wife. I have enough wives, I said. How many do you have, they shouted. One, I said. The white woman didn't understand our language. I rode with her down to a gulch, where I stopped the horse, told her to get off the horse to the ground. She did what I told her; then I got down. She was scared. That white woman was very scared. I stepped toward her, and held out my hand to shake. 'Go,' I told her, English. 'Get out of here, go with your life.' A few years ago I met her again, an old lady. She gave me six dollars. After I sent her running up the trail, I rode to the village. I entered the tipi and told my wife I could have made a half breed today. 'What are you telling me?' she said. I said I gave a white woman a ride on my pony. 'You were with a white woman?' my wife said. 'She rode on your horse with you!' I asked her, 'Do you want me to go to war or not?'"

Another man was drunk the night before. Black Feather said that many men were drunk. "Old men as well as young men, many braves. But I was never counted as a warrior, never went into real fighting. After the White Bird fight I had a gun, and so did many others who made no great use of them. If we did shoot, it was at good distance and from close hiding. I never went ahead a brave man. I followed. I never made myself a brave man. Never did anything of worth."

*

General Howard wrote about the battle in his smooth book on the Nez Perce war. He described how Joseph knew the cavalry was coming: he used a telescope, a "glass"—and then vetoed his chiefs' strong pleas that The People escape across the Salmon. No, said Joseph; the enemy is there and I will strike him. The Nez Perce warriors, Howard wrote, outnumbered his troops three to one—odds as bad, or worse, than any faced by Robert E. Lee in the great War of the Rebellion. To his officers, Howard said it was a loss that for the numbers present was as bad as the Custer massacre at Little Big Horn last summer. Joseph was a fierce and formidable opponent who used his warriors well, possessed superior arms; as a tactician and strategist, he rivaled Lee and Grant. Howard personally would assume immediate command and take the field himself. The Nez Perce would break; they were weak in character and did not possess the will and fibre for a hard campaign. Look at their practices, he said: they're bigamists. Joseph himself has several wives. The nontreaties are obscene in their very essences, he said; and this will sap their strength. The Dreamer faith is no faith; it is delusion—delusion born of self-indulgence. "Do you believe that, General?" His new immediate second in command, Colonel Lucullus Jones, First Cavalry, had known the Nez Perce many years.

"I do. Enough to fight a war at least, I say."

Respectfully the Colonel pointed out there was no good alternative to Nez Perce practice. "The women outnumber men two-to-one or more. Monogamy would mean they'd have to reproduce like Catholics—all due respect, Sir."

"I am not a Catholic, Sir!" the General retorted, closing their introductory conversation. Jones had brought two companies of his regiment at Howard's call for troops. Five companies of the Twenty-first Infantry had come from Oregon by train and wagon; Battery E, Fourth Artillery, would march along as Infantry. In two days, more troopers and more infantry would augment Howard's immediate command to four hundred. Within a few weeks, Howard was to have at his command a thousand men. He also sent a dispatch to his old fellow Union Army officer, John Gibbon, three hundred miles away, to ready his Fifth Infantry in case the Nez Perce broke out into Montana.

Out West the infantry had one advantage over cavalry—that being speed. A man is more efficient as a marcher than a horse: a man is two-fifth legs; a horse is only one-tenth legs. True, cavalry far outdistances infantry the first three days, but gradually the walking men catch up, and in a few weeks or so the infantry and cavalry are neck-and-neck; but then the troopers fall behind. Their grain-fed horses tire, throw shoes, get lame and tender-footed. In short, a horse cannot stand nearly as much war as a man.

The U.S. Cavalry lost thirty-four men killed at White Bird Canyon, a minuscule Gettysburg if you compare percentages. Lee's army lost a third in Pennsylvania, as did Howard here in the morning shadow of the Bitterroots—but Howard's third were all killed, only four men wounded: Lee's killed were only one-fifth of his loss. No Nez Perce was killed; all three wounded recovered, even the gut-shot man, whose mother, it was said, sang medicine songs over him.

The young warrior, runner, Shore Crossing and his battle partners, strong Eagle and Red Moccasin Tops, pledged each other that next time they met Howard's soldiers, all would wear red. "To make good targets," Strong Eagle boasted; "to show the whites that we look down on them."

"Bright red," Shore Crossing added; "bright red all over our bodies, not only shirts."

"Your wife can make us blanket coats," Red Moccasin Tops exclaimed to Shore Crossing. "Blanket coats all the same. We three will be called the Red Coats for all time, at campfires of The People forever!"

But White Necklace shook her head. "Go ask your mother to make your three coats. A mother makes the clothes for boys."

"Boys!" Red Sunset barked indignantly. "We three, you call boys? We rode through the soldiers like weeds and cut them down! The soldiers do not call us boys."

"Then make your boasts to them!" she cried, tears coming fast.

"Wife!" said Shore Crossing. "What is wrong?"

"You will be killed! All of you, all three of you!"

"No, my dear one. Medicine for us is strong! We will not die. The white men will die."

"Boasting will not make it so!"

"I do not understand. To tell stories of bravery—of exploits—to promise great deeds—is this no longer good?"

"This is no buffalo hunt, my brave man."

"It is better than buffalo hunting!"

"You are not yourself when there is man-killing!"

"I am, dear one." He put his deadly hands on her shoulders. "My dear one, the war will not last long. Maybe even now the whites are deciding no more, no more war with Nez Perce warriors. We scattered their dead like seeds in the wind!"

"You must not exult. I heard Joseph say this afternoon out on that field of dead, we should not exult. A field of dead men is never a good thing."

"Joseph is no warrior."

"He is a chief."

"I have no love for him. He is crafty, says things that confuse your mind, makes you think what you do not think."

"Husband, you are the same for me. When I look at you and touch you, my mind goes away and only my heart thinks. If you die, I must die with you."

Two great warriors returned from buffalo country—Rainbow and Five Wounds—as the five tribes set up camp along the full and rushing Salmon River. Seven more strong braves, good fighters, came back with them. The chiefs met in Joseph's tent, sitting down in a circle. Should they cross the Salmon? Should they stay and fight the soldiers again?

White Bird spoke. "We have defeated them badly. The smell of their dead made foul my canyon. But I do not know what they will do now. Will they give up and let us live in peace, will they send to make a treaty again, or will they bring more soldiers until they kill all the Nimiipuu?" He looked around the circle.

Toohoolhoolzote said, "Joseph, you understand the one-armed General."

"He is a white man. He will come after us."

"Then we must fight," said Toohoolhoolzote.

"No," said Ollokot. "To fight him would be foolish. We have defeated him only once. He will bring more men next time."

"He will come himself," said Joseph.

"The two brothers," White Bird grunted; "they never want to fight."

"They were not afraid to fight in White Bird Canyon," Two Moons said. "I saw all day. It is not true what you say about them."

White Bird nodded, frowning. He looked over at the great buffalo hunter. "What do you say, Rainbow? What must we do?"

The big man fingered the brown horn handle of his knife. His long hair, not braided, hung down past his shoulders. "Let us go to Crow country across the Bitterroots, to our friends. The whites in Montana have nothing against us. We can live in Montana free, like the Crow."

"There are soldiers there, too," said Ollokot.

"You say no to everything," White Bird said.

"They are not the same," Red Elk said. "Howard will not cross the mountains. He is Army chief from here west to the ocean."

Ollokot returned, "Are not the whites across the mountains more afraid of Indian people even than the whites here—after what was done by Crazy Horse and Sitting Bull?"

"They were not Nez Perce," said Rainbow.

"And Sitting Bull has gone to Canada," added Five Wounds.

"You hunters like Lakota Sioux. You even look like Lakota." Toohoolhoolzote felt his braids and the men laughed. "But the Lakota are not our friends."

"They are friendly enough," said Rainbow. "Anyway, we do not need to be afraid of them!"

"We have enough war here," said Joseph.

"The Cheyenne," Red Elk added. "They are not our friends."

"No, they are not our friends," conceded Rainbow. "But we do not need to fear them either. They will stay below the Yellowstone anyway. We are friends with the Crow, the Blackfeet, the Flathead. Enough buffalo for all, always."

"Must we go?" asked Joseph.

The chiefs nodded reluctantly. "All The People?" White Bird asked.

"Yes, all The People," Joseph said.

Again, the chiefs nodded, saying "Huh!" emphatically.

"How then will we stay ahead of Howard?" Joseph asked.

"Don't stay ahead of him," White Bird said. "Fight him."

"Send the women, children, and the old ones across the river," Two Moons put in. "Keep the warriors on this side to fight."

Red Elk shook his head. "The women would be helpless on the other side. White settlers and Indians would steal our herd. We cannot leave our women."

"We need them," said Ollokot. "Our numbers are greater with them, our warrior strength, because they bring fresh horses and take the hurt soldiers' guns." Joseph frowned. Ollokot concluded, "We all cross together."

No one disagreed.

"River's high. Fast. It will be difficult. The herds."

"If it will be only difficult," said Toohoolhoolzote, "we can cross in four hours. If you had said it will not be possible, then it would take two days!"

The men all laughed—all but Five Wounds, who squinted. "Huh. Two days. I have a thought."

"Howard will follow us," said Red Elk. "He will cross the river too."

"Yes," agreed Five Wounds. "That might not be bad."

*

During this time the five bands had been moving toward the Salmon. Howard had assembled his force, and five days after the battle of the 17th of June he started with his cavalry. At noon the next day they bivouacked at a ranch near Cottonwood, the next day moving on to Grangeville and Mount Idaho, where the Norton-Chamberlin survivors had found refuge. And finally, nine days after the battle, Howard took the cavalry with cautious carefulness toward the pass at White Bird Canyon. Three miles up the scouts signaled—sitting their horses impassively—the first dead regular. Lucullus Jones rode off the trail and saw what was left of the man. The body lay in long underclothes in the high June sun, face huge and putty-like, gape-mouthed, and black from days of burn. The colonel's horse, throwing its head, shied and backed and then the smell hit: a gulping sick and overpowering wave. Jones had smelled it first at Antietam, the body-thick field, and many other places during the War. More lately, in Apache country under the hot Southwestern sun: the smell of human bodies decomposing had come back—a stench worse than anything, unlike any other rotting flesh, worse than the horse-piss thick smell of dead mounts, a smell called "sweet" but sweet the way you'd call vomit sweet or a soldier's mildewed foot sweet, or the heavy syrup smell of blood sweet. He rode back to the halted column, told Captain Jarret of L Company to detail some men, and said to Howard, "It's not a pretty sight, General."

"It's war, Colonel," the one-armed veteran observed.

It sounded wrong from him, thought Jones, but true enough. "There will be more, that's certain, between here and the field proper in the canyon."

They found two more left from the running fight between retreating troopers and the warriors in taunting, whooping pursuit. As they neared the narrow pass to White Bird Canyon, Howard told the colonel to send out some men, not scouts alone, to secure the elevations and reconnoiter up ahead.

"Hostiles are long gone, General."

"I won't lose more men needlessly. See to it."

As they rode out into the valley the soldiers saw two miles of field, the upper portion littered with a dozen and a half blackened, bloated bodies.

The Colonel ordered E Company to bury them. "I don't want Trimble's boys to have to look at their friends and bunkies," he told Robertson, the captain.

"Wouldn't recognize 'em anyway, Sir," the captain said. "We'll see to it directly."

The men of Jones's First Cavalry were combat soldiers—hadn't spent their time policing peaceful Nez Perce, but had been participants in a long, slow, nasty skirmish against fierce Apache and Arapaho recalcitrants. But burying these rotted troopers proved difficult. The men would not touch the mushy, disintegrating bodies. A soldier's diary entry reads, "Marched down the canyon and were ordered out to bury the Fourth Cavalry's dead. They was laying out there in the sun nine days. Some say coyotes had been eating on them, but I say Nez Perce women cut them up just like Apaches do. Ain't never seen sights more sickening than them soldiers—what was left of them. We dug holes beside the bodies then took and rolled the corpses in with our shovels. Every minute you had to run off and breathe. We'd long lost the inside of our stomachs. We covered them and laid stones on top to keep coyotes from digging them out again. There was plenty of stones, and plenty of coyotes around."

Later in the afternoon as they were finishing, a thunderstorm came up over the canyon walls, thunderheads high and white above, bright white and edged with the sun's gold, hard gray like gun smoke underneath. Bushes and rushes in the dark swale along the creek began to blow and then rain drove in. The soldiers jammed their hats tight on their heads, opened saddle bags and unrolled rubberized canvas slickers, but then the storm was moving fast, its shadow sweeping like a reaper down the valley, darkening the draws and bluffs on the way to Salmon River. As the rain was letting up, a soldier found another man's remains. The corpse had been an officer, his blue jacket still on though unbuttoned wide open.

"That's Theller's jacket," Captain Parnell said when Robertson called him over. "Wrap him in a blanket before you bury him."

"Still got a ring on," Robertson remarked. "Looks to be Masonic. Superstitious redskins didn't want it, I guess."

"Take it off and I'll send it to his family."

"I doubt it, Captain," Robertson said. "Who's going to take it off his hand? Recommend we make the grave and then if anyone wishes to disinter the skeleton next year, they can."

"You're a son of a bitch, Captain," Parnell said.

"Apaches do that for you. Are you saying you are willing to remove that ring?" Parnell walked away and Robertson ordered two men standing to the side and listening, "Find a spare blanket and wrap the body. Display proper respect toward the body of an officer."

Reinforced to 400 soldiers, Howard's command arrived at Salmon River on June the twenty-eighth. Amazed to find the Indians had crossed the river, evidently taking all their non-combatants—and most incredibly of all, their herd that numbered, he was told, almost two thousand horses and considerable cattle—Howard settled down to serious campaigning. He sent unnecessary wagons and supplies back to Fort Lapwai with Captain Perry and his company as escort, ordered preparations made for crossing; stationed one hundred sharpshooters on the ridge behind him with instructions to harass and kill the Indians across the stream, composed a dispatch full of confidence assuring his superiors that Joseph had now made a fatal mistake by delaying to cross the river, and at his headquarters tent caused to be raised the American flag. Across the river simultaneously, a group of observant Nez Perce warriors raised a blanket on a pole—red, of course; and soon a sundry gathering of Nez Perce braves appeared to taunt the soldiers, shouting insults and impugning their ability to cross the swollen stream.

"We called to them," an old Nez Perce survivor told a white man many years later. "We called to them in English, 'Come to us, you assholes! We will give you breakfast! What, you sent your wagon train away? You have no food, cannot invite us back? Poor soldiers! Assholes!' We wanted them to think we wanted them to cross there, at that place. It really was the best place."

But General Howard would not take the bait, marched back along the river looking for a better place, and then began the process of getting men, horses, and Army mules across. First a squad with great difficulty got a rope across, secured it, and used it to get back. The soldiers constructed a small raft and then commenced to ferry Howard and command across—the feat needing forty-eight long hours, adding to the time the Nez Perce had to approach the looming Bitterroots with horses, cattle, and six hundred human beings. Howard's force of four hundred fighting men required two days to cross; the Nez Perce had done it in three hours.

Nez Perce Christian scouts shadowed the five bands, staying on their own side of the river—until they topped a rise and confronted four warriors waiting for them silently a hundred yards away. Five Wounds had sent them back across the river. The Christian scouts pulled up, and one of them put on a shield of boldness, calling, "Why do your people run from the Army? You cannot get away!"

"You have four hundred white men behind you, with guns on wagons."

"Cowards!" the Christian shouted.

A warrior answered, "You call us cowards, we who are trying to defend our land, our wives and children, and our old people? You, growing fat on government food, scouting for the whites who murder us and steal our country! Come closer and we cowards will kill you!"

"We have no rifles."

"The soldiers do not give you guns? Christians do not trust Christians?"

"The soldiers are our brothers!"

"You are their sisters!"

"All Christians are brothers!"

"Go," called the warrior; "tell your brothers to behave like brothers!"

The scouts turned their horses and slowly rode back the way they had come. The warriors watched long after the Christians had gone, staying where they were.

Joseph was the camp chief, organized all the families and their possessions, tipis, furnishings, supplies—the first time ever that The People moved in such a hurry with so many. "How did we cross the Salmon?" Yellow Bird was asked in later years. "Same as we crossed all other deep, swift-moving streams with all our families and goods! We knew those rivers and knew how to manage. At this crossing we had only one course. Did we take The People over a few at a time, as the soldiers did? No! We crossed over all at once. I will tell you how we managed that. We made hide boats using buffalo. The big skins with hair side up were spread flat on the ground. Across the hide were laid green willow and whatever limber poles we found, about the thickness of your thumb. The hides and poles were bent up and lashed to other poles to form a circled rim. And that was all. Such boats carried big loads. The children and old people rode on top of those packs. Everything was ferried in those boats—our tipi covers, cooking pots, pans, blankets, everything. No paddles used. The boats were hauled by ponies in the water, guided by men—two ponies, maybe three or four, for every boat. Two other men swam beside the boat to steady it. Then we swam all the animals across.

The horses spread almost a mile downstream, but it was easy to get them. So all The People crossed quick; it was not difficult for us. All but thirty warriors went ahead. We stayed behind to watch the whites. Howard's soldiers did not cross where we had crossed. The whites could not swim their horses as the Nez Perce could. But they did not give up. They went looking for some other place, and when they were on our side of the Salmon they came after us fast."

*

"Why did they cross the Salmon?" Howard asked his scouts. "Are they headed south?" The Christian Nez Perce scouts could not know what The People intended. Maybe they will circle south of us and double back to their land. They do not want to leave their land. "I know that," Howard said. "That is why we are at war with them."

He turned to Colonel Jones. "It matters little where Joseph goes or why, for I shall follow him, and we shall round him up!"

"And then, Sir? What shall we do with them once we have caught them? Shoot them?"

Howard stiffened, not knowing whether he was being trifled with. "My orders are to drive the Nez Perce onto their reservation, and I shall execute those orders."

"General, I meant no disrespect. I was only musing on the difference between how things are here and what our superiors imagine."

"You have stated it exactly, Sir. Of course I wonder the same myself. It will take some time for you and me to grow accustomed to each other—our different tones, one might say."

"Yes, Sir. I was being ironical, Sir."

"Jones, I do have a sense of humor. I can be a man of humor. When pressed." Howard smiled. "Be at ease, Colonel. We shall get along very well."

"Like Herod and Pilate, Sir!"

Howard darkened and turned away. After a few moments' silence he turned back. "I have prayed for us, Colonel. Now I believe that will be all."

The soldiers, having crossed, knew that the hostiles were very near. In bivouac they were issued forty extra rounds of ammunition, told to expect to be engaged with Joseph tomorrow. That meant, wrote a lieutenant later, "the usual variety of soldier behavior facing imminent death. In camp—singing old songs in chorus, telling stories, swearing carelessly, but little card playing. Card playing was too much like battle, I think. It felt like all luck, when what you wanted was not luck. A soldier accepts horrible things, corpses mutilated on the field—ours or theirs—ghastly forms—killing, itself. On the night before a battle it is time to write to sweethearts, mothers, wives. You joke about being killed. You talk about 'my body,' not to look for it, as if without thinking. Old soldiers feel the dread as much as new recruits—more, I think, each fright worse than the last. As you near the field, you want to get out of it, wonder how you got into it. Each soldier thinks he will escape, yet this is when the soldier thinks about immortality, prays to God, prays to Jesus, rues that there's no time to change his ways, makes promises. You seldom think the enemy is doing just the same, praying to God, maybe with a different name."

Yellow Wolf said later, "Next morning scouts brought word the soldiers crossed, were on our side of the River. This was good. Immediately we crossed back to the north side."

III

Camas Prairie

Looking Glass was forty-five or thereabouts in June of 1877, some gray streaks running down his braided hair. A handsome man of middle height, he wore brass earrings and adorned the braid that ran down beside his face with shiny, twisted brass. Two feathers or a white man's black hat would decorate his head, but never would he wear a war bonnet, the large head-dress that dominates the portraits of Cheyenne and Lakota. The thing that people noticed was a necklace that suspended a metal or glass mirror—that and his small hands, more like a woman's hands than those of a warrior as famous as he was. In buffalo country he had fought the Cheyenne for the Lakota: he made his reputation there. As brave as Custer, he was not a war lover, knew that any war against the whites was hopeless war; as intelligent as Howard, he was honest, holding to no hope for anything for Indians any more, a dreamless man with a mirror.

After Howard's May council where he showed the rifle, Looking Glass and his chiefs, Red Owl, Red Heart, and others decided to divide themselves away from Joseph, White Bird, and the five bands camped on Camas Prairie, and return to their own land along Clearwater River—land already safe within the boundary of the new, smaller reservation ordered for them by the white man's government. This way they showed that they were peaceful Indians; this way there would be no trouble.

And that is where they were in June, back home along the Clearwater, where they plowed land and grew potatoes, corn, squash, cucumbers, melons, beans—and raised milk cows like the white people, and gave the milk to their children. Eleven large tipis, lodges, stood along the river, housing twenty men of warrior age and another hundred twenty women, children, and older men and women. When battle rose in White Bird Canyon, it rose without them; these people did not learn of it until reports were brought to them two days after. Looking Glass was the chief's white name; his Nez Perce name was *Alalimya Tekanin*, which was the name that Joseph used months later, at the end when he made his famous speech beginning, "Hear me, my chiefs, my heart is sad and sick," and ending with, "From where the sun now stands, I will fight no more forever." It was of course a translation when Joseph told them simply, "Looking Glass is dead."

The boy Red Heart was son of a treaty chief whose band lived on the reservation. His buddy Red Coyote was a warrior's son of Red Bird's buffalo hunting non-treaty band. The two would fish, swim, and ride in springtime before White Bird's people left for Montana. This June the two shouted to each other, whooping, the news of raids against the whites and rumors of a great battle down in White Bird Canyon. The two boys stripped for war and rode to find adventure. In early morning's light they saw a white man's stallion grazing in a hazy field, a ghostly cream white breeding stud ready for the taking. They haltered it with Red Coyote's halter, leading it as carefully as quail hunters, then breaking for the open spaces. Where to take it? Not to Red Heart's band, the Presbyterians—and White Bird's people, maybe on the run, were somewhere to the south of Salmon River. Let's take the horse to show our cousins up at the Clearwater; it might be Looking Glass himself will tell the elders what braves we are.

Of course the white man and his neighbors tracked them. To a Native Person, a horse means sustenance and wealth, honor, pleasure, and love of beauty. To a white man, a horse can become a matter of principle. The white men tracked the horses far enough to see where the hoof prints led. Soon Howard received reliable reports that Indians of Looking Glass's band were stealing horses and probably would go on a rampage as the other non-Christians had—Joseph's band, that is. Howard wrote that twenty braves had gone from Looking Glass's band to Joseph's; later, after contemplating the groundless outrage he had unleashed on Looking Glass within the reservation, he doubled the number, claiming it was forty "bucks." The man who founded or helped to found two colleges for Black ex-slaves and led the Freedman's Bureau for a time now used the same word for young male Native People that Southern slavers had used for Black people.

Those twice-twenty bucks were dangerous and Howard offered to believe what he was ready to believe. "Colonel Whipple, you will take two companies together with two Gatling guns, conduct a night march to the village of Looking Glass, surprise that chief, capturing him and all that belongs to him."

Whipple was a California veteran. Cited for "faithful, meritorious service" there, Whipple next worked in Arizona with the First Cavalry. But this night's forced march did not proceed propitiously. At dawn, the moment Army tactics specified as that at which you charge a sleeping village, Whipple was still miles away. At seven, as the Indians were breakfasting, Whipple showed up with his Whipplets and the rest is history, recorded in the words of Peopeo Tholekt, Bird Alighting, a buck in Looking Glass's camp: *"My wife had given birth and I was staying with her at Lapwai, but when I heard the news of war, I went up quickly to Clearwater, to the village of my chief, Looking Glass. Next morning it was Sunday and some Indians had gone down to the Kamish Dreamer church. I was in Looking Glass's tipi, where the chiefs, conducting a traditional Sunday breakfast, got word that soldiers were coming down the mountain just across Clear Creek. Our village stood where Clear Creek joins Clearwater River. My chiefs said to me, 'You better go and meet the soldiers. Tell them, Leave us alone. Tell them, We live here in peace and want no trouble.' I mounted, rode across the creek, and met the soldiers. A scout the whites call a squaw man greeted me in good Nez Perce, and I gave the message that we want no trouble. But the soldiers would not listen, and came near to killing me. One said to me, 'You Looking Glass?' He jabbed me in the ribs with his gun muzzle. He jabbed me hard. Another soldier said, 'Hold on! This is not Looking Glass! Only one of his boys!' I went back and entered Looking Glass's tipi. Some Indians there had watched and seen the soldier strike me with his gun. They said the soldiers mean to kill the chief. So Looking Glass would not go, sent me again instead. An old man, Kalowet, went with me. Looking Glass raised a white cloth on a pole between his tipi and the creek. I told the soldiers, 'I am Peopeo Tholekt. Looking Glass is my chief. I bring his words. He does not want war! He came here to escape war! Do not cross to our side of the creek. We want no trouble!' The old man, Kalowet, spoke for peace, said they had not been at White Bird. But the same mad soldier struck me with his gun again and said, 'This Injun's Looking Glass! I will kill him!' I told myself that I will die a brave man. But another soldier said I was too young. I was not Looking Glass. Then their commander took some men and went with me and Kalowet across the creek to Looking Glass's lodge. He was not there. The chief had disappeared. As we were talking some white men fired across the creek and wounded Red Heart in the thigh. At this the white men whirled their horses and rushed across the creek, and then the soldiers opened fire on us."*

The soldiers poured their fire into the tipis. Some Nez Perce men were killed outright. A woman with her baby rode her horse into the river—all three drowning in the roiling stream. Bird Alighting admitted that his horse was bad and would not move and then commenced to buck. Then the warrior got shot—a bullet hit him in the leg like a club—and the horse stopped.

Bird Alighting drew his rifle from its case and hit the animal on the head, which made it buck again, and now the young man clobbered the horse until he cut the bucking and agreed to go. The brave rode along the corral fence as bullets struck the wood like hail, clubbing the horse toward the river where others were running to find cover by the bank. He overtook a warrior trying to get away, who pleaded that Peopeo Tholekt take him up behind on the horse. The brave shouted 'No! My horse is bad!' but saw death for that man if he didn't help. He pulled him up behind.

"Soon I felt something was wrong. I could not see very well. I felt my body, breast and shoulders, found no wound, said 'I'm all right,' but quickly everything turned yellow—then all color, all light went out. I went out of my senses and the man I helped held me up, kept me from falling. He saw blood running over my moccasins, felt for my wound, found that the bone was not broken. We rode like that a quarter mile when I came back to living and could see. I saw the soldiers close after us. My partner was scared. I thought that we would die. And then we saw a woman riding toward us, ready with a rifle to attack the soldiers. She fired shots, two, three, four, five. The soldiers now were busy with our tipis, breaking our copper kettles with their boots and bayonets, stealing our robes, trying to light the tipis on fire. The woman helped me with my wound; she wrapped it up tight with cloth. She wore a wolf's hide wrapped around her shoulders and she called herself Arrowhead. She was a brave woman. If Looking Glass had been a man, he would have gone to meet the soldiers even if they would have killed him! There was a fine boy named Nennen Chekoostin, or Black Raven, a handsome, good boy—seventeen snows old—shot through the thigh as I was. He travelled almost three miles on his feet. He got weak. He sat down with his back against a tree. Some women came by and wrapped up his leg, but could not stop the blood. Then I saw him. All color and light left Black Raven's eyes. He had an empty six-shooter—it slipped from his hand, he felt for it. 'Where is my gun?' he asked. I put it in his hand. Then he said, 'Tired, tired! Now I sleep.' The soldiers stole nearly all our horses, more than six hundred. They rode away and left us nothing but our tipis. They took or ruined everything they could—even burned two tipis. We wanted peace. We ran away from Joseph, White Bird, and Toohoolhoolzote, but now, when they came near, moving to go north of Salmon River on the way to the Bitterroot Mountains, we joined them. There could be no going back."

Howard reported that his troopers successfully destroyed Looking Glass's village. Regrettably Whipple had not carried out Howard's orders to arrest Chief Looking Glass and bring his people in. This caused Howard, he wrote, disappointment. The war on the non-treaty bands had now become Looking Glass's war.

In Washington a new president sat in the chair of U.S. Grant. Rutherford Hays had not been elected fair and square. His party, the Republicans, had cut a deal with Southern Democrats when the close electoral count threw the decision into the House of Representatives: Agree to Hays and we shall end Reconstruction, pull out all Federal troops from the defeated South, and let you handle your government and your Negroes as you see fit. You have a deal, you damn Yankees, said the former Rebels; and the "swindle"—as Mark Twain named it—brought the nation together, a grand reunion after a bloody civil war. Now Mr. Hays had his attention turned to the far West.

Newspapers had picked up the story of another Indian War. Settlers had been murdered and property destroyed; and now a battle had been fought—fought and lost, grossly mishandled, troops killed. The latest word was that an innocent village had been massacred by clumsy officers and undisciplined troops—friendly Indians, the tribe that helped Lewis and Clark. The President told Sherman, "You must see to this: If General Howard can't suppress these Indians, find someone else who can! There shall not be another Custer debacle while I am president, nor shall I allow these hostiles to go unpunished. These savages who terrorize civilians must be made to feel the full weight of the United States armed forces. Let General Howard understand that his career is on the line. Make him understand this is war. I remember Howard from the war. The Christian Soldier. Get someone ready to replace the man."

White volunteers from Cottonwood and Grange had organized a company and chosen Darius B. Randall captain. He was a veteran of the Civil War, had seen what war was all about, and he knew how to make decisions and give orders. He knew that Howard was still two or three days south, but the Nez Perce were back near Cottonwood on their way north toward Looking Glass's camps and Camas Prairie. With his fifty volunteers and a squad of U.S. Cavalry, he'd keep an eye on Joseph, at the same time showing force enough to discourage the hostiles from swinging near the settlements. Sending two white cowhands ahead as scouts, he ordered Lieutenant Sevier Rains to take his squad of cavalry toward the high ground five miles north, and look around.

The cowhands were Pick Foster and Chub Blewett—"Pick" because he'd hunted gold with pick and shovel several years and swung heavy tools for the railroad before that, and Chub was so thin he had a dent where most men kept a chest. They saddled up and rode out while Rain's troopers groomed their horses, checked their tack, and lined up for ammunition. The morning sun shone in a wide sky; ahead for miles was open country cut by draws, small gullies, and rock outcroppings. Then farther on ahead the land began to rise and somewhere up there you'd find several thousand head of ponies driven by skedaddling Nez Perce. There would be war parties out there, too, keeping a lookout. "You don't figure to argue with them, do you, Chub?"

"Not if we see them first. Depends how many, though. One or two, just might go collect a scalp, a souvenir. Won't be much chance of that after this one blows over."

"That's what I thought you'd say." Pick Foster fingered the reins and mused, "You're the scrappiest character I've run up against out here."

"I grew up scrappin' and anyhow, I ain't afraid of redskins. Can't shoot good enough to plug me—ain't got enough meat on me to hit."

"Well I'll let you go first then if we spot any of 'em. You know Looking Glass is up there somewhere."

"Looking Glass! You see, Pick, with them Indians it's like fighting children. The men are all Big Buffalo and Running Wolf, and the squaws is Pigeon Feather and Dancing Rabbit—names some child would think up. They ain't got proper names. Slow up a bit." The two dropped from a trot to a walk, then halted entirely.

The Indian they saw watching them was called Red Spy. He sat his horse motionless among some Cottonwoods, maybe three hundred yards away.

"You can't hardly see 'im," Chub said quietly; "but he's had his eye on us a long time, I'll bet." He began to draw his rifle from the case in front of the saddle.

"It's a long shot, Chub."

"Yeah," Blewett agreed, letting his rifle slide back. "Let's go up a bit, see what happens." The two walked their horses forward. The warrior still sat motionless.

"Hold up," Blewett said. "Suppose there's more?"

"Doubt it. He's a lone scout. We get much closer and he'll make the coyote call." Blewett smoothly drew his rifle out and put it to his shoulder, cocking it. "Whoa." He said quietly, as his horse side-stepped and lowered its head, recognizing the sound of a rifle's hammer cocked. Blewett fired. The Indian didn't move; then kicking a leg over his pony's neck, he jumped lightly to the ground with his rifle, bracing it in the cradle of a branch.

"Oh, shit," Foster said.

"Don't worry, Pick. Them Indians can't use sights. But let's do move apart so he don't get lucky."

Pick touched a spur to the horse's inside flank as he heard the distant crack of the Indians rifle. An instant later Chub exclaimed, "Christ, I'm hit!"

Foster saw him drop the rifle, clutching at his chest as he went off the horse backwards, but didn't look further. Using his spurs, Foster flailed his horse back toward Cottonwood. Racing back the shortest way, he bypassed Rain's squad going out down along lower ground, the two not catching sight of each other.

Back in the cottonwoods Red Spy, never having killed a man, began to chant a rising, falling repetition—part exultation and part lament.

Scouting with Red Spy a quarter mile away, Yellow Wolf put his heels to his pony's sides and galloped toward the wailing song. Closer, he saw Red Spy remount his horse and trot toward the white man on the ground, whose shying horse trotted and circled, then broke at a run toward Cottonwood. Yellow Wolf pulled up beside Red Spy, who was standing silently over the dead man.

He looked up at his friend: "Go back for Five Wounds. The other white man rode back for soldiers."

"I saw the soldiers," Yellow Wolf said, "riding this way down there." He pointed toward the draws and gullies to the southwest.

"Let's go and wave the blanket," Red Spy said, stooping down for the white man's rifle, and pulling the pistol that was tucked inside his belt. "No ammunition."After they had signaled, the two remained on the higher ground. Before long a string of hard riding braves approached. At their head rode a strongly built man of near middle age, painted and stripped for war. As he came closer, the two young warriors saw the grim and angry determination in his face, light in his eyes.

"How many? Where?" His deep voice was calm but forceful.

Yellow Wolf pointed: "Ten, twelve. Soldiers, not settlers." Pointing up the other way: "Red Spy has killed one white scout—there. Another scout ran. He will bring more soldiers." Five Wounds cradled his rifle across his lap, looking toward the gullies and draws, then over toward Cottonwood. "Good!" He nodded. "More soldiers, good, yes. Rainbow is leaving camp now. He will be here this afternoon with twenty warriors. First we will kill the ten, twelve soldiers down there." He looked in the direction Rains was coming. "I smell Long Knives," Five Wounds said.

"I, too," said another man.

Yellow Wolf tested the air. If the breeze came right, you could smell soldiers. Unlike the Nez Perce, white soldiers did not wash themselves often. They smelled of sweat, smoke, urine, unpleasant food. Red Spy shook his head, but Yellow Wolf nodded.

Five Wounds turned around on his horse and pointed at Strong Eagle, who wore a long blanket coat of bright red. "You ride down and let them see you, then ride back toward these two—" pointing at Red Spy and Yellow Wolf. "You two stay. Hold the soldiers if they get this far. We will ride down out of their sight and let them come to us. When they pass, we will take them from behind."

Yellow Wolf and Red Spy looked at each other as the Warriors rode away. "I was afraid," Yellow Wolf said many years later. "But you did what Five Wounds said."

*

The soldiers rode from Captain Randall's camp out toward the place where Foster left his pal, to bring the body in and to get a sense of Nez Perce strength and where they were headed. Three miles or so out from the entrenched camp they spotted something moving up ahead—maybe a mile, just part of some scattered rocks and near a stand of cottonwoods and oak. They chucked their horses to a jingling trot to take a closer look, and sure enough it was a hostile—but could you figure, a Nez Perce in a blanket coat, bright red, on this warm day. The Indian sat his horse watching them, then slowly turned away.

Rains drew his breath to shout, "Full gallop!" but breath caught in his chest—Indians everywhere, out from these trees and up from nowhere, up from the gullies Rains's men had skirted. "Get out of here!" Rains shouted once his breath returned, and all wheeled horses, galloping back toward Cottonwood, an impossible five miles away now.

But Lieutenant Rains was confident that if his men could keep a little distance from the Nez Perce they would be met by Captain Randall leading out a force to rescue him. He knew that Randall had his eyes on him, that several pairs of field glasses discerned the situation. The troupers lashed tired mounts with reins and spurred the lathered horses, Rains and five men in a pack at the front, the other six on slowing horses strung out behind, bent low and forward, shouting, pleading toward their horses' plunging heads.

Then streaking out ahead of the Nez Perce warriors, a bull-like man with red-streaked face and chest caught the last man, who at the final moment turned his head to see the enraged face and pointed carbine. The point blank discharge blew the soldier sideways and his body rolled and jolted like a broken doll across the rocky ground.

Five Wounds touched his pony with his heels and surged past the riderless cavalry horse, overtaking the next man, who having heard the shot turned, drew his revolver, fired twice, his arm waving crazily with the aimless pistol, held the pistol now along his horse's neck and turned with white eyes to see Five Wounds fire—and horse and rider tumbled rolling hard onto stony ground, the bullet having cut through the man's body and lodging in the horse's driving shoulder.

Now Five Wounds slowed his winded pony and several warriors galloped past, kicking to a dead run. Two shots pitched the next man forward on his horse; he swung down, caught by the stirrup, his neck cracking with the shock of dropping and his head punching along the rocks. Yellow Wolf and Red Spy saw the strung-out soldiers fall. They rode down carefully, picking their way, then finding level open ground they chased the soldiers from the other side, still several hundred yards behind Strong Eagle riding up along the line of trees. Three more soldiers, one by one, were felled by Five Wounds and his warriors. And now the half dozen troopers in front found rocks the size of tables on a rise. The soldiers pulled up, jumped from their horses, and dropped down behind the rocks. Yellow Wolf and Red Spy halted too, unsure of what to do but choosing not to ride at soldiers aiming from the ground. Already Five Wounds had turned his warriors off and down the rise behind the enemies; he pointed once like lighting up at Strong Eagle a quarter mile away and Yellow Wolf understood. He motioned once to Red Spy and the two dismounted. They left their horses hobbled and, running low, they quietly approached the soldiers.

Strong Eagle rode along the tree line, raising his rifle, chanting his war song. Volley after volley, the soldiers fired toward him. Too far, Yellow Wolf thought; the enemies have panicked now, and they think we are all up in the woods behind Strong Eagle; they will not see us until we are close. Wrong to kill unsuspecting men by shooting at the backs of their heads. They murder us, they kill our children; but no, we will not be like them. We are not fighting the whites in order to become like them.

He felt his medicine bag, worn like a necklace—prayed his Wyakin for help to kill but not to soil his spirit. Perhaps the grandfathers watched: they would know what to do. The soldiers all were turned toward Strong Eagle, shooting up toward the trees from behind their rocks. One of them dived forward, throwing out his arms as if embracing the stone; the shot was Five Wounds—and the other soldiers, seeing this man shot from behind, all turned, their eyes bulging; they worked their sweaty hands to jam cartridges into their carbines. Yellow Wolf and Red Spy rose up and fired; others on the rise aimed from rocks and fired—perhaps twenty shots fired at the soldiers.

Randall saw it all, three miles away—saw the last six regulars surrounded and shot down—could see rifle smoke, riderless horses; he understood what was happening to Lieutenant Rains. But all he saw were some dozen hostiles. He believed a hundred more were out there waiting and he dared not leave the cover of his rifle pits and howitzer to get cut off. These dozen braves were decoys, Randall thought; they meant that Joseph and his whole force were now in front of him.

Yellow Wolf stood and watched for movement, then with the others walked toward the dead whites. He raised his right hand at Strong Eagle, who had circled on his horse to bring the two hobbled ponies. All stood looking at the scout and soldiers lying in front of the rocks. Blood pooled and ran down in rivulets along the hard, dry soil. You could smell it, thick, heavy, dizzying; and the soldier sweat was bad.

Strong Eagle rode up, leading the two horses. Five Wounds said to him, "You did well, Strong Eagle; but now give that blanket to an old woman. If you wear it in battle, you will be shot and then you will die from a small wound as the white soldiers die from their small wounds. Fight naked as your people fight, and you will not die from a small wound. You are young; listen!" Strong Eagle nodded.

The buffalo warrior spoke again, to the others: "Not one of us killed. Not even hurt. Understand: our Wyakin have been powerful today." Without being told, the warriors began to take the ammunition belts, carbines, and revolvers off the soldiers. They could use their shirts and trousers. No knives came out; no brave cut or scalped. Yellow Wolf had picked up the rifle lying in front of the soldiers' volunteer scout, who lay curled up on his side. Suddenly the man sat up. His back against a rock, the man, who had been Pick Foster, looked around.

Yellow Wolf stared aghast and let the carbine drop. The white man's face ran with blood: between his eyes in the middle of his forehead, a hole spilled blood. The man raised both hands to his face and washed his face with the blood; then dropping his hands he made noises like a chicken. "Cluck! Cluck! Cluck! Cluck!" The warriors stood silent.

Then Red Spy said, "Who is this man?" Strong Eagle dismounted and walked to the man. "He can't live. He is too bad hurt!" All noticed then the two soaked bullet wounds in the man's chest. Five Wounds grunted disagreement. "He can live if he wants to. He has a power; he is like one of us!"

"Let us see if his power saves him!" said Strong Eagle.

Red Spy said, "He cannot live. No power can save him. He is too bad shot. He is shot in the forehead!"

"I want to see," Yellow Wolf said.

Then an older warrior, Smoker, who carried an old flintlock musket, grounded the stock and poured powder from his old horn down the barrel. "We shall not leave the man like that. He suffers! He will be too long dying!" Smoker took a large lead ball from the pouch suspended on the rawhide thong looped across his chest, then rammed the bullet home. He primed the musket, pulled the outsized hammer back, and standing to the side raised the weapon halfway, aiming at the dead man's chest. The flash was bright and the bang loud against the rocks; the discharge knocked the man back down on his side. When the smoke cleared, the man sat up.

Again the man's hands rose to his face; again he washed his face with blood; again he made the noise—"Cluck! Cluck! Cluck! Cluck!" The warriors stood silent. Then Strong Eagle said to Smoker, "See! We all have told you that your musket is no good!" But no one laughed.

Slowly Smoker grounded the musket, poured the powder, thumbed the ball and rammed it home. This time he stood in front of the dead man. Again he pulled the hammer, lowering the weapon to Pick Foster's chest. He fired. The body jolted in the smoke.

He sat, his hands down at his side. He raised them to the face and washed it with the running blood. "Cluck! Cluck! Cluck! Cluck!" He seemed to look around with his bloody eyes, no battle rage left on his face, nothing but dripping blood from his forehead and the glaring noon sun. Strong Eagle came forward with his war club raised; he struck the head with all his strength.

The man drooped forward, head hung down, and Yellow Wolf cried "No! Let's save him!"

Five Wounds put his hand on Yellow Wolf. "We have no doctor. Poor fellow! How he suffers! Let us put him out of trouble." He raised his club and struck. "There was not one of us that did not strike," said Yellow Wolf in 1930, fifty some odd years later. "And not one of us who were there have ever forgotten it."

Now Five Wounds said, "It is enough. We have killed thirteen enemies, and none of us is hurt. We will fight no more today." But the sound of horses came, and soon a line of warriors single file. At their head rode Rainbow, the great Plains warrior. White paint blazed his face, streaked with red, orange, yellow. His pale horse bore red paint on its chest; around its left eye was drawn a white circle, and black paint circled its right eye. He rode into the grim group of warriors standing over the dead body and stopped his horse. Saying nothing, he raised his right arm, pointing up toward Cottonwood.

*

Some two days south of Cottonwood, Howard and his force of infantry and cavalry— four hundred soldiers and their scouts—marched north following the five bands' wide trail worn deep by herds of horses and cattle.

The chiefs had sent two groups of warriors west to strike at Cottonwood to screen The People's flight to north and east, protecting their left flank from soldiers known to be on watch or marching from the west. The Nez Perce sent small parties out to watch for couriers and sometimes knew what Howard's orders were. The General stuck to the trail, still confident that he and several hundred soldiers could catch up to Indians with children, old people, and herds.

With Howard's troopers rode the doctor, John Fitzgerald, whose careful wife wrote pictures from her heart to him nearly every day. Each day he wanted one, but usually they came in bundles tied by hasty sergeants; so most days went without her voice. Emily helped with nursing at Fort Lapwai, both whites and Indians, and wrote her husband:

Dear, you mustn't let the savages keep husbands from their wives. I mean the officers of course, the generals and what-not ordering you about. Tell General Howard you've a note from me that authorizes only one week's absence from your wife. Dear John, be diligent returning to me when you've corralled Joseph and Associates, but drag your feet while putting miles between the young doctor and his pining wife. Do keep good cheer, my husband, remembering no matter what hardships you must endure—fatigue of march, heat of sun, cold of wind—that I and all your comforts await you here; your old chair vacant by the lamp, adoring wife, clean sheets and Western cooking vouchsafed daily, cheaply, by the hands of conscientious, Christian Appaloosa squaws. Must say I wonder at their superstitiousness, much as that our big politicos in Washington will really leave them anything after we have made America of everything out here—even their reservation. Suppose some antiquated forty-niner pans up gold or stumbles on a silver streak near Lapwai here, on Nez Perce land. What then? The Indians shall have to move—and move again, whenever anything is found we want, until they move at last into the waters of the Pacific. But what else can be done? Our millions need this land; the days and ways of yore are gone like Hiawatha and Evangeline, and all these beaded savages shall be but words in some poor child of Longfellow's pen. And savages they are, my Dear—I see them every day here at the fort, the Christian Nez Perce; I wouldn't change my place with theirs for anything, they live so meanly, day to day—not mean in comforts merely—mean in education, culture, hope—and science too: you've seen their medicine, such as it is. And fashion! The salons of Paris would be scandalized by things we see. But here, you see, you take your naked children (pardon me) running all the day, spring, summer, fall—healthier than you or I by far—until tuberculosis comes, of course, brought, of course, by you and me and ilk of ours. And take your nearly naked warrior (pardon me)—when he is wounded he recovers, while our soldier boy lies languishing with wounds gangrenous, pyemic, and

all other horrid things you treat. And why? Because our civilized soldier wears
clothing: bullets push dirty rags into the wounds. And so our soldier boy dies of
modesty, quite literally. Modesty and comfort—the evidence of Christian civi-
lization. It's too complicated for me, Dear. Well, I shall puzzle it out whilst you
are roughing it. Please give the General regards for me, and tell him—won't
you, Doctor?—he must take a cup of spirits for his stomach's sake—quoth St.
Paul, General Commanding. Love—

Howard ordered Perry up to Cottonwood with infantry and two new
Gatling guns—instruments of firepower that worked by crank, like a mill—
the first machine guns though limited as yet in usefulness because they were
as big as cannons, needing caissons, limber chests, and teams of horses. But
these auxiliaries, Perry had, and what the warrior Rainbow saw and pointed
at was Perry's column coming in to Cottonwood, the Gatlings gleaming in
the sun. Not many years later on the banks of Wounded Knee, the army
would use Gatling fire to murder Big Foot and his sleeping families one cold
December dawn.

Understanding what they meant, the painted warrior Rainbow said
to Five Wounds, "You must fight again today. For they will come, now that
they have the guns. We stop them here, or they will bring their guns to the
families before they can cross Clearwater and the Camas Meadow. If The
People reach the Bitterroots, they will be safe."

Five Wounds nodded. "We will die here, then. We can defeat soldiers
but not those big guns."

"Maybe they will not bring the guns today. Their wagon horses have
pulled many miles. Maybe they will plant them up there." He swept his arm
toward the hills behind Cottonwood. "Then they will feel brave enough to
send out more soldiers."

Strong Eagle, standing straight, chest forward, looked up at Rainbow.
"I am not afraid of their big guns."

"I am," Five Wounds said behind him.

"I will ride behind them and kill their horses."

Rainbow silently regarded the young warrior, then remarked, "And
they will not see you, bright red. Young man, we are going to war. Leave the
coat here."

"I told him," said Five Wounds.

Strong Eagle looked up at Rainbow angrily. "Why do you older warriors try to humiliate us? I have sworn an oath with my friends. We-—" He
stopped speaking when Shore Crossing rode out from the warriors who had
come with Rainbow.

His friend was stripped for war, the usual red paint covering his
face and chest. "Strong Eagle," the wide-shouldered young man said, "he

humiliated me too—with good reason. We must become grown men today. If we play with our lives like boys, we play with our families' lives. Leave your coats and come fight with me."

"Put it over that battered white man," said Five Wounds. "Maybe your coat will keep the prairie wolves away, and please the Spirit."

"My mother made this," said Strong Eagle.

"My mother made *this!*" laughed Shore Crossing, pointing to his breechcloth. "Come fight with me, my friend."

*

At Cottonwood, command had changed. Perry, holding captain's rank in the regular U.S. Army, assumed command. Randall called for volunteers to go with him out to bring the thirteen bodies in, expecting his whole company to saddle up, but only sixteen men agreed.

"Very well," a tense and angry Randall said, "Seventeen of us will go."

"I won't stop you from going, Randall," Perry said, "but I can't come out to help you if you bite off more than you can chew. Until General Howard arrives, we are all the troops these people have. I won't come out from these fortifications."

"Suit yourself," Randall said. "Boots and saddles," he told his bugler. "Play it one last time."

*

Thomas Sutherland was twenty-two years old. A graduate of Harvard, Sutherland expected success, and for a journalist success was having stories run back East in papers like the *New York Herald*, *Harper's Weekly*, and the dailies read in Boston, Washington, and Philadelphia. This, Sutherland set out to achieve. The news that Easterners paid money for this year that followed Armstrong Custer's massacre at Little Bighorn—was news from the West: hot news of Indian battles, Crazy Horse, and Sitting Bull. The Bicentennial Year was over now, and Custer's killers stood at bay—so Sutherland looked farther West and found his war in Idaho. He would be first to ride with fighting troops, be first in U.S. history to be "embedded" as they call it now, and send dispatches out from where the action played.

One morning bright and early Sutherland appeared before the tent of O. O. Howard, one-armed hero of the Civil War, the Christian Soldier. He'd studied up on Howard, learned all about the Freedman's Bureau, read the citation for his Medal of Honor, knew not to ask about Chancellorsville or ever mention Stonewall Jackson. But best of all, he'd gone to Temperance meetings, learned the talk, and could recite the Bible verses pertinent to abstinence all day, need be, as repetition gratifies the Lord.

Howard had been praying for some help against his enemies back home in Washington: he knew his job was on the line. His orderly came in reporting. "Correspondent here to see you, Sir. Name's Sutherland, says you have sent permission."

"I have, and thank you. You may send him in." Tom Sutherland was sunshine with a pen to the beleaguered general, a smart man from New England like himself, whose cheer shone from his fresh young face and pure green eyes, a sober man of energy who wished to brave an Indian campaign with him. "I'm honored just to be here, General," the young man said.

"A pleasure," Howard answered honestly, and after pleasantries got down to business. "What do you know—that is, what are your impressions relative to the situation I have here."

"Sir, I have concluded from what news I gleaned from the White Bird battle that in Joseph and the Nay Pairsay—"

"Pronounced *nezz purse*, Mr. Sutherland."

"Ah! Thank you, General. My French instruction refuses to conform to Western preferences."

"I understand."

"In Joseph, General, you face a foe more desperate and cunning, and more able, than any faced by Grant or Sherman during the late war. However, it is clear to me that you have got him on the run, that Joseph and the purses are fleeing precipitously north before your troops."

"You flatter me, Sir."

"Not in the least, Sir."

"Well, I do feel confident that we have Joseph where we want him. At Cottonwood, two days from here, I have placed sufficient force to hold Joseph while I come upon him from the south and crush him. The Nez Perces must be punished, Sir."

"Indeed, General."

"Tell me, Mr. Sutherland: in the East, how do people view this Nez Perce conflict?"

"They are unfamiliar with it, Sir—a condition I propose to change. I can tell you that the public wants no further Custer massacres."

Howard winced almost and cleared his throat. "There shall not be another, Mr. Sutherland, I can assure you. Confidentially—strictly not for print—the late Colonel Custer acted with poor judgment."

"My impression also, for what little it's worth, General."

Howard nodded. "Tell me, Mr. Sutherland, if I may be so direct: what are your sentiments as to temperance? To the consumption of liquor?"

"Sir, I'm not a temperance man."

"Oh." Howard frowned.

Sutherland continued, "But I firmly believe in moderation—severe moderation; and when working, I abstain entirely. And I regard this campaign as work, Sir, until it ends."

"Good. I appreciate your point of view and even more, your honesty, Sir. Another, lesser, individual would have lied to me, Mr. Sutherland, to curry my favor, seeking the permission you seek. My sentiments are very well known."

"Yes, Sir."

"I assume you knew I am for temperance, abstinence, Mr. Sutherland."

"No, Sir."

"So you are here because there's war in Idaho."

"And because I know your record, I admire your work with the Bureau—and, if I may say so, I have read some of your communications and admire the dry and subtle glimmers of New England humor that evince themselves, Sir."

"Excellent!" Howard smiled, then repeated "excellent" some little doubtfully. "You may certainly carry on your work with my command. Are you Presbyterian, by any chance?"

"For generations, Sir."

"Excellent. I'll have my orderly bring your belongings to Dr. Fitzgerald's tent—an educated young man currently lacking a tent mate. You will enjoy his conversation. Good Presbyterian."

*

"Of course I'm a good Presbyterian!" John Fitzgerald laughed. "As good as I must be to keep peace with our stupid General. How about you?"

"Splendid!" Sutherland said, sitting on a folding cot that Howard's orderly had set up. "I'm a splendid Presbyterian! But tell me, do you really think Howard is stupid?"

"Any religious fanatic is stupid. You don't have to agree."

"I do, on principle. But I don't think Howard's stupid."

"We'll see. Does your correspondent's instinct tell you whether we'll be out here long?"

"I'd say five days. If Howard can't catch several hundred Indians with all their baggage and old people, well, then I'm as Irish as you are."

The doctor smiled. "You don't know the Nez Perce."

"Indians are Indians," Sutherland said, lying back with hands behind his head.

Fitzgerald looked up from his portable desk. "Then Christians are Christians. Go to sleep, so I can finish my letter."

"To whom are you writing?"

"My wife."

Sutherland sat up. "Your wife! I'd thought surely a young buck like you were single, and could show me some squaws!"

"Not at all, Sutherland. My wife's a dear girl and I miss her. I hope you are right about the five days. But I don't think so."

*

Five Wounds and Rainbow watched the soldiers dig and build stone walls and place their Gatling guns. Red Spy turned to look the other way: far out on Camas Prairie trailed the miles-long line of families moving north. He saw distant, stretched-out masses—their herds. The People on their horses, pack horses, the old and sick on travois, were too small to see. *Move fast!* he thought, and as he looked a bit of dust or rock enlarged, becoming five riders.

Far off behind them, beyond The People moving, rose a ragged line of blue and gray, broken northward by a fold or cut, extending far beyond the sight and rolling, he knew, for miles toward buffalo country. Those mountains were the Bitterroots, wild and endless, broken by the Lolo Pass. A long way to go.

The riders were closer now and Red Spy could make out the almost black Appaloosa in the lead. "Ollokot is coming. Four warriors with him."

Rainbow turned his horse's head and walked toward higher ground. He sat looking, thinking. When Ollokot rode up, it was only he and Fair Land, his wife, leading three horses. Ollokot gave two halters to his wife and walked his tired horse forward. "It's good to see you, Ollokot," Rainbow said.

"And all of you. Do you need more here?"

"No," said Five Wounds. "The soldiers are building shelters."

"But they will send out a strong group to take their dead," said Rainbow; "and to test our strength."

"They can see The People with their spy glasses," said Five Wounds. "But they will not ride out in force to bother us. They can't see how few men we have down here in these gullies."

"Howard and maybe four hundred soldiers are two days south of here. The herds are spread apart for miles; the young boys have never managed so many ponies so fast and so far. All the warriors are helping with the herds."

"We can send half our men to them," Rainbow said.

"You can't let the soldiers get past you."

"We won't," said Shore Crossing, walking his horse forward. "I would die first."

"I don't want you to die," said Ollokot. "How many should stay?"

Rainbow looked around. "The younger men. I and Five Wounds. Twelve men."

"I will stay with you—I and my horses."

"It's enough," said Rainbow. "The soldiers here are waiting for Howard; I am sure of it. Afraid."

"When Howard gets here, he will have six hundred men," said Ollokot. He looked toward Cottonwood. "That's why I spoke hard to the chiefs, saying we should camp where we are and all the braves come out and fight these soldiers, wipe them out while we can."

"There is no water for herds on Camas Prairie," Five Wounds said.

"So said my brother and White Bird. I am sorry that they are right. We need to reach Clearwater and camp some days to rest, feed, and water the herds."

"Howard will catch us there," Five Wounds said with no expression. "It will be war."

"Maybe we can talk to him. He will see that by moving to Clearwater, we have moved onto his reservation."

"It will be a big fight there," said Rainbow. "We have made the one-armed soldier angry."

"We would be fools to fight six hundred soldiers and their heavy guns," said Ollokot. "We have only two hundred warriors, two hundred twenty with Looking Glass."

"Looking Glass?" asked Five Wounds.

"The soldiers have attacked his camp. He will meet us at Clearwater."

"Good!" said Rainbow.

"I think it is bad. Looking Glass will want to tell us what to do," said Five Wounds.

"Look!" said Red Spy, pointing. "The Soldiers."

"Smoker, take the older men but start slowly," Five Wounds said. "We will call you back if there are too many."

"Seventeen men," said Red Spy. "Eighteen. They look like mail carriers, scouts, not soldiers."

"Settlers," Rainbow said. "No love for us in them. They are brave."

"Foolish," Shore Crossing said.

"You and your friends come with me," Rainbow ordered.

"No," said Ollokot. "Let them come to us."

"Good," Rainbow agreed. Strong Eagle coughed angrily.

"Listen," commanded Ollokot.

*

Randall rode in front of his column, Luther Wilmot, his lieutenant, riding beside him. The volunteers were riding in pairs. Wilmot looked back, then said to Randall, "We ain't no cavalry, Colonel. The men is bunched in back."

"Perry is cavalry, that cowardly son of a bitch, and look what he's good for."

"Not one single damn, Colonel."

The two rode on, but it was plain the Nez Perce were waiting for them. Strung out more than a quarter mile, a dozen braves faced them in a line across the road. "What are they thinking, Lew?"

"Nothing at all, Sir. They just figure to scare us into turning back. Tryin' to screen us from herds yonder, which we can see the dust of as plain as day."

"Believe you're right. Let's show the bastards we're no cavalry. Go for the big Injun on the black horse straight ahead! *Hyah!*"

The two whipped up their horses and the bunching column galloped forwards.

Ollokot dismounted, slowly aimed his rifle, fired, then mounted in no hurry. As the volunteers began to fire from charging mounts, he backed his pony, rearing it, then dashed away not fifty yards ahead of the two officers leading the volunteers. The column pounded on, one dead man and a bucking horse behind them in their dust.

The other braves watched, sitting their horses or dismounted behind them, until the volunteers galloped past them. Then quickly turning, mounting, the warriors rode converging behind the volunteers. Now Randall realized what he had done by charging through the Indian line: he was cut off from Cottonwood.

"Up there!" he cried to Wilmot, pointing toward a rise—but now there was no hurry, for the Indians had slowed behind them, cantering, trotting. The citizens rode up the rocky ridge just as a bullet struck the Colonel off his horse. Ollokot had dismounted just ahead and having hit the officer now raised his rifle in one hand, taunting the white men.

"Don't go for him!" Wilmot cried, but several men had turned to ride down the Indian who had shot their Colonel. Ollokot led them off and two braves followed. Firing from their horses' backs, the citizens could not hit Ollokot, but one lucky bullet cut a hamstring of the big black pony.

Four volunteers now dismounted, three of them turning to shoot at Strong Eagle and Shore Crossing, who had followed Ollokot and now swerved sharply, choosing to dismount themselves. But Ollokot had tumbled hard with his wounded horse. The white man facing him, an excited young cowboy, fired fast without carefully aiming.

As Ollokot rose to his knees two horses pounded toward him. Looking up, he saw his young wife Fair Land leaning down to throw a halter rope. He seized the halter as she galloped off, swung up, and followed her toward higher ground. "You gave me a good pony!" he shouted after her.

When he dismounted among the rocks, he realized that he had left his carbine where he fell. He felt his face—stinging, rubbed with gravel—and his head seemed turning. Horse hooves coming, and Yellow Wolf leapt down with two carbines. "Ollokot! You forgot something!" The young brave handed him his carbine and then helped the chief sit down behind a rock. "Rest a little while. We boys will shoot the whites who came after you."

After everything stopped spinning, Ollokot got to his knees and looked over the rock. Up to his right the young brave waited, looking for a clean shot now and then. The small group of white men shot from rocks and low ground. One of them lay wounded. Higher up, the larger group of whites had settled into good cover, but all around them warriors waited, firing carefully and letting the whites shoot off their ammunition.

Lew Wilmot looked back toward Cottonwood, where not two miles away on heights behind the outbuildings, Perry and his men were plainly visible. "Damn the goddam cavalry!" he shouted. "Damn the coward Perry! Stop your shooting! Damn you men!" He shouted louder. "Save your shells!" he screamed. His men turned to glare at Wilmot. "Cease firing boys! You see the redskins don't waste their ammunition. We might be here 'til dark. Oh God," he moaned, realizing the truth of what he said. "And I don't know what then."

"There's no more firing," Perry said to Captain Whipple. The soldiers had watched for an hour, seeing Randall's volunteers ride out, become surrounded, and take their stand on a ridge among the boulders. Twice Captain Whipple had implored Perry for permission to mount his company. "It's no use, Whipple," Perry said. "You couldn't assemble and mount fast enough to save them." The second time he'd said, "They want to draw me out, for God's sake! A hundred bucks are waiting in those draws. We are the last defense of these civilians!" Now silence.

Back in the ranks the privates started talking loud enough for officers to hear. "Say, Shearer, if you ever get your German ass in trouble like those volunteers out there, don't whistle for the First Cavalry. It won't do you no good."

"*Ja*, Guterman," the soldier answered. "I think I remember you are German too. I say we get our German asses on our horses and go out to help some Americans!" The two men, George Shearer and Paul Guterman, Dutch One and Dutch Two as known to their messmates, saddled up. The officers except for Perry looked the other way.

"My wound is mortal," Randall said to Wilmot. "Can you spare some water?" Wilmot lifted Randall's head to his canteen.

"We'll get the sons of bitches, Captain. Take it easy, now."

"My wife and baby, Lew."

"Don't worry about them."

"I have a baby two days old!"

"She'll be all right. I'll see she gets along real good."

"Thanks, Lew." Wilmot laid Randall's head back down. "How many we got killed?"

"Two so far, Captain. And two wounded like yourself." The volunteers had resumed firing an hour ago, but sparingly.

A young brave named Rider tired of hiding in the rocks and whistled up his horse, a red-speckled Appaloosa. Strong Eagle called to him, "Rider, stay down under cover!"

"I have no rifle!" Rider held up his short horn bow. "I need to see them better!" He leapt up and the red horse bolted for the two men who had followed Ollokot—the two remaining. One turned, hearing Rider galloping, and raised his carbine just as Rider veered the pony, drawing back the strings. But Rider recognized the volunteer, the son of J.M. Crooks, who was a good friend of Chief Joseph's band. He eased the string just as the young man fired. The horse, shot in the foreleg, collapsed and Rider, bow in hand, jumped free as Crooks shoved another cartridge in the chamber.

Rider shouted as the boy took aim, "You, Charley Cooks! Take your father's rifle home!" The bullet crashed through Rider's shin bone. Down on his knees, the brave picked up his arrow and as Charley pushed another cartridge in he rose to one knee aiming but the bullet young Crooks fired struck him, breaking a rib and Rider sprawled on his face, dust and gravel in his mouth, a bullet through his heart.

Strong Eagle rose with his rifle, screaming rage—a bullet seared the muscle of his thigh and he too fell, his rifle clattering. Ollokot and Five Wounds both shot Charley Crooks, who crumpled, spitting blood and teeth. The man beside him hunched back down and slid a cartridge in.

"Shorty!" Wilmot shouted from the rise above him, "keep your head down! There's help comin'."

He had been watching two troopers galloping out from the stables at Cottonwood. As they approached, Ollokot ran forward without his rifle, crouching but running straight for Rider's body. Behind him came a shrill cry, and when Ollokot reached the body and lifted it, three horses came down at a dead run. Fair Land leaned down along one horse's side, veered off and sent the other horses toward the volunteers. Ollokot raised the dead man to his shoulders, stood and made his way under the burden toward the rocks, the warriors all firing now to keep the white men down.

Shearer, fifty yards from Wilmot and his squad, leaped from his horse as it was shot, and ran without his rifle toward the volunteers while Guterman rode right to the rocks. Both men pointing—Shearer gasping for breath—they crouched beside Wilmot. "*Ganz schlimm!*" said Guterman.

"*Verdammt schlecht, sogar,*" said Shearer as he caught his breath.

"You goddam Dutchmen," Wilmot said, "God bless you both."

"Ve taught odders come. Shame," Guterman said.

"Look behind!" Shearer exclaimed. Fifty or sixty men at Cottonwood were running for the stables. A crew was limbering a Gatling gun.

The men of Whipple's company were saddling up. Perry had given in when Sergeant Bernie Simpson said that he would take a squad to follow the Dutchmen whether Perry court marshaled him or not. Perry told Whipple to mount but watch his flanks and come back if redskins looked like they were cutting in behind, as they had done to Rains's and Randall's men. The Gatling crew was ordered out but given similar instructions. His company assembled, Whipple ordered *Forward at the Run!* Now the dozen warriors started to withdraw, but several hundred yards short of Wilmot's men, Whipple got suspicious and waved down his men into a trot and then a halt. "No firing from the Injuns. This isn't good," he said.

Sergeant Simpson cantered forward, "God damn it, Captain! Are we going to get those men or not?"

"You watch your language, Sergeant!" Whipple barked, turned in his saddle. Behind the sergeant and the other troopers, a courier was galloping. "We'll wait," he said. "Look there."

The courier drew up, saluted, handed Whipple a note. "Break off and return," he read aloud to his lieutenant, Simpson overhearing. "They mean to turn your flank. —Perry." Whipple said, "That settles it. Perry's not giving me any orders. Let's go!" He turned and spurred his horse toward Wilmot's men, the company at full run following behind.

*

The news story Sutherland sent in for approval came from Howard's dispatch to McDowell, his superior: "The battle fought at Cottonwood the other day resulted in one officer and two enlisted men's deaths, with several troopers wounded. The hostiles are reported to have suffered at least ten killed and twenty or more wounded. General Howard's advanced blocking force of hastily gathered farmers from nearby settlements, along with two companies of U.S. Cavalry, numbering a hundred fifty men, were unable to thwart Joseph's full force, consisting of upwards of two hundred well-armed warriors. The Nez Perce threatened to cut off Captain Perry's brave and isolated command from General Howard's rapidly approaching army. The hostiles, concealing themselves in numerous ravines and canyons near Cottonwood, attempted to draw Perry and his command out from the cover of his Gatling guns. The Captain did not take the bait. The desperate and wily Joseph, thus screening brilliantly with overwhelming force the Nez Perce escape, is headed now towards Clearwater River. General Howard intends to catch the hostiles there, before they slip away across the river." The story received Howard's approval. To Sutherland Howard observed, "I tried in every way I could to keep the Nez Perce pacified, and give the savages benefit of the doubt. I believed in Joseph's good faith. The Nez Perce are a people replete with interest, intelligent and, I thought, amenable to civilizing influence. But reading Perry's dispatch I am horrified and sickened at the way these savages abuse and mutilate the bodies of our fallen. One civilian volunteer the savages evidently harbored animosity toward was found mangled to a crushed and horrid mass of flesh. These Indians are Indians, Sutherland, make no mistake. They are the Philistines in this good land, and we must replace them as in the days of old. We must conquer and subdue them!"

Next day at Cottonwood the Army gave full military honors to the body of the fallen Captain Randall. The Brave Seventeen, he and his men were called—though only thirteen lived to tell the story of that day, when seventeen civilians and their gallant captain held their own against at least three times their number of Joseph's chosen men of war.

Captain Randall's body in a coffin of planed pine lay in the stark sun of afternoon. Surrounded by his grim survivors, all the garrison's volunteers and troopers, officers in the best uniforms they could produce from their small chests of war, the chaplain chosen from the citizens of Cottonwood in mourning black—a robe he used for funerals and solemn feasts of the Episcopal Church.

Beside the coffin's head, in long black dress and veil, the Captain's widow stood as still as stone but holding in her arms a baby boy. Behind her stood her weeping sister, also married to a veteran of the Civil War. He stood with bared head, his farmer's hands rolling and straightening his old felt campaign hat's weathered brim.

Around them all the citizens of Grange and Cottonwood stood in the breezeless heat, wearing their best—the women in pressed linen dresses, calico and muslin, holding parasols with black-gloved hands; the men in tightly fitting coats of wool that smelled of mothballs, coats they wore at Christmas, weddings, and their families' funerals.

"'I am the Resurrection and the Life,'" the chaplain said, "'and whosoever lives, believing in me now, shall never die.' So reads the Word of God, whose promises are life to us. Dear friends and family of Darius B. Randall, Captain, we are gathered here to lay to rest our fellow child of God. The Lord be with you."

In answer two or three among the gathered citizens, and the widow and her sister, murmured back, "and with thy spirit." The Captain's wife's lips moved at the words, but soundlessly.

"Now let us pray," the chaplain said, and officers removed their hats. "O God, whose mercies none can number, hear our prayers for thy servant Darius, and grant him entrance to the land of light and joy, where all our tears shall be forever dry, and none shall hear the voice of mourning raised through all eternity, through Jesus Christ, thy son, our Lord, who lives and reigns with you in heaven, now and evermore."

Again a scattering of voices came, "Amen."

"I read again God's Holy Word: 'The Lord is good to them that wait for him, the soul that seeketh him. He will not cast us off forever. Though he cause grief, yet will he have compassion. New every morning, his mercies never fail.'"

The chaplain drew an old harmonica from his coat pocket, played the first few bars, then sang: "*O God our help in ages past, our hope for years to come, be now our guide while life shall last, and our eternal home.*" The widow murmured the first few words, but then broke into sobs. Her sister reached for the child and cradled him while the young woman gasped alone her grief under the glaring sky.

The hymn sung, the minister looked up and said, "Do any of you wish to speak?"

The widow's sister nudged her husband. He cleared his throat and said, "I do." He cleared his throat again; he took a breath; and then he looked out past the crowd of people toward the East, beyond the distant blue of the Bitterroots: "Randall was my friend. He was the best comrade a man could have. We were messmates. We drank from the same canteen. We got through two years of the war together, until he was wounded. I figure the most you can say about anybody in this world is that you were at Gettysburg together. Well, we were at Gettysburg, Randall and me, together." He glanced down at the coffin, coughed and cleared his throat. "I know he was a good husband because he was a good man. And I know he would have been the best father." He swept his eyes quickly across the people behind the soldiers. "We're going to take care of that boy. We're all going to help you raise him, even me. You and him are never going to want for anything as long as you live in Grange. Your boy's going to have fifty fathers. But all of us put together won't be as good as what he would have had if this hadn't happened."

The widow, weeping softly, groaned.

"Well, I ain't going to say more, except 'Rest in peace, Captain. I hope to God we'll all meet again.'" He stepped back and his wife, holding the child in one arm, put her other through her husband's and he covered his face with his hat.

The chaplain, open book in hand, looked at the lowered faces in the crowd: "The holy Gospel of the Lord." He squared his shoulders and recited, "Let not your hearts be troubled, for in my Father's house are many mansions. Were it not so, I would have told you. And if I go to prepare a place for you, I will come again and take you to myself, that where I am you may be."

The chaplain bent and filled his hand with dirt. He poured it in a sandy stream as thin as dust upon the coffin. "In the midst of life we are in death. Deliver us, O Lord, from the bitter pains of eternal death. O Thou who raised up Jesus from the dead, raise also this our brother Darius and grant us life in Jesus's name. Now we commit our brother's body to the ground, earth to earth, ashes to ashes, dust to dust." He closed his eyes.

*

Across the Camas Prairie along the bank of the Clearwater, The People spread their camp to rest and feed their horses—three thousand spotted ponies grazing on two miles of flowing grassland by the river. A thousand cattle, tended by the growing boys, fed or settled in the summer sun; four hundred dogs lay in front of tipis or loped along with the boys. Women washed clothing in the river, and men rode miles hunting wild game to kill and dry. Eight hundred people lined Clearwater River, six bands gathered for the first time.

All the chiefs met before the lodge of Toohoolhoolzote, the old man having sent his braves with word for all the others. From the Wallowa band came Joseph and his brother Ollokot, grave and solemn, hair braided with coyote fur, forelocks brushed high and tinted with white grains of paint, clean buckskin shirts fringed with twists of rawhide trailing white braids of wolf and sheep's hair, horsehair medallions with twenty lengths of twisted hair suspended down their breasts and worked with threads made of buffalo hair. Bright striped blankets wrapped them from waist to moccasin, done in beaded patterns—lines and diagonals of shining white, blue, red, black, and yellow. With the brothers came Two Moons and Red Elk, warriors with black necklaces of bone and shell—tall and strong, muscles taut, faces calm and eyes keen, standing as if listening for distant horse's hooves and the roll of soldier's weapons.

White Bird brought Shore Crossing and the other two Red Coats, Strong Eagle and Red Moccasin. Rainbow and Five Wounds, great hunters of the buffalo, warriors feared by the Lakota and Cheyenne—these and many others stood in the council circle. And, the last to come, Looking Glass stood now among them, his penetrating raven eyes, wild and beautiful, resting on the chiefs and warriors as if taking their measure, stalking for the weaknesses and strengths of each.

It was Looking Glass who spoke first, addressing the old chief who called them there. "Toohoolhoolzote, you are the oldest among us."

"I am, and I still am strong enough to ride at the head of a war party, but it is for all of us to choose the paths to take. You were not with us before, Looking Glass. Why have you come now?"

"Two days ago," the younger chief began, "my village was attacked by soldiers. I tried to surrender every way I could. My horses, lodges—everything was taken from me. Now, my chiefs, as long as I live I will never make peace with the Americans. I am ready for war."

"Today is not a day for war," said Joseph.

"No?" Looking Glass regarded Joseph with a look of patient irony. "What is today?"

"These are days to make one People of our six bands. We cannot fight the soldiers as we are."

"I have heard news of your five bands defeating the soldiers several times," said Looking Glass.

"At White Bird," said Ollokot, "we faced a hundred whites, and yesterday we faced a few soldiers and after that only settlers. Now we know that the One Arm General has five hundred soldiers, cannons, rolling guns; and many more soldiers will join him soon. Together, we have two hundred warriors—and your twenty or thirty."

"Together," said Joseph. "Never have all The People fought together, all the warriors together, all The People moving together."

"Maybe we should not be together," said White Bird. "The bands could go their own ways across the mountains. Howard cannot chase us all."

"He can and will," Joseph said. "I know his heart. He has the heart of the badger; he will go down any hole and follow any trail, blind and slow but with his nose. If we divide the bands we will all die separately. Let us die together."

"Are you sure that we will die?" asked Looking Glass, a sad smile at the corner of his mouth.

"I have had a dream," Joseph said quietly. "I do not understand it yet, but I believe I have been shown that those who do not die will wish they had. I saw our fathers' land on fire, a fire as big and wide as I could look, and birds like our people scattering into the canyons of the clouds. In my heart I feel as though to die."

Looking Glass put a hand to his forehead. "I know it is true. But I will fight to the death. I do not want to outlive our people, to see The People become whites, become Americans. We must all fight. Together. Chief Ollokot, think of something to do. You have hard thoughts."

"He has thought of something already," said Joseph.

"Hear me, my chiefs," said Ollokot. "Until yesterday our people expected to run away with all our lives. The first Nez Perce was killed by soldiers yesterday."

"Whose band?" asked Looking Glass.

"No band," Joseph said. "He is a Nimiipuu."

"Before, the family and the band of a dead warrior grieved and made his funeral. Tomorrow all will make a funeral for our fallen warrior. Then The People will understand."

*

The Nimiipuu were drawn up along the banks of the Clearwater, band by band and family by family, in front the warriors in paint, buckskin shirts, and leggings, holding rifles or the tough short bows made of ram's horn: each warrior with one war feather in a braid turned downward. Behind them stood the old men and old women; behind them girls, and boys not watching ponies or cattle. At river's edge was heaped a pyre of fragrant hemlock boughs with dry wood of oak and walnut crossed beneath to raise and sustain the flames, to make them dense as glass under the dead warrior, a window to the Ghost Road so that the spirit may go where it sees—the land of the fathers and mothers.

At the farthest end of the watching People, Chief Ollokot sat on a speckled pony, holding a rawhide halter to a white horse harnessed with a travois on which a red blanket wrapped a body whose face, exposed, reposed in wild white roses, lilies of the valley, late honeysuckle. Now as Ollokot paced the horses forward, behind the still body walked Rider's wife, Meadow, a daughter at one hand, the smaller son at the other; behind them Buffalo Song, his father, and the basket woman Healing Tree, his mother; his brother and two sisters. Five boys led five horses, the best of the herd, for Rider was a gentle breaker of horses. They heard his voice and came to him, and had talked to him in his dreams: horses were his *Wayakin*, his guardian and companion spirits.

Now the first to come forward was a basket woman, the youngest of them, Sees to Mountains, still unmarried, strong in body and in inner sight; and she sang a death song: "Oh People, People of the Spotted Horse, come and see our greatest tamer of ponies, our giver of war herds whose doom is our People's doom! See our beloved Rider and see how we will die. Our first man dead! As our first has gone, so all of us will go before winter—cut off from our fathers' and mothers' land, to die where snows come at the harvest moon, or where the sun is as strong as turning horses in the dreams of dying buffalo!"

At her song women wailed and men chanted, moaning their laments for a warrior, greatest of the Nez Perce for what other peoples know the Nez Perce to be: People of the Spotted Horses. So Ollokot led the horses with the singers of their sorrow behind, though wife and mother were silent. He passed the warriors with fringed arms raising rifles and bows; passed the chiefs all together: White Bird, Joseph, Toohoolhoolzote, Looking Glass, the great hunters Rainbow, Five Wounds, Two Moons, Red Elk; passed young braves—the Red Coats: Shore Crossing, Strong Eagle, Red Moccasin Tops; and Yellow Wolf, the bravest of the young men, whose mother could shoot deer and buffalo and who brought her son's repeating gun hidden in four pieces within her robe from the burning village of Looking Glass.

When Ollokot reached the bier he stopped the horses, sitting quietly. The dead warrior's wife, Meadow, came forward, leaving the children holding her mother-in-law's hands. She knelt beside the travois, reaching out with a groan to cradle her husband's head, to touch her forehead to his forehead; and she sang low, "Oh husband, husband, let me die with you; oh husband let me die with you! Our children, may they die with you, for if our daughter lives, she'll be taken as a slave to raise a white man's garden; and our brave boy if he remembers you with his brave heart, will die beneath the white man's iron horse. Oh husband, husband, let us die with you, let us die with you. We could not say goodbye to each other, lying side by side. Oh husband, let me die with you!"

His mother lifted up the moaning woman, gave her to her own father and mother, knelt down beside her son, and laid her hand on his smooth forehead. "Now go, my son, where our People will follow one by one, up where the long road rises in the stars, to the place of my mother. What have I now? I have you again, fresh as morning dew, you and flowers, forever. Go, my son, to where the Great Spirit walks. Wait there for me, and I will see you again. My son, my son, fresh as morning dew." She bowed her head and her husband, Rider's father, raised her to her slow feet.

Now The People bore the body to the bier, lifted it upon the boughs, covered the resting face, and all stood back as Joseph came forward, his face as sad as hills. He lifted his hands and prayed, "Great Spirit above, Father, Mother, Brother, Sister, Friend—Maker of heaven and earth, send the fathers down to take our brother by the hand." His voice rose clear and strong, not loud but deep, like thunder rising in the mountains. "Let him ride in happiness! Let him be a free man!"

All night the pyre burned and warriors danced before the red-ribbed flames. Yellow cinders rose toward the sparkling Ghost Road, rising up above The People's sight. In the morning Rider's father, Buffalo Song, gathered his son's warm ashes, folding them into his own blanket, and carried them into the river, wading out until the water washed his chest, and sang what only he could hear, spreading the thin dust across the flowing water, and the families watched. All day boys and warriors raced their ponies, competing for the prizes offered by the dead warrior's father—buffalo robes, rifles, strong horn bows, and horses—fast, tall, spirited ponies tamed and trained by the horseman first to fall in the long war. And so The People buried Rider, breaker of horses.

*

In the afternoon a young officer rode out wide from Howard's column to scout for the days-long disappeared Nez Perce—veering miles northeast from the long line of army mules, men marching route step, cannons on their rolling caissons, wagons creaking, troopers with their tin canteens clanking, horses snuffing, men mumbling, talking, chewing and spitting tobacco. The lieutenant topped a lonely ridge and saw below three thousand horses, cattle lowing tended by breech-clouted boys; a wide, long village of lodges, tipis yellow-white in the afternoon light, and farther up the plain along the river warriors racing ponies, boys behind them keeping up on barebacked Appaloosas, thundering the ground and raising whirling roses of red dust. And below him—he tied his horse and crept down a slope through cottonwoods—bathing in the river, naked Indian women, laving water on brown skin shining like bridal satin in the warm golden sun.

IV

Clearwater

Lieutenant Wilmot raced his horse across the rolling, grassy hills of Camas Prairie, back toward Howard's plodding column. Sound of Running Feet, who had been bathing with the women, saw the white man as he watched and crossing arms across her young breasts had waited, shivering, among the cottonwoods. She saw him as he crept and peered; she saw him turn and, crouching, lope back up the hillside, catch up his reins; and then she ran for her buckskin dress, calling to the women and pointing back toward the slope. Atop the ridge a mile away the young man Going Alone had seen the white man too—had seen him galloping across the prairie. He ran his horse toward the village just as Running Feet was shouting to the lodges, and the chiefs not racing ponies ran to meet her. Joseph, Ollokot, and Looking Glass listened to her breathless urgency and seeing Going Alone riding at full speed toward them understood that time had run out.

Joseph held his daughter in his arms as Ollokot and Looking Glass ran for the horses tethered at their tipis and galloped off to stop the races, gathering the warriors and the fighting chiefs. At Toohoolhoolzote's lodge the leaders gathered with some younger men: Rainbow, Five Wounds, Shore Crossing. The old chief called to Joseph as he came walking fast with his rifle, "Are you certain?"

Joseph nodded, saying "Sound of Running Feet was not mistaken! The young man Going Alone saw the white scout too!"

Ollokot pointed at the high ground. "They will take the ridge unless we get there first."

"With all our men," said Rainbow.

"Yes," said Joseph. "Howard can put his big guns there."

"We must move the herds now," said Looking Glass.

"That will keep half our men busy!" said Toohoolhoolzote.

Joseph shook his rifle. "Let us stay here! Take our men and meet Howard."

"Joseph," smiled Looking Glass, "that is not like you, a man of peace!"

"No peace now," said Joseph, "We have no choice but to fight."

"Defeat Howard now," said Ollokot. "Attack him coming up the ridge with all our men."

"Attack five hundred soldiers, ride into five hundred rifles with two hundred braves?" Looking Glass shook his head. "We hold the soldiers with half our men, move the herds and our People toward the mountains."

"I would die before leaving our land," said Joseph. "Let us fight him now."

"Defeat him now," said Five Wounds.

"We must choose one chief," the old warrior Toohoolhoolzote said. "One voice for battle."

"Listen," Looking Glass said quietly. "Victory means nothing here. They have the open prairie behind them to retreat across."

"Get around behind them!" Rainbow urged. "Cut them off!"

"No," said Looking Glass. "We would leave the village open if we did that. We have too few men to hold them in place while we go behind."

"We have enough men," said Five Wounds.

"It doesn't matter," said Joseph.

"It matters, Joseph," said the old chief. "I know your devotion to the dead. But you must serve the living. Listen to Looking Glass. Joseph and White Bird, you must get The People out of here. We will take half the warriors and hold Howard on the ridge."

"Defeat them now!" said Rainbow.

"You younger men must control your fighting hearts," said Looking Glass. "Victory is not victory here. We would lose too many men, and still have to escape across the Bitterroots. Who would help the women, the old men, and herd the horses? Who would hunt buffalo for six hundred people?" Looking Glass threw his hand out toward the high ground. "The dead braves we leave on that ridge? We do not have to defeat the soldiers to win. What is winning but to survive?"

Joseph nodded. "My spirit sickens at your words, but you are right." Looking Glass nodded somberly. "We will never return," Joseph added quietly. "You and I will never come back—to our land—to our father's land."

"I know," said Looking Glass. "Maybe our sons and daughters will. Joseph, move The People. Say goodbye to your family quickly." The war chief looked at the men's faces. "Will you do as I ask today?"

"We all must," said Toohoolhoolzote. "Or else the soldiers will kill us separately, band by band."

*

The correspondent Thomas Sutherland saw Wilmot coming, as he rode alongside Howard at the column's head. The General spoke an order and the train of men and mules and ammunition halted while the volunteer with heat refused to talk to Perry, whom the general had sent ahead to get the scouting citizen's report. Sutherland, amused, rode forward far enough to overhear Wilmot's angry voice, and then an enraged Howard galloped up to shout, "What is the matter here? Captain!"

Perry, mortified, told Howard, "This man refuses to deliver his report to me!"

"I'll not report to this damn coward!" Wilmot said.

"What?" the General cried. "Such lack of proper respect positively sickens me. I'll have you arrested, Sir!"

"General," Wilmot said, "I've seen the Nez—"

"Silence!" ordered Howard. "Address yourself to Captain Perry, Lieutenant!"

"I will not, Sir! This man allowed my friends to be massacred at Cottonwood within his sight and refused to leave his rocks to send relief."

"I wouldn't jeopardize my base, General!"

"All right," said Howard, holding up a hand. "There is no time for this now. Sir, report to Colonel Jones!"

"Colonel," Wilmot said, careful not to show relief or satisfaction, "this column is headed wrong. The Nez Perce camp is directly east, across those two ridges—that way."

"Are you certain if was not a small war party or a treaty band?" the colonel asked. "How many Indians?"

"I can't be sure, but—"

"How close did you get?"

"A hundred yards, maybe less."

"Did you count tipis?"

"Not exactly, but—"

"Then what the hell were you doing out there?" shouted Jones.

"At least a hundred tipis!"

"A hundred?"

"Maybe more. A thousand Indians, their whole herd, five hundred, six, cattle—"

"Why there?"

"It's along the Clearwater, Sir. The river's just over there."

"How far's the camp?"

"Just under five miles."

"Did they see you?" Jones asked, satisfied now with the report.

"No, Sir. I don't think so. They would have pursued."

Howard walked his horse up.

"General, shall I order a change of march?"

"Make your dispositions, Colonel." Jones saluted and rode back along the column. "Rejoin your company, Sir," Howard ordered Wilmot, who saluted and cantered off.

"Captain Perry."

"General?"

"Do you credit the volunteer's report?"

Perry hesitated, then nodded. "I do, Sir. The man's reliable."

"Thank you, Captain. You do yourself credit."

"Yes, Sir."

"Get your company in hand, Captain. We'll be fighting the hostiles within an hour."

"Thank you, Sir." Perry saluted and as Howard raised his hand the Captain turned his horse and galloped down the column.

"Did you hear all that, Sutherland?"

"Yes, General, I did."

"I wish you hadn't. I think it serves the public ill to read about our officers quarrelling."

"I'll not breathe a word of it in my story, General. It appears there will be sufficient material to write about shortly."

"I do appreciate it, Sir." The correspondent nodded pleasantly and touched his hat brim. "Mister Sutherland, I hope you will be careful to stay back a prudent distance from the engagement."

*

Joseph quickly walked to his tipi, his hand tightly enclosing the fine hand of Sound of Running Feet.

"Father, Snows Resting can go with you. I will stay here with mother and the little one."

"No, no. I won't leave you to pack and drop the lodge alone."

"Father, this is women's work."

"Soldiers are coming."

"Your place is not with us. The People need your voice. We have your voice all the time." She smiled and laughed at Joseph's frown. "Too much!" she said. "Too much. You tell us everything." He clasped his daughter to his chest. "Don't cry," she said.

"My People shall not see me weep—not if you are careful and are safe." He looked down at her face. "Life would be nothing without you, Pitty Pat. The sun is nothing compared to your brightness."

"Mother and I will take care of each other."

He laid his hand upon her head.

"Are you blessing me, Thunderhead?"

He smiled. "If only I could. But you don't need it!" He looked up and called toward the tipi. "Springtime! Are you there?"

His first wife pulled the flap aside and stepped into the sun, the tiny baby in her arms. The shock of brightness made the infant cry, and Joseph took the child into his arms. The baby cried still more and Springtime said, "She's frightened by your frown and bobbing feather!"

"Oh Springtime, she's too young to see!"

"She feels that you are red for war—she knows already!"

He held her closer, gently in his arms. "Hush, Little One, I will not go to war today. My place is with the families today. Hush, hush." He kissed the child; her cries were quieter.

Now Sound of Running Feet, a stiff sad smile playing on her lips, said, "Father, do you think you'll love her more than all the rest of us?"

He placed his hand upon her head again. "Love any child more than you?" He shook his head. "I will die first."

He gave the baby back to Springtime and moved to touch his head to hers. "Springtime, you must go quickly and go safely. I would surely not know myself without my sit-beside-me wife."

"Don't worry about us Chief Thunderhead."

Joseph said aloud as he walked to his hobbled pony, "Now my whole family calls me Thunderhead." He smiled and as he threw the halter rope over his horses' neck the smile became a great light on his face.

Leading a string of three ponies Joseph's younger wife, Snows Resting, came toward him. Her deerskin dress was tanned nearly white, beads on her long necklace glistened. She smiled to see Joseph, but then as he walked to her and put his hand upon her knee a look of sadness passed between them.

"You are well-named," she said. "Your joy and sorrow are high as mountains and deep as thunder."

He looked into her strong and wise young face. "We are the happiest two on earth, you and I. And I have everything here, now. I have a family to love, my father's land, most beautiful, and I have you, my very heart. My heart of hearts."

She touched his braided hair, then let her hand fall on his. She said nothing, but looked into his eyes. He breathed deeply, filling his broad chest. "I must lead our People across the river, and when we cross the water it will all be over."

She rubbed his hand softly. "Not all. Not all."

He looked up at the sky.

"Do you think the Great Spirit led the whites here?" she asked.

"I think the Great Spirit weeps deeper than thunder." He took the halter in both hands. "There is no more time."

Snows Resting pointed down the river. "The young men and the boys already drive the herds into the lower ford."

"We'll take our People to the upper ford."

Half Man Half Woman ran to find the lodge of White Necklace and Shore Crossing, side-stepping hurrying boys too young for paint leading strings of horses for their families, old women bundling blankets with rawhide ropes to tie on horses' backs, younger women pulling down stout sheets of weathered buffalo hides from smooth-hewn tipi poles standing crossed and skeletal against the cloudless sky. The slender brave caught breath in front of Joseph's lodge, and panting, asked Sit Beside Him Wife if she had seen any braves of White Bird's camp—if they had gone up the ridge to wait for the soldiers yet.

She shook her head and laid a gentle hand on the unpainted brave's shoulder. "Don't go," she said. "We need you with the families. The boys can't manage all we have to do and our good chiefs can't be everywhere at once."

"I have to go!" the brave replied. "This time I must fight! I'm going to fight in Shore Crossing's place!"

The wife of Joseph lifted her hand and touched the center of her chest. "What you feel here, you must do, but I am afraid for you."

With lilting indignation now, the warrior stood before her, tall and calm: "I understand, dear friend of many summers, but remember I can ride and shoot a rifle with the strongest of the men."

"But killing men and killing buffalo are not the same. Your gentle heart might not permit you to shoot white men."

"I have no heart today! I am told in a dream—goodbye, dear friend." The warrior touched her head and smiled with all but eyes, and left her anxious with grief.

White Necklace saw her warrior friend approaching as she tied a roll of buffalo canvas from the tipi she and Shore Crossing had shared for many loving summers. Rising to her feet, she faced the look of dismay on Half Man Half Woman's face. "I am too late!"

"Too late for what, my dreaming friend?"

"To stop Shore Crossing! I must fight today in your husband's place!"

"Oh, tender brave, be still and help me take our tipi down. My husband won't act recklessly today—he promised me, and my love always keeps his promises."

"White Necklace, I have had a dream!"

A look of fear leapt from the young wife's face; she caught her breath. "What was the dream? I fear your dreams!"

"No, no, White Necklace; I won't tell you what my spirit told me—but maybe everything will be all right if I fight for Shore Crossing."

"What did you see? Oh!—" She looked inside her tipi, ran to snatch a rifle lying on the blankets she had folded only moments ago.

"No! No!" Half Man Half Woman cried. "I saw you both together, fighting, your husband hurt and you with his rifle, firing! Oh!" The warrior grasped her shoulder hard. "White Necklace, kill me then before you go! For my life itself you must not go! I will go for you. I—will go for you."

"You saw us together—in your dream."

"Yes. In the dawn's earliest light. The two of you side by side."

"Our men will fight the whites today and tonight, and still tomorrow morning, then. Maybe if I go with the families—if I am not with him in the battle. Maybe your dream's only a warning, not what must be—or only your fear—"

"Yes!"

"But I want to be with him, fighting at his back, protecting Shore Crossing!"

"White Necklace," the warrior said as calm as death. "I am White Necklace. I am you. I will be Shore Crossing's twin spirit. What you would do, I will do. White Necklace, if you would die, I will die."

Through her tears the young wife stared into the firm and loving face. She clasped the warrior, holding hard. "My tender brave," White Necklace said again. The warrior stood immobile, holding tears back. Quickly White Necklace let go and bent down for the rifle. "Take this. Take my horse. The black and white. The one we used to ride."

*

The doctor, John Fitzgerald, saluted Colonel Jones and turned to move his two assistants in behind him with their wobbling pack horses. "We'll set up in those trees yonder," he called, pointing.

Tom Sutherland rode up beside the doctor, frowning. "General Howard sent me back here."

"Good!"

"I want to be up front watching. How can I write the battle if I don't see it?"

"Do what you always do."

"And what might that be, good doctor?"

"Why, make it up! What else is battle writing?"

"Insulting my integrity and journalistic verisimilitude is no way to get into my whiskey tonight, John."

"Oh I'll get into it all right. I know you hate to drink alone. Be glad you'll be back here tonight instead of hunkered down behind a pile of rocks."

"Or shot."

"Shot? You? In those civilian clothes? You look like some Parisian gentleman—and smell like his professional amour, I must observe."

"As if the Indians would give a damn how I am dressed—or shoot fine enough to avoid me even if they did."

John Fitzgerald sniffed and shook his head, serious. "You don't know these Nez Perce at all, do you?"

"What do you mean?"

"You'll find out soon enough. Meanwhile, here comes good Brother Luther."

"Wilmot? Why is he riding back to us instead of scouting up ahead?"

"You're the reporter. Ask the good citizen when he gets here."

But Wilmot was not in the mood to stop and talk. "That goddam self-appointed missionary," Wilmot shouted as he trotted by. "You wait and see—he'll claim he whipped three times as many braves as Joseph's got!" He reined his horse to a full stop as if he couldn't help it. "And *you*—" he pointed hard at Sutherland—"you'll be the one to write the glorious news."

"I'll tell the truth!" the journalist replied.

"He always does," the physician added with a smile.

"We'll see," said Wilmot. "There's all the difference in the world between that damn fool and the truth!" As if to mark his words with exclamation points, the angry man put spurs to horse and jolted past the staring assistants and their fly-whisking animals.

"Now what do you suppose set old Lew off like that?"

The doctor shook his head: "Just touchy, I expect. You leave a man and his friends out surrounded by Indians like Colonel Perry did, and that man's nerves get exercised."

"That wasn't Howard's fault."

"My friend, this whole thing is Howard's fault."

The journalist picked up his reins. "No doubt. I'm going up to take a closer look."

*

Going Alone had turned to Yellow Wolf before the soldiers showed themselves above them on the ridge: "I smell their dirty wool."

His friend grinned. "A heavy wind brings their smell across the ridge and down to us!"

"Look there!" The young warrior pointed south along the ridge.

"I don't see as far as you," Yellow Wolf said.

"Here they come! Ride back and tell the chiefs. They come from the south. Wait! Look! They have big guns. Ride and tell them."

Hard-faced, Yellow Wolf pulled his pony's head around and struck his heels against its flanks and set off at full run back toward the river. As he approached the village, the young brave saw tipis coming down and women folding hides while children held pack horses. Dogs ran behind young men going for their ponies. In the distance by the river, boys dashed here and there on horseback waving sticks but he could see they were too few to start the shying ponies at the edges of the herds. A group of chiefs and older men were trotting toward him, riding in a line behind two men in the lead. Old chief Toohoolhoolzote had stripped for war and streaked five lines of black paint down his wrinkled face and weathered chest. Beside him rode Looking Glass in full buckskin. "Going Alone has seen the soldiers! There—" Yellow Wolf turned and pointed south. "Along the ridge. They are bringing their big guns."

"You saw their guns?" asked Looking Glass.

"Going Alone saw them."

"He sees well," Toohoolhoolzote said to Looking Glass. "He is an eagle."

"If they have Howitzer-guns and fast-firing guns, it is not farmer-soldiers. It is One-Arm General, Howard. Four hundred, five hundred soldiers."

Toohoohoolzote pointed up where the ridge became a bluff opposite them, its riven face cut twice by deep ravines. "Let them come closer. Half the men go north of the bluff and stop them, get around behind; half go south and do the same. We'll drive them off the bluff."

"No."

The old chief stiffened. "No? Why do you say no? Those of us who have fought the soldiers have defeated them each time. We have lost only one man. We will defeat them again here!"

"We can't defeat them with a hundred men."

"If we defeat them, we will not need to move!"

"If we defeat them, what will happen then? Do you think the whites won't send another army bigger than this one? If Sitting Bull and Crazy Horse could not stop them with two thousand warriors, what can we do?"

"We can defeat them again! The white soldiers are only men!"

"They are men without number! We will never defeat them. We can only try to get away."

"Get away, then! Look!" Toohoolhoolzote gestured toward the village where clusters of warriors having caught horses were mounting, some already trotting up the trail. Rainbow, the great hunter, painted red and white on face and chest, rode fast with the Red Coat warriors—Shore Crossing and his friends. Behind them Five Wounds rode, cradling a rifle across his pony's back. "I will have enough young men," the old chief said. "You take your braves and help Joseph and White Bird get away. I will die here with my warriors!"

"Foolish old man! We will need all of our warriors to cross the mountains, to fight again. The war will not end here!"

"I will fight them here!"

"I am the war chief!" said Looking Glass.

"So you have spoken! I will take half the men and fight. You and Joseph take the rest and go. As you have said."

Looking Glass stared south toward where the keen-eyed brave had seen the soldiers, then turned his pony toward the village.

Toohoolhoolzote, his face a sharp-eyed blank, held out his hand toward Yellow Wolf. "Young man, wait here for Two Moons and Five Wounds. Tell them to take as many men as come and go north to that ravine and up to the ridge." He touched his horse into a trot, and all the men followed him, riding past Yellow Wolf in single file painted and stripped for war, rifles resting across their ponies' backs—Rainbow first, and at the last Shore Crossing, looking back down toward the village where White Necklace had said good bye.

"Your wife will be all right," Red Moccasin Tops called back to him. The husband turned and raised his rifle.

Toohoolhoolzote and his warriors dog-trotted their tough ponies to the foot of a ravine that rose like a stubbled scar into the bluff, and there the old chief shook his battered muzzle-loading rifle toward the ground, signaling the men to jump down and tie their horses to trees. From there they climbed the slope, sometimes on hands and knees, clambering on rocks and boulders after the old man, who sprang with fierce grunts from foothold to foothold, his anger at the soldiers coming to attack the families giving him the strength of the cold Bitterroot itself as it dashed and tumbled through its wintry gorge.

"Old Chief!" called Rainbow from behind, "you had better steal a carbine from the soldiers and give up your grandfather's buffalo-hunting rifle. The soldiers will fire faster than you can!"

"Uh!" the old man grunted. "I like the old ways!"

"All rifles are white man's rifles," shouted Shore Crossing. "Let's kill them all and then we can throw away the guns, all of them!"

"We will have to," said Rainbow; "there will be no one to make bullets."

"No cotton or wool for shirts or blankets," called Red Moccasin Tops. "We all wear cotton shirts."

"Not today! We are naked today," said Rainbow.

"And dead tomorrow," barked the old chief. "Come on, you chattering children! We must beat the soldiers to the bluff!"

"Ha!" Red Moccasin Tops was looking back and pointing down the slope. "Look who has become a warrior!" Half Man Half Woman, far below, had begun to climb, clutching a horn bow and a brace of arrows.

"No laughing," Shore Crossing said quietly—then louder: "Any man who laughs I'll kill." Up at the top, Toohoolhoolzote threw himself against a rock and braced his old gun. He fired—a smokey crack—and singing out a chanting cry he shook his rifle in the air.

*

"Fire that god-damn thing, you lazy sons of bitches!" shouted Captain Trimble as three men wrestled with a howitzer—a stout, stubby mouth of brass held on its wooden cradle by its own weight.

"You can't depress the tube, Captain!" said a sweating man. "We're aiming into thin air!"

"Drop shells on those damned Indians—now!" The Captain spurred up to the other crew. "Get that god-damn gun into service! Haven't you men been trained to use that thing?"

"No, Sir," a bearded youth about eighteen replied, calm as the moon.

"No, Suh," an older man offered. "We're new to this contraption."

"Well fire the damn thing anyhow!"

The Captain galloped off as the second man observed, "Take orders from some damnyankee officer."

"He fought with Stonewall Jackson," said the younger man. "That's what they say."

"Like hell he did. I ain't never seen him."

The other howitzer now thumped its hollow whump and up above, a streaking black shell arced toward the river and the families. "Good!" said General Howard, riding up to Trimble. "Bring up the Gatlings, Captain, and we'll make short work of it!"

Saluting, Captain Trimble cantered back down the column of artillerists, pack mules, and plodding horses.

"You see," Howard said to Sutherland, who had ridden up beside the general, "the shells exploding in their camp will raise a panic and drive their warriors up this way. We are deploying along this bluff in front of us, cavalry ahead and infantry here, to funnel the hostiles toward the center. We'll open on them there with the two Gatling guns. I've yet to see the hostiles who'll stand Gatling fire."

"Or damnyankees either, I expect," said a voice behind. Howard turned, his face a storm, as a civilian removed his hat. "Samuel Trimble, Sir, Ginrel. Of *The San Francisco Chronicle*."

"Trimble?"

"Precisely, Sir."

"Are you any relation to Captain Trimble?"

"Hell, yes!" The man exclaimed.

Howard eyed the young man dressed in gray wool pants, new boots, and red plaid shirt. "You are welcome here. But you must bridle your mouth, Sir."

"Yes, Sir. I shall, Sir. Thank you, Sir," Howard's eyes narrowed again.

"How did you get here?"

"The paper sent me to Grangeville, Sir. Missed you there by half a day. I rode to Harpster, missed again, and when I got to Walls your trail was warm."

"You are persistent, Mister Trimble."

"I have followed all your victories, Ginrel. Wouldn't give up now."

"Victories?"

"I wrote up Missionary Ridge and Lookout Mountain for the *Richmond Examiner* during the Late Unpleasantness, Sir."

"Those were Grant's and Sherman's victories, Sir."

"You are a modest man, Ginrel."

"You're too young to have been a reporter during the war."

"I was a boy, Sir," the reporter said evenly; "all our men were in the army." The two looked steadily at each other.

The General spoke: "You may stay with us. You will accompany Mister Sutherland here. One more thing, Sir. Know that I disapprove of you personally."

The Southerner removed his hat a second time. "Thank you, Ginrel. You have my profound thanks."

As a Gatling crew trotted past, the General turned his horse and cantered away. The other howitzer at last discharged its shell.

As the two reporters' horses shied, Sutherland said, "Samuel, are you really kin to Captain Trimble?"

"Just by way of Eve and Adam, if you please. Who is this Captain Trimble?" Sutherland pointed. "Up there with the Gatling crews."

"Just what, if I may show my ignorance, is a Gatling?"

"Half rifle, half cannon, works like a coffee mill. Turn the crank, it shoots rifle bullets. Cuts down anything in front of it."

*

Joseph's wife Springtime screamed when the first shell exploded in the air over the packing village. "Husband!" she called, then knew that Joseph was across the river, he and White Bird leading out the first few families and seeing to the herds. She knew that Joseph wanted bravery from his older wife, but who can keep a calm and steady heart who has an infant child? The soldiers always come for her—they come in dreams, and when the child is grown the soldiers will be in her dreams also. Always soldiers, always pounding horses, always hard white faces. There will never be anywhere there are not soldiers. She sat and took the baby in her arms. The sun is so bright! She pulled the little cotton blanket farther forward so it shaded the little one's eyes. Don't cry; Mother will hold you, Mother will rock you. See? We will stay here and rest. There will be shouts, my little one, shouts up in the hills, and loud noises that will not hurt you. You lucky baby, you lucky one—it is a world you never knew that now is coming to an end. Here, I shield your eyes. Rest now; we are going to that new world of yours. We both will rest. We will not go from here until your father comes to take us there.

Ollokot and Two Moons led forty warriors upstream and then into the second ravine that cut the rocky face of the bluff. Two miles downstream, Five Wounds and thirty warriors rode to the other rising cleft piercing the massive, broken table land. Seventy warriors would surround the soldiers,

thinly spread and hidden, some lying down in grass with weeds and branches tied to their heads, some in shallow hollows, some few behind what rocks
the broken landscape offered. They must fight like whites, like soldiers, staying where they were, not showing bravery by riding or running into groups
of firing soldiers. Careful, careful; patient.

Ollokot took a few braves to wait around the only spring for miles,
up near the top of the ravine. The day was bright and hot: the soldiers will
want water. But long before these warriors reached their places the braves
with Toohoolhoolzote must stop the soldiers, stop their column, make them
stand where they are, and then must hold the center when the soldiers gather in the middle and make their charge. Ollokot looked down and saw the
lodges, herds—the horses, cattle—hundreds of dogs. A few families moved
along the river, not enough of them. To move The People, Joseph would
need all day, all night; and still tomorrow families would wake inside their
tipis where they stood now. We must defeat the whites and drive them off
this bluff, or stay another day tomorrow—but there will be too few tomor-
rows left. Hurry, Brother; we can't afford to die before The People ride into
the mountains.

*

Riding with the Gatling crews, Lieutenant Otis turned in his saddle:
"Captain Trimble! How about that rise ahead?"

He pointed to a shallow knoll and Trimble shouted, "Set 'em up there,
Harry, and give 'em hell!"

As Otis waved his sergeant forward toward the knoll, Toohoolhoolzote's first shot struck the sergeant in the collarbone, blood and bone splin-
ters bursting from the man as he was hammered from his horse. The old
chief's muzzle-loader threw a heavy slug of dirty lead with force enough
to kill a buffalo; the sergeant, stunned unconscious falling on his back,
lay spurting bright blood from his neck's artery. He gasped convulsively
through a shredded windpipe as Lieutenant Otis leaped from his horse and
knelt, reaching to lift the dead man's head.

The second shot from Toohoolhoolzote creased through the back of
Otis's blue jacket, pitching him across the sergeant's body as it severed the
lieutenant's spinal cord. A flash seared through his brain and he lay panting
face down with the dusty, grainy earth in his mouth. "Company B!" Trimble
shouted from behind. "Get your asses up there on the gallop! Bugler!" But
the bugler took a bullet in the chest just as he lifted the brass piece to his

mouth. "Major!" Trimble ordered, "Move 'em up there! Cover those Gatling guns! Move! Move!"

The troopers galloped past him as Trimble waved them by with his hat. Then dismounting, he walked to Otis, pulled him off the sergeant, and laid him on his back. "Medical!" Trimble shouted. "Fitzgerald! Where's that goddam doctor? Surgeon! Private, get the doctor—find the son of a bitch! Move! Move!"

Now Trimble's horse took off running back the way they had come. On foot, booted, the Captain looked around him. His troopers, dashing toward the Nez Perce warriors emerging at the top of the ravine, began to fire their carbines and revolvers from the saddle, stopping, turning their horses. "No! No! You sons of bitches! Ride them down! Ride the sons of bitches down! Damn!"

"Captain!" General Howard's calm voice called him from behind. "Curb your temper, Sir. You have done splendidly. Your men will keep them busy while the artillery goes into battle. Then we'll give them a taste of Gatling fire."

"Is the surgeon with you? Fitzgerald?"

"A surgeon does not belong here under fire, Captain."

"I don't give a God damn—this is Harry here! They've shot Harry all to hell."

"I'm here, General," Fitzgerald said, riding up.

"Resume your proper place in column," Howard ordered, but the doctor had dismounted, saying "Nez Perce don't shoot doctors." Howard looked away, ordering his aide, "Give my respects to Major Young, instructing him to detail forty men to set up a defensive barricade three hundred yards to the rear of the artillery. Use the packs as breastworks. That shall be my headquarters."

"Yes, Sir." The aide saluted, turned, and spurred back toward the column's rear.

"Thank you," Howard said after him.

"You should not have moved him, Captain," John Fitzgerald said, kneeling beside Lieutenant Otis.

"I couldn't leave him on his face!"

"His back is broken."

"God damn it! Have I killed him?"

"It's no matter, Captain. The wound is mortal."

"Mortal!"

"Let's call some men to move him back. The sergeant's dead."

"Can you give Harry some whiskey?"

"He couldn't swallow it. He's all right, Captain; he can't feel a thing."

"Harry!" Trimble said.

Above him, Howard calmly ordered, "Take command of your troopers, Captain. Occupy that section of bluff a half mile ahead. I'll use the infantry to support the guns." He saluted. Trimble stood, saluting.

"My adjutant will lend you his horse, Captain." Howard turned and rode back down the column.

*

Around Toohoolhoolzote, the warriors spread to any cover they could find. When the troopers came at them they waited, then loosed a fusillade that stopped them, milling, firing wildly from their saddles. One soldier clutched his saddle screaming, shot through the hip; two others, shot full in the chest, rolled onto the ground like salmon punctured by bear's claws and thrown up onto land.

Shore Crossing raised his rifle but a bullet struck the rock under his chest and he ducked down. Ashamed, he rose and fired from one knee, then, still exposed, fed another cartridge to the chamber; fired again. The second shot went through a trooper's body, and stunned with agony, the soldier clutched his middle, doubling to his horse's neck. Shore Crossing raised his rifle, whooping a high victory cry.

Behind him Strong Eagle called, "Get down and save your breath! Shoot one of them for me. I can't hit them while they ride around so crazy!"

"He didn't mean to hit that one," called Red Moccasin Tops.

"Shut up, you foolish children!" The old chief pointed: "Look there! Big guns!"

Up to their right some several hundred yards the soldiers were unlimbering two Gatling guns—unhitching the horses, turning the big wheeled barrels. Between the warriors and the knoll the horse soldiers now galloped, driven by a shouting officer—racing toward the bluff where Ollokot and Two Moons were climbing their ravine. Here Toohoolhoolzote shouted, "Groups of two and three, charge the guns! Take them before they fire! Hurry!"

"Red Blanket!" shouted Strong Eagle. "We will show the chief how to capture white men's guns!"

Red Moccasin Tops, closer than the others to the guns, called, "Follow me, my friends!" He stood and ran, the two others thirty yards behind, across the dry and stony table land toward where the soldiers took their places at the guns. The first burst of bullets from the left piece cut the air above the warriors with rushing knots of *ssst! ssst!* sounds—then the fire lowered toward Red Blanket, whose body seemed to break in two in a spray of blood. Shore Crossing screamed, stopped still—"Run!" shouted Strong Eagle. "Run!"

But then something like a knife slashed Shore Crossing through the inner thigh. He didn't feel his fall, but knew himself to be staring at the sky. He looked along his body toward his leg and saw a spurt of blood leap into the air. Exhaustion, dizziness washed away the world as he felt a hand push against his thigh, and then he knew nothing.

Half Man Half Woman bent over Shore Crossing, weeping open-mouthed, pushing both hands hard against the wound to stop the blood. One hand free was not enough to rip the buckskin tunic that Half Man Half Woman wore—must use both hands—blood spurts again—the buckskin torn—a long, wide strip—two desperate bloody hands break twice an arrow, hook the buckskin—wind the thigh—turn tight—hold. Man Woman holds sticks and hide as shouting warriors run past, does not hear bullets hissing for him—waits, weeping; holds. Now, knees skinned and graveled, Man Woman carefully on hands and knees moves the half-dead warrior—slowly—slowly—toward, and to, and behind two rocks—goes crawling, then crouching, then running, for more stones, rocks, piles them up in front of them, puts hands back on the drying buckskin, raises a salt-streaked face to the Great Spirit: *Father and Mother of all, Look down! Save!*

All afternoon, all evening, the hundred warriors held their places. Four hundred soldiers, surrounded, fired back at clumps of moving grass, kept their heads down. Howard, down behind the barricade of packs and shot dead animals, received reports from his officers, ordered the howitzers to continue shelling the village, and prayed for his thirsty men.

Ollokot and Two Moons with their warriors held the troopers back from the only spring, and on the other end, more than a mile away, Five Wounds and thirty warriors held the soldiers in a tightening semicircle. The night turned cold; warriors in breechcloths shivered behind rocks.

One by one the older braves inched back down the ravines to meet and talk. In the center Yellow Wolf, who had followed Toohoolhoolzote, crawled up the ravine. Two women, whispering, were moving back and forth. "Careful!" he whispered, "Why are you here?"

"My husband, Young Raven! Have you seen him?"

"He was shot by soldiers."

"I know! Warriors told us. Where is he?"

Yellow Wolf pointed, then wondered why warriors had left the battle to tell anything to anyone.

Far down the ravine White Necklace, wife of Shore Crossing, climbed carefully, a long Navy revolver in her hand. She heard labored breathing and then saw a figure coming down, half carrying a large man in both arms—buckskin tunic torn and ragged. "Oh Friend," she cried in a whisper. "Oh Friend!"

Half Man Half Woman settled with a groan and laid the body down. "My husband," cried White Necklace. "My love!" She bent over Shore Crossing, couldn't breathe, clasped his face.

"He is alive," Man Woman gasped. "He is alive."

"Oh!" White Necklace threw her arms around Man Woman, clasping hard. "Oh, you Friend, you Friend. I knew something had happened to him! I felt it. I felt it. Oh, you Friend." She looked down at her husband, put both hands out, caressed his face. "How did you carry him?"

"I went a little bit by a little bit. I started as soon as it was dark. Now we can carry him together."

"I will never let him fight alone again."

"We'll make a travois when we reach the village, and we'll carry him across the river."

*

Howard's orders placed the men at five yard intervals. The line was only one half mile from flank to flank, but two miles counting all the convolutions, zigs and zags, and ups and backs. Howard wrote that his men suffered terribly, exhausted but not discouraged. Overhead, the bright stars in the clear air above the distant mountains shone along the Milky Way, the Spirit Path, the Ghost Road, picturing the families of souls' ascent into the hunting-grounds of dreams. Sleepless soldiers heard the Indians piling rocks for barricades, heard women wail twice, and hoped for water and some food by dawn. Surgeons Newlands and Fitzgerald applied field dressings to the wounded, awaiting water, daylight, and a way to transport helpless men. Newlands asked Fitzgerald, "Notice that the wounded are too few?"

"Too few? So many are too few?"

"Two wounded so far for each killed. Should be four or five. Not complaining."

"Those Nez Perce shoot to kill. Take their time, use their pieces well. These aren't your Sioux or Cheyenne."

"They did well enough against us last summer, my Sioux and Cheyenne—well enough against Custer."

"They had ten to one against Custer."

"What do you think they have here? Two to one?"

"We've got them three to one at least, four maybe. Otherwise we'd all be dead or running back to Grangeville."

"Not according to the General."

"Don't believe him."

"You think highly of these particular Indians. But I don't care who takes my scalp."

"The Nez Perce don't take scalps."

"All Indians take scalps."

"Not the Nez Perce."

"Christian Nez Perce do not take scalps, perhaps."

"Christians take scalps, in my experience."

"Fitzgerald, are you a Christian?"

"I am."

"You seem critical of Christians and laudatory of these non-Christian Indians."

"Do I?"

"You do."

"Then I am."

"If you had seen that hillside by the Little Big Horn strewn with our dead—naked and cut up every way possible—you would change your mind."

"Is that why you're here?"

"I wanted to be transferred to a quiet spot. I dream of Custer's men. Almost every night."

"I haven't seen anything like that here."

"You will, if this war goes on long enough."

*

Behind a little ridge down at the base of the long bluff, The People years ago had built a lodge of stone and muddy mortar. Here now the older men come down from fighting were gathering to talk. The smoke of pipes was heavy in the crowded space, the only light an orange glow that made the painted faces look like heads protruding from a teeming lower world. Husis Kute, the old leader of a Palouse family, spoke quietly: "The young men have hurt the soldiers, but four are killed. Why? What good does it do to lose our warriors one by one? Let us quit this fight, take the rest of our families, cross the river."

"Why are so many lodges standing? Why have not the women taken the last ones down and crossed?" Looking Glass refused a pipe.

Two Moons shook his head. "No. I told my people to stay and to tell all to stay. If all lodges go, the young men go; they fight only to protect their families."

"Is that bad?" asked Looking Glass. "What else should we fight the soldiers for?"

Two Moons nodded. "I know how you think: fight awhile to give the families time to get away. Fight and run, fight and run. I tell you, the whites will never give up following—unless we kill this One Arm General and all his men. Let's kill them here! Enough running. I am tired of running. They will fight us running and they will fight us here. Either way fight. Why run, too? Ollokot, why do your brother and White Bird lead The People to Kamiah?"

Joseph's brother answered quickly: "They are smart. My brother does not want to fight at all. He says we cannot beat the soldiers, staying here or running. To fight is to die."

Two Moons' eyes narrowed. "What kind of talk is that?"

"It's true," said Looking Glass. "But we have to fight anyway."

Then Rainbow, youngest of the men, rose quietly, handing his pipe to Ollokot. "I will tell you what I will do. I will go to my family and take them up the river."

"If you go," Two Moons objected, "all the young men will follow."

"I hope they do," said Looking Glass; "it's time we got away from here."

"You men are cowards!" Two Moons threw down his pipe; his face went into darkness. Only his voice seemed present. "Kill them or be killed! Cowards!"

"Fool!" said Husis Kute.

"I am ashamed of all of you!" Two Moons rose. "I am going back to my men."

But when Two Moons went back up the ravine he found fewer than half his men. Hair Combed Over Eyes was making his way down when Two Moons caught his arm. "Are you a coward too?"

"I am no coward, Two Moons. The cowards have left while you smoked. Now the brave must go too or die for nothing, leaving The People helpless. You should go. Leave your pride here."

At dawn, some twenty-five Nez Perce remained strung out before Howard's soldiers. The General ordered Captain Miller to take seven companies, supported by another six of Parnell's, to storm the spring and fetch water for the cooks. When this was done, a hundred men moved on the head of that ravine. Ollokot and three men watched them, fired a scattering of shots, then slipped away.

In his report Howard would write, "The assault was carried off in splendid style, the men advancing smoothly under fire in good alignment. The spring and several stone fortifications were captured. The cooks now had their water, General Howard among other officers participating in a make-shift company of canteen carriers, and in two hours all the men had rations of fresh bread, their first of any kind since the battle had been joined."

At two that afternoon, noticing the slackening of hostile fire—though two of his own men shot each other accidentally—Howard ordered an advance along the whole line.

Yellow Wolf and Tired Now were the last two Nimiipuu in the center as the soldiers came. "We skipped away like running lambs," Yellow Wolf said years later, talking to a white man who befriended him, and who did not believe the old reports. "We got away from there! Four of our warriors had been killed and still we didn't know what we should do."

The General finally had a victory, finally drove the hostiles from the field. The newspapers and Washington, until now busy with criticisms of Howard, whose command was nearly taken from him, had Howard's numbers and Sutherland's story. The Army lost twelve killed in battle, two more soon to die of wounds, another missing—found in 1900 with the canteens he had been sent to fill: for fifteen dead and twenty-five wounded—one to lose a leg. Howard's report had twenty-three dead braves and "at least twice as many" wounded—braves whose bodies no one ever found and men whose families never knew they were gone. The Nez Perce mustered, in the bold imagination that inhabits career Christian soldiers' recollections, three hundred warriors plus perhaps fifty squaws—a monumental force.

But best of all was Sutherland's news stories—circulated in the papers from the West Coast way back East, that pitched Howard, one-armed hero of the Civil War, against the wiliest of leaders—resourceful beyond Robert E. Lee; audacious beyond Stonewall Jackson: the great Chief Joseph, unschooled military genius—a force like nature, perfectly suited to the unimaginably difficult terrain. How had Howard beaten him at all? Some things simply cannot be explained. Call it Howard's devotion to duty; call it perseverance mixed with intelligence; call it right makes might or anything you please, but there's the fact—wrote Sutherland, a writer with the subtlety of Virgil, who wrote what the emperor desired—the glories of the dutiful and pious—but whose harping elegiac lines still tender us the sadness and death in duty heartlessly performed. Success is failure in the *Aeneid*, a necessary loss of everything worth winning—so that posterity may enjoy peace and wealth, inheriting the sin and grief of history. So Sutherland's public in the old United States admired the Hero of Gettysburg but all their yearning hearts wished Joseph's people to escape.

Yellow Wolf and Tired Now caught the ponies they had tied, and splashed across the narrow river at the ford below the village. The People had been packing up and leaving slowly, reluctantly, all yesterday and this morning—digging holes to cache the things of their lives, hoping to return: dried meat and salmon, coffee, flour, pots and frying pans, bundles of blankets and buffalo robes, beadwork on buckskin. But when the last warriors came running, riding through, those left behind to finish threw down their shovels, ran from tipis, caught up horses and galloped for their lives. Tired Now saw that his family had left their half struck lodge, and galloped down beside the stream to follow them. But Yellow Wolf heard crying, someone calling for her husband. Riding to an unstruck tipi the young man slid to the ground and looked inside. Springtime, cradling in her arms the infant daughter still unnamed, looked up and cried, "I need my husband!"

"Quick!" said Yellow Wolf. "Soldiers are coming down from the bluff!" He held out his hand. "You must get up and come with me!"

"The baby's sick! She will die. I can't ride with her!"

Yellow Wolf reached down and took the baby from her mother's arms, knowing that Springtime must follow now. He went out, slung up his horses' bridle, and holding carefully he leapt onto the pony's back, the baby held like flowers in the wind.

"I will carry her!" Springtime cried, running to her spotted pony saddled with the high wood pommel and stay women used to ride.

"After we cross the river you can carry her!" The warrior touched heels to his horse's ribs and started away in the steady, even dog-trot Nez Perce horses were taught. He looked toward the bluff and saw the soldiers on their horses carefully stepping down the ravines. "Are you coming?" he called, and saw that Springtime trotted after, her bony knees looking like clubs on each side of her horse's ghostly gray-white face. For the first time Yellow Wolf felt death all around.

During the night, with only breech-clout and moccasins to keep him warm, Yellow Wolf had crept back from his little rifle pit of rocks, shivering. Not knowing where to go or why, he found himself down by the smoking lodge, the place, he said later, where the "no-fighters" stayed that night. Seeing his cousin No Heart lying on the ground asleep, he lay down next to him. No Heart awoke and Yellow Wolf said, "Brother, I will freeze to death. May I lie next to you to warm myself?"

"Stay here and fall asleep."

Hearing the voices, a woman crept toward them. "May I stay with you? I have no blanket and I'm cold!"

No Heart said, "Come here, lie between us. We will keep you warm."
She knelt between the two men and lay down. Feeling her warmth, Yellow
Wolf thought of what the old men said: In war a man must not sleep with
a woman. If he does, it is possible he will be killed. So getting up, Yellow
Wolf made his way back to his rifle pit and lay there, curled up and cradling
himself, shivering, no shirt or leggings, stripped for war, almost naked as a
baby from the soft, warm womb.

He said, "I saved my own life. What the old men told me was right:
my cousin No Heart died. He was killed at our very next battle, our terrible
battle at the Big Hole."

*

"You might not wish to report this sadly demoralizing scene," General
Howard remarked to Thomas Sutherland as they walked together through
the shambled village. "It is my feeling that it reflects badly on the Army
and our civilian friends alike." Sutherland replaced his little notebook in
his pocket, looked deliberately at his stub of pencil and then threw it on the
ground.

"You find 'em like this," a man dressed like a shopkeeper said to another as he thrust a ramrod into the ground. "You poke around until you
feel something soft. With all the fresh holes, it don't require much lookin'."

Seemingly out of nowhere, wagons driven by civilians had appeared.
Drawn by the sound of rifles and artillery, the settlers knew that Indian
clothing, food, and even gold would be available for nothing but the taking.
Soldiers put aside what they had found and looked for more, then discovered their bundles gone when they returned, appropriated by sharp-eyed
civilians. "An army that stops to loot deprives itself of speed, the ability to
pursue."

"I shall remember that, General."

"You need not report it," Howard said. "But I repeat myself."

"Could the cavalry go after Joseph? I speak as an amateur."

"I am about to see to that." Howard turned to his aide. "Find Lieutenant Parnell and give him my respects. Please inform him of my desire for
him to collect his troopers as soon as practicable, mount them, and feel
forward for the hostiles' trail. Instruct him to proceed with caution, not
bringing on any engagement until I have come up with the main body." He
turned to Sutherland. "I shall press those people."

*

Joseph was already at Kamiah, a settlement of treaty, Christian Nez Perce—a short-haired people dressed in white men's clothes. They tilled their garden plots, sat in a wooden church, and were educated in a school taught by missionaries from the East. Joseph, Sound of Running Feet, and People from two families rode their ponies to the school, dismounted, and stood waiting.

"Running Feet, did Mother really send you to me?"

She looked at him steadily, full in the eyes and not down at the ground like an ashamed child. Her face, a frank and open face like his, was finer: where Joseph's looked like honesty itself, his daughter carried shades and nuances like summer rain dashed with points of sunlight in the evergreen forests of the Wallowa, where in the spring, fragrances of spruce and fir come sometimes fresh and sometimes deep, as breezes off the light and drifting showers rise and fall. "No, Father. Mother did not send me."

"She sent you to look after your young brothers and sisters, didn't she?"

"And I know they are well cared for by Ollokot's family. You know it too."

"I do."

"But who takes care of you?"

"Snows Resting takes care of this old man." Joseph smiled a gentle, sheepish smile.

"No, Father. You are in love with her, that's all."

"My daughter, remember never to have children who are smarter and wiser than you are."

"You are not made to be happy, Father. So I must take care of you. And I will take care of Snows Resting, too, and children you will have. I am strong."

"Oh, Daughter, you take care of everyone. You care for everyone."

"Because I am like you, Father. Daughter like father."

Joseph rested his hand lightly on her head, then stood quietly. At last he said, "I can't do anything."

"You can do anything."

"You don't still believe that, do you?"

"No, but it is good to say and good for you to hear. You lose heart quickly, like the coyote."

"We are children of the coyote."

"You have to be a wolf now, Father, an elk, or a wild charging buffalo."

"Our brother buffalo is not smart."

"Not a buffalo, then. But an elk."

"Good. I will be an elk. What can the elk do now?"

"You know, Father."

"I do not know. I am here to ask the Christians to let our People use the large ferry to cross the big river. If they say Yes, we leave our own country, our ancestor's graves, the beautiful land. If the Christians tell us No, then we stay where we belong and die. Nothing is good."

"Cross the river, no matter what they say." Joseph breathed deeply and sighed. "You are like the whites, Father."

"What? Running Feet!"

"To the whites, land is everything."

Joseph smiled. "To the whites, it is land. To us, it is The Land."

Now one of the men waiting with Joseph put his hand on Joseph's arm. "Never have father and daughter talked so much. The Christians are coming."

Seven elders from the Presbyterian church walked from the white building toward the school. In front, an old man named Reading Smith came with long strides; his look was grave. "Joseph," the man said, offering his hand, a gesture the chief accepted.

"Thunder-Rising-in-the-Mountains," Slow Horse corrected curtly.

"Joseph to us," said Reading Smith, "and to the whole white nation. You are known for trouble everywhere, Joseph. We do not want it here."

"We did not start the trouble."

"Your young men did. Change your ways, Joseph. We will welcome you here, as Christians. But if you come among us as wild Indians, you will bring the Army with you."

"You have nothing to fear from the Army."

"It is the time, Joseph, where the sun now stands, to forsake the ways of war and seek peace."

"I did not want war!"

"Then surrender! Then you will not have war."

"We are going away from this country; we want to go away from war. Help us to go, and there will be peace."

"The United States Army would not see it that way if we helped you."

"We need to cross the river. We have many old people and young children. The soldiers are close behind."

"You may not use our ferry."

"Is that what a Christian says?"

"We want no trouble."

Joseph nodded. "We will make no trouble for you. We will cross by ourselves."

"God bless you, Joseph; and may he teach you his ways."

"I know his ways. Reading Smith, what makes a Christian different from others of our People?" Smith gave no answer. Joseph said, "He is someone who thinks that God is a white man."

Two hours later, the Nimiipuu chiefs met by the River's shore: White Bird, Ollokot, Joseph, Two Moons, Rainbow, Toohoolhoolzote, Looking Glass, and others. Joseph had made up his mind.

"The soldiers have beaten us because we would not fight," said Toohoolhoolzote.

"We should not have fought more than one day," said Looking Glass. "The People could have moved yesterday. Who told them to stay?"

"I did," said Rainbow. "All the men with courage wanted to stay."

"I have no courage?"

"Rainbow has no wisdom," White Bird said.

"The soldiers," Joseph said quietly.

"What of the soldiers?" Two Moons demanded.

"They are coming."

"Slowly," said Looking Glass. "General Howard has one arm when he fights, and one leg when he moves. There is no need to run quickly."

"What do you say, Brother," asked Ollokot.

"I am tired of Joseph's words," said Toohoolhoolzote. "Always talking, never doing anything."

"You are angry about getting beaten by whites," said White Bird.

"We were not beaten," Toohoolhoolzote said. Then he added, "All right, Joseph, what can you say that does something for The People now?"

Joseph answered the old chief: "I say that unless we learn to agree, The People will die. Soon."

Toohoolhoolzote said nothing, then nodded.

"You have agreed that I am our war leader," said Looking Glass. "Now you must learn to follow my orders."

"Like the whites," said Rainbow.

"Yes," Looking Glass said. "Like the whites."

"What do you say, then?" asked Toohoolhoolzote.

"We cross the river, cross the mountains, and live in Buffalo Country."

"I can agree to that, like a free man," said Rainbow. "That country is good."

"I will stay," said Joseph quietly.

"You have just now said we must all agree," said Looking Glass. "What do you mean?"

"I will die rather than leave my country. I promised my father I would never leave his grave. I mean to keep my promise."

"No," said Ollokot.

"The People remain together," said White Bird. "It is our way. The warriors could escape the soldiers, but we will not. All of us go, or no-one goes. We will not abandon one old woman, one child—and we will not divide again!"

"I and those who choose to die will stay. We will hold back One Arm General and his soldiers while The People escape."

"You do not need to hold them back, Joseph," Looking Glass said calmly. "They are slow."

"Brother," said Ollokot, "I know your heart. Listen. The whites use a word—duty: you know what you must do because you must, not because you choose. You have duty to The People. You may choose no more."

"It is a white man's word," said Joseph.

"Our country is the white man's now," said Ollokot. "You choose to die but you must live. The People need you."

"We need everyone," said Looking Glass.

*

U.S. Grant, the former President, sat smoking while two reporters introduced themselves, commencing to ask questions about his old friend Sherman, about the new President (no response), about the South, about Robert E. Lee ("a gentleman"), and then one of them brought up Howard. This Howard fought under you at Chattanooga, did he not? "He did." How did he do? "Followed orders." The reports from Idaho say he has won a brilliant victory over the Nez Perces. Have you seen the papers? Grant nodded, "I have." Some people say you almost fired Howard when you were President. Some say this Clearwater affair was not a victory but a disaster—because he let the Nez Perces escape. Do you think it was a brilliant victory? The former President's cigar was out and now he took another from his inside coat pocket, brought out matches, tried to light the cigar, failed, deliberately lit another match but failed to draw, went for another match, and the reporter said, Sir, I beg your pardon, but do you think it was a brilliant victory? "A brilliant victory of course. Howard says so himself."

*

Oliver Otis Howard stood by his horse on the south bank of the river, while Major Campbell shouted to the Nez Perce warrior on the other side. "You gave us Joseph's pledge yesterday that he would come here to surrender!

We have been patient! General Howard instructs me to ask, Where is Joseph? Why is he not here? Why have you come back instead of Joseph? The United States Army shall not be patient with you people indefinitely!"

"Well stated, Major. Thank you," Howard said quietly.

For answer, the warrior dismounted, turned his back to Howard and slapped his buttocks.

"It's a sign of contempt, Sir; disrespect."

"I know that!"

"I believe that Joseph never intended to meet us here and surrender. We lost two days waiting. We've been bamboozled again by those savages, Sir."

"I have suspected it, Major. I knew it all along."

Howard had sent for reinforcements, and when he crossed the river he had seven hundred fifty men. Another four hundred fifty were on the way from Fort Spokane, and to the east, across the mountains in Montana, Colonel John Gibbon, who fifteen years before had commanded the Iron Brigade, would receive a message from Howard. If Joseph and his hostile Nez Perces succeed in crossing the Bitterroots, Howard following, Gibbon was to march south and intercept him. Most likely they would camp at the Big Hole, and there a thousand soldiers would converge and crush them.

Across the Clearwater later that day a band of Nez Perce families came fording. Their leader, Red Heart, rode directly to the Army camp, bringing two rifles to surrender. With him rode seventeen braves; waiting at the river, twenty-eight women and children watched. Ten other Nez Perce stood apart from them: the warrior Three Feathers, a few young men and boys, women. None of these was treaty; none Christian. Howard sent his adjutant and Major Campbell to parley with Red Heart and his long-haired riders. All of them were dressed in buckskin leggings, shirts of calico and plaid; there was no war paint on faces or on horses. No warrior carried a rifle.

"They've come across the mountains," Campbell said to Howard while the Nez Perce waited. "Been to buffalo country—Montana. On their way down here they ran on Joseph, about a day north. This Red Heart could name all the big boys—Looking Glass, White Bird, that old chief Whats-His-Name, and all the rest. Saw them, or knows them. Says they told him about the war and asked him to join. Says that he declined with thanks, no war for him; that's why he turned his rifles in. Those other long-hairs are Joseph's—fed up with the war, want to come in, live on the reservation. I told him we would escort him onto another part of the reservation. Funny thing, Joseph was on the reservation when we hit him. Maybe that's why so many of them stayed two days in that village."

"Arrest them."

"Arrest? Yes, Sir. Which ones?"

"All of them."

"All. Yes, Sir."

"Detach one of Parnell's companies to escort them to Fort Lapwai. Secure them in the jail there. All of them."

"All."

"We've captured Joseph's rear guard."

"Have we, Sir?"

"Yes, Major."

"Another victory, General."

"See to it, Major Campbell. Those are orders."

*

The Nez Perce families—three thousand horses, a thousand head of cattle, the old people, children, several hundred dogs; girls and boys, men and women riding spotted ponies at the dog-trot that the Appaloosas could keep up all day—stretched out for miles along Clearwater River, out onto the prairie, led by Joseph and White Bird toward the mountains. The black Bitterroots waited to the east, most of their snow gone now in midsummer, the needled trees dark as midnight when light came up behind them. As the land rose, the leading families made camp—here, in the first foothills, where they could turn and see the land they left almost every summer, the land they always came back to in late summer with fresh buffalo robes, dried meat, and stories to tell in their lodges through the snows—land of coming back to, land they would never see again. In the photographs, Joseph is always looking at that land, always looking back the way he looked that evening leaving Kamiah prairie, looking the sun straight in the face, beyond wailing, beyond mourning chants, dead silence in his soul.

As Joseph stood that evening, wrapped in a wool blanket against the chill gusts coming down from the dark, endless mountains, the young warrior Yellow Wolf rode up from three days following The People, catching up and slowly doubling the stunned and trotting families, asking, "Where is Joseph? How far ahead is Joseph?" He slowed his pony when he saw the still figure standing, then slipped down onto the sandy soil. He walked to Joseph; waited quietly a moment. Then he said, "Hinmatooyalahtqit." Joseph shuddered. "Your daughter is dead."

*

In Montana, John Gibbon slept soundly, not yet having received the orders that would send him to the worst two days of his life. Behind, Howard's infantry and troopers used a day to cross the Clearwater—after what one soldier called "considerable humbugging" with their horses, many of which "had to be towed across, as usual"—the artillery following, and took up the pursuit.

V

The Mountains

These are the Bitterroot Mountains. They rise in the forests of hemlock,
pine, and blue spruce that once covered the Idaho wilderness
following rivers that ran clear in those days, and flowed cold three seasons—
Snake River, Clearwater, Salmon, Wallowa, descending northwestward
down to the green and uncut woods and the endless soft meadows
once called the land of The People, the Nez Perce, tamers of strong horses.

These are the Bitterroot Mountains; but where are The People who crossed them
bound for the buffalo country, traveling into summer
over the mountains and into the plains of Montana?—riding their
spotted Appaloosa ponies that could pick their way across rocky
mountainsides and swim the steep-falling and boulder-tight streams,
find in the rising forests the paths of the pacing bull elk, narrow
trails of the long-eared and alert deer. Where are the Nez Perce, The People,
farming and hunting the headwaters of the Columbia, peaceful
friends of the Palouse and the Crow, but fierce to invading Shoshoni?

Gone now—no lodges by rivers or farms in the meadows, no buffalo
running on the long-sky-land of summer; now only the long story,
memory of the Long-Travel War. This is our own American
story. Tell us, Spirit, our darkening tale of frailty and sorrow.

*

The Bitterroots go on forever, a jagged, stony sea of hazard, one hundred
fifty miles as hard and steep as grief and despair—ascent after ascent,

an ocean of cold at the peaks, snow on the sliding old trails, and straight ahead another mountain, hewn and indifferent, forever. Blades of shale and granite rise ragged, tall as thunderheads up one side of half-vanished paths—two paces away, descents fall like whirlpools, rising maws with pine-spiked and serried throats.

The People led their ponies walking like grim Israelites between wild walls of eternity, Death and its sister Peace churning like the raw, ravenous chaos of the night out of which they had come. Joseph and his warrior brother Ollokot led the stunned and wounded People up the trails, the visionary at the head, the warrior watching, turning, slow and sharp-eyed, the stinger of the scorpion's tail, watching through Bitterroot mists for the dun blue of cavalry and mules, for the bearded one-armed general, the floating smell of sweat and wool stronger than the odor of ponies, more sickening to the stomach than urine in the sun. "Come on, forward," Joseph urged unfeelingly and quietly, The People's fear and haunted yearning pushing him, who thought while walking every gray stone, *Were there not enough graves in Wallowa Valley, that we should bury our hearts in these mountains?*

Ollokot told Four Blankets riding wounded in the chest, "It does no good to see the future. I had a head and a heart and knew that once we fought the soldiers, we would have to go to the mountains. And now I know that many will die, maybe all of us, running and fighting, or living far from home. I know, yet can do nothing to stop it. I can only run and fight, like an animal. Yet I will fight hard. I will fight these whites who make us do what we must!"

Walking at the head of Four Blankets' pony, an old man called Daytime Smoke looked back at Ollokot: "It is not these whites we see who make us move, but many whites, long ago, whites without number, all born from the hand of the Great Spirit. Your grandfather saved my father, a white man, Clark, who would have died on this trail without The People's food and horses. It was he, my father, William Clark, who brought these whites here looking for land. The whites are all homeless, children of the sun, moving east to west. Am I one of them?"

"We are children of the moon," said Ollokot. "We pale and die before the sun. You are one of us, Daytime Smoke. See—you walk toward the morning, like your mother."

"My mother loved a white man. I could never find why. She told me that Clark did not force himself upon her. She gave her heart to that white man. My father. Where she loved, I hate. I am not my mother's child. I have no mother or father. I belong nowhere."

"You are The People, what we are now," said Four Blankets.

"Your wound hurts you," Ollokot said quietly.

"My wound will always hurt me."

"No," said Daytime Smoke; "you only want an excuse to ride, while we old men have to walk, you lazy Indian!"

Then all three laughed, hard and long, as they climbed the steep and narrow trail into the cold. The Bitterroots rise seven thousand feet like broken saw teeth, snow lying on the north edges down well below the timber line. Winds—not winds but tempest gusts—uproot tall trees and leave the deadfall sprawled, strewn, across the Nez Perce trail that stitches elk and bighorn paths meadow to meadow. Generations of Appaloosa ponies have grazed the meadows, rested there by The People, families, passing one by one to buffalo country, passing back to the Wallowa Valley—until the trail is rutted deep and filled with scree and jumbled branches. Never before now have hundreds of Nimiipuu passed at once, three thousand horses with them. Through cold rain The People climb on muddy, slick slopes. Up front on dry, sun-blanched ridgelines the horses and people raise clouds of sticky dust breathed by those behind. In the rear, Ollokot and his warriors walk quietly with four families of Joseph's band, listening for soldiers. Any feeder trail could bristle with Howard's Christian scouts, Nez Perce cousins, not brothers any more, soldiers behind them riding.

The first night Sun-on-Water's baby cries. She cannot comfort him. He cries, then screams even though she bares her breast and tries to feed the child. She cradles him so tenderly in soft doeskin arms, sways gently, whispering and murmuring a song. A brave creeps to her, saying, "Please still him, Sun-on-Water! The whites could hear and know that we have taken this trail."

She quickly strokes the baby's raging face. "Be still. Still!" She rocks the child and sings a little.

Again the warrior comes. This time he pleads, "Still him, Sun-on-Water! Feed the child! He's hungry!"

"I have fed him," she whispers. She prays and groans, holds her hand to the child's mouth but he squirms away screaming.

At last Ollokot comes. He thinks perhaps her husband's ghost, he dead at Clearwater, torments the child. "You must still the baby!" he tells her. "Hold my medicine over his heart." He gives her the small bag he has carried on a leather necklace over his heart since he was a boy. "Still him or our People will die!"

She winds the necklace around the baby's neck, holds the medicine against his heart, the beaded pouch of soft deerskin. "Go!" she says to Ollokot. "He will be still."

Ollokot nods and rises, walks to the horses where the braves are holding shirts and blankets over jittery ponies' muzzles. Sun-on-Water's baby screams, screams; and the mother rises, holds the baby's forehead to her own, closes her eyes, speaks to him, then strikes his head against a tree, strikes again, strikes a third time, then settles to her knees, rocking, rocking, gasping, sobbing quietly, kissing the bleeding, still head.

Ollokot has heard and realized what she has done and runs to her, his face streaming tears. He kneels beside her, wants to cry out "No!" but understands that she has given what she has given. She begins to unwind the necklace but he puts his hand on hers and tells her, "Bury it with him. Our hearts will be buried with yours in his grave."

Before the next sunset all The People will know.

At dawn Ollokot tells his braves, "Twelve of you will stay with me here to watch and wait at the grave while the families go on. You, Red Moccasin Tops, take four men and go back down the trail. When you see whites, send two of the four to me. You three defend the trail for one day. Death is in these mountains now."

*

Correspondent Trimble said, "You ought to speak with Clay sometime."

"And just who is Clay?" asked Sutherland.

"Major Clay Wood, my friend—Howard's adjutant."

"Major Wood? You call him by his first name?"

"You know I don't take these damnyankee officers for officers."

"The war has been over for some twelve years."

"But I keep it up. Not out of feeling, of course, but just for fun."

"I'm a damnyankee, you know."

"I know it, Tom, but now and then it doesn't show."

"I suppose that's a compliment, coming from you."

"Not particularly. All I'm saying is, you could just about pass for a Southerner if you'd had proper upbringing. Hell, you can almost pass for anything."

"What is it you are trying to say, Trimble? Come out and say it."

"Well Tom, it is not a gentleman's way to point out that you have your lips squarely planted on Otis Howard's posterior."

"Why, you son of a bitch."

"Just so you know, I don't call the man Otis. It's General Howard, Sir. He recognizes sarcasm quicker than you do."

"We are fellow correspondents, *Sir.* Why do you take it upon yourself to insult me? Is it jealousy, *Sir*?"

"Now don't get ugly, Tom. If I mean to insult you, you will know it. I speak only for your good, with your welfare in mind, Tom."

"How is that?"

"Tom, you are too good a writer to destroy your career."

"How am I destroying my career? My stories run in newspapers all over the country!"

"And nobody believes them anymore."

"How would you know?"

"Tom, you'll cover yourself with embarrassment and humiliation when this Christian Soldier of yours finally fails to catch these Nez Perces—or worse yet, if he catches them, old people, children, and half of them women, and shoots them down like dogs."

"Howard won't do that."

"Oh like hell he won't. You scratch that Christian Soldier deep enough, you find another Armstrong Custer."

"Some think of Custer as a martyr. Maybe not you Southerners."

"At Appomattox Custer tried to steal General Longstreet's horse, and as I see it, he only went downhill afterwards as a moral being. Custer was a squaw-killer, Tom, to state it plainly. Why do you think the redskins called him Son of the Morning Star?"

"Reluctant admiration, I suppose." Trimble smiled wryly. "Why, then?"

"Because he'd charge into a village before the sun came up and shoot the sleeping families right through their tipis. I didn't despise Custer for being a Yankee: he was worse than any Yankee ever was."

"What did you want him to do, halt his men outside the village and invite the braves to get up and shoot it out fair and square? How many Indians is one soldier's life worth?"

"So that's it, Tom. You people have no sense of irony. You Yanks made no end of fuss about the Negro being just as much a man as you and me, sent troops to occupy my state to make sure every Negro got a vote because a Negro is a man—and now you've found another word for 'Negro:' *hostiles, redskins, Indians*—make them dead or make them white: they're no good as they are. No wonder most of them fought for us in the War."

Sutherland said nothing for a while, and then he said, "I've got nothing against these Nez Perce. I admire them. I wouldn't want to be in their place. I am looking out for myself."

"Then do yourself a good turn, Tom, and speak with Major Wood."

"Howard has forbidden me to talk to any other officer until his plan is put into effect."

"Well Tom, you might as well put on a dress and powder up your face."

"How is it you could talk to Wood?"

"I never ask permission."

"Howard doesn't talk to you. He talks to me."

"If you want to know the truth, speak with Wood."

"He probably has orders not to talk to me."

"All right."

"I would have thought you wouldn't want the truth to fall into my hands. Aren't we two here competitors?"

"A Yankee is a Yankee. To tell the truth, I've had a stomach full of this and reckon to be shut of it once Otis follows Joseph to the mountains."

"I happen to know that we're not going into the mountains. We're going south. Joseph is turning south to get around us, heading back to his country."

"That's what Howard thinks, but Howard is a fool. After a week or two he'll figure out that there's no choice for Joseph but to run."

"Run where?"

"Canada, where Sitting Bull has gone."

"Then why not go north now, straight north?"

"The Blackfeet are up there. Blackfeet and Nez Perce are blood enemies. They'd be more trouble than Howard. Joseph will go east to Crow country and then up. Howard and you all will plod along behind."

"You aren't coming?"

"Might could join you, other side of the mountains. I'll take the road, though, from Spokaine."

"That's the long way around."

"No rush. Give my respects to Clay."

"I'll talk to him when and if we go into the mountains."

*

General Howard did move south, awaiting re-enforcements and intending to cut off The People when they turned back west. He sent several treaty Nez Perce scouts to shadow Joseph's trail, which seemed to lead east toward the Bitterroots. The four he sent were James Rueben, a nephew of Joseph's; a man named Captain John, whose daughter walked with Joseph's people; Horse Blanket, whom whites called Sam—whose father by another woman was Yellow Wolf's father; and Sheared Wolf, known as John Levi to Howard's soldiers. These four followed the long, deep trail The People made—the families, their herds and cattle—into the foothills of the Bitterroots. On second thought Howard sent some thirty men behind the scouts—civilian volunteers under an officer's command—in the unlikely case that Joseph really had gone eastward up into the towering Bitterroots. There Red Moccasin Tops and his friends waited.

The slow approach of horses through the trees far down the trail brought the five braves listening. In the lower distance they could see a climbing line of white men on the trail, the officers and volunteers; but here at hand not sounds of white men but of braves dismounted, working through the trees and brush beside the rutted trail. Moccasin turned toward Winter Horse and Sleeping, and they moved without a word back from the three remaining and then loped up the broken trail. The three moved forward down the trail and when they found close-grown trees, stopped and waited. Almost without sound the four Christian Nez Perce came closer, sidling together as they understood something wrong. "Put down your rifles!" Red Moccasin commanded them.

"Where are you?" asked Captain John.

"Here," said Five Wounds upslope from the trail.

"How many are you?"

"Enough," said Yellow War Shirt quietly down from the other side. The four scouts laid their rifles carefully upon the rocky, branch-littered ground. Red Moccasin Tops stepped out with carbine leveled; then the other two emerged.

"Three of you?" said Sheared Wolf, called John Levi.

"Yes, only three," answered Five Wounds; "three guns pointed at your bellies. If you pick up your rifles, we shoot three of you. The fourth might take aim but two of us will shoot him down. You decide what is best to do."

"We will not pick up our rifles," said James Rueben. "We will talk."

"No, you will listen!" said Red Moccasin Tops. "We are relations of yours! You should be ashamed!"

"Your skins, your hair, your faces, and your bodies are the same as ours!" said Five Wounds. "Now you scout for the Americans, great friends of yours, who have stained our land with the blood of your relations."

"The white man has spilled Nimiipuu blood for years," said Red Moccasin Tops. "Our chiefs have put their nerves between their teeth to keep peace with these whites!"

"We do not want this war," said Levi.

"Neither do we!" said Five Wounds. "And we don't want our cousins and brothers helping soldiers to kill us!"

"We will go back home," said Levi. "Let us take our rifles and we will quit this war!"

"We have given you enough chances to act like People," Five Wounds said. "Why should we let you go?"

"We promise," Levi said. "We promise not to raise our hands against our brothers in this war. Let us go and we will tell our people of your mercy and your courage."

"You are white now," Moccasin replied. "You make white promises."

"As Christians, as men, as Nimiipuu warriors, we promise," said Captain John.

"We do not want to kill our own People, even Christians," said Five Wounds. "We will let you go, but without rifles!"

"Then kill us here," said Reuben, "because if we return unarmed, the soldiers will know what has happened and will put us in their prison! We will not use our rifles."

"Go," said Five Wounds. "Pick up your rifles and go."

"But if we find any of you helping the soldiers again, we will kill you quick!" said Red Moccasin Tops. "If any Christian People help the soldiers, we will kill them! Tell that to The People at Kamiah!"

"We have given you our word," said Captain John. The four picked up their rifles, turned one by one, and walked single file back down the trail.

"Let us go," said Red Moccasin Tops, holding his rifle across his chest.

"Wait," said Winter Horse. Five wounds nodded. A long time the three waited, not moving. Sunlight and shadows moved across their faces as they looked down the trail and listened.

"They are gone," came the quiet voice of Captain John from below. The three listening warriors raised their carbines and fired down the trail. A cry of pain rose up. The three loaded and fired again. Another cry—John Levi: "They've hit me!" Crashing below, the sound of stumbling, running, and dragging told the three braves that two men had been hit. When they came upon John Levi, lying where the others had left him, he looked up and said, "I have news to tell you!"

"You may tell it in the spirit world," said Moccasin. He pushed a cartridge into the breech of his carbine, lowered the muzzle to Levi's face, and fired.

*

Far up the mountain, Looking Glass had heard the shots. He turned his horse's head and slowly picked his way down through The People strung along the trail. Five warriors followed, turning one by one.

Closer, Ollokot moved with his dozen fighters down the trail. Halfway to the three braves he met Winter Horse and Sleeping. Ollokot left one man to watch the picketed horses, and fourteen fighting men trotted down the trampled trail.

At the same time, Lieutenant Johnson and his thirty volunteers reached Rueben, slightly wounded, walking gingerly, the other two beside him carrying his cartridges and rifle. "How many of them up there?" Johnson barked, and Captain John said, "Three, but more behind them, coming fast. Go back down."

"The hell I'll go back down!" Johnson retorted, but as he spoke a fusillade above them crashed through the branches and the volunteers went running down the trail. The sergeant caught a few of them, so Johnson, the three scouts, and several men took up position behind trees and boulders each side of the trail. They waited for the hostiles but in an hour the lieutenant called it off. Ollokot would not send his warriors straight ahead into the soldiers' rifles; instead he sent two groups to right and left, but before they went forward, Looking Glass arrived.

After hearing what had happened he told Ollokot, "Do not attack them. Let us rest here."

"We can kill them!" Ollokot insisted.

"What use would killing them be? A few would run and tell the one-armed general we are here. Send five men after them when they retreat, and let the five make noise."

"Howard will come with all his soldiers."

"Let Howard think we are only few, not all The People here. I will take twenty fighting men back down to Kamiah and punish those miserable Christians—burn barns and run off their horses. Howard will think we have turned north. He will not know what to do. He will go north. It will be many days before he understands that we have left for Buffalo Country."

"I thought we were turning south after crossing the mountains!"

"We will speak of it together after I have visited the Christians."

*

Thunder in the Mountains and his brother Ollokot looked from a mountain meadow at the peaks ahead of them, dark woods covering the view below as far as they could see. Steep abysses cut ragged slopes. "Do you think One-Arm Soldier wants to follow us?" asked Ollokot.

"He wants to catch us, but he does not want to follow us. He wishes to subdue us, but he does not want to fight us."

"He is called the Christian Soldier, but I think he is mostly a white man, and he will follow to the death. An Indian would count his coup and let us go."

"Not a Christian Indian."

"No."

"Why do the Christians hate us?"

"They want our land. It doesn't matter if they are Christians or not. They are white."

"They will take the land, never let us go back."

"I would rather die fighting them in these mountains with our women and children behind us than wander all our lives I know not where."

"Even the young men do not talk that way, Brother."

"They do not see the end, as they did not see this when they began this war. Now we run and are killed running. Might as well be killed standing."

"What does Looking Glass think?"

"He thinks we will escape to Buffalo Country and live happily forever there. As if there are no soldiers there, or Howard will give up. I know Howard's heart: he will send us all to his heaven by killing us."

"He is a strange man."

"The whites think we are strange. All who lose the place they belong are strange to the rest."

"Where did Howard belong, do you think?"

"I do not know. Maybe there was never a place for him."

"His heaven is the place for him."

Thunder in the Mountains rubbed his cold hands together. "I think Howard does not hate us. He is afraid of us."

"He has many soldiers, and we are few."

"He is afraid that we are good, and do not need his heaven."

"We are not good."

"You are not good, Brother. I am good."

"I forgot again."

"Ollokot, I do not know what to do."

*

Far up the trail that night it rained—a short cloudburst of nearly freezing spray, up-drafted so The People lying under buffalo skin spread from bush to rock were drenched shivering. All lodgepoles had been left behind; families made shelter as they could—some, like White Necklace and her husband Shore Crossing lying close, wrapped in a single skin of buffalo.

"How is it with you, Beautiful?" he asked as cold rain blew over them and they lay covered head to foot under the hide. "Warm and well, My Heart, safe in your strong arms."

"But the child?"

"Our child will be all right, Heart. It will be many months before it is big enough inside to be hurt by such traveling. He will be a strong brave, healthy like his father and mother."

"I think that he will be a girl. She will be like her mother. Stronger, better, than her father."

"No one is stronger or better than her father."

"Shall we fight over who is right?"

"Oh, Heart, I do want you so."

Later in the night, as dawn began to touch the tops of pale gray mountains, Shore Crossing lay dreaming of the endless flowering meadows beyond the Bitterroots under the wide, long sky of Buffalo Country. Then he saw soldiers, soldiers running, riding, shooting. He and his companions, the Red Coats, raised their rifles but he heard himself chanting, not a war song but his death song, and then he saw the wide sky and the face of his beloved weeping over him.

He awoke and White Necklace was soothing him, stroking his face, hushing him, saying, "Husband, Husband, what have you seen? What were you crying out? What song have you sung?"

"My death song. It was my death song! I saw myself killed in Buffalo Country! I will be killed, Beloved! I will not live to see our baby born!"

"Hush, hush. It might not be! It might not be! Sleep again, Heart. Maybe you will have a better dream, a healing dream."

But neither slept. Painfully and stiff, they turned in each other's arms, until Shore Crossing said, "It is wrong, our going to Buffalo Country! We must turn back! We will all be killed!"

As White Necklace watched, afraid, the warrior rolled out of the covering, stood unbalanced, then walked toward the other families camped in the small meadow. Tufts of grass were stiff with ice; the families lay close and shivering. "Wake up!" Shore Crossing cried as he limped along the trail. "Wake up and hear me! I have sung my death song! I have seen myself killed! We will go to Buffalo Country and many will die. I will die! Soldiers will kill us. My friends, take care of my wife and child. Do not let them suffer or starve! I will be killed! I have seen myself killed." White Necklace rose and went to Shore Crossing's side, holding him.

"Oh my Beautiful!" he cried, his face against her neck. "Oh my Beautiful! I do not want to leave you!"

"Hush, hush, My Heart. It is all right. You will not leave me. I will go with you."

"No! No!"

"Hush. It is all right. Heart, it is all right."

*

In another meadow in the early light as a hard sun struck the waking People, the old warrior Four Blankets, wounded at Clearwater, his chest wrapped in calico cloth strips, walked to Joseph's shelter. The chief and his daughter, Sound of Running Feet, stood looking across the mountains. Below, seven hundred of The People and their herds spread back across the trail and meadows. Sound of Running Feet looked toward the sunrise. "Thunder in the Mountains!" Four Blankets said, "I have something to tell you!"

"We must not go to Buffalo Country."

The warrior stared at Joseph amazed. "That is what I wanted to tell you!"

"I feel it. I know it in my whole spirit. Have you had a dream, Four Blankets?"

"No, Thunder in the Mountains. But I do not feel right. My heart does not feel right. My spirit did not sleep last night. My guardian spirit told me, Do not walk toward the morning sun. We are walking into darkness."

Joseph nodded. "We will not go to Buffalo Country. We will go back to our own country and die fighting for our fathers' graves, for our wives, for our children!"

"But Father, who will protect us if you die? I don't want to live in our old country if you and all the braves are dead."

"Sit Beside Me Wife says, Go back."

"Think of what the soldiers will do to us when all you men are gone! We have to go toward the morning sun."

Four Blankets spoke up: "Thunder in the Mountains, you must tell us what to do. You always know what to do."

"I don't know what to do!"

"You must go seek the Great Spirit. You must seek a dream, for our People."

"I have had no dreams. I have had no sleep."

"Go ahead of us. Go alone."

"I cannot leave The People now, Four Blankets. If the Great Spirit wishes to give me a vision of what to do, I will receive it here among The People, where I must be."

"You have to be alone to see a vision."

"It may be that the Great Spirit can do anything, can even give a vision to a crowded man." Joseph smiled at Sound of Running Feet, and Four Blankets laughed.

"You and your daughter always think alike. But not this time. What does it mean?"

"It means my father is sad."

*

Oliver O. Howard was at Grangeville welcoming his son, who had come with Wheaton's regiment from San Francisco. Frank Wheaton was at Gettysburg fourteen years ago, then had been stationed in the South seeing to the Reconstruction of former Confederates until politics in Washington concluded the experiment and let be what would be for Blacks and whites down there. Now Howard had around a thousand men at his command, including Guy, his son, who would serve on his staff.

"You'll note the water didn't part for Joseph and his savages when they escaped across the Clearwater," the General told his buck.

"Nor for you, either, Sir," the young man said. Anger and surprise fought for control of Howard's face. "I mean no disrespect, Father—Sir. I only represent to you what the newspapers say."

"What papers? What do they say?"

"I brought a stack of them, Sir. I shall have my trunk fetched."

"What are the papers saying about this campaign, Guy?"

"Well, Sir, except for what that correspondent Sutherland reports, they say that Joseph has the advantage of you, Sir, and will get away. They say that you have no heart for such pursuit."

"We'll see what heart I have. Joseph and his hostiles will be brought to bay, I assure you, Guy. Now that Wheaton's regiment is here, I can put my plan into effect. Pursue Joseph we shall not. With some hard marching, we can achieve success without bloodshed. I shall leave two hundred troopers here to protect these settlements, send Wheaton north along the Mullen Road to cut Joseph off when he emerges from Lolo Pass, and parallel him to the south with our main body, ready for him if he turns south along the Bitterroot to come around and return to his home country. If I know Joseph, as I believe I do, that is exactly what he will do—and he will run directly into us—infantry, cavalry, and artillery—waiting for him."

*

But next day Looking Glass and twenty warriors struck Kamiah settlement. By evening Howard had the news, and also had orders from the commander of the United States Army, William Tecumseh Sherman. Sherman had said that war is hell and understood how to make hell come home. "Exterminate them," he ordered—meaning Indians—men, women, children—"with vindictive earnestness."

After last year's Custer so-called massacre, Sherman wasn't going to let any hostile Indians get out from under his authority. It was Custer's death last summer that secured the tragedy enclosing the Nez Perce this year. A week after the Cheyenne and Lakota fought a drawn battle at the Rosebud, Custer and a portion of the Seventh Cavalry rode toward the Little Bighorn River—what the Lakota called the Greasy Grass. At least ten thousand, maybe as many as fifteen thousand—half the whole Lakota population, held a long and last encampment at the call of their great leader Sitting Bull—warrior, visionary, and the center of resistance to the whites. Crazy Horse was there, a doomed Achilles of his people; his friend He Dog; the war chief Gall; Black Moon, Big Road, Wooden Leg, Crow King—twelve to fifteen hundred fighting men and their families. Not at the Rosebud, Sitting Bull presided at this weeks-long gathering, and as five hundred of his friends were fighting George Crook's thirteen hundred at the Rosebud, the staunch prophet received a vision: soldiers and their horses falling headfirst from the sky into the Lakota village. And then a warning voice: "Take nothing from them." Sitting Bull knew his vision meant a victory, but even he did not expect it to be so soon.

In eight days Custer led his companies toward a big Sioux village reported to be camped on the Greasy Grass, past several ridges ahead. He didn't send his scouts ahead to see exactly who was there, how many, or precisely how prepared they were. Lieutenant Colonel George Armstrong Custer had been a young, aggressive general of cavalry during the Civil War. At Gettysburg, shouting, "Come on, you Wolverines!" he'd led his Michigan troopers in crashing charges on the storied horse soldiers of Stuart, Hampton, and Fitzhugh Lee. He had been in on the kill at war's end, his brigade among the men of Sheridan who blocked the last retreat and hope of the devoted soldiers of Robert E. Lee. But his own officers called Custer arrogant, vainglorious, "a circus rider gone mad," wearing velvet trousers and a wide-brimmed hat.

At post-war rank no general, he craved attention and success—success as it was measured by the body counts of Indians. Long Hair, some of the Lakota called him, wearing as he did his golden tresses snapping in the wild west wind—though not in his last campaign. He wore a buckskin jacket, fringed along the sleeves and back, over dark blue, gold-striped tight trousers and blue officer's blouse. His boots were shiny black, and light tan leather gauntlets finished his look.

Wanting to catch the Indians that Crook had missed at Rosebud, Custer had pushed hard two days, force-marching his men and horses. His scouts reported a big village ahead. Dividing his force like a pincers, he sent Major Reno's and Captain Benteen's troopers to swing around to the south and charge into the helpless village. Custer himself with the remaining companies continued north to hit and bottle up the panicked savages from the northeast.

When Reno struck, the first two volleys from his carbines killed both wives of Chief Gall and one of his daughters. Galloping hard to rally and direct his warriors, Gall gave no sign of what had happened to him except to fight with stricken abandon, or as he said later, "like a wild animal." But still his mind was cool, and soon he ringed his warriors halfway around Reno's troopers, now dismounted, running for what cover they could find, then remounting their tired horses to stagger up a ridge and dig a circle to defend. Gall and his warriors would have killed them all, but then a brave came running his horse to the chief and shouted that more soldiers in a column had been seen behind another ridge.

Leaving enough warriors to pin down Reno's sweating, wide-eyed men, Gall rode back through the big encampment shouting for warriors to join him. At the north end, Crazy Horse with several hundred fighting men rode out to circle down and strike Custer's companies from that direction. Gall shouted for his men to make two groups—more than a hundred each, and hit both sides of Long Hair's column. As is well known, Custer and but fifty men finally dismounted, made a stand of desperation, firing their revolvers and carbines from behind their dead or dying horses, while the better shots and fury-brave Lakota and Cheyenne finished them off down to the last lone man.

Did they take nothing, the offended Lakota and their allies? No, they took everything. Boots, carbines, clothing, photographs, money, and whatever those dead soldiers once had carried became theirs—and then the enraged women moved among the dead and cut off ears, jabbed out eyes, stripped the filthy underwear and slashed off private parts, gashed faces, cut off hands and feet, left only Custer whole to see and hear and feel what he had done to his blind and screaming mutilated men whose homeless ghosts would terrorize him until the sun goes back into the dark wolf's endless maw.

The warriors did not finish Reno's surrounded men, nor Benteen's. Some braves had seen a large approaching column of the walking soldiers, and the chiefs—Sitting Bull and Gall and Crazy Horse—decided that the people must be led to safety. So the whole encampment packed up tipis, gathered herds, and with ten thousand horses moved away and left the naked, bloating, sun-blacked bodies scalped and gut-spilled, lying on Last Stand Hill.

The walking soldiers were John Gibbon's Seventh Infantry. They came upon Custer's bodies the next day. It was they who masked their mouths and noses with their handkerchiefs, and they who gathered up the body parts and buried them; and they, posted now up at Missoula, would get Howard's order to march down and cut off Joseph and his people.

*

Cold rain had made the trail a muddy slide and when Snows Resting and Sound of Running Feet had packed the horses with reed baskets and tough bags of hide, the horses would not go. Many times The People had come over these mountains, band by band and family by family, but never all together, never with a need to hurry. Horses never would be driven into heavy mist where they could not see, but Joseph had told his band that they must lead and show the other bands that this time they must not be leisurely. "Come, help me pull the lead horse's head," said Snows Resting.

"You can do it well," said Sound of Running Feet, standing at the head of the next horse.

"Then would you let me take your horse, and you come up here and make mine move?" Sound of Running Feet smiled a smooth smile to herself and walked forward, took the halter rope from Snows Resting's outstretched hand, and waited for the young woman, walking carefully beside the slick trail, to reach the second horse.

"Now, Gopher," she murmured to the wide-eyed horse, "let us show these fine women that we are not afraid of some little cloud. Come. Come, Gopher." But the horse held up its head, its forehooves wide apart. Sound of Running Feet slackened the halter, talking to the horse. "Everything is up to you, my friend. All the families stand waiting for you to show them how to be brave. You know the way. I know you are not afraid. You are the best horse of them all, do you know that? No wonder you are first this morning. Be a good boy, Gopher. Come on. Come on, Gopher. Oh, you stupid, stupid horse! No wonder you are called Gopher! Move! Come on!"

Snows Resting waited quietly, until Sound of Running Feet said, "He won't move! Bring White Woman. Let her lead the way."

"I don't think I can get around you here," said Joseph's younger wife. "The slope is steep."

"Where is Mother?" cried Sound of Running Feet.

"Oh, she went ahead with Father earlier!"

"Snow, you have to leave White Woman and come here and help me."

"She won't move if I leave her, Running Feet!"

"We have to do something!"

"All right. Maybe we can start the horses one at a time." But as she let the halter fall, the white mare stepped backward, slipping hard across the muddy rocks and going down with a piercing neigh. The horse lay churning its forelegs against the wet stones, raising her head, the whites of her eyes bulging; grunting. "Hush, hush," said Snows Resting, trying to hold the horse's head.

A boy scrambled alongside the trail, staying clear of the thrashing head. "Is her leg broken?"

"Sun in the Morning! I think so."

"Maybe not. I want to help!"

"Help me wrap her eyes." Snows Resting took off the cotton shawl that draped her shoulders, handing one end to the boy. Together they tied the cloth around the horse's head, and then she lay quiet, head lifted, moaning.

"Do something!" called Sound of Running Feet. "Get her up!"

"I think she has a broken leg!" Sun in the Morning called.

"She can stand," Snows Resting said quietly.

"Then what?" asked the boy.

"Help me bring up her head," said Snows Resting. "But only with your hands—stay back."

The boy reached out and firmly took the horse's head. "Up, gentle lady," he said calmly. "We will help you."

Snows Resting held the shawl in place and tried to lift the mare's head. The murmuring horse found a hold with her forehooves and pitched herself half up, hindquarters on the stony ground; then with the two still holding her head she flailed one leg, struck the side of the rutted trail, and brought herself full up, panting, blowing.

"Good woman," said Snows Resting. "You brave White Woman." But the horse's rear leg was lifted up, the hoof turned outward. She stood on three legs, grunting and panting in pain.

"Now what?" asked the boy.

"We have to get her off the trail."

Sun in the Morning looked up at Snows Resting, tears at his eyes. "Leave her?"

Snows Resting put a hand on the boy's head. "You have a good heart, little brother, and you are strong and brave. You will be a good chief, like

Joseph. I think when you are old, you will lead all The People, like my husband. Not in war; in peace."

"Move her!" shouted Sound of Running Feet.

"Quickly!" said Snows Resting to the boy. "Go find a big, knotted stick!" Sun in the Morning started out, looking at the deadfall lying everywhere below the trail, and Snows Resting laid her hand against the panting horse's face. "I am sorry, my friend. I am sorry. The People must move quickly or all will die. I hope we will meet on the Spirit Path!"

The boy returned solemnly, holding up a gnarled stout stick spurred with broken fragments. "Let me do it," he said, but Snows Resting shook her head.

"I have to do it." She took the branch, moving from the horse's head.

"Take your shawl!" the boy said. "It's cold!" but Snows Resting made her way behind the horse's good leg.

An old woman, Hands Laughing, met her there. "I will do it. I am strong as a bull buffalo."

"You are not," said Snows Resting.

"Strong enough." As if to prove what she had said, the older woman with a firm look seized the stick. "Stand behind me, Snows Resting!" She raised her arm and struck the horse's flank. The white mare whinnied, lurching upward on her good rear leg as if to raise her forelegs, slipping sideways as the boy pulled off the shawl—sliding for a frantic moment then going down and sliding, kicking, on the steep slope's scree. Slipping into mist, the white horse screamed twice and then was not heard.

The older woman threw the stick against the hard mountainside, and Snows Resting took her shawl absently, then walked with strong and reckless strides forward to where Sound of Running Feet stood waiting at her horse's head. She wrapped the long shawl harshly with strong hands around the horse's head, tied a hard knot, and said, "Help me pull him." Together the two young women brought the animal forward, and The People started.

*

Yellow Wolf and his friend Going Alone had ridden back with Looking Glass to raid Kamiah Settlement, and now they helped herd four hundred horses taken from the treaty Nez Perce. The sharp mountains rose before them, their broken teeth high in afternoon sunlight, gray and gold and touched at northern edges with hard tips of lingering white. Yellow Wolf had been watching Going Alone as they rode into the rocky, wooded foothills rising to the Bitterroots. His friend ignored the horses, dropping back to walk his black and white pony, then catching up, then slowing down again as if listening. Yellow Wolf at last dropped back and rode to his friend. "What is it, Going Alone? Do you smell soldiers?"

The young man shook his head, but doubtfully. "It is not soldiers. Yet there is something in the west wind. I can't tell what it is. I know we are followed."

"We would see and hear soldiers or white settlers. They would make a big cloud of dust. They would send fifty men."

"Someone follows. Maybe just one or two. You and I should have waited and watched. Now we are in the trees."

"Let's wait now."

"Tell someone, then come back." Going Alone dismounted there and led his pony down into a little draw. When Yellow Wolf returned, his friend stood watching with his rifle held across his waist. "Stay on your pony, Yellow Wolf. Wait for him in plain sight. If he makes to shoot you I will kill him, but I think he comes without a gun. He doesn't care if he is seen or heard."

"One man?"

"Only one."

"A crazy Christian riding after us to get his horses back."

"He has courage. Or he's crazy."

"I see him. Look."

In a few moments one rider came through the trees, his horse dog-trotting. He wore cotton shirt and trousers, but moccasins with beadwork showed on his feet. "A short-haired Indian," said Yellow Wolf. "An old man."

"A Christian Indian: a horse with webbed feet."

Yellow Wolf held his rifle down across his horse's back and raised his other arm. The lone horseman raised his arm and kept coming. "I know him," said Going Alone. "It is Speaking Thunder's father. He is a good man."

The old man rode up to Yellow Wolf and stopped his horse as Going Alone led his pony out from the trees.

"Going Alone!" the old man exclaimed.

"With Cyclone!" responded the younger man, adding, "Here is my friend Yellow Wolf. Why have you followed us? Will you join us?"

"I want to talk to my son."

"He is with us," said Going Alone.

"I know. I saw him running off my horses."

"Looking Glass will give them back."

"I don't want them back if Speaking Thunder stays with you. He will need them. But I must speak to him."

"I will find him and bring him to you here," said Yellow Wolf. While his friend and the old man talked, Yellow Wolf galloped to the herd, where Looking Glass and two warriors waited looking down the trail.

"It is an old man named With Cyclone," said Yellow Wolf. "He wants to talk to Speaking Thunder, his son."

"He wants Speaking Thunder to go back with him," said Looking Glass. The chief's small mirror caught the low bright sun and struck Yellow Wolf's eye. The young brave shifted and Looking Glass turned to the warrior next to him. "Go up; tell Speaking Thunder."

"His father is a Christian, I think," said Yellow Wolf.

"Speaking Thunder is not."

"It is hard to understand."

"Joseph's father was a Christian," said Looking Glass. "A Presbyterian. But he quit."

"Thunder in the Mountains was never a Presbyterian, was he?"

"He is a Dreamer. What he sees, I do not know."

"I think I am a Dreamer too."

"Dreams will not help you."

"Dreams tell me what to do sometimes."

"You never know if they help you. You cannot know what would have happened if you didn't do what you think the dream told you."

"It is better than nothing, I think."

"There is nothing."

The young warrior looked again at the mirror. "Perhaps your Wayakin and the Great Spirit will bring you out of this alive," said the older man. "But I will walk the Ghost Road soon." Looking Glass turned his horse to stare up the foothills.

Before long, the warrior Speaking Thunder came riding down, skirting the strung-out herd, cantering his brown-faced spotted pony. Yellow Wolf raised his rifle, turned his horse, and the two young men trotted down the trail. When they got down to Going Alone and Speaking Thunder's father, With Cyclone, the old man said, "You took the best ones, Son."

"I left your favorites, Father. They are the best ones."

"I know. You should have taken the best."

"I didn't want to steal your best horses, Father."

"I know. But I wanted you to have them. You will need the best." With Cyclone rode slowly to his son until his knee touched Speaking Thunder's knee. "Son, I want you home with me. Death awaits you on the trail you are taking. I see the future. It is dark with blood! I do not want to hear that you are killed. All who go with Looking Glass and White Bird will die or will see bondage."

Speaking Thunder said quietly but deeply, "No! If I am killed it will be all right. I want to go with my brothers and sisters."

"Your brothers and your sisters are at home."

"Father, my brothers and sisters are free. I will go with them up into the mountains. Maybe they will need me there."

"We need you at home to farm!"

"I will not look back, Father. No one who takes the rifle in his hand can look back."

"It is not too late! Live! All will welcome you home, and you will be safe."

"Let me be a free man, Father!"

"Even if you live, you will lose your freedom."

"But you die now!"

The old man said nothing for a moment, then he raised his hand over his son's head. "Go with God. May Jesus walk with you, my Son, my Son!"

*

Chief Joseph's band came first to the high ridge The People called The Path in Clouds. Behind them stretched for miles the bands of Toohoolhoolzote, White Bird, Looking Glass, and all their horses. On this high ridge, small late-spring meadows bloomed in grass and colors that below had bloomed two months ago. The People family by family spread out to camp alone so that their horses would have grass enough. Old Summer Dove camped with her daughter Playing Voice and granddaughter Early Dove, and often Joseph and his brother Ollokot would help them raise their small tipi, for Playing Voice's husband had been killed at Clearwater. Now, without lodgepoles to frame their heavy buffalo hides, the three contrived to spread their shelter over living bushes and uprooted trees. This afternoon Joseph helped lift tightly bound bundles of hide from the family's horses, and the old woman asked Joseph, "Are we going to Buffalo Country, or will you turn us toward Shoshoni country once we reach the Bitter River?"

"I want to turn down, not go to Buffalo Country, but almost all the other chiefs want to go on."

"If we go on, our friends the Crows will help us find the buffalo."

"The Crows are smart birds," said Joseph smiling a wry smile. "They know the soldiers will not like their helping us."

"But we have left them back in Idaho, the soldiers."

"Soldiers are everywhere, on both sides of the mountains."

"Then I want to go to the Spirit World," said Early Dove, the little girl; "there are no soldiers there, and my Papa is there."

"I want to go there too," said Joseph, squatting down to look her in the eyes. "But our People need us, Early Dove. I know your Mama and your Grandmama would be sad and lonesome without their happy little one."

"I am not happy anymore."

"We will all be happy again one day."

"Will you be happy, Thunder in the Mountains?"

"My wife and Pitty-Pat, my little girl, make me happy when I am with them."

"Why do you not walk with them now?"

"I have to go ahead and up the mountain for a little while to listen. I hope the Great Spirit will tell me what to do for our People."

"Will you tell us what the Great Spirit says?"

"I will come back and tell you, my friend. Will you smile when I come back?"

"I might. I don't know. Will you tell Great Spirit to kiss my Papa for me?"

Joseph straightened up and turned away. "I will ask the Great Spirit— to kiss your Papa."

Joseph took three horses for the journey, riding when he could, but at night walking carefully by moonlight and starlight across the deadfall and scree that filled the ancient trail where wolves and mountain sheep had picked their way before The People had come with horses, before The People knew the buffalo—but not before The People themselves. The wolf was not as old as the coyote, from whom The People came. The wolf came from the dog, and The People brought the dog to the forests and the foothills. The People brought sheep, from whom these wild mountain sheep had come, wandering ahead of the Nimiipuu toward where the sun arose. Only the buffalo was as old as the Nimiipuu, for The People were older than memory. Before Abraham was, they were. Before the Christian book, before the white men and women knew their God, The People were. The People went each by themselves to listen to the Great Spirit, who made them from the coyote's bones and the soil of the Mother Earth, who speaks truth and wisdom and goodness, who loves The People and all the spirits, all creeping ones and walking ones, those who swim and those who fly, the wind, the water, the forests and plains and mountains, the whole earth and sky, the moon and stars and sun, and the ancestors, and those who are to come, and this man, Thunder in the Mountains, who does not know what to do, where to go, whether to live or to die fighting for his promise to his father, for his love of his home or his love for his People—family and friends—or for love of this earth; for love of the Spirit who walks, the Spirit who calls.

So Joseph, Thunder in the Mountains, prayed and walked. He brought no food, but only water, did not sleep, stopped only to rest the horses, and went up to Grandfather in the Clouds Mountain. He left the trail and went up, his horses tethered in a tilting meadow; went up walking past the timber line, wearing the coat Snows Resting had made, decorated with quill beads from her grandmother, all the colors of the earth and sky. He carried the old horn bow his grandfather had made for him when he was a young brave, and his father's knife; he wore his medicine bag on a deerskin thong around his neck, and in it were the small coyote bone he found as a boy on his spirit quest, two eagle feathers, and soil from his father's grave in the beautiful valley where the sky blue river runs.

He climbed as the sun fell toward The People's homeland, snow above him brilliant white, the mountainside golden, all the colors of the earth below him and the sky pale and endless, a star already in the darkened band that spread wide across far-off Buffalo Country. He climbed in starlight; and before the snow began Thunder in the Mountains sat and pulled the coat around himself and waited, talking sometimes in the cold wind. Before morning, clouds moved in below and mist surrounded him; and he sang in the mist. His death song would not come; instead he sang of the earth and walking, of his dying People, of the little girl and her father lonely in the Spirit World.

Two days and two nights had passed since he had left The People. In the morning, the sun seemed to burn away the mist, and the man stood, and he saw the Great Spirit, the Old One, who came as a golden eagle burnished by the morning sun. The great eagle circled above him, and circled below, and the sun was warm through the stillness. Thunder in the Mountains watched until the grandfather eagle went back into the light. He left his father's knife and then began his long way down; and his thought was, "I do not hear the Spirit speak in this country."

*

Cold night rain had washed the families of sleep and kept the horses huddled close. At dawn the shivering People stood stiffly from their hard bedding and with trembling fingers took blankets, elk hides, buffalo skins— tried to brush away the ice. It was no use to try to kindle breakfast fires under blowing drizzle, so they chewed salted game and dried salmon, folded sodden shelters and loaded sluggish horses, then shook their wet blankets and led their ponies up the trail. They laid their coats and blankets on their horses soon because the walk was hard work: deadfall glistened black and slippery and horses must not step on the slick trunks and branches. Everything must be picked up, so fighting men and children walked before the women leading horses, lifting out the fallen brushwood, limbs, and slides of shale. Behind the first few families the trail became runny mud on angled stones, so some warriors went back to help their wives and mothers lead balking horses forward.

Shore Crossing led and pulled the first horse of their string, telling White Necklace to hold tight to the rope across the pony's face and not to fall. "I walk as well as you," she said. Shore Crossing gave no answer, grimly watching the treacherous path before their feet. The sun had been out some time and felt almost hot through the thin air, but gusts of rain kept blowing up across the rising trail and showering from blown branches. Shore Crossing looked down, brushing soaked hair from his face.

"Does your dream lie heavy on your heart?" White Necklace asked beside him.

"No. That was four dawns ago. I have forgotten it." The two walked on beside their struggling horse.

"It is warm but it is wet," White Necklace said. "It is strange to have both sun and rain at the same time."

Shore Crossing grunted, looking forward. The two walked on, watching their steps and holding the pony steady. Blowing hot breath, the animal labored against its fright and the slippery slope leading higher toward the dark, distant Grandfather of the Clouds.

"Not all dreams are true," White Necklace said.

"I do not think of the dream at all!" The horse was hesitating and Shore Crossing pulled roughly on the halter rope. "Come on, you sheep!" the warrior said.

"You shouldn't pull sharply like that," White Necklace said. "You scare her more and soon she will not move at all."

"Who is saying what people should do?"

"What?"

"Don't stop. I'll pull her more carefully. Walk."

A little later White Necklace said, an angry tremble in her voice, "What did you mean?"

"When?"

She looked away, and the two walked ahead. "You think the child will replace you."

"I do not. I do not think so childishly."

"I won't walk any farther."

"Half The People are coming behind us."

"Then tell me what it is. I am tired of guessing."

"Nothing." Shore Crossing looked back at his wife, then looked away. "You are with child. You are wet."

"The child does not show yet. Not for two, maybe three months."

"Your breasts are becoming larger."

White Necklace looked down and then stood still.

"Walk! We have to move."

"I will not walk with you."

"Then walk with the horse. We have no choice."

She resumed walking and said, "I thought you were different from all men, but all men are the same!"

"We are not! You say that and I will strike you!" She looked up at him, eyes wide with rage. "You know I will never strike you," he said through his teeth.

"But you want to."

"No. I only want to know why."

"Why what?"

"Why you like to show men your breasts."

"Oh!" She walked quickly ahead, then she turned. "I am pregnant and my dress is wet!"

"You wear it tight. It's thin."

"It's summer! Do you want me to wear a winter dress. A coat? Do you want me to wrap a blanket around my breasts so that only you can see them? No! You will not tell me what I may wear."

"It is not the Nez Perce way, to be immodest."

Her dark eyes flamed. "Who are you to tell me what is the Nez Perce way? Who are you!"

"Nez Perce women do not show themselves to every brave—"

"You will not make me feel shame! I will not feel shame!"

"—every brave, every boy, every old man—"

"Old man! What do you mean, every old man? How can you speak of it! You, who were right there to see it!"

"I see it every night. I see that man's old fat body, his hairy—every night I see it, every morning I see it. I see the look on your face."

"I tried not to scream! He would have killed you if you had jumped at him—or killed me."

"I can't help what I see and what I saw."

"How can you think as if it is my fault?"

"If you did not dress the way you do, the white man wouldn't have had his eye on you!"

"How to I dress, Husband?" He gave no answer. "I have breasts! Do you want me to cut them off?"

"No."

"You will not make me feel shame! I feel shame every day!"

"I see him every day!"

She was quiet for a moment, then she said, "There was one thing that has saved me, one thing that kept me from killing myself. Do you know what it was? I have always thanked the Great Spirit that of all the Nez Perce men who could have been there to see it, it was you, because you love me, and because you understand; you understand everything."

Shore Crossing looked up the trail. "The white man is destroying us."

After a while she said, "Why didn't you say anything, anything at all, all these suns?"

"I could not; I must say nothing. I see your suffering. But I suffer too."

White Necklace started to say something, then stopped herself. Shore Crossing said, "What is it? What do you not want to say?"

"Maybe women and men should not live together."

The warrior looked long and carefully at her. After a while Shore Crossing said, "Maybe you are right. Maybe men should not live with women." White Necklace looked up at him. He nodded, resolved. "I will find myself something else. I will find a gray goose."

"What? You!"

"I will. I will find a big gray goose and do you know what else, my beloved wife? I will make sure that my she-goose has big tits!"

"I could kill you!" She struck him on the buttocks hard. "You would be jealous of every gander!"

"I would not, because I am not a goose."

"Yes you are! But you will not make me happy with you. Make the woman laugh: men are all the same."

"That is how I feel about them, too. I do not care. I am going to get myself a nice goose."

"She'll be jealous. You'll look at every young goose. I've seen you look at the girls."

"I only look at them to compare them to you. None ever compares or ever will. It is like looking at geese."

"You will not make me happy again."

"Never? As long as we live? I think if you struck me again you would be happy."

"Let us see," she said, striking him harder.

"Ow! You are strong. When braves look at you I will say to myself, Shore Crossing, how beautiful is your wife and how lucky you are!"

"You are lucky I don't kill you."

"That is what I meant."

"I will kill you some day."

"I know."

"Your dream has made you think that I will belong to another man after you are dead."

"Yes."

"I have told you that I will die with you."

"The child."

"You will not tell me what to do, Husband."

He laid his hand gently on her shoulder. She glanced at him and then looked ahead. "I am not happy with you yet."

"I know. I am not happy with you either." He looked at her cautiously. "But I love you with all my heart."

*

When the first families reached the flat part of the trail crossing the foot of Grandfather of the Clouds Mountain, Joseph was waiting there. The little girl, Early Dove, saw his haggard face, which brightened but not enough to make her smile. "Did you see my Papa?"

"No, my child, I did not see him, but I asked the Great Spirit to kiss him for you."

"Did you see the Great Spirit?"

"Yes, I saw the Old One."

"What does the Old One look like?"

"The Old One was an eagle, a great gold eagle full of the morning sun."

"An eagle? Is that all?"

"The Great Spirit is not an eagle, but can come to us as one. The Spirit is neither man nor woman nor child, but can be anything—a man, woman, child, eagle, or an elk or a bear."

"Or a crow?"

"That is what the Crow people think."

"I saw a crow this morning."

"Up here? In the mountains?"

"Yes."

"Then maybe the Great Spirit came to you as a crow."

"It didn't say anything. It just cawed."

"Sometimes you have to think about it. But sometimes it's what you think right away."

"Did the Great Spirit talk to you?"

"My child, now I know that we must do the best we can. We must love each other, and help each other."

"It's what you said before."

"Yes."

"You did not come back happy."

"I am tired, Early Dove. I did not sleep while I was gone."

"Then you should sleep, Thunder in the Mountains."

"I want to, little one."

"You can sleep with us tonight."

"Thank you, little one, but I must see about my wife. She is very sad because our baby did not get well. I will send one of my daughters to play with you."

*

When all The People passed the last high ridge and the long trail began its last descent, Looking Glass rode forward where the trail widened, passing families of Toohoolhoolzote's and White Bird's bands, talking with the old chiefs and going on to overtake his friends Ollokot and Joseph at the far front of the exodus. Today the brothers walked together, leading their careful horses, lifting branches from the trail with young men of Joseph's band.

"Have you seen our one-armed friend?" asked Ollokot. "Is he behind us?"

"The war is quit," said Looking Glass. "Howard has not come onto the trail. He will stay in Idaho, protecting the Christians and gathering an army big enough to keep himself and all the settlers safe. He thinks that we will turn and double back, as you would like to do, Thunder in the Mountains."

Joseph turned to Looking Glass, his firm face only a little showing the new sadness that now would never leave the eyes that saw the Great Spirit soaring in silence. "I will speak of it no more."

Looking Glass studied Joseph's face and nodded. "Good. We will go down the trail to the four hot springs, take our time, rest and bathe, send messengers to our friends the Salish that we are in their country. I know the white settlers in the Bitterroot Valley and they trust me. There will be no trouble. In Stevensville the store men will sell us whatever we need."

"At high prices," said Ollokot. "They are nice men. When we have plenty of white money."

"We have plenty, and the whites will be happy and afraid. The only trouble to be wary of would come if our young men drink. All the chiefs must keep them away from white men's whisky."

"The whites would be fools to sell whisky."

"They do anything for money," Joseph said.

"Then we will go to the Place of Ground Squirrels, and rest a long time. We will talk with our friends the Crow people."

"Do you think the Crows will share the buffalo with us?" asked Ollokot. "Things are not as they were."

"They will not share what they no longer have," said Joseph.

"Mountain Thunder, you always speak the bad side of things."

"You know too well," said Ollokot, "white hunters have been killing buffalo until the plains are spotted with them and the sky itself stinks."

"True, but also true that there are too many buffalo even for the whites."

"I think there are more whites than buffalo," said Joseph, "and they can make ammunition until the sun burns out. They mean to starve us. The whites mean to make farmers of the Crows. Of all of us. Of the ones who are left."

Looking Glass smiled. "The one thing that matters, Thunder in the Mountains, is that we have peace again. We will take our time, and see about our friends the Crows."

Ahead, far down the trail, a rider picked his way up through the trees. "Who can that be?" asked Looking Glass. "Not Salish."

"I asked Red Elk to take two young men and scout the trail ahead."

Angrily Chief Looking Glass regarded Ollokot. "That was not my idea. Not necessary."

"I know how you feel," said Joseph blandly. "He never listens to me either. He thinks for himself." Joseph looked calmly down the trail, then smiled a small smile at Looking Glass.

The war chief took his time. "All right, Thunder in the Mountains. You are right. I am sorry, Ollokot. You did a good thing."

Ollokot smiled broadly. "Even though it was not your idea?"

"It is hard to believe," said Looking Glass with no smile. "But it is true." He nodded toward the trail ahead. "It's not Red Elk."

"Horse Travelling. One of the two young men."

"He's hurrying," Joseph observed.

"Maybe he has word from my friend Charlot and the Salish people."

The three mounted their horses and rode to meet Red Elk's messenger. When they reached him he pointed down the trail and said, "Soldiers!"

VI

The River

"*My dearest husband John,*" wrote Emily Fitzgerald, "*I am so happy that you have not gone chasing savages across those terrible mountains. Just knowing you are safe this side of them helps me to pass from day to day without such terrible anxiety as I suffered last week. Everyone here wishes the Indians would be no more and we could all live normal lives again. Tell General Howard that he is a prudent man, that we admire him for it, and that had he gone across the mountains all here would fear for our lives.*"

"There's more, Sutherland," said John Fitzgerald, folding the letter. "But it's rather personal. Now you know what the civilians think. They're out for safety, not for Nez Perce blood."

"I think I heard some of each," said Sutherland, "but knowing people understand the General's priorities helps me to frame my articles. Say, do you know this Major Wood?"

"A little, why?"

"Oh, Trimble said that I should talk to him."

"Hasn't Trimble left?"

"Before he left, he said talk to Wood. I've wondered why. It would be a risk, as General Howard gave me to understand that my talking to his officers would not meet with approval."

"Wood is a no-nonsense officer."

"What is his opinion of General Howard?"

"I couldn't say."

"Do you think I should talk to him?"

"I do."

"And do you think we'll go after Joseph through the mountains?"

"I do."

"But we're a good ten days behind him now."

"Howard's your hero. Ask him."

"Now John, I hear a note of irritation in your voice."

"It's lack of sleep. I am a pessimist and believe anything that parts me from my wife will come to pass. Howard has enough troops to protect Idaho and still take seven hundred men or more to follow Joseph and his 'savages,' as my worried wife calls them."

"But Montana is outside Howard's command. It's Sheridan's department."

"We both know Howard has got his orders from higher up, Sherman himself. You know what that means."

"What do you think it means?"

"Follow Joseph to the death—him and his people. In any case, Howard is too careful of his reputation to allow some other officer to capture Joseph."

*

"Mister Sutherland, the talk and rumors you have heard are false. I have no desire to build my reputation by hunting Indians. My reputation can speak for itself. I am disappointed, Sir, that you have credited these rumors."

"I do not credit them, General."

"I can show you a copy of my message sent to General Sheridan, requesting that Colonel Gibbon be sent to cut off Joseph if he emerges from the mountains and bears east. Here it is. I shall read it: 'I would not advise you to wait for me but to delay, parley, or maneuver only if you get no opportunity to attack. I think the Indians must be short of ammunition, so you can smash them in pieces if you can get them to stand and fight. Your judgment on the spot will be better than mine.' So you see, Sir, that I have no desire for glory. Let Gibbon have it; he seems to have enjoyed it during the War."

"He did, Sir?"

"I only mean that several times he found himself in noteworthy places. He commanded the so-called Iron Brigade, as you know."

"I wasn't aware of it, Sir."

"And Pickett attacked Gibbon's division at Gettysburg."

"To Pickett's destruction."

"Gibbon enjoyed considerable help from Hays's Division. Still, one must say that he always handled his troops well."

"Fought them well."

"Yes, and fought them well. If he can delay Joseph, I can spring upon his rear and destroy him, Sir."

"With all respect, General, I thought your intent was to capture the Nez Perces, not destroy them."

"I shall do whatever the Lord lays before me. My personal preference, often stated, is to avoid unnecessary effusion of blood. Many have mistaken this preference for timidity. I assure you, Sir, that it is not. If General Sherman orders a policy of destruction, I am the man to carry it out."

"Yes, Sir."

"Mister Sutherland, have you been speaking with any of my officers?"

"I would not dream of it, Sir."

"Sutherland, I shall take you at your word. But one thing, Mister Sutherland."

"Yes, General?"

"I might appear to you as a man who does not discern subtlety. I am a straightforward man, an earnest one, and a military officer. But I do discern subtlety. The Book of Genesis reminds us that the subtlest of beasts was the serpent. I discern subtlety, Sir, and many who did not appreciate that fact have lived to regret their underappreciation. Let a word to the wise be sufficient."

"Yes, Sir."

"Major Wood is a personable man."

"Is he, General?"

"He is a sound officer, very sound. But he has conceptions."

"Conceptions? You mean—"

"I only say, be perspicacious. Be discerning. Keep a sharp and astute mind."

"General, I have not spoken with Major Wood."

"I would very much like to believe that."

"You may, General. You have my permission."

"You have been talking to someone!"

"Humor, Sir. I know you are a man of humor, and I thought you might appreciate a little repartee."

Howard smiled. "And so I do. I am under a great deal of pressure and I sleep little."

"I hope you get sleep tonight."

"I hope to, Sutherland."

"Good evening, General."

"Sleep well."

"Sir? Are we going to follow Joseph across the mountains?"

Howard effected a tired smile. "I wouldn't be surprised, Sutherland. But don't write it yet."

*

Dr. Fitzgerald did not look up when Sutherland entered the tent, but continued to write a moment. Still looking down, he asked, "What did you learn?"

"That General Howard believes Chief Joseph reads the newspapers."

*

Some call John Gibbon's Iron Brigade the greatest unit of the Civil War. When Abraham Lincoln was elected and the South attempted to secede from the Union of the States, unwilling to brook the possibility that the new president would bring about the end of Southern Negro slavery, and fired its cannons on the National flag—then northern men rose up and volunteered to shoulder arms and put the great rebellion down. President Lincoln would say amid the war that the struggle was for government of the people, by the people, and for the people; and that the nation was conceived in liberty and dedicated to the proposition that all people under God are created equal. For what Lincoln called the last, best hope of humankind, the sons of liberty and equality battled Southern rage and Southern shot and steel, dying in their thousands to the burly music of the Battle Cry of Freedom and the Battle Hymn of the Republic and the summoning thunder of God's guns.

John Gibbon's Black Hat Brigade fought their first battle in Virginia, outnumbered two or more to one by Stonewall Jackson's troops, the most famous in the Confederacy. They fought in straight line shoulder to shoulder, firing at Lee's veterans not eighty yards away, slugging it out as light waned, standing in the smoke and muzzle flashes, Gibbon and his colonels walking up and down behind the line shouting "Steady men! Fire low and cool, men. Pour it on them! Give them hell, boys!" As night came down, both sides withdrew and left their dead and wounded on the field. One third of the Black Hats lay in the hot August night, but Stonewall's brigades lost twice the number, full certain they had fought a whole division at least, not one mere re-enforced brigade of the despised men in blue. Those Yankees had earned their dignity, fighting to be called free men—whom Southerners considered an inferior race, mudsills and the dregs and scrapings from the alleys of Europe, hypocrites to boot, factory drudges, shopkeepers, laborers and ditch diggers, incapable of courage, honor, and sacrifice.

Two weeks later, those mudsills in black hats stormed up a wooded mountainside and earned the famous praise, "They must be made of iron!" And so named, at Antietam on the bloodiest day in American history, they led the Army of the Potomac's dawn attack—charging through a cornfield into the teeth of bayonets and bullets, under solid shot and bursting shells— Gibbon himself dismounting and showing a gun crew how to aim a brass twelve-pounder with the enemy mere yards away. Later, when Texas general John Bell Hood was asked by Stonewall Jackson, "Where is your division, Sir?" his answer was, "Dead on the field."

And then came Gettysburg. By that July the depleted brigade—Gibbon gone, promoted to command a division in another corps—stood again and gave their lives, buying time, setting up Robert E. Lee's confident, unvanquished Southerners for a defeat that turned the tide of war, standing by their tattered, bullet-torn flags morning and afternoon, Southern bravery and Southern slavery dying before the muzzles of their muskets. Two days later Gibbon himself held his division steady as a half-mile wide high tide of Southern valor charged across the burnished fields, rank on rank Pickett's grand Virginians, Pettigrew's Carolinians and Tennesseans, trailing blood and glory—Gibbon standing with his thin blue line, firm for the cause of "liberty and union": "Give it to them, boys, and hold your ground!" If there was glory anywhere, it rested on that thin blue line at Gettysburg; if there was glory anywhere out West, surely it beat within the resolute heart of John Gibbon, soldier blue and soldier true.

*

"Colonel Gibbon was the greatest soldier in the Army of the Potomac, in my opinion—with the possible exception of Winfield Hancock, Lieutenant." Captain Charles C. Rawn of Company I, Seventh United States Infantry, tamped the tobacco in his pipe and lit up. "It is an honor to serve under him. Those are my feelings plain and simple, Sir." He singed the top of the tobacco, squinting, then tamped it down again. "I think," he said, then interrupted to strike another match, draw deeply, eye the little flame, draw again, and wave out the match. He blew smoke and said, "I think he is a better man than Howard, Sheridan, Sherman, and all the rest."

"President Grant, too?" Lieutenant William English had already lit his pipe while Rawn was talking. The two sat smoking, tilting back their folding chairs against the cottonwoods they sat under.

"English, I'm not dealing in superlatives. First Grant. He won the whole damn War. And then Gibbon. If any one brigade deserves the name of iron, it was Gibbon's Black Hats. The Iron Brigade. They were the best—in either army."

"Either?"

"All right, English, either Eastern army. I know you served in that Western army."

"Army of the Tennessee."

"I always seem to forget the name."

"It was Grant's army, Captain, Sir."

"Before he got promoted to my army, the Army of the—what?"

"Potomac, I believe you said, Sir, or something like. Pot something."

"Both of you lads are most amusing, I'm sure," broke in Captain William Logan, "but as Captain Charlie had a point, and as I served in the Army of the Cumberland, and as I have no pipe, I'd feel obliged if you'd get to it."

"Call us lads, Bill?" said Rawn. "I'm forty years last month."

"And I, my lad, was born in Scotland lo, forty-seven years ago—to fanfare, mind you, fanfare and gratitude. More than can be said for either one of you. Now, my esteemed Captain, what are the god damn orders?"

"I was about to get to that. Have you noticed—" he said aside to English, "that the foreigners are so mightily impatient?"

"Indeed we are. Get to the bloody bleeding point, my friend."

"Colonel Gibbon, great soldier that he is, has made an error. My orders are to march I Company immediately to the Bitterroots, collect civilian volunteers, and throw my force across the redskins' path—delay them so that Howard can catch them from behind. Your company and five others, as soon as practicable, are to march down east of me to the Big Hole meadows, where Joseph's people always camp when headed east."

"Why, if you are to cut them off fifty miles west of there?"

"It remains unsaid, but Gibbon must think Howard won't come up in time. And I will be annihilated or dispersed."

"Not you. We," inserted Lieutenant English.

"In any case," continued Rawn, "it's bad business. Dividing his force. Why not strike with the whole regiment?"

"Charlie, how many civilian volunteers?"

"Three hundred, maybe four. The Colonel says that all of western Montana is on the scare. Civilians say they want to eat Nez Perce for breakfast."

"Civilian volunteers aren't worth a tinker's dam," said English.

"The Colonel thinks highly of volunteers, if handled with respect and firmness, as he says, and well trained up."

"And what do you think, Charlie?"

"The Colonel was implying that as these settlers won't be trained, I had better watch my step. He told me, after I had read the order, 'Delay but don't engage them. Give me time, Rawn, then fall back on me at Big Hole.'"

"Well, he's an honest man. Must be that Sheridan has told him what to do and he doesn't like it. A Scots-Irish name, Sheridan; pity that he's not a finer specimen. What do you think, Charlie?"

"I think those settlers will run, the Nez Perce will surround and attack me, and it will be another Custer massacre."

"Very sorry that I asked."

"Captain," English said, "I disagree. You're a better man than Custer ever was. It will be the Rawn English massacre, famed and celebrated in its own right."

*

An orderly came to the Colonel's door and rapping softly, heard the sharp, frank voice: "Get in here, Sergeant. You don't need to knock." The soldier introduced a man with rusty hair dressed in a baggy, rumpled suit of dirty black. "It's Correspondent Trimble, Sir, the man who telegraphed."

Gibbon looked at Trimble with piercing blue eyes, narrowing as he took in all the nuances of the man's puffy face. "How did you get here, Mister Trimble?"

"Over the Mullen Road, Colonel. I hired a pair of horses."

The soldier nodded an admiration skeptical and cool. Trimble removed his narrow-brimmed black hat. "What can I do for you?"

"I'd like to go along with you, Colonel, and cover your expedition against the Nez Perces."

"Singular."

"Thank you, Sir, but it's something any good correspondent would undertake."

"I mean the term 'Nez Perce.' The plural's never used. Permission denied."

"On grammar, Sir?"

"I don't need a newspaper correspondent to help me fight Indians. Good day."

"Sir, may I say one thing, respectfully."

"Yes."

"Sir, I have come from General Howard. He has a correspondent with him, name of Sutherland. You might have seen his work. It makes General

Howard look rather good, Sir. To the detriment of other officers. Such as yourself. I would like the opportunity to redress—"

"Mister Trimble, I do not give a good god damn about my reputation with civilians. This is a dirty business and I will perform my duty as I am ordered. There is nothing more to be said. Good day."

"Yes, Sir. Good day."

"You have insulted two officers of the United States Army."

Trimble curled the bowler's brim in his hands. "I should like to apologize, Sir, sincerely and regretfully."

"Accepted. Exit."

*

"How many soldiers? Where are they?" Ollokot asked Horse Traveling, instinctively half turning his pony to gallop back up the trail to get his rifle.

Looking Glass did not believe it. "They are only settlers. They have heard rumors from Idaho."

"No. Soldiers!" exclaimed the young man. "They are building a fort!"

"How many?" asked Joseph.

"Twenty soldiers, more coming. Hundred fifty white settlers, twenty Salish."

"Salish? No!"

"Yes, Salish, Chief Looking Glass! They are building a fort across the trail in the canyon a half day this way from Lolo. Salish!"

"Now what shall we do?" asked Joseph.

"We go and see," said Looking Glass.

"Traveling Horse, ride up the trail and tell what you have seen," Ollokot directed. "Get ten warriors and come after us."

"I will go with him," said Joseph. "We will bring more than ten men."

*

The company of Captain Rawn had made the march down from Missoula, gathering civilian volunteers and picking up along the way Chief Charlo and his twenty Flathead warriors. When they reached what Rawn thought was a defensible part of the trail that came across the Bitterroots from Idaho, a narrow canyon flanked by heights both sides, he set his men to work cutting down trees and making a log barricade—one log laid down in front of a long ditch, another log placed carefully on spacing branches, which gave a gap just high enough to place a rifle and look through. Four of Rawn's scouts had seen the Nez Perce warriors on a ridge above them farther up the trail, and hurried back to tell the Captain that the hostiles were coming. All morning well-armed settlers from Missoula south as far as Darby had been coming up the trail and joining in to make the barricade, a hundred now and more coming—and then to Rawn's surprise a company of mounted infantry, riding on civilians' horses. "Logan!" Rawn saluted. "What is Company A doing here? I am damned glad to see you!"

The Scottish captain touched his hat, dismounted, and shook hands. "Your hero, Colonel Gibbon, had a change of heart and sent us after you. I bring his compliments and orders not to let the hostiles pass until receipt of further instructions. And there you have it, William. I recall your mentioning George Custer."

"Things might not be as bad as that. We have some decent volunteers and twenty Flatheads."

"The surly gentlemen with white rags tied on their heads and arms?"

"So we don't shoot them down for hostiles. Their chief's a friend of Looking Glass, who's up the trail about two hours, I suspect."

"We shall be ready."

"I am very glad you are here, Captain."

*

Riding up the trail, Joseph was surprised to see the old chief White Bird making his way down on a stout pony. "I grew tired of walking so far behind," he said to Joseph. "Some of our old women are anxious, bad dreams of soldiers, so I have come ahead to look."

"There are soldiers."

"How far?"

"Not far. Looking Glass and Ollokot are going ahead to talk to them."

"Talk to them? Looking Glass will not want to fight them."

"You can catch up to them if you hurry." The old chief kicked his heels into the horse's ribs, and Joseph watched him go. The old brave had brought his rifle.

*

Three officers stepped over the barricade and walked out to meet the three Nez Perce chiefs waiting for them with a white cloth tied to a lance. Behind the soldiers came Chief Charlo and two of his Salish warriors. White Bird, Looking Glass, and Ollokot stood silently, the old chief with his rifle held in both hands across his chest. The three officers noted that the Nez Perce chiefs, all dressed in beaded shirts and buckskin leggings, had no war paint streaked on their faces.

"The young one must be Joseph," Rawn said quietly. "The old man is White Bird, and the mirror means Looking Glass."

"I'd make sure," said Logan. The officers raised right hands, palm outward to gesture peace, and Looking Glass stepped forward to shake hands. He introduced himself, White Bird, and Ollokot; then Rawn gave rank and name for the three soldiers. Chief Charlo said nothing.

"I am glad to see that all three of you are well," said Rawn. "You had plenty war on other side of mountains."

Looking Glass nodded.

"Now," continued Rawn, "your people are plenty hungry and plenty tired from coming over big mountains."

White Bird said, "We are well. Our People are well."

"I see," said Rawn. "Well. Gentlemen—chiefs rather, I am here because General Gibbon has ordered me to stop you and collect your weapons."

"Who is General Gibbon?" asked Ollokot.

But Rawn's attention shifted to nearly twenty warriors riding down the canyon toward them. Two of them rode forward while the others, holding rifles, sat their horses well within their weapons' range. Rawn looked back and saw both companies now standing up behind the barricade with rifles held at present arms. One of the Nez Perce riders dismounted.

"That one's Joseph," English said and nodded toward Rainbow. The warrior sat his war horse while Joseph came forward to shake hands.

Captain Rawn said, "I think you are Joseph."

The chief nodded but said, "*Hinmatooyalahtqit.*"

"Yes, Sir," Rawn said, shaking hands. "As I was saying—"

"Who are you?" asked Looking Glass. "Are you Idaho soldiers or Montana soldiers?"

"We have come through Fort Missoula. It is a Montana post of the United States Army."

"We have no fight with Montana soldiers. The war in Idaho is done. We are not at war."

"Nevertheless," said Rawn, "my orders are to not let you pass."

"We must go to Buffalo Country to live," said Looking Glass. "If you do not allow us to go peaceably, we will do what we must." He gestured toward the barricade. "If the officer wishes to build corrals for the Nez Perce he may. We will not go into them. We are not horses. We are men and women, like you. I think we are as smart as you."

"Be that as it may," said Rawn, "if you insist on going through, I must collect all your rifles and all your ammunition. Those are my orders."

Rainbow said loudly from his horse, "Do not tell me to lay down the gun! We did not want this war! General Howard kindled war when he showed the rifle in peace council. We answered with the rifle and that answer stands to this sun! Some of my People have been killed, and I will kill some of our enemies and then I will die in battle!"

Logan stepped forward. "We do not want anyone to die. Let us think this matter over and then meet again tomorrow. Tomorrow noon."

White Bird lifted his chin. "Officers! We will talk again tomorrow. But know that we will pass. We will go through peaceably if we can, but we will go through."

Rawn looked at the old chief, then nodded grimly. The chief nodded curtly in reply. The officers turned to walk back to the barricade.

Looking Glass said to the chiefs, "Wait up there with the warriors. I want to talk to my old friend." He held up his hand toward Charlo and the Salish chief nodded.

As the officers walked back, Rawn said to Logan, "I hope we've bought one more day, at least. We'll have a hundred new volunteers by noon tomorrow, I think."

"They don't want to fight," said Logan.

"I think that old chief wants to fight," said Lieutenant English. "They will all fight if they have to. They've proved that."

*

A short while later, Looking Glass came striding back to where the warriors and chiefs waited. His face a storm of anger, he said to Joseph, "Now I know why the whites call them Flatheads!"

"Charlo will not help us?"

"They are afraid the soldiers will kill them and their families. Twenty Salish warriors will fight with the soldiers. Charlo says his people will fight us unless we pass through quickly."

"How can we pass at all?" asked Two Moons, holding his horse with the young warriors.

"I will talk to the settlers," said Looking Glass.

"Talk to them!" exclaimed White Bird.

"I know them," retorted Looking Glass. "They know me well. I will tell them that we want to go through their country peaceably, as we do every year. They will leave the soldiers and go home."

"I will believe that when I see it," White Bird said.

"You will see tomorrow."

"Look up there," said Rainbow, nodding toward the ridge. "We can get up there and shoot down on them."

"We can get up there and go past them," Red Elk said, standing behind the braves. "The small trail behind the ridge is not so bad."

"What do you think, Brother?" asked Ollokot.

Joseph looked from face to face, then lifted his shoulders. "It doesn't matter to me. I don't care where we go or what we do. We are strangers away from our home. No difference."

"Do you think we should go back?" asked Ollokot.

"I want to go to the river, go along it to the southern trail back through the mountains, and return home—but I know it is too late for that, and none of you wants to do that."

"We can go north instead of south," White Bird said.

"That old idea," said Looking Glass. "There is only one way for us to go—to Buffalo Country. We can live there. We know the country, and we have friends there, the Crow people."

"The Salish were our friends," said Joseph.

"I will talk to the settlers in the morning. Let the women and children go behind the ridge, warriors go in front. There will be no war here. If we get by, then I am right, and we go to Buffalo Country."

"We can hunt and live free there," Rainbow said. "Peace or war, we must go there."

*

During the afternoon and evening fifty volunteers came to the barricade, so in the morning Rawn had nearly two hundred fifty men—thirty-five soldiers, almost two hundred citizens, and twenty Flathead fighting men. He knew that he could not move out and maneuver with his volunteers, but they could hold a fixed position. The Flatheads would fight if attacked. Not bad, considering the hasty preparations.

*

Chief Looking Glass rode toward the barricade about midmorning, carrying no rifle and holding up a white cloth on a lance.

"Go see what he wants, English," Rawn ordered. When the lieutenant approached Looking Glass, the chief dismounted and held out his hand.

"I come only to talk," he said. "I know many of these merchants and settlers. I would like to see them."

English reported to his captain, who thought Looking Glass among them would ensure that no attack would come. "Let him come, and welcome," Rawn said. "Maybe we can buy another day. I hope he is a loquacious fellow."

Looking Glass was loquacious indeed, greeting many citizens by name, assuring them that The People would pass in peace as always, buy supplies as always, trade buffalo robes and buckskin jackets for calico and salt and flour as always, because the war is done. "We have no war with friends."

Well, the settlers said, Chief Looking Glass is more honest and reliable than these army officers, and better for business. And if we stay we'll only aggravate the redskins anyhow. By noon a hundred fifty settlers had packed their gear and left to get back to their lives and wash the terror off, so Rawn walked out to talk with only eighty or a hundred men behind him.

"Gentlemen," he said while waiting for the chiefs, "they'll have to ride right over us, and that will cost them and they know it. Maybe they have had their fill of war."

"By damn, I wouldn't count on it," said Logan, looking up. On the steep ridge that overlooked the barricade, a long and slowly moving line of Nez Perce warriors on horseback rode, rifles at the ready.

"God damn," said English. "Who'd have expected there to be a trail up there? What now, Captain?"

"Now they shoot us down like dogs," said Logan.

"No, they don't," Rawn said. "We act magnanimous and tell them they can pass."

"You'll be court marshaled," English said.

"Isn't that a pity."

"I believe Colonel Gibbon would approve. We'll let them pass and go down the Bitterroot and take their time—and we'll take the shorter route straight west and join the Colonel."

"Capital idea, William. The press will vilify you."

"Let them. I am laying up treasures in heaven. Now, pluck up a little courage and let's look peaceable and genial."

And so Fort Fizzle, as it came to be known, was circumvented by sharp Indians and abandoned by sharp whites. The People passed above the barricade all day, braves and soldiers eying each other, and all marched to meet their rendezvous at the Place of Ground Squirrels, also called the Big Hole.

*

"Say what you might, the Rawn affair's a disgrace—despicable behavior for an officer and inexcusable in any man." General Howard put the telegram down and stared at Major Wood, his adjutant, as if expecting contradiction.

It came instead from Colonel Jones, facing Howard with a slight stoop as he stood against the tent's pitched roof. "If I may speak freely, General—" tilting his head toward Sutherland, who slouched at the tent flaps alertly.

"Of course, Colonel, you may speak freely, as always. We are all free Americans."

"I think his alternatives were unacceptable," said Jones.

Wood nodded but said nothing.

"What can you mean, Colonel Jones? He had but one alternative; it was to fight. I am a fighting general," Howard said to Sutherland, "and cannot but condemn an officer who will not fight. My telegraphed request was that Gibbon hold Joseph until I can fall upon him."

"He would have to hold him two weeks, Sir."

"How is that, Colonel?"

"Joseph began crossing the mountains two weeks ago. We are going up today."

"We shall not require two weeks, Colonel."

"How many days do you expect the mountain crossing to require, General, if I may interrupt?" Sutherland brought out his pencil and his memorandum book.

"Five days!" the General snapped. "No more. I could have left five days ago but I have waited for the fifty civilian axmen. Either way, ten days, but my way shall ensure my men and horses easy travel. It is not only more humane, but we shall arrive in Joseph's rear fresh and in good fighting trim. The enemy will have to stop and rest a good long time. We shall catch him and we shall defeat him."

*

"Do you believe him, Sutherland?" Fitzgerald asked that noon as their effects were packed up around them.

"Not only do I accept Howard's estimate, and applaud his motives, but I have sent my story in, complete with frank condemnation of Captain Rawn."

"Congratulations. You work fast."

"Thank you. Like General Howard, John, I am a man of humor and subtlety." Fitzgerald smiled. "And I perceive your skepticism. But I write what I believe. This time Howard's right."

"Are we crossing the mountains?"

"You know we are."

"Well then?"

"All right, John. I will see Major Wood."

*

"I will not talk to you," the major told Sutherland immediately. "I am General Howard's adjutant. It would not be proper for me to speak to a newspaper reporter."

"I understand, Sir. But I was wondering only what your opinion might be regarding this pursuit of the Nez Perces."

"Have I said something you do not understand, Mister Sutherland?"

"What do you mean, Sir?"

"I mean that I just told you I would not speak to you. Is there something about that you do not understand?"

"Well, yes, Sir."

"What? What could it be?"

"How you can assent to General Howard's orders and carry them out when you disagree with them, Sir."

"A soldier executes his orders, Sir, whether or not he happens to agree with them!"

"Thank you, Sir. I appreciate your honesty."

"Honesty about what?"

"Your honesty about disagreement with General Howard, Sir. I shall keep it to myself."

"You damn well better! Print any of this and I will have you shot! Get the hell out."

*

That afternoon Howard's force of seven hundred fifty soldiers, three dozen Indian scouts, and fifty axmen commenced ascending the trail. A cold and steady rain began as soon as the column got under way, making the axmen's progress difficult. The slippery ground caused laden pack mules to balk, and infantry had to help rotate wheels on Howard's artillery caissons. Men began to wrap themselves in blankets, shivering in their summer campaign jackets. Before nightfall, the column camped. Oliver Otis Howard was now a full day behind his schedule.

*

The Bitterroot runs north beside the mountains with its name: a dark blue tumbling stream between long stands of sun-struck evergreens, narrow meadows peppered with wildflowers—wild and beautiful and pure, cold and clear, some places rocky and knee deep, where you can see slowly finning, hunting rainbow trout, their dark backs the color of grey stones and their sides, when they rise, glittering like silver and gold, streaked red and speckled blue and green and orange like Indian beadwork. At its banks long-legged elk bend tufted necks strong as birches toward the moving water; deer drift like pollen to the stream; coyotes trot like businessmen looking side to side, suspicious owners of the level ground and panting grandees of gophers, groundhogs, and the star-nosed mole; while overhead hawks ride currents of rising, falling, curling air and drop like arrows onto dusky shrews and field mice; meadowlarks, lyrical and lean, seem to while away the day sunny and eternal; the grizzly rises up beside the stream to shake its heavy head and smell the air, itself its Wayakin, then drops to all fours waiting, and lightning-strong jolts its claw into the water through a writhing, bending rainbow—agony in evening bronze, an armored Trojan pierced by a Greek spear through plated ribs, oval mouth gasping in the sudden air, eyes comprehending earth and the whole domed sky, and the wine-dark river rushes forward. At night the Ghost Road crosses the water.

*

Gibbon's column reached Missoula, then turned south to parallel the Bitterroot, three days behind the Nez Perce families. Pack horses carried pieces of a mountain howitzer—a small cannon capable of firing solid shot, exploding shell, and canister. Managing one of the horses, on foot beside its head, Private Jewell Washington, a Buffalo Soldier, as Native People termed Black troops with their tightly curled hair, talked to the God of Abraham.

"About a dozen mile today, the white man say—'a dozen mile a day on nothin' but hay, in the Regular Army-O,' and Lord, Lord, I'm talkin' 'bout the Seventh Infantry. Can't complain; can't complain because it ain't no use; so I complain to you, Sweet Jesus, knows the sorrows, knows the sorrows—"

"Washington!" Riding up beside the chanting soldier, Sergeant Eli Grover said down to him, "Sing one them slave songs—sing out loud and clear. Maybe the boys'll take it up. We could all use a little cheer. Sing it out, Private!"

"Slave song, slave song, can't remember no slave song, Sergeant—ain't a slave no more, no more—sing out by the waters, by the waters, by the waters here in Babylon, yes Sir, I remember now, oh, yes indeed—but I'm a colored soldier in the U. S. Infantry, ain't a slave no more, no more—"

"Yeah, that's it, Washington, somethin' with a refrain like that," Grover said. "Ain't no slave no mo', ain't no slave no mo'—that's the stuff."

"Ain't a slave no more, ain't a slave no more. Mista Lincoln set us free, now I'm in the Infantry. Some say ain't a slave no more, no more, but the Black men know what the white men don't. Ain't a slave no more."

"That's it, Washington. Come on, boys!"

*

A hundred miles by crooked mountain trail southwest of Gibbon's column, Doctor John Fitzgerald wrote his wife,

Dear Emily,

Last night was an unpleasant time, though not the worst we've had thus far, because we went to bed without our tents—they being back a mile or two on worn-out, dragging mules. About midnight the ever-present clouds began to rain on us again, so I got up and fashioned up a shelter with a piece of canvas I had laid upon the ground beneath me as a kind of mattress. No more mattress then, and ground as hard as rock, tilting like a rooftop. I bunked with Doctor Newlands and it took a while to crunch in cozily but tired enough for five or six men, we slept like babies 'til the morning. Up at five a. m., we waited six hours before the column moved—cooked our breakfast, checked our horses fifty times, and finally got walking. We made only eight miles but saw the nicest mountain scenery, the views extending miles in three directions, we were so high, and all that beautiful country spread below us. The weather turned fine in the afternoon and we could see the Dales of Arcady, or something like. Captain Spurgin and his handy axmen have finally caught up with us, and we go like Hannibal, especially because this afternoon we got our beef rations. But the poor horses and the mules eat no beef, and must go hungry. For three full days there's been no grass. The meadows all are trampled by the Nez Perce herds—trampled and grazed clean—so some men peeled the trees of bark to feed their mounts, which I believe will have results like colic and perhaps the leafing out of horses' ears. Some mules are just about done in, not used to wire grass and wild dwarf lupine, so we leave them on the trail, sometimes with their big packs beside them like the boulders you find up here as if left over from the catapults and military engines of Milton's war in heaven. But Joseph's horses are not supernatural: we find their broken down ones here and there abandoned on the trail and wandering like homeless Arameans. I think the Indians feel pressed and have

*been hurrying, despite what General Howard says. One officer has estimated
that our force, including baggage, is stretched a full five miles along this trail. At
night it takes nearly three hours for the hindmost to come into camp. Then the
men dig level places for themselves so they don't roll down the mountainside in
their sleep. I am not exaggerating, Dearest, about that. It is a wonder we don't
lose more horses, mules, and busy correspondents to the slant of the world up
here. Greet civilization for me. I hope we will return by summer's end.*

While Fitzgerald wrote, not far from him beside a lantern, Correspondent Sutherland made a few notes in his memorandum book:

*General Howard scared himself again this afternoon. Sent some cavalry down
the mountain toward the sound of firing. Thought Joseph's rearguard was shooting someone. Turned out to be a splashing salmon stream. Men dismounted,
rigged up lines, and fished. I think Howard believes Indians are everywhere and
I expect he dreams of them. Howard now has a thousand men to hunt Joseph,
Gibbon's infantry included. If Gibbon catches Joseph before our Christian Soldier does, the war will be over in a day.*

*

John Gibbon now was on the Nez Perce trail, his scouts' reports precise and accurate because the whites along the Bitterroot kept careful count:
they watched the Appaloosa ponies being driven by, The People's cattle, and
they noted minutely everything The People wore and carried—beaded leggings, soft white deerskin dresses, tunics, war shirts, buffalo robes and arrow
cases, women's saddles, bear claw brooches, bright necklaces and headwear
plaited with eagle feathers. Might be good to follow, see what happens, when
the Army comes through after them. But most of all they noted how well-
kept, clean, even polished all the rifles looked, held firmly by the warriors
or reflecting sunlight from hide cases resting across the horses' backs. The
People rode at a dog trot in perfect discipline. "Fine-looking Indians," some
settlers said. But Gibbon's infantry would catch them if The People stopped
to camp for several days—exactly what they planned to do after passing
through Stevensville and other towns along the Bitterroot. They'd buy supplies as always, then turn from the Bitterroot moving directly east to the big
meadows along Big Hole Creek—The Place of Ground Squirrels, they called
it, the place Colonel Gibbon knew they'd stop.

Captain Rawn and his thirty-five men joined the Colonel's column
south of Lolo Pass, so Gibbon had about two hundred fifty men, his Bannock scouts included. Before the Iron Brigade, John Gibbon was an artillery
man, had written a manual the Army used, and to this day he kept his eye

for fields of fire; and he made sure that especially good care was taken of the disassembled mountain howitzer whose lead horse Jewell Washington led by the bridle.

"Morning, Corporal," Gibbon said, riding up beside the humming soldier.

"Morning, Colonel Suh. A pleasant morning by the river, Suh."

"How is our friend the howitzer today?"

"He like the valley air, Suh, like it fine. Howitzer a happy soul, Suh. He like to sing, sing his trouble, Suh."

"What troubles does a brass tube have these days, Corporal? He doesn't have to walk, won't get hungry, has a man to take good care of him and sing to him."

"Yes, Suh, I am like a wife to him, a wife, just like a wife to him, but when I going to find a wife my own? The tube get lonely sometime, Colonel."

Gibbon smiled, lifted his hand to touch his hat brim in salute, then held up, saying, "You're going to fire that gun into an Indian camp in a few days, Corporal. Can't tell what you'll hit. Do you understand?"

"Yes, Suh. We gon kill some little chillun, Colonel. Ain't nothin' that the good Lord Jehovah ain't done to the Philistines and suchlike folk, time immemorial."

"You're a praying man, aren't you Corporal? Who do you pray to?"

"I sing, Suh, I sing to Jesus. He understand it all, been kill by that Jehovah too, one day on Calvary. Ain't it so, Suh?"

"I—I don't know, Corporal. I couldn't say."

"Were you there—were you there, when they crucify my Lord?"

"No I wasn't, Corporal. And glad of it."

"You be there, Colonel, Suh—you be there when we open with this howitzer, Suh."

*

Near Stevensville the settlers had a fort—a mud and sod enclosure named Fort Shaw, that for almost three weeks had housed the hundred fifty residents of town plus another hundred farming families round about. Ever since the first reports from Idaho, replete with tales of murder, burning, theft, and battle, culminating with the dread likelihood that Joseph and his hostiles would cross the Bitterroots, these citizens had holed up for security, the town's merchants boarding up their stores. Now the whole Nez Perce column, its warriors veterans of battle with the U. S. military, were seen approaching down the Bitterroot and going into camp three miles away.

Next morning, Looking Glass and seven braves rode to the entrance of the fort and called the names of settlers that he knew, to come out and talk. The whites conferred, then opened the gate. A delegation of twelve armed men walked out to the dismounted Nez Perce.

*

The night before, The People's chiefs had met in conference. New families had joined them days ago—the band of Eagle from the Light—who years past had moved east and stayed here in the valley, happy to be far from Idaho's encroaching settlers. Eagle from the Light was dead; their chief was Lean Elk, a quiet, sinewy man with large, soft eyes, a hunter who knew Buffalo Country as well or better than Rainbow, Five Wounds, and Looking Glass. The whites knew Lean Elk well and trusted him as far as merchants ever trust a customer. His band, with sixteen warriors and hundreds of good fresh horses, were welcomed by The People and had traveled with them four days.

What brought the chiefs together was the appearance of three young Nez Perce men who had been scouting for the U. S. Army in Montana against Lakota and Cheyenne. One of them, Grizzly Bear Youth, had told as many chiefs as he could find, "You would be fools to go to Buffalo Country!" So now the chiefs gathered to hear the three men out. Old Toohoolhool-zote, White Bird, Joseph, Ollokot, Looking Glass, Rainbow, Red Elk, Five Wounds, and Lean Elk stood quietly as the young men told them what they had seen. "Too many whites!" the big young man exclaimed. "There are settlers everywhere—farmers, ranchers, and we know how many forts and long knife posts there are. There is no end to walking soldiers and horse soldiers. When more are wanted, more come. Enough to destroy the Lakota, enough to finish the Cheyenne—enough for us, who are so few."

"Where do you think we should go?" asked Looking Glass.

"Old Woman Country," said the young man. "Go back north, down this valley through Blackfeet Country, to Canada. Sitting Bull has gone there and is safe. Easy travel."

"We should go," said Toohoolhoolzote.

White Bird agreed, nodding his assent, but Ollokot spoke up: "We can-not go through Blackfeet Country with our old men, women, wives, and children—and our herds. Blackfeet will fight us all the way. We can defeat soldiers, Cheyenne, Lakota, but the Blackfeet are too many, they hate us, and they are treacherous."

"He is right," said Pile of Clouds, a hunter and a friend of Rainbow and Five Wounds. "Let us go back to our country. The Crows will fight for the soldiers."

Grizzly Bear Youth nodded. "They scout for the soldiers against the Lakota. They will scout against us. The buffalo are now too few to share."

"They will never be too few," said Looking Glass.

"Already they are too few," said Pile of Clouds.

Rainbow spoke: "We have no choice."

Pile of Clouds said, "Buffalo Country is all open, no place to hide our families, no place to shelter our herds. Let us go up the valley, then back into the mountains on the lower trail. There we can fight."

"What do you say, Toohoolhoolzote?" asked Ollokot.

"I hate the soldiers. I would kill them all if I could, but they are too many."

"You always hated the soldiers," said Looking Glass. "But we have peace with the Montana whites. We found that out in front of Lolo Pass. We made peace with the soldiers from the Missoula fort."

"Whites never will make peace with us."

"You are too much for war. Your young men began this war." Toohoolhoolzote stood silent, as if thinking over whether to speak his mind.

"Tell us," said Ollokot, "whatever is in your heart."

"I have not spoken this because of shame," the old chief said. "Howard had me locked up in his prison."

"We do know that," said Looking Glass.

"What you do not know, what I have told no one, is that Howard commanded his soldiers to dress me in woman's clothing, bride's dress."

"No!" said Rainbow.

"Is it true?" Looking Glass exclaimed.

The old warrior continued, "They laughed, the soldiers, and I could do nothing. I am an old man and a warrior and a chief. The white soldiers are not men, the whites are not people. They are not animals. I don't know what they are. Perhaps they are a disease. We are in their prison. All we can do is go out of their prison, get away, to Old Woman Country."

"We wouldn't get there," said Looking Glass quietly.

"My Chief," said Ollokot to Toohoolhoolzote, "you are not shamed. Only what a man does shames him. What is done to us by others does not shame us. It shames only them." The old chief nodded. Lifting his hand to the younger man's shoulder, he pressed his thanks.

White Bird said, "There are some who have not spoken."

Lean Elk looked around at the men. "I have joined you only days ago."

"I know you," the old chief said. "I know what the whites call you. Poker Joe."

"I do not walk by that name," said Lean Elk. "It is the name of a drunken Indian."

"What do you think?" asked Ollokot.

"I think Rainbow is right; we have no choice. Going back, we would die in the mountains. Going down the valley, we would die among the Blackfeet."

"Then we go straight to Buffalo Country," said Looking Glass.

"I think we should go up the valley, and go across the pass down there," said Lean Elk. "Fewer whites."

"Rest at Big Hole, The Place of Ground Squirrels," said Looking Glass.

"And then keep going," said Lean Elk. "Go through Montana up to Old Woman Country."

"We can stay in Montana," said Looking Glass.

White Bird looked at Joseph. "You have not spoken, Thunder in the Mountains."

His face drained blank of feeling, Joseph said, "It does not matter where we go. Where all of you decide, there I will go, I and The People with me."

Looking Glass said, "We have decided. I will show you that everything is all right. Tomorrow I will ride to the white settlers' fort, tell them we are peaceful, and it will be all right. We must buy flour and supplies from them. They will sell."

"Our young men will cause trouble in the town."

"I will keep the peace myself."

And so, next day, Looking Glass and seven men rode out to talk peace to the settlers at Fort Shaw.

*

A tense, uncertain silence lasted but a few moments, for Looking Glass had no intention of receiving or giving offense. He raised his right hand, saying, "Friends, old friends of many summers, we have come again in peace, as always. Henry Buck—" he nodded toward a young shopkeeper, "it is good to see you. We want to buy supplies in Stevensville."

Buck nodded, glancing at the men beside him. "You are welcome, as always. We don't want trouble, either."

Another man, removing his straw hat, scratched his matted hair and said, deep voiced, "Of course we will have to discuss among ourselves whether it would be good to open our stores."

"Hell, Edwards, we'll open," a man with hands in his pockets said. "What do you need?" he said to Looking Glass. "We got it, we'll sell it."

"We must have flour. We will buy salt, sugar, calico cloth, tobacco, ammunition, clothing. We have gold coin, gold dust, and greenback dollars to pay."

"No ammunition, and no whisky," Edwards, the deep-voiced man, said.

The other man, still with hands in pockets, smiled at Looking Glass and said, "You send your squaws in tomorrow, and we'll see they get what you need."

"We have almost no flour in town," said Henry Buck, "but you can buy it at the mill yonder." He pointed past the town toward the creek.

As the warriors rode off a few minutes later, Buck turned toward the man who had smiled. "Simmons, if you sell as much as a drop of whisky to those Indians we'll string you up without hesitation."

"Oh, I'll be careful. Besides, you know I don't sell the stuff—normally."

"You ladle it out free to attract business. We won't take time for hanging; we'll shoot you down on the spot."

"Now Edwards, you know I hate to be threatened."

"Any kind of trouble just might set those Indians off," said Buck.

"Won't be any trouble." Simmons finally drew his hands from his pockets and rubbed them together. "Still a little early for this chill, ain't it?"

*

The next morning Arrowhead, the woman who had saved Bird Alighting when Looking Glass's camp had been attacked in Idaho, came with several women into Stevensville. She rode her pony to a knot of store owners—Buck, Simmons, Edwards, and two others—and announced, "We will buy what we need today, with gold, but if you do not sell, we will take what we need just the same."

"Nearly all the stores are open," Buck said.

"We'd be glad to have your business," Simmons added.

The women went from store to store, buying cloth and clothing, cooking implements, tobacco, salt, and sugar. But at noon Looking Glass rode into town at the head of a hundred warriors armed with clean, shiny repeaters.

"A better set of Indians I've never seen," wrote Buck later; "decent, noble-looking men, well-dressed and for the most part quiet. The older men were friendly with us, clearly wanting peaceful relations. But the young men wanted whisky and got it."

Townsmen closed Simmons's store but quietly, fearing that a shooting or a hanging would excite some kind of melee.

The next day Simmons would load up his buckboard wagon and drive out to the Nez Perce camp—to find himself behind two other merchants already selling ammunition. But the single incident this afternoon arose when a young brave, having found his whisky somehow, strutted toward a storefront where four white women watched the goings-on. He called out, approaching, "One of you women come with me! You come to my lodge tonight!"

He got no further when a lashing quirt slashed across his neck. It was Looking Glass, who leaned from his pony and grasped the young man's hair. Walking his horse, he led the grimacing brave down the street to his pony. "Go back to camp and stay there! You shame every Nimiipuu woman!"

All afternoon Looking Glass sat his horse in the middle of the street at Stevensville.

*

Mid-afternoon the next day, The People rode past Stevensville, processing in column drawn tight, disciplined, no gaps between families, each band marshalling its herds of horses and stock. "I watched them as they passed," wrote Henry Buck. "They went along in Indian style, the horses at a dog-trot. Wanting to keep a count of some sort I took out my pocket watch. From end to end the Indians required an hour and a quarter. Riding their best ponies, sitting straight and easy, they passed with a grandeur I have never seen since, attired in their finest, with no disorder or confusion. I found I had removed my hat, and almost had forgotten to look at my watch as the last warrior passed by."

Joseph, Thunder in the Mountains, as camp chief rode first, dressed in a coat of red blanket wool, quill beads sewn along both sleeves, a glittering cascade of white and blue interspersed with tiny mirrors; fringed deerskin leggings underneath beaded down both sides, moccasins covered with blue and white beadwork; a deerskin war shirt, sleeves hung with rows of ermine tassels in the fashion of the Crow people; in front a necklace hung with twisted horsehair tassels. His hair, brushed up in front, was colored white over the forehead, and long braids knotted with ermine hung down along his chest. In his right hand, bone bracelet on the wrist, he held a Sharps repeating rifle laid across the withers of his Appaloosa, whose halter rope was hung with beaded deerskin strips. Behind him rode Springtime, his Sit Beside Me Wife, straight in her wooden saddle box, a small child bound against a wicker board tied to her back. She wore a red cloth shawl over her long dress of elk skin fringed around the bottom where her moccasins showed careful floral beadwork, yellow, red, and orange. At the dress's yoke hung deerskin tails knotted tightly at their tops with light brown strands of pony hair. Around her waist a supple leather sash was cinched, and from her neck and shoulders hung six loops of necklace strands of copper tubes, glittering stones, and bright quill work. Beside her rode their oldest daughter, Sound of Running Feet, whose shorter dress was light deerskin, fringed and beaded, and her necklace was a single strand of mica pieces reflecting light like mirrors. Behind her rode Snows Resting, her soft dress of deerskin almost white. Her moccasins were covered with white beadwork; her necklace was one strand of braided rabbit hair suspending a stone polished by the Salmon River, glistening with pastel colors like a pearl. Next rode Springtime's mother, and then boys and girls too small to tend the horses following behind the families of the band.

Ollokot rode next, his wives and family behind him. He too wore a Crow war shirt; his hair, dyed red in front, was brushed high off his forehead as his brother's was. He wore no coat, but on his shoulders rested a small stole of coyote fur—for The People all had come from the Coyote when the Old One chose spirits from whom to draw the different children of Mother Earth. The war chief of his brother's band rode a war horse with pale reddish face and dark spotted forelegs. Behind this family rode all the rest of Thunder in the Mountains' band, their herds following, tended by adolescent children and the families' high-headed, loping, nervous dogs.

White Bird came behind Joseph's band, wearing an eagle-feathered war bonnet he had captured years ago from the Cheyenne, and a belt of rifle ammunition slung across his chest. His medicine bag hung at his breast, and showing from his bison belt a thick, bone-handled knife in a heavy hide sheath was fastened at his side.

Toohoolhoolzote's band followed, the old chief's white hair in two long braids far down in front festooned with hawk feathers quill end up. Across his back a quiver hung, and a stout bow made of sheep horn; his right hand held a Remington carbine, its barrel pointing up, its stock resting on the warrior's thigh. Behind this family rode Shore Crossing, strongest of all the young warriors, red coat open, bear claw necklace large and heavy on his chest, fringed leggings, war shirt, and moccasins of dark elk hide. Beside him rode the elegant White Necklace, spirit-eyed, her soft-braided hair hanging longer than the necklace made of abalone shell that rested on her breast. Behind the young husband and wife rode Man Woman, warrior's hair brushed high in front, fringed dress worn over light cloth trousers; behind rode Red Moccasin Tops, his red coat closed and crossed with two ammunition belts.

After Toohoolhoolzote's people rode Looking Glass, mounted on a white horse with painted black circles around the eyes, red streaks across its haunches, black lines down its throat from jaws to chest. The war chief sat upon two blankets, one of curly buffalo, one white trader wool. His dark brown elkskin leggings set off light moccasins whose tops were worked with bright white beads. His deerskin war shirt streamed with foot-long fringes painted black and white; a hair-pipe choker tightly ringed his throat, its rows alternating black and white. He wore a short-rimmed black hat tilted forward down his forehead, decorated with a black fox's tail fastened to the crown. And large as a man's palm, a mirror hung suspended on a rolled buckskin necklace, sewn against a dark buffalo hide star: the sun glanced from its brilliant face and looked away as the procession passed the white townspeople watching by the Bitterroot.

Great warriors passed—the hunter Rainbow, tall like the pines, and his friend Five Wounds, sitting their war horses straight as eagles, rifles resting lightly on the spotted ponies' shoulders. The chiefs all passed—Two Moons, Red Owl, and the others, passing with their lodges—families of wind and water, salmon rivers, valleys running with wild horses, of buffalo running on the prairie like clouds receding on the dry late summer wind, people of the blue white-shouldered mountains, full-grown children of the deer, elk, and coyote, Great Spirit's sons and daughters, children of the waning moon. Lean Elk rode last with his people, sinewy and canny, bearing his white name Poker Joe like a defilement but tall, raven-eyed, dove-voiced, singing quietly the death song of a people passing on their horses into stories told beneath the smoke-dimmed Ghost Road, the last time all together, talking to each other, passing, riding toward the place of slaughter called Big Hole.

VII

Big Hole (1)

The People passed the other towns along the river, turning east to cross a steep but easy pass through the Anaconda Range into the valley, going slowly, Looking Glass made sure, to rest their horses and their herds of cattle. Nevertheless White Bird rode impatiently, and one morning shouted, "Looking Glass, you are playing with death! We must move fast through this country! I can feel the wing of death coming close."

But Looking Glass said, "No, The People must be rested, must dig camas root and cut more lodge poles. We must prepare ourselves to make a new life among the Crow people in Buffalo Country."

Years later, Yellow Wolf said many People felt foreboding, and men with strong medicine powers saw many dying. But then The People came into The Place of Ground Squirrels and their old camp ground lay welcoming, its lush grass green along the marshy creek's swale, clear water moving lazily among willow bushes and tall reeds, the familiar hillside huge and wide and full of good grass, fragrant woods of spruce and pine above—a good place, a place to stop. And so The People rested.

*

The Seventh Infantry, now mounted on wagons, mules, and horses, marched quickly, though from time to time the command halted at the orders of its commander, who appreciated fish and game and knew the limits of his men's endurance. More than once the whole command enjoyed a lunch of fresh-caught brook and rainbow trout. Gibbon and many of his fellow officers had brought their flyrods; all they had to do was wet their lines in waters filled with fish and in no time at all caught heavy strings of perfect speckled trout.

One day around noontime, Colonel Gibbon took an orderly to carry his rifle and, himself armed with a shotgun, went horseback hunting in the woods. As he told English, Logan, and some other officers that evening as they sat at campfire eating roasted venison: "I hadn't been out more than ten minutes, thinking of nothing in particular, when I passed a little grove of green quaking aspen. Happening to cast my glance off to the left, I saw a sight that made me check my horse and grasp my gun. There hardly fifty yards away lies the most lovely white-tailed buck, his thick and velvety rack pointed straight at me and his great, soft, dark brown eyes just looking at me questioningly, as if asking why I was disturbing his cozy, nested sleep. Strangely enough, he did not rise, but looked at me from his noonday bed, lying there like a magnificent, uncomprehending, wild brown child. I'm so excited that I rush my loading and the shell jams in my breech. I feverishly try to force it and it's stuck. I fear some exclamation escaped me—"

"He said 'shit!'" English explained to Logan, who replied,

"Or worse—all due respect."

"I wouldn't dream of it. Perhaps 'land sakes' was what I said."

"Undoubtedly," said Logan. "'Land sakes' probably is Philadelphian for something indelicate."

"You interrupt," said Gibbon. "So at whatever I said he slowly rises to his feet, stalks off, the most beautiful, the most graceful animal I ever saw. I jump down from my saddle, drop the shotgun, run back to my orderly, take my rifle from him, slip a cartridge in, and run back forward. There's the deer, walking slowly and calmly through the timber right toward us, completely unaware of his danger. A sharp crack of the rifle echoes through the woods, he plunges forward and falls right at our feet, a splendid, magnificent, fat buck, shot through the heart. And gentlemen, tonight's bill of fare, spread out before you, reflects the grandeur of my successful day's hunt."

"Bravo!" said English. "Never liked our bully beef—or buffalo either, for that matter."

"Detest buffalo," said Logan.

"Don't worry," Gibbon said; "they're disappearing fast. A rangy, belligerent animal, not suited for driving or for farming."

"But as I see it," Logan said, "is not destruction of those vast and shaggy herds by our diamond-ring-wearing Eastern swells a wanton travesty of sportsmanship? They shoot them from trains!"

"Nothing wanton about it," Gibbon answered. "Practically deliberate. Simply kill off those herds, the Indians have nothing to depend upon but government supplies—no reason not to live on reservations. Fence off the high plains, make cattle ranches and cattle barons, feed the surplus beef to Indians."

"And to us," said English.

"You sound a bit offended by it all," said Logan. "As am I."

"The Indians must go," Gibbon observed. "One people displaces another people, a process old as history, old as the Bible. Still, the history of our two races is a continuous series of frauds and impositions."

"But we know better than anyone what cruel savages they are. Look what the Sioux did to Custer's men."

"The blind rage of Indians mutilating an enemy is no different from the cold warfare of what's called civilization. Cump Sherman said 'War is hell' and he's right. I've never believed that the only good Indian is a dead Indian, but they'll surely be exterminated. They can't hope to fight civilization."

"They're fighting us," said English.

"Almost scientifically," remarked the colonel. "Dispatch from Rawn said the Nez Perce put a force in front of you to screen the main body, which went around your flank and got away."

"Perfectly true," said Logan. "But I wouldn't say they got away, exactly. It made no sense to fight them with our thirty men—and as many badly frightened settler volunteers."

"And we're alive to fight them with you, now."

"If they let us," Gibbon said. "Undoubtedly they've scouts out everywhere and know exactly where we are and how fast we're coming."

"I am not sure of that," said English.

"Nor am I," said Logan. "The way they talked—that chief Looking Glass in particular—as if they think the war's behind them, they left it in Idaho. They think the war was with Howard, not the United States Army. They think Howard's stayed behind."

"Howard is infinitely behind," said English. "Two weeks."

"Five precious days waiting for a company of axe men!" Gibbon exclaimed. "But let us not speak of it."

"Howard is a hero, after all," said Logan. "Hero of Gettysburg."

"Hero like hell!" Gibbon snapped. "Howard is a sanctimonious fool, a self-important, self-promoting—but there's an end to it. Fellow officer. I'll not speak of him this way again, and neither shall you."

"Yes, Sir," said both English and Logan, as the others silently nodded like reprimanded school children, glancing at each other surreptitiously.

*

Surrounded by tipis of Charlo's band of Salish Indians near Stevens-ville, a Christian mission stood—a weathered wooden structure, not adobe like Catholic churches in California, but complete with European priest and mission bell. Here John Gibbon and his adjutant, Charles Woodruff, stopped to wait one night while their command marched to catch up to them. Gibbon spent hours talking with the priest, Father Rivalli, writing later that thirty-five years here "in the wilderness" had failed to suppress or tarnish "the graceful cordiality of a past age." The priest, "a charming old Frenchman," received his guest sitting in bed, a skull cap on his head, spec-tacles resting on his nose, for he served as a doctor to the Indians and, as Gibbon noted with surprise and admiration, had been reading medicine by light of a dim lamp. "Whilst wondering in my worldly way," wrote Gibbon, "whether the good priest had wearied of doing good," Father Rivalli said, "I thank God that I shall in time lay down my bones with these poor Indians."

The Colonel said his duty was quite different, although it might involve the lying of his bones "with these poor Indians of Joseph's band."

"How different, my Colonel, is duty, as you say, from the call of God."

"I think it adds up to the same thing, when you are at the sharp end of it."

"Oh no! Oh no! Duty, it does not absolve a person from deciding to obey or not, but we pretend it does. It is a grand excuse, this duty. Napoleon orders it, so I shall lead my men into cannons. But who is this Napoleon? Does he speak for France? And if he did, does this France speak for God? Ah, no, my Colonel. Who speaks for God? You must do so yourself. You feel and you hear the call, but you never lose your doubt. You never know you have fulfilled your call. The responsibility is always yours. A soldier who fol-lows orders never is damned, in the theology *militaire*, but I am constantly damned."

"Damned if you do, and damned if you don't?"

"*Non.* Saved if I do, and saved if I don't. Alas, there is no heaven for soldiers, only a heaven for sinners."

"Then with all due respect, Father, what good is a call? I prefer duty. Duty is imperative and clear."

"Not always clear, I think."

"Always. You have orders; you execute them."

"Who makes the orders, Colonel?"

"In this case, I do; but I have orders to pursue and to engage the fugi-tive Nez Perce."

"The question, then, is how."

"Exactly, Father."

"Ah. But you must engage them?"

"That is my duty, Sir."

"My son, how many troops have you?"

After a moment's hesitation, Gibbon answered, "About two hundred, give or take."

"Ah, *non*—you must not attack them, Colonel. You have not enough. I count the other day about one hundred sixty warriors—and they are splendid shots, these *Nez Percé*, and they have bought much ammunition. Now I say, Colonel, 'with all due respect,' you must not fight them."

"I have to fight them."

"So it is fate, a tragedy, and not God's will."

"An officer is trained in ways to make up for inferior numbers."

"The element of surprise."

"Perhaps, Sir."

"I have read the maxims of Napoleon. To surprise these people, you must attack when they are not ready, and that can mean only to strike them when the warriors are dispersed among the people, completely unsuspecting."

"Very good, Father."

"No, very bad. You will kill them all together, indiscriminately."

"I will try not to."

"But you have your orders." Gibbon nodded. "You do not want to do it."

"No matter."

"It is all that matters. Colonel, you have seen a great deal of killing, *non*?" The officer stared back impassively. "Quite as I thought, *mon Colonel*." The priest nodded thoughtfully. "My son, history will not forgive you. But the Sacred Heart of Jesus, which you wound, may forgive you. You are a good man, Colonel."

"But that is not enough, is it, Father?"

"*Non*, not enough at all. That is why I am here."

The Colonel wanted his pipe.

"Go with God," pronounced the priest. "But do not attack them."

*

"My shaking heart tells me trouble and death will overtake us if we don't hurry out of here!" Lone Bird, a warrior who had stayed to fight the soldiers at Clearwater, rode among The People as women unfolded bundled cloths and hides and unpacked cooking pots and pans. The men, leading their horses to go out and hunt, stopped and listened.

But Looking Glass confronted Lone Bird. "Look around you! We have no lodge poles to make tipis, no food to carry with us, no strength in our horses. We will stay a few days. We will cut the poles, dry them, dig camas root and bake it, hunt, and let our horses drink and graze. Stop this talk. The war is behind us. We stay."

Next day the women would cut down small trees on the hillside and peel the bark, and let the poles dry for the long drag into Crow country, but tonight no tipis were set, and The People slept in hide shelters or under the deep mirror of the wheeling sky. In the morning Wottolen, a warrior with strong medicine power of second sight, woke from a dream, rose, and walked among The People stirring from their sleep around him. "I dreamed of soldiers, walking soldiers! We are in danger here! Many will die!"

He went to Red Spy and Red Moccasin Tops. "You young men must go back up our trail, go back and look for soldiers!" The two went to gather friends, found ten of them, but they were all young men who owned few horses, and the two or three they had ridden were tired from the long trek through the mountains. But one man owned hundreds of horses, strong and fresh, and two race horses that the two lead scouts should ride. Burning Coals, an old man, no longer fit for war and tired of his wives, gloried in his herd—some said a thousand with the ponies he had left behind—and in his money. Burning Coals, the richest of all Nez Perce, Christian or non-treaty, was said to have buried his gold dust deep in some hillside along the Snake River—a treasure undiscovered all these years—and the man said No. "You young men will not ride my horses dead. You can ride your own!"

So Red Spy now took Yellow Wolf with him, the young brave trusted by the older men, to talk to Looking Glass. They found him eating flour cakes with his friend Yellow Bull. "We must scout back over the mountains," Red Spy said. "Too many men have dreamed of soldiers. We need to borrow fast horses."

Looking Glass regarded him a moment and stood up. "Have I not said the war is quit? Did I tell you to go scouting? Howard and his soldiers are behind us."

"But seven suns ago we saw walking soldiers in wagons, and four suns ago, coming fast."

"I know that. You don't have to tell me. How many of them, since you know so much?"

"A hundred thirty, forty. But they will gather up white settlers. They have Indian scouts."

"The Salish will not fight us. And the Montana settlers are our friends. They agreed with us at Lolo Pass that no war would be fought in Montana. We will rest here. If we act like we expect war, we will get war. We have beaten five hundred soldiers with fifty warriors. These few walking soldiers will not dare to attack us. Go eat. Tell your friends to stop dreaming."

Therefore no scout was made, no watch mounted.

That day the women cut lodge poles, dug camas root and roasted it, bathed in Ruby Creek along whose thicketed and willowed bank the tipis of The People now began to rise, shocks of bright white in the sun like bleached and dried wheat. The families put up their lodges near friends regardless of bands, a long line on the little river and a second, shorter line angled off, making a bending "V" with apex at the south. The tipi at the bottom tip was put up for mothers of new infants—three babies had been born this week—a place of sleeping, nursing, and noonday quiet for soft songs and lying still. The horses were gathered in several herds; the largest led onto the hillside facing the long camp across Ruby Creek and the sluggish slough next to it. The grassy hillside, bounded by clean-scented woods of thickly growing lodgepole pine, would warm quickly in the morning sun, be cool in late afternoon, and formed a perfect natural corral.

Joseph saw Springtime, his Sit Beside Me Wife, comfortably settled in their tipi with Sound of Running Feet and the three other children. He and Snows Resting talked outside the lodge a moment. Ollokot, whose wife and three children set up lodge next to Joseph, was out hunting. "What are you looking at," Snows Resting asked.

He nodded toward the couple several tipis up the row. "The young man Shore Crossing should be out hunting, not touching his beautiful young wife's face." He smiled his warm, wistful smile and she put her hand up to his, that rested on her cheek. "You are lovelier than White Necklace, my beautiful one."

"I am not."

"And I will die twenty winters before you—thirty maybe. Women live longer than men."

"I am your wife, Sadness-for-the-Mountains. When you are gone, I will raise our memories like children."

He touched his forehead to hers. "Maybe we will never be separated," she whispered.

*

Watching Joseph part from Snows Resting and lead his pony away, Shore Crossing held White Necklace gently. "Would you want to be old?" he asked.

"Heart, our spirits have grown old together already. There is nothing more to ask the Great Spirit for. Tonight I will lie in your arms."

As the two talked, the young brave Strong Eagle rode up, his face painted with streaks of red and blue.

"Squaw man!" he said by way of greeting. "You should come hunting with me, not stay here love-making."

"Come down off your horse and call me squaw man. I will kill you."

"That is why I stay up on my pony. But come with me and hunt deer. White Necklace will give you to me for that long." He smiled down at her, nodding.

But Shore Crossing looked at him with sudden blankness on his face. "I will not be alive much longer, Strong Eagle. I do not want to spend my last suns hunting."

"It was only a dream, my friend."

"I am a dreamer."

Strong Eagle reached down and Shore Crossing took his hand. "You look as fierce as your name. You will scare the deer."

"We will dance after the hunt. I want to be ready." He brought both hands to his halter rope. "I hate to hunt alone."

"Bring Man Woman," White Necklace said.

"Man Woman is sick. Must have eaten white man's food. Sick as a dog."

"Our poor friend," Shore Crossing said. "I will go look."

"Vomits like a dog."

*

Snows Resting watched her husband as he led his horse toward Lean Elk's tipi. The tall chief of the Bitterroot band waited before his lodge, a spotted pony standing still beside him. She caught a glimpse of Morning Sun, the boy who in the mountains had helped her and Sound of Running Feet. She raised her hand and smiled. He raised his hand, putting heels into the sides of his small pony. He was riding to herd the cattle grazing farther down the valley. "Quiet and strong, like Thunder in the Mountains," Snows Resting said within herself. "The People will depend on him."

*

"He never wants to hear a thought that he hasn't had himself," said Yellow Wolf. "He didn't listen to Red Spy."

His friend Going Alone looked unconcerned. "The war is quit. Why do you worry? Worry about finding deer."

But as the two rode northwestward over the hill that looked down on the camp, Going Alone pulled up his horse, turning his face sideways to the breeze.

"You smell Long Knives."

"No, not Long Knives. No stinking wool. White settler."

The two rode forward at a walk until they saw two white men trotting their horses on the wide and worn trail The People used. The white men hadn't seen the warriors yet. Going Alone carefully slid his rifle from its buckskin sheath.

"No," Yellow Wolf said. "Looking Glass said we are not to harm whites unless they try to kill us first."

"Looking Glass is in the village. Watch me kill that one on the big horse."

"I think I know who he is."

The brave lowered his rifle. "I should shoot from the ground." Going Alone lifted one leg forward over his pony's withers and dropped to the ground.

But now the whites saw the two warriors. They stopped their horses, and one of them waved.

"His name is Browning. He sells in the dry goods store in Stevensville. Better not shoot him."

"Better that I do."

"He is here to find us so he can bring his wagon."

"He is here to spy on us for the soldiers."

"No, the Flatheads are their spies here. Better not shoot."

"I want to shoot."

"You will start another war, like Shore Crossing and his drunken friends."

"They weren't drunk."

"Peace is better than war."

"Not with whites."

"You are not going to shoot."

"No."

"You see, the whites are waving."

"They know we saw them." Neither warrior raised an arm, and after a moment the two whites turned their horses and rode slowly back the way they had come.

*

"He thinks the whites will not attack us here or anywhere this side of the mountains. What do you think?" Joseph sat his pony watching five young boys herding some horses toward the little stream that ran through the valley.

"I know the whites as well as he does," Lean Elk answered. "We should be hurrying, not resting here."

"Hurry to where?"

"It doesn't matter. All that matters is that we hurry, and keep hurrying. The whites will never make peace with us. We should go to the Grandmother's country."

"I do not like to run."

"It is better to run than to fight. Anything is better than fighting."

Thunder in the Mountains looked at Lean Elk carefully. "You are not afraid of whites."

"No. I hate them. But we have no choice."

Joseph nodded. "Tomorrow I will talk to Looking Glass."

"Take White Bird with you."

"I do not need White Bird. Tomorrow I will tell Looking Glass what to do. In the morning."

*

Colonel John Gibbon, with a hundred forty officers and men plus thirty-five Indian scouts and volunteers, had doubled distance on the slowly moving bands each day. Now his mobile infantry was making the ascent up through the pass that overlooks the valley called Big Hole. The horses carrying pieces of the small but heavy howitzer needed help, so Jewell Washington the driver, two cursing privates, sergeants Frederick and Daly, and a corporal, Rob Sale, took turns shouldering the cannon's smaller parts. But going was slow, and they fell behind.

"Give that lead pachyderm a little shoulder, Washington," said Daly, an Irishman from Limerick. "Put some spirit into it or I'll be teaching you what for."

"Yassuh."

"And why not give us a song there, to boot."

"Working too hard, Suh."

"I expect you are—now," said Daly. He turned on the two privates, John Gale and Mack McGregor from Glasgow. "Look alive, you sons of bitches. And don't be thinking you'll sit down to rest before I tell you to.

We've got to bring our baby to the Colonel before night. He loves his baby you know, the Colonel."

Late that evening they staggered into camp, not long before a scout John Gibbon brought from Fort Shaw, Henry Bostwick, came riding in shouting for the Colonel. The camp stirred up like dust under by bootheels, and before long the order came from Gibbon through Charles Woodruff: "Sergeant Daly, Colonel Gibbon wants the howitzer to follow close behind the infantry until you're told to halt. Wait there and come up fast as soon as our fire commences."

"Yes, Sir. We'll be marching in the dark, then, Sir."

"We're moving out immediately."

Gibbon's orders were to leave the horses, excepting his and the howitzer crew's, climb the next ridge and join the company he pushed ahead to look for the hostiles, sending them forward when he realized that the Nez Perce had not been watching their back trail. Perhaps they didn't know Gibbon and his soldiers were closing up on them. The message that Bostwick had shouted down to Gibbon was, "We've got them, Colonel. Got them!"

*

That evening The People celebrated their short, successful hunt for game and their escape from war. They roasted venison and later, warriors who had spread bear fat on their chests and faces, colored it red and black and white, danced before the high fires as sparks rose toward the flames of heaven. These were the young men, men who now had stories to dance, stories of their war with soldiers back in Idaho, stories of travel through the dark and spirit-haunted mountains. Old men and women told their grandchildren of hunts out on the plains where they were going, told them of The People's friends the Crows, told them stories of the Lakota and Cheyenne who also hunted buffalo and who had fought the white soldiers; but most of all the children wanted stories of Coyote, the crafty animal spirit from whom tTe People were descended. Tell us how Coyote fooled great Grizzly Bear, made him leave his fresh-caught salmon on the warm coals to go find the Spirit of the Salmon Waters. Tell us what Coyote told Crow when Crow had found the agate in the stream and sat with it in his beak, not letting go. "Tell us how The People came to be."

One of the stories told how Coyote gave birth to the Nimiipuu, The People. One morning Coyote awoke early, smelling something in the winter wind. "Wind," he asked as nicely as he could, "tell me what you are carrying, that smells so sweet." But Wind refused to say, and went his way. "I must find out what Wind is carrying," Coyote said. He saw Eagle soaring high above where Wind had gone. "Eagle," he called, "you must tell me what Wind was carrying!" But Eagle said nothing. Coyote saw that Eagle was hunting, looking down intently, and would not be bothered. So Coyote shouted to him, "Tell me what Wind is carrying, and I will catch a rabbit for you. I can reach into their holes."

"Reach first and show me the rabbit, and then I will tell," said Eagle, who knew not to trust Coyote. Coyote loped off to the valley of the Bitterroot where he knew rabbits lived, wondering how he would catch one by reaching into a hole. He could catch them easily when they were out, but it was winter, and the rabbits stayed below where it was warm. He stopped at the first hole and called down, "Come out, and I will give you camas root. I promise not to eat you."

A muffled voice came from far down inside. "Promises from Coyote are nothing."

So Coyote went and dug camas root up with his forepaws. He had never worked so hard, but it was for the sweetness on the wind. He dug a very large pile of the good-tasting root and laid it at the mouth of the rabbit's hole. The rabbit cannot see far in the winter but it can smell, and it was hungry from staying inside so long. So it came out. *Snap!* Coyote's teeth closed on the scruff of that rabbit's neck.

"You promised not to eat me!" the rabbit cried.

Coyote said between his teeth, "I will not eat you." So the rabbit hung limply and Coyote brought it under Eagle, who came down and grasped it in his big claws. "I kept my promise," said Coyote. "Now you must keep yours."

So Eagle told him, "Winter Wind is carrying the Seed of Promise. He will plant it; in springtime it will blossom."

"I want it," said Coyote. "I will follow Wind until it rests." And so he did. Coyote followed Wind across the prairie, over mountains, crossing rivers and running on the snow. Coyote had never worked so hard, but it was for the sweet scent on the wind. At last Coyote found Wind sleeping at the green end of a bank of snow. The warmth of Sun had made Wind tired. No animal was as quiet as Coyote. He crept up on Winter Wind, waiting to move until a cold sigh blew. After three days Coyote gently laid his mouth around the Seed of Promise. He jumped up with it in his teeth and ran. Wind rose and blew and stormed but Coyote kept running.

He ran for days until he found Eagle. "How do I plant it?" Coyote asked. But Eagle didn't answer. He was hungry again, circling in the sky. Coyote said, "I promise I will bring you another rabbit if you tell me how to plant the Seed." Coyote thought the Seed would bloom forever with the sweet scent Winter Wind had carried, and he was willing to work hard and keep promises.

Eagle called down, "I know that you keep promises now, so I will tell you. You plant the Seed by swallowing it."

"Will it bloom forever?" Coyote asked, for the seed was very large, almost as large as a rabbit.

"Tend the blossom and I think it will," said Eagle. Coyote thought a long while. The Seed was too big to swallow. Maybe it would grow even bigger in his stomach. So he went to the Bitterroot River where a mother grizzly slept, and laid the Seed of Promise at her nose. The bear awoke and sniffed. "It is Coyote," Mother Grizzly said.

"I've brought a salmon for you to eat," Coyote said. "You must be hungry, for you have slept all winter." Mother Grizzly Bear was hungry. She could not see well, but she sniffed and said, "This is no salmon. Go away and let me sleep."

Coyote thought for a while, then took the Seed of Promise to the Bitterroot River. Seeing a salmon swimming in the cold water going upstream, he said, "Come rest and I will tell you something that will save your life." The salmon flopped up on a rock, and Coyote rubbed the Seed along the salmon's slimy side. It felt good to the tired fish, who lay warming in the sun.

"I must go back and breathe," the salmon said. "Now tell me what will save my life."

Coyote kept his promise, saying, "When you come to the black boulder upstream, go deeper toward the middle of the river. A hungry bear is awake there." Coyote took the Seed of Promise back to Mother Grizzly, laid it at her nose, and said, "Wake up and eat the salmon I have brought." The wonderful smell of salmon came to Mother Grizzly's nose and with one huge gulp she swallowed it. But it was not a fish and she was still hungry, so she went to the river. She caught many salmon, but not the first that passed, for Coyote had kept his promise and his salmon friend swam where the bear could not catch it.

A long time later Mother Grizzly gave birth, and the child was first of The People. Grizzly nursed it, and then Coyote took it to the Wallowa Valley, taught it how to hunt and fish and breed good ponies, how to dance and sing, tell stories, and how to keep its promises. And so We The People are all children of a promise.

That is why Thunder in the Mountains is so sad. He promised his father not to leave his grave, but here we are, said Talking Asleep, the father of Fair Land, Ollokot's wife. Ollokot had listened to the story and he said to the children, "We must live the best we can out here, and someday maybe we can keep his promise and return to our valley." Fair Land took his hand.

"You always can see the best in things, no matter how bad they are. I have never seen you cry, not even when your father died."

"Father was a hunter. Now he hunts again, and no whites bother him."

"He never has cried," said Talking Asleep. "I remember this strong warrior when he was a child. Not even then did Ollokot cry. We called him Frog, because he was so cold."

"He isn't cold," said Fair Land, smiling up at her husband. He shook his head at her.

The two great warriors, Rainbow and Five Wounds, had stood and listened to the stories by the dying fire, remembering two friends, their fathers, who had died in battle with Shoshoni warriors the same day. Now these two friends, their sons, remembered the promise they also had made, to die the same day fighting, as their warrior fathers had died.

Farther from the fading midnight campfires, lying in their lodge, Shore Crossing and his wife White Necklace lay talking in the dark. "One night," he whispered lying on his back, his arm around her as she dozed beside him, "we will lie together for the last time, and we will not know it." He turned his face to her. "I think it will be soon, My Love."

Stirring, she said still half asleep, "Heart." Then the two slept. In his dreams Shore Crossing could hear a far-off rushing as of water falling, quiet, distant, soothing, restful, then closer, as when in spring the river swells, racing with the melted mountain snow, carrying first branches, then whole trees, now sweeping over banks and cracking tall evergreens like rifle shots, and Shore Crossing heard the raging voice of Looking Glass: "Wallitze! Talp-sic-ill-pilp! Um-til-lilp-cown! You Red Coats, this is a battle! Soldiers shooting us! They are not asleep like the whites you murdered in Idaho! You started all this war, now wake up, come out and fight like men! Now you can kill right and left!"

Shore Crossing lurched up to his knees. Looking Glass was screaming outside, "Better that you trouble makers die than the other warriors! Come out and fight!"

Bullets ripped through the lodge and Wallitze picked up his rifle and tumbled out the tipi's flap. White Bird, standing between two tipis as men and women ran, shouted in his old loud voice, "Why are you retreating? Brave men fight for their women and children! Should we run away while white soldiers kill our women and children before our eyes? It's time to fight! Better to die here! These soldiers can't shoot better than the ones we killed in Idaho! Fight! Shoot them down!"

Shore Crossing looked toward the creek and saw the soldiers firing their rifles. He ran toward them shouting his death song, with White Necklace running beside him.

Young White Bird, a boy of nine, was playing with his friends that night as warriors danced in front of fires and drums repeated in high country air the knowledge of the grandfathers. Dancing dreams and memories, the warriors prayed in turning patterns, drummed and chanted, old men singing *hay ay ah yah, hay ay ah yah* underneath the clear Montana sky, for ancestors and for their Wayakin whose powers rose with orange cinders streaming out of sight; and the boys played with dry bone cubes and sticks, snatching them with quick young hands, casting them rattling on the beaten ground—songs, drum beats, and bones late in the fresh night at summer's end. Once White Bird, who survived—as one might say—and told of it years after, got up and ran to fetch another blanket from his family's tipi, and saw two men standing distant from the fires wrapped head to foot in gray blankets; and he saw white, just a little white below their hat brims, knew they were white men, but ran back and played and when he looked up again the two men standing still at the edge of night were gone. Someone had seen a white man riding earlier, perhaps a miner riding back from working, or a rancher looking for a calf, and no one thought of Hair Combed Over Eyes, who dreamed the night before of soldiers, smelling death in his dream; so the boy, grown stumbling drowsy, went back to his lodge with father, mother, sisters, crawled underneath blankets and four hours later as if dreaming, crawling on all fours next to his mother outside the lodge, heard her saying Keep down, when someone shooting naked children and their mothers fired his gun again and White Bird's mother, her clenched face now down against the ground was saying to him, "Crawl quickly to the creek! I am wounded and I can't go with you." He dashed for the low willows, tumbled in, and hiding in the water to his chest now heard the voices of chiefs Looking Glass and old White Bird—did not hear their words at first but now he knew: *soldiers!*

*

The young man Yellow Wolf, nephew of Joseph, would have gone to Joseph's lodge with other relatives to sleep, but, tired from dancing, stopped to sleep with a friend's family down close to where the line of tipis ended, next to the young mothers' lodge, and heard while half asleep, mostly asleep, a horse crossing the creek slowly, walking deliberately, and heard it pass along the tipis up the line. And later, dreaming—or was he waking up?—he heard a shot, a rifle sounding far away, another shot, and then four shots together. Jumping up and seizing his war club he bolted from the tipi as a long fusillade of firing opened from across the creek, and then two more and he was lying flat against the ground, a woman next to him crying, "Why aren't our men shooting them? Why don't the men shoot back?"

Bullets ripped through tipi hides and Yellow Wolf heard shouting around his uncle Joseph's lodge. Up and running, Yellow Wolf stumbled over an old man, Last Crane Flying, crouching, holding one hand at his side, his bare waist running with blood. "You are shot!" The old man nodded, gripping the barrel of a new rifle. "Give me your rifle and bullets. I'll shoot the soldiers down!"

"No!" cried the man. "I need it to defend myself!"

Hearing bullets all around like hot bees, Yellow Wolf jumped up and ran. Ahead, his uncle Thunder in the Mountains, wearing only a shirt, no moccasins, carrying no rifle, ran for his horse shouting to a young warrior, No Heart, "The horses! They will run our horses off! Come on!"

A soldier splashed up like a grizzly from the creek but as he raised his rifle firing, shots came from behind Yellow Wolf. The soldier spun and fell against a willow, cursing. Yellow Wolf dashed toward the willows raising his war club. He struck the soldier's head, clutched the man's full ammunition belt, unclasped it, seized the army rifle, and ran back toward the tipis. His friend Going Alone ran toward him, arms flung out and face gaping disbelief, shouting, "Rainbow is killed!"

*

Red Wolf, a boy of five, awoke to shots and horses neighing. His two brothers ran from the tipi as his mother took up the baby sister in her arms and reached to grasp the boy's hand, pulling him along out through the tipi flap into the night. Pulling, she ran after her sons, the father loping along beside. They passed two men as they fired toward soldiers dashing around the village. He heard a bullet strike; his mother stopped and, looking down at him, sank to her knees and then fell forward. The bullet had gone through the baby's body into her heart. The boy's father bent over her, then tried to grasp her son's small hand to lead him toward the willows, but the boy pulled back, refusing to leave his mother, so the father threw their buffalo blanket on his son and ordered him, "Lie still! Don't move!" The boy heard guns firing and wounded people's screams but did as he was told.

Ninety years later it was he, Red Wolf, who turned the first shovel for the building put up at the battlefield by Gibbon's government to house the relics and the memories of what the small boy saw. The building overlooks the creek bank where his mother once lay in a shallow grave. He died a hundred one years old, the last survivor of the hell Big Hole became as White Bird shouted, "Kill them! Shoot them down!" and soldiers carrying a hundred rounds of ammunition each fired low into the tipis and walked through the village shooting.

*

The infantry had walked three hours in silence, stumbling over downed tree trunks and mucking up to shoe tops in the low spots, marshy swales, and stream beds. The starry night was dark enough that lagging marchers lost their way if they dropped from the column, and their company delayed while the man caught up. At one o'clock, the soldiers came in view of a wide valley and they saw what looked like sparks spread out about a mile ahead. Indian campfires, lots of them.

Behind the infantry by several miles, the howitzer and crew went into camp. "Ain't no special reason I done it," Private John Goale replied to Corporal Sales. "Wanted to see the Great American Desert, I expect; kill Indians; have adventures I could talk about. And you?"

The corporal thought awhile, then said, "No reason."

"By God, there's a reason for everything," said Daly, one of the two sergeants. "You had a reason for enlisting whether you knew it or not."

"What was it, then?—since you know so much."

"If nothing else, to come here in the dark and cool your brogans until we get the order to move up. So there. I'll not have my inferiors tellin' me there's anything but reason, God above."

"'Inferiors!'" the other sergeant cried.

"Inferiors," repeated Daly.

"The Irishman means us," Mack MacGregor said.

"I'm not an Irishman to you, I'll have you know. I'm your sergeant, you son of a bitch."

"Sergeant or not, you god-damned Irishman, you'll not address me in such a manner."

"I may be a god-damned Irishman, and proud of it. We'll settle this another time. We may all be killed tomorrow, so might as well not argue. But you'll obey my orders, Irishman or not."

"And if we don't?" MacGregor said.

The sergeant drew his pistol, pointing it at the Scot's face. "I'll shoot you down as if you were an Indian."

"Maybe I'll shoot first."

"Say, Sergeant," John Goale interrupted, "what have you got against us, anyhow?"

"You're cowards through and through, the both of you."

"No man, much less an Irishman, calls me a coward," said MacGregor. "Yes he does," the other sergeant said. "He'll call you any name he wants as long as you're a private and you're under his command."

"Well by God," said John Goale; "that's just what I did not join the U. S. Army for—to be ordered here and there and up and down by anyone above me. It's not American."

"Ha!" MacGregor said, but added nothing more.

Goale said, "You'll see we're not cowards, Sergeant. We're new recruits. That doesn't mean we'll run."

"You'll run. You'll run like jackrabbits the first armed redskin in his war paint takes aim at you."

"I ain't afraid of savages."

"You should be," Sergeant Frederick put in.

"I bet youse don't know how to fire the gun," Daly said. Neither private offered to answer. "That's what I thought."

"Well hell, Sergeant, no one ever taught us, only told us do what you said."

"And I am saying now, shut up."

"Freedom of speech," MacGregor said. "The First Amendment to the Constitution, what we are fighting for."

"We're fighting for our arses, plain and simple, like the redskins. What thinks you, Boy?" Daly suddenly shot toward Washington.

"Yes, come away from them horses, Corporal," said Frederick, "and tell us what you think. What's an ex-slave out here fighting Injuns for?"

Washington emerged from the horses, lifted his arms over his head in a slow stretch, and spat tobacco juice off to the side, where Sergeant Daly sat. "Why, I am out here so I can obey the gentleman's orders, Suh."

"By gentleman you mean just what?" Daly asked.

"Why, I mean the Sergeant here," nodding toward Frederick. "I'd mean you, Mister Daly, too, Suh, but a man that calls me Boy is no gentleman."

"No?"

"A man that calls me Boy might get shot one day. By Indians I mean, Suh."

"I'd like to see you try."

"Now listen all you gentlemen, whatever you want to call yourselves. We're short of sleep, we're tired as Methuselah, we're hungry, bored, and scared. But we are the U. S. Army and tomorrow morning nothing else will matter. I've never heard so much pointless jaw-flappin' from such a small group of men."

"Suh, Sergeant, Suh, all due respect, I don't see it pointless when somebody calls me Boy. We been here longer than him. I will not fight beside any man that calls me Boy."

"Well, fight beside me then, tomorrow, because sure enough we'll fight as soon as we hear Gibbon's rifles. I think you'll find this drunken Irishman to be the friend you need when Indians start coming at us. And come they will. One round from that brass baby and they'll send some braves to pick us off. And if they notice that mule with the ammunition they'll come like vultures to a rotten corpse. What say we all shut up and get some sleep? Sergeant?"

"I say Amen to that. Let all cowards, gentlemen, and others hereby shut up and sleep. Corporal Sales, post picket guard, by which I mean yourself. And Private Washington, Sir, why don't you regale us with a song, a lullaby, a lovely old slave song?"

After a cool nod of his head, Washington strolled to the horses half mumbling and half singing,

> *Oh the drums would roll, upon my soul,*
> *This is the style we'd go,*
> *Forty mile a day, on beans and hay,*
> *In the Regular Army-O.*

"That's no lullaby," called Daly. "And it's a cavalry song to boot. We go twenty miles a day. Carry forty pounds on our backs and walk twenty miles, by God. Won't you do better than that, African Sir?"

"*Hush little sergeant, don't you cry;*"

"That's better, Washington."

"*You know tomorrow, gonna die.*"

"Not a hell of a lot better, though."

"*All my trials, Lord,*
soon be over."

"Better."

Washington began another song, deep and low at first:

> *I have seen Him in the watch-fires of a hundred circling camps,*
> *They have builded Him an altar in the evening dews and damps;*
> *I can read His righteous sentence in the dim and flaring lamps:*
> *His day is marching on.*

And then more and more softly,

Glory, glory, hallelujah!
Glory, glory, hallelujah!
His truth is marching on.

At first Colonel Gibbon thought they might be marching into a trap, for no hostiles would fail to put out scouts to raise alarm. Ahead along their route of march a hill obscured the campsite. Emerging from the wooded crest, Gibbon and his men almost walked into shapes—large and moving—a huge herd of sleeping, grazing horses, several hundred of them seeming like a thousand. Walking his horse forward, Gibbon saw the campfires spread ahead a quarter mile. The horses by the tens and dozens neighed and whinnied but then simply moved aside as silent white men with their Bannock scouts walked past them. About fifty Bitterroot volunteers were moving in the dark with Gibbon, commanded as a group by John Catlin—a man who thought that Gibbon hated his civilians and who had no use himself for career soldiers.

Back in the valley of the Bitterroot two brothers had stepped forward, bringing sharp knives to "lift scalps," as the younger, Tom, wrote later. Older brother Millard Sherrill, aged twenty-four, went by the nickname "Bunch" for reasons lost to history and legend. Bunch wore drooping handlebar moustaches like a drawing done for Eastern newspapers, and brother Tom, whose wavy brown hair topped a thoughtful face, kept a modest duster on his upper lip. Both packed revolvers like gunslingers, in holsters hung from loaded leather belts, and carried rifles neither one had shot with anything like systematic practice.

When Gibbon halted the column and ordered the men to spread into line of battle, Catlin with his Sherrills formed on the left, beyond the center of the village whose tipis in the starlight looked ghostly white. Eighty-six lodges were strung out along the far side of the creek that Gibbon's two hundred men walked toward in nervous silence. The guide from Fort Shaw, Bostwick, told Gibbon, "If they don't get wind of us, you will see the tipis start to glow with fires inside just before daylight as the squaws get up and pile on wood."

"That's when we'll go," Gibbon ordered, nodding to Woodruff to pass on the word. "We move up to the creek and halt. Daylight should come in about two hours. Three volleys fired low into the tipis and then charge. Shoot the war ponies and burn the tipis."

Logan, Catlin, English, and two other officers overheard the orders. Logan asked, "What's to be done with prisoners?" and Gibbon answered,

"We don't want prisoners."

When Catlin reached his volunteers he announced, "Boys, now we know what to do. The General says no prisoners."

The soldiers and auxiliaries walked in line of battle through the bottomland—slow going in the dark, slogging through water in low spots and soggy patches, shoes covered in mud—and cold, for Gibbon had ordered that greatcoats and knapsacks were to be left behind. Tom Sherrill later said, "We boys were mighty eager to eat Indians for breakfast, but the cold and wet dampened our appetite some. Boys got mad that they had come along at all. But worst was when the order came to stop and wait. Then we sat shivering two hours waiting for daylight, nervous as rabbits and real hungry."

Sherrill and his brother Bunch sat back to back keeping warm, their loaded rifles cradled across their laps. At first they heard babies crying here and there, awakened by dogs set off when those horses whinnied; and they heard mothers soothing them, voices talking; but then everything settled down in earthly silence under stars you'd see on early winter nights, wheeled around now overhead as the night became far spent.

Without light increasing noticeably, you could begin to see the tipis plainer a half hour before sunrise, about four o'clock. Tom Sherrill and his brother crouched behind a thicket now, alert because they heard a horse's muffled hoofs, its breathing in the stillness coming closer. They saw a lone, old Indian riding straight at them. Ten yards away, not seeing them, he'd ride right over them and call alarm, so Bunch and Tom raised rifles just as someone else nearby fired; both fired, then three more men shot at the Indian. The bullets knocked him from his horse. It was the old, nearly blind Natalekin riding out to check up on his horses in the hillside herd. "They shot him down like a coyote," Joseph said later.

Those shots became the signal for the whole line to rise up. They volleyed once—a ragged shock of smoky blasts—reloaded all along the line, raised rifles to their shoulders, fired again; and one more time fired, aiming low into whatever tipi stood before them. Then with a line-wide shout the soldiers and civilians rushed forward, some splashing across Ruby Creek in shallow places, others wading into holes up to their stomachs—shouting, loading, shooting.

In dim grey light they saw Indians disgorged from tipis, running in all directions. Some few men were shot at. A man was knocked back into the creek, a bullet through his chest, by a shot fired from the ground by a prone Indian; his buddy returned fire, got shot; and now a group of men around them fired together and then stormed across, running past dead Indians and into the mad scene of old men, women, children running everywhere. They heard a couple of loud-voiced Indians shouting angrily, but so far there came few shots fired back at them. They burst into tipis, firing down at blankets, in two or three cases being shot full in the face by old men cradling rifles. One man, fired at by a terrified squaw who missed him in her panic, blasted her through the heart and then reversing his rifle clubbed the body's face; then seeing an infant next to her brought up his heel and smashed its head. A soldier burst in next to him and fired—the first man hadn't seen the other squaw, half naked tangled in a blanket scrambling for a knife but now her brains were flecked along the buffalo skin.

Splashing across the stream in shallow water, Sergeant Steinbruch from Hessen, brandishing his six-shot sidearm, gripping a carbine by the barrel in his other hand, saw a naked Indian boy run toward him, making for the creek. He pointed the revolver and the boy stopped, wide-eyed; Steinbruch aimed down to nail the boy between the legs but his excited finger twitched the trigger an instant too soon, the bullet striking through the stomach; the sergeant pulled the hammer back and fired again at the gut-shot boy. This time the youth was knocked on his back by the bullet cutting through his chest. Steinbruch's last sensations were blunt, blinding crashes against his head and Captain Logan shouting, "Stop shooting women, men! Don't shoot the non-combatants!"

Logan saw Steinbruch being clubbed to death by a raging Indian swinging like a madman shouting, crying, still chopping with a stone war club on Steinbruch's head though he had fallen. Logan saw it was a woman in a deerskin dress, rushed to pull her off but saw a man's face or what looked to be a man, shouted out a cry of hatred and disgust and swung his rifle like a club, knocking the thing down and as he swung again a bullet smashed his skullbone, cutting through the brain, and the man that used to be known as the kindly Scotsman who could take a drink lay on his back, dead, five yards from the creek, while farther downstream Tom Sherrill spotted two cowering squaws.

One of them held a papoose tightly in her arms while the other stood transfixed. "I pulled my pistol and took aim at the old squaw that held the child," he later wrote. "I was a good shot and aimed right at her head, but she did not waver a particle. She looked me in the eye, and say, I began to think. Why should I shoot an Indian woman who had never injured me a bit in the world. I put up my gun and left. A little later in the day I heard a fellow bragging he had killed those two women."

The soldiers and civilians walked from lodge to lodge and scouted along the bushes and willows; and some followed orders, striking matches from their pockets—tried to light the thick, damp hides that covered tipi frames. Captain Catlin complained later that they wasted precious time attempting to ignite the stubborn hides. But some success was gained, for many tipis burned, and charred corpses of some old invalid Indians were found later as proof.

Sitting on his horse, Colonel Gibbon watched as the first sun cast light across the gunsmoke-swathed expanse of Indian lodges, running half-clothed figures, soldiers shooting and shouting—eighty-six lodges, a lot of Indians, eight hundred maybe. He saw that once the shooting started, all the herds of horses ran towards each other like a bunch of sheep, and soon he saw braves mounted, riding back and forth, herding them, riding out to shepherd running children, squaws clutching blankets, and confused old men and women. Soldiers who couldn't light damp tipis lassoed them and pulled them over, exposing bedding, cookware, clothing, and cowering Indians. And then he saw a soldier fall and pretty soon another. From outside the village, one by one, shots cracked—one from somewhere on a rise that loomed several hundred yards to the south, some behind him, some from the winding creek beyond his flanks. "Splendid shots," Father Rivalli had said; and the guide Bostwick had said two hours ago, "Keep your men together, Colonel; you aren't fighting Sioux." At each crack of a rifle, Gibbon wrote, a soldier fell.

Dismounting, the Colonel realized his horse dripped blood behind a foreleg. He looked down at his own leg and saw the strange dull sensation he had felt had been a bullet cutting through his calf into the mount. His impulse was to run, which he did for three steps, then stumbled to his knees and Woodruff helped him up. The Colonel drew the pistol from his belt but saw noplace to fire. Not twenty warriors had their guns, ten or a dozen staying back to shoot at soldiers, but these fired carefully, not wasting bullets.

Lieutenant English tried to keep his men under control, but his soldiers ran everywhere among the tipis mixing with other companies. He walked with pistol drawn, shouting, "Together, men, keep together! Stay with me, boys!" Down at the south end of the village two men pulled a tipi down, uncovering two young squaws and what looked to be a papoose two years old, maybe less. Thirty yards away a group of soldiers in the creek took aim at girls and boys and women huddled, backs toward them believing they were hidden. Here the creek bent and the Indians crouching there at first did not know where the shots were coming from that knocked them forward. The water there became tinged red with blood, and Gibbon later observed, "the greatest slaughter took place" there.

Some boys and old men ran into the creek with knives and clubs to stop the soldiers' fire; now hand-to-hand they fought, the soldiers shooting pistols point blank, clubbing muskets, and dead bodies white and Indian floated down the stream. An officer with pistols in both hands fired left and right. Shouts, groans, screams, and curses mixed with barking dogs and blasting rifles. Indians jumped into the stream with coats and blankets, hiding under them, but as one soldier wrote, "As soon as we discovered this trick we only had to notice where the blanket raised up slightly and a bullet at that spot would be sufficient for the body to float down the stream."

Another soldier, stunned by a spent bullet, woke up face to face with an Indian woman dragging him into a tipi. Kicking her away, he grabbed a rifle lying there and with one shot "dispatched her," as he said. The Colonel saw three women in the creek who raised their hands when they saw him; he shouted they were safe and beckoned them toward him, but they stayed stock still in the water. Gibbon's gaze was lifted by a volley from a dozen men: a woman whose husband was shot had killed his murderer, an officer, and drawn this fire that tore her up.

North from there Tom Sherrill and the volunteers from Bitterroot walked the line of wrecked tipis toward the soldiers, driven by the slow, deliberate shooting of three warriors somewhere out there hiding in the tall grass. Six volunteers were down, including the guide Bostwick, killed outright, and only three wounded, proof of deadly marksmanship. The Colonel looked behind him to the wooded hillside, then back across the creek where many of his men crouched down on one knee looking out from the village trying to see where shots were coming from. With every distant pop a man went down.

VIII

Big Hole (2)

Great and Holy Spirit, sing the death song of Wallitze
and his beloved White Necklace; sing the broken
summer of their earthly love, sing sorrow, sing the story
of their last sunrise, last passion, last wounds, and last embrace,
and take them up forever in the song,
O Great and Holy dreamer of the dead.
How they ran together toward the willows tell us, sing
how in the first eternal light they ran into the teeth
of battle, across wild grass that grows between the empty
lodge poles and the creek where willows still stand rooted
in the bank's blood-haunted soil.

Shore Crossing, running faster, saw low ground and fallen branches and threw himself down; White Necklace a moment later lay beside him pushing up a branch in front to brace her husband's rifle. They lay not twenty paces from the heavy thickets where white men cautiously were walking through. "White Necklace, go back! Beloved, hide with The People!" She raised herself a little, fell back down, and a moment later she said, "Husband I am shot! O Heart—." He saw her soft breast in doeskin drenched with blood, her now drowsing face in its last pain looking through a grey cloud at him. He cried out, "My wife is shot to die! I will not leave her! I will stay here until I am killed!"

Half Man Half Woman coming out of sleep hears the cry a half dozen tipis away and with a sobbing groan grips a war club and comes running; the great warrior Rainbow hears Shore Crossing's cry, takes up his rifle; families

199

waking, running, hear it; Joseph and No Heart, starting toward the herd on fast war horses hear it; and Joseph's wives Springtime and Snows Resting hear it—one holds a girl, the other a small boy, to pounding breasts.

Alone, Shore Crossing turns and fires his rifle at a soldier hastily reloading in the high bushes. The soldier, bullet in his brain, stands stiff against the branches, dead, eyes open glassy like a fish, his rifle on the ground. A man behind him has seen the Indian's rifle flash and smoke, and as Shore Crossing rises to an elbow working a cartridge into his Enfield's chamber, the soldier aims and shoots. His forehead crushed, a bullet in his brain, Shore Crossing falls face in the dusty grass before the hide-walls of the wailing camp. His wife has seen it with dimming eyes, drags herself forward to her husband's ready rifle, lifts it across the branch, fires at the soldier—and a man named Albert Schmidt not long from Hanau, Germany, stumbles backward falling into water writhing, gut shot. His comrade Ernest Broetz, a giant nearly seven feet, roars like a speared boar and fires at the squaw lying on the ground. His bullet entered at the base of her throat—so Yellow Wolf, who helped to bury her, said many years later—and ran through White Necklace's body, exiting, a bloody mass, from the small of her back; and she fell across her husband's form, hands holding him, the child inside her killed, their hearts dead together.

> Old One, Lover of the dead, Singer, Dreamer of the dream of life,
> may they lie together until the raging universe burns out,
> then walk together in the long meadow
> where Dreamer and the dream are one.

Now they lay in their blood as Rainbow running raised his rifle at the giant soldier pushing in a new bullet; the warrior's rifle clacked, no fire, and the tall soldier snapping off a quick shot from the hip hit Rainbow through the heart: the warrior's knees buckled and he fell onto his back, arms thrown up and out; and his face dropped sideways with blood running from the gaping mouth. Broetz, replacing the hot, spent casing, looked up and saw the warrior Bad Boy Grizzly Bear, Hohots Elotoht, run toward him raising up his rifle like a club—the young man had no bullets for the gun—and swung his Army rifle, both weapons flying from the two men's sweating hands. The big man grasped the brave, picking him up and crushing him in heavy arms. The warrior cried out to his Wayakin for help and squirmed away; but Ernest Broetz grabbed him again and threw him on his face, bending up his arm behind his back until it cracked, pulling a knife from his Army belt, but Man Woman reached him, swinging with both hands, the round stone of the war club cracking Boetz's temple. As the soldier's eyes and nose ran blood, Woman Man swung again, knocking the giant forward on his face, then swung again, again, until Elotoht, catching the war club, said, "That's enough! Go help the others—there!"

He pointed toward the last tipis, down where the mothers' lodge stood and soldiers approached the shallow creek. Man Woman got up running and Bad Boy Grizzly Bear, an arm hung down dead, stood up, turned and saw a scattered group of men and women watching him. None had come forward; not Towassis, Bowstring, able-bodied but no warrior, or the Yakima who, though traveling with The People, never fought soldiers; and three women watching. They turned and ran toward the open meadow.

*

Joseph and No Heart rode toward a shallow place beyond the farthest white man and crossed the creek; but already two warriors up at the village's north end fifty yards past the Army's flank jerking up their picket ropes and jumping on their war ponies, heard an old man looking toward the hillside shout, "The Bannocks steal our horses!" So splashing across the creek the two young warriors see in half light Joseph and No Heart riding in the moving herd and fire their rifles. No Heart, hit twice, hurtles from his pony skinning his dead face and shattered chest across the hillside's weedy grass.

"What have you done!" cries Joseph and the warriors recognize the thundered voice. They cry out, heel their ponies toward the dead man on the ground where Joseph kneels. "What have you done?" he asks again, "Why did you shoot?"

"We heard an old man shouting that the Bannocks or the Salish were stealing our horses! We couldn't see!"

"You have killed him. My nephew is dead. Look at him. You young men are killing us all."

"We are sorry!" cried the young man, Passing Overhead, and the other, called Black Trail, said, "We wanted to protect the herd."

"I understand, but you have to see better to shoot. Now follow this herd and drive all the horses to safety. I will take my nephew's body up the hillside." They stared at Joseph, so he said, "Go now. No Heart's spirit forgives you."

"Does yours?" asked Passing Overhead.

"I will. Not now. Go."

He gestured eastward with his hand; the two turned toward the herd and followed the ponies, spotted Appaloosas pounding downhill toward the low ground, manes and tails making a disappearing stream in the rising sun.

Joseph quickly laid the body across his horse, ran with it up the hill, and laid No Heart among high thickly grown bushes just over the hill's crest. He laid one hand on No Heart's head, the other on his chest, and prayed that the watching Spirit would guide the young man to his ancestors. Remounted now and topping the hill's crest, the grieving man saw spread before him tipis burning; soldiers walking and firing rifles into lodges; ten warriors, no more, spread behind the tipis shooting; another eight or ten men on their horses riding here and there with rifles, two coming up the hillside toward him. Soldiers everywhere—these could not be Howard's men. Where did they come from? How many more will come? *We must get all The People out of here.* He saw his brother, Ollokot, with White Bird and Toohoolhoolzote. Not far from them Lean Elk and Looking Glass were running with their rifles toward the higher ground across the way, facing the hillside. Joseph rode his pony fast down the slope and around the last tipis. When he reached Ollokot he shouted, "Brother! Can you hold the soldiers here while I take The People out?"

The war chief shouted, "Take them quickly! We will hold the soldiers down!"

"Most of the warriors have to come with me; maybe another army waits for us."

"I'll bring my men and come with you!" White Bird shouted.

Joseph saw the valley covered, so it seemed, with People running—old men, women, children, everyone still able, some wounded, streaming toward the sun.

"Fair Land is shot!" Ollokot cried. "We must take back the village!"

"Kill these soldiers, murderers!" Joseph shouted.

Smoke from burning lodges rose with strands of rifle smoke, rolling eastward, following The People. Down among the tipis screaming, crying People crawled or fell or tried to run; and in the stream the firing of the soldiers in every direction went on. Joseph kicked his horse hard, galloping up the hill toward Lean Elk and Looking Glass, both on one knee carefully aiming at the soldiers near the tipis.

"Look at what this man has done!" cried Lean Elk as Joseph stopped his horse. "You, Looking Glass, you fool! You have gotten all of us killed!"

Leaping from his horse, Joseph said simply, "Lean Elk, you and Ollokot must take charge here while I and White Bird get the People away. Looking Glass, drive the soldiers back across the creek."

"I'll die with my young men!"

"You are not to die, Looking Glass! You must fight again another day!"

"Go," said Lean Elk to Joseph. "We will kill these murderers! Get The People out."

"My wives and children might be down there still," said Joseph, pointing toward his tipi.

"No one comes out," said Looking Glass. "Your wives and children are away on foot. Go after them. I will run to your tipi."

Joseph mounted, shouting, "Don't run down there!"

"I am a free man!" said Looking Glass. "I go where I want to go."

"You're no good dead!" called Lean Elk, but later when Joseph and The People came back to the village and Joseph ran to his tipi it was Looking Glass who met him there.

*

Yellow Wolf had come upon a soldier crawling on all fours, "as though he were drunk," the warrior said. The soldier had been shot through both lungs. Spitting, drooling blood, the man saw nothing but the ground in front of him. The warrior clubbed him dead and took his rifle, ammunition belt, and pouch half filled with bullets. "This is understood in war," Yellow Wolf explained many years later. "I had no gun, and soldiers were burning lodges with our sick and old people inside."

A wounded warrior named Red Heart approached the young brave, bent and carrying his gun in the wrong hand. "I'm shot," he said, and kept walking. Yellow Wolf could see the man had taken a bullet in his right arm, which hung dripping blood off the fingers; what he did not notice was the spreading blood at Red Heart's stomach. He would die two silent, sight-swimming days later, in too much pain to call upon his Wayakin or understand when told his mother had been killed but her body had not been found.

The voice of Scattered Human Bones now rose above the shrieks and screams of wounded and fleeing People: "My brothers, stay and fight! Resist! Our tipis are on fire!"

A round of war whoops answered him—not more than ten thought Yellow Wolf, though in that part of camp a hundred soldiers worked to burn or pull down lodges, shooting anything that moved. The young warrior knew that few of the men had thought to take their guns when they ran out of their homes.

He saw a warrior, Five Fogs, standing out beside his lodge using a hunting bow. A group of soldiers ten paces from him pointed their rifles at him, fired, but all had missed and Five Fogs "stepped about a little," shooting down a soldier, and the white men fired again, all missing him again. He shot several more arrows; meanwhile Yellow Wolf took aim and dropped a soldier, wishing Five Fogs had a rifle. Reloading while the soldiers fired again and missed, Yellow Wolf shot down another white man and this time one of the soldiers shot Five Fogs dead.

Yellow Wolf killed a third soldier, thinking it was better to die here defending families and freedom than be led away by force some place you didn't want to go. The warrior picked up the hot guns those three unskillful men he shot had carried, giving them, and ammunition, to three warriors who had left their rifles in their lodges. He thought now maybe twenty warriors still were near or in the village, carefully shooting, and the soldiers, some of them drunk with terror, seemed to be helpless against the long-range fire aimed in from all directions.

Moving at a crouch toward the willows, Yellow Wolf saw a soldier shooting with his back toward him. "I'll touch the man alive," the young brave thought, coming up close behind. The man turned suddenly, perhaps sensing something wrong, his rifle raised, so Yellow Wolf fired point blank at four feet killing the white man with a bullet to the chest. But looking ahead, the young man saw a soldier calmly standing in the willows. Bringing up his rifle, Yellow Wolf took aim wondering that the soldier didn't move—then knew the white man had been shot, was dead, was stiff in death. Looking where the soldier faced, Yellow Wolf saw Wallitze and White Necklace, and not far from them the mighty warrior Rainbow dead upon his back.

Falling down to his knees, Yellow Wolf caught sight of big Wetyetmas Likleinen, Circling Swan, beside the body of his wife, shooting rooted there, not moving—hit by bullets, going down like a strong buffalo. The young man with a war cry rose and ran up toward his uncle's tipi, looking for his cousins.

Farther up the row of tipis an old man called Tobacco sat before his lodge and smoked, watching the soldiers running past—until finally a soldier walking saw the old man, lowered his rifle and shot his bullet into the white-headed Indian. Tobacco did not move, and smoke continued to curl from his long pipe. The soldier calmly put another cartridge in, raised his barrel, fired. This shot too struck the old man's war shirt, but he still sat and smoked. "Say!" the soldier called to another. "Look at this redskin smoking pretty as you please! I've put two bullets in him and he sits there like a cigar store Injun."

"Shoot again," the other said, and then both fired. Their bullets struck the old man, but still he sat up. In all, a half dozen soldiers shot bullets into Tobacco's ribs and limbs.

"Wonderful thing we saw," said Yellow Wolf. "The wounds gave out steam, nothing more, like fog after rain. He did not feel the shots, and two suns later the old man rode horseback from there. The wounds did not grow.

He died next year at the Hot Place where the soldiers took The People after the chiefs surrendered. The story is true. He sat on his blanket like a spirit."

Another old man, Allezyahton—father of Two Flocks on Water, who later took a white man's name on the reservation—tried to make his way to shelter under the bank's tall growing bushes. He was seen crouching by a volunteer from Bitterroot and shot. Just minutes later Yellow Wolf found him dead, water washing around his legs. "We called him Allezyahton, an old name whose meaning was known only to the oldest Indians. He wanted peace, did not fight, and now there is no one left who can tell what his name meant in the days long ago."

Helping Another was the wife of a man who had been killed in Idaho. Asleep inside her husband's parents' lodge she heard the crack of rifles, and as Looking Glass and White Bird shouted to the warriors she shook off her blankets and crawled out to see. Some soldiers had already crossed the creek and walked among the tipis shooting while terrified women and their children tried to dash toward shelter in the willows. She waited for a moment hoping the soldiers wouldn't see her, then made for the creek bank as fast as she could run. On her way she picked up a small girl toddling alone the wrong direction, coming toward her. With the child in both arms, Helping Another ran toward the creek. She half slid, half jumped down the bank into water waist-high, holding up the little girl, but realized that soldiers crossing would be able to see her easily. So she waded downstream toward an inward-sloping section of the bank and, holding the child close, she nestled against the crumbling soil trying to keep the little girl between her and the earth. The silent child clutched her dress and pressed her face against the woman's pounding chest. Helping Another looked up just as a soldier without aiming squeezed a shot at her but kept on splashing toward the bank. Hearing the child's stunted cry, she looked down. The little girl had taken the bullet near where the shoulder joins the neck. Without another sound the girl lay dead, eyes still open looking up at her deliverer. Helping Another moaned and rocked the child there where she lay, rolling side to side, calling to her dead husband.

A few yards from her a boy lay on some stones at water's edge, his blood from two wounds spreading like ribbons in the stream, his mouth and his eyes open. Not caring what would happen to her, Helping Another clambered up the bank, the little girl still in her arms, and started walking through the village. A mother lay dead upon her back, an infant crying on her chest. Helping Another stopped and looked: the child's arm had been mangled by a soldier's bullet and as the arm swung back and forth a little hand flopped, hanging by a shred of pink-white meat. There was nothing she could do, so the woman stumbled on.

Wetatonmi, wife of Ollokot, whom on the reservation in old age the whites called Susie, recalled at nearly ninety what the bullets sounded like as they sliced through damp tipi hides: like angry bees but heavier. She stayed to gather blankets and a pouch of water while her husband and his other wife, Fair Land, together ran from the tipi. The younger woman emerged from the lodge to see Fair Land fall. Running to them, Wetatonmi shouted to their husband, "Ollokot! Ollokot! You take that rifle and fight the soldiers! I will care for Aihits Palojami." Looking down with wild eyes, the warrior chief nodded quickly then ran toward the screaming voice of Looking Glass. Wetatonmi saw her sister-in-law had a wound between two ribs low down her side; and already Fair Land breathed in short gasps. The woman bent down over Fair Land, lifting her shoulders and her head, shielding her with her body.

A ten-year-old son of Chief White Bird awakened to the sound of bullets ripping through hides, and then his mother pulled him from his blankets, pulled him through the big flap of the tipi saying, "Go that way—run fast as you can!" He ran from the lodge seeing tethered horses shot and falling, people leaving tipis stunned and terrified and running. Young White Bird saw a low place in the ground and ran to it along with several women. As he laid himself down flat his mother pushed herself in next to him. As yet they saw no white men, but a man called in a loud voice, "Soldiers are right on us, in our camp! Get out, get yourselves away somewhere or you'll be killed or taken." Young White Bird's mother grabbed his hand, got up saying "Come on, Son; let's run!" A bullet struck their hands and cut off White Bird's thumb and two of his mother's fingers, but they kept running to the creek. "Get down into the water!" she commanded, pushing him, and they tried to make their way through the waist-high water, forcing their legs forward as in a nightmare, everywhere men shooting—pushing thick, heavy legs—push enough to burst your heart, but the legs are as heavy as the dead, heavy as dying buffalo.

The boy looked toward the other bank and saw a woman digging frantically with clawing hands, trying to scoop out a hollow place to shelter in. Then he saw his first soldier: the man was turning hasty like a squirrel, trying to see everywhere, loading, firing, and reloading, shooting every Indian he could. White Bird's mother pushed the boy down in the water until only his head was exposed, and she sat down beside him. The useless cover of a flimsy bush was all that stood between them and the soldier, but five more people came beside them, two women and three girls. The soldier now turned and fired at them. The bullet hit a small girl in her arm, missing the bone and going through. She screamed, held up her arm, and White Bird could see through the hole. The soldier's attention was caught by the woman digging across and up the stream. He took aim calmly and shot. The woman slammed against the bank, cut through her left breast, then fell face first into the water, thrashed her feet and right arm, floating, trying to turn upright.

Then three more soldiers came and leveled rifles at the group of mothers and children in the water. "Only women!" White Bird's mother called in English, standing up and raising both hands high. An officer behind the soldiers shouted something; all four lowered their rifles and moved off toward the tipis. The woman shot in her breast now floated past and White Bird's mother caught her, pulled her toward them turning her over, then laid her head and upper body onto a gravel bar in the water. The woman breathed with weak coughs gurgling water, and then couldn't cough. Her face stopped moving. She looked beautiful, the young boy thought, the first sun on her shining forehead, brown eyes lit with gold, and parted lips seeming about to speak. He saw water around her coloring with blood; her hair waved softly, streaming around her head.

A boy of twelve named Sleepy woke, like Young White Bird—to his mother pulling him from blankets while bullets whistled through their tipi hides. Outside a man was shouting, "Wake up, People! Soldiers right here shooting at us! Wake up!" His father, Likinma, Last in a Row, thought fast enough to snatch his rifle. Leading out his family, the father warrior pointed to a shallow gully, telling them to run there and stay down no matter what. But once there, Sleepy put his head up to watch what was happening, and saw his father shooting at the soldiers. "I saw one woman killed—my mother," he told a white man taking notes four decades later. "She was the first killed. Then I saw my father shoot and drop a soldier—maybe the man who killed my mother, I don't know. I looked around and saw the other four women lying dead or bad wounded." He said to his brother, a little boy, "We must get out of here!" They jumped up and ran for Ruby Creek, drawing the soldiers' fire, two naked boys without so much as hatchets in their hands. "The soldiers fired at us. I do not know how many shots—as many as they could until we dropped out of sight" behind the low bank of the creek, where a dead body lay, a man with no gun beside him. The brothers huddled with him while screams and smoke and bullets passed over.

Pohit Patikt was a little boy, son of the warrior Grizzly Claw, who jumped up and pulled his wife from the tipi telling the three boys—Pohit, his older brother, and a cousin—to stay hidden under blankets. A soldier burst in soon, failing in the early dawn to see boys under blankets; but he shot the small boy's dog before he left. "Get up!" his older brother said. "Bring your blanket with you! Come!" The three boys ran from the tipi toward the creek. "The guns are so loud!" thought the boy—and so much smoke. The three jumped down behind the bank and stayed there as soldiers fired. The air smelled strong of powder smoke. The boy heard warriors yelling, and the soldiers cursed and shouted. "I was scared! Bad scared!" he said. Bullets whistled near his head as the three boys crowded in their small space in the bank. Pahit's brother cried out, rose up, and was shot two times. His body splashed into the water. Pahit's cousin grabbed the little boy and held him tight against the bank; but then little Pahit thought of his blanket. He'd dropped the blanket running from the lodge. Twisting out from his cousin's grasp, the small boy ran to get his blanket. He picket it up and saw his father riding on the hill behind the soldiers. He looked around and saw the wreckage of the camp—lodges down and bedding everywhere; tipis burning; ponies lying dead still tethered; men and women crying over bodies, many crying. He could not understand why so many men and soldiers had lain down on the ground and why so many, "oh, so many" women and children lay there too. "Afterward I understood," he said.

An older boy, almost a warrior at fifteen years of age, ran toward the bushes, crawling the last yards on hands and knees. Next to him an old woman was shot; he heard the bullet hit her chest. She fell on her side, saying to him, "You better not stay here with me." "Grandmother!" he cried, grasping her, but she said, "Run for your life. I'm shot to death. Go!" He ran and hid behind the bushes, watching as soldiers and civilians in the camp shot down whatever Indians they saw—bullets like rain, he said, and many little children dying in the storm; men and women shot inside their lodges, women shot down in the water, boys shot running after parents, girls following like partridges, shot down. He saw a young man with wide eyes and gaped mouth run to the creek with his two wives. They swam downstream side by side, the man between the women; came to a willow thicket and the man laid down between his wives while they sat guarding him. The man's name was Crying Bird. He cried again two months later when Thunder in the Mountains refused at first to surrender. The teen aged boy watched him in the willows now, and then jumped up to run and seize a dead soldier's gun.

Red Moccasin Tops and Strong Eagle, two of the three Redcoats, heard Looking Glass shout as soldiers crossed the creek. Each took his rifle from its place tied at the center lodgepole and ran outside to fight the soldiers. The two braves saw each other and then ran together toward the south end of the village. Red Tops, or Sarpsis Ilppilp, fired once at soldiers upstream; without reloading he ran on, at one point fighting two soldiers with clubbed rifle until Strong Eagle came up and shot one white man. Then Sarpsis Ilppilp overcame the other, throwing him down and clubbing him to death. The two ran on to higher ground beyond the birthing lodge and watched for clear shots at soldiers just two hundred yards away. These two alone accounted for a dozen soldiers killed or wounded down at that end of the village. "Shoot officers!" said Sarpsis Ilppilp—"then the soldiers won't know what to do."

"Too many officers and two few soldiers," said his friend.

"Let's go around them, shoot them from the back." He knew that soldiers feared above all else to be flanked or surrounded. When it happened they'd draw back their lines. These two alone, prone in the grass and moving constantly, turned the right flank, driving in the rightmost company to mix with soldiers attacking in the center. Carefully the two took aim; unerringly they shot. Seeing a mounted officer, Strong Eagle made a shot. The tall grey horse spun around and in a moment the white soldier leapt down favoring his leg and looking at the horse's gushing wound. The officer went to the creek to wash his wound, then limped back to the horse, from where he watched his men across the creek.

The two Redcoats would have shot the officer again, but women's cries and rising smoke kept their attention fixed on soldiers ransacking the village. They saw two chiefs and several warriors shooting from the higher ground up to their right, while mounted warriors rode around the village toward the slope behind the creek.

Another warrior, here to earn his name of Wounded Head, dashed from his tipi, leaving his young wife and little girl, like Shore Crossing and White Necklace throwing himself down to shoot at soldiers crashing through the willow thickets. Looking back at his tipi, he saw his wife and child come out and try to escape toward the horse herds down the valley. Without seeing which soldiers fired, the father watched the little girl fall forward; then his wife, a bullet in her back, pitched to her face. Another bullet creased his scalp, a blow that felt like a stone war club on his head. When he got up he staggered toward his wife, who still lay with their daughter face down. He wondered why the soldiers had not shot him yet, then saw Hair Combed Over Eyes and Looking Glass shooting. They stood near the two bodies shooting at soldiers behind Wounded Head. The warrior found his wife and child still breathing; he turned them carefully and touched their wounds. His daughter's hip was mutilated and his wife's right side showed a pulsing exit wound. The chief and Hair Combed Over Eyes carried the woman to the lodge as Wounded Head took up his little girl.

Inside the lodge the chief said, "You must leave them and come out with us to shoot these whites. They will both die."

The warrior shouted "No! They will not die! I am their husband, father! I will stay and nurse them even if I am killed here!" Her wound bound up and shivering body covered, and her terrible thirst assuaged by Wounded

Head, the mother lived. Their little daughter cried weakly for water all day, became fevered, and in the night she died.

When Looking Glass and Hair Combed Over Eyes reached Joseph's lodge its canvas sides were charred. The soldiers had slashed it and tried to light the heavy cloth, but damp with dew it would not light. Some of the other lodges, whether made of canvas or hide, were flaming in the village; sick children and old people screamed as fiery canvas dripped on them and lodgepoles fell. Soon after Looking Glass and Hair Combed Over Eyes entered the lodge where Joseph's family had slept, the younger man came running out to find a horse. He ran the whole length of the village and at the northern end encountered Thunder in the Mountains, who was riding back to see about his family. One look at the young warrior's face made Joseph kick his horse's ribs and gallop along the line of smoking tipis. Startled soldiers falling back from sniper fire looked up then crouched again as shots cracked from the flanks and higher ground.

Before the tipi, Looking Glass was holding Joseph's daughter in one arm; his other hand gripped his Winchester. Joseph leapt down from his horse, but as the other chief transferred the small girl to her father's arms, a fusillade of bullets shivered the air around the tipi. Joseph's horse screamed and tried to rear, then fell on its side with a heavy gasp, its wide-eyed head thrashing and its large teeth champing.

"Run for the creek!" Looking Glass shouted. "Any man who tries to fight them here is killed! I'll run and shoot at them beyond their aim."

Pressing his daughter close, the father made a dash to the creek. Reaching the bank, he jumped into the water and then hunching with his daughter to his chest began to wade downstream where the willows draped into the creek. There Yellow Wolf encountered him, the younger man running to the thicket looking for a safer place to shoot. "Uncle, why are you here?"

"I have no rifle to defend myself!"

"Stay down! I will shoot them, Uncle!"

Here and there soldiers singly or by pairs and looking neither left nor right began to dash back across the stream. Some fifty yards behind Yellow Wolf a soldier wading toward the village stopped in midstream, unsure whether to go on into the village or back away. Seeing White Bird's mother, he went to her and held out his hand to shake. The startled woman took his hand and then the soldier waded toward the standing tipis.

Downstream, several women and a medicine man tried to shelter children with their bodies. One of the women cried, "Do something! Stop the soldiers' killing. You have power! You have strong power!"

But the old man answered, "I am helpless! I have tried, but I can do nothing!" He spread his hands. "I am helpless!"

*

The Colonel, standing at his wounded horse's head, reins looped loosely in his hand, saw the first men coming back across the creek. "Bugler, sound recall!" he ordered. Turning to Woodruff, he said, "If we start running they will slaughter us. We must keep together." Gibbon looked behind him toward the bare slope. "Too bad we've no artillery—and where the hell is the howitzer?" He pointed toward the trees covering half the hill. "We can get some cover up there. Lead the way and I will stay here till the last man crosses."

But when the bugler sounded recall the men did not fall back in order. Most simply made a break for it, running through the village, jumping in the creek and splashing up the near side—never turning to fire, then slopping through the swampy mire they'd come through three hours earlier. Three braves came after them, running up behind, guns raised like clubs and beating down Gibbon's soldiers. Some hundred citizens and troops ran frantically and the enraged Colonel shouted, "Turn and fight god damn it! I'll stay here by myself if I have to, damn it!"

*

The three braves, Yellow Wolf, Going Alone, and Five Wounds, seeing that in among the whites they would be killed, slowed to a walk and watched the soldiers streaming toward the woods. They took aim carefully, avoiding shots that might carry into the trees, for they had seen three mounted warriors ride around and up into the wooded hillside. The soldier in a yellow coat who had been mounted bawled like a bull buffalo, limping behind the other soldiers, waving his crushed hat. "Don't shoot him," Five Wounds said. "He is their chief. I want to find out who he is and where he came from. He isn't the one-armed fool."

*

"Drive those god damn bastards out of the trees!" Gibbon shouted. "Give them a volley, charge them!" He turned to see if more men followed him but only one officer came walking calmly up the slope. The Colonel waited. "I've always liked Wisconsin men, Lieutenant. I commend you for keeping your head."

"Thank you, Sir." George Wright, a Civil War veteran, had tried to count the men he saw ahead of him. "We've left a good third of our men back in that village, Sir. A lot of wounded. I hate to think—"

"The Nez Perce don't take scalps, I'm told. We'll see."

"After what we have done, I wouldn't count on charity, Sir."

"How did we lose so many men, Wright?"

"They whipped us, Sir. They beat hell out of us." Wright smiled pleasantly. "We'll soon be famous, Sir."

"Damn it, Lieutenant, this isn't another Custer massacre. Not yet it isn't."

"Very good, Sir."

Gibbon's voice quieted: "Get these men digging. We will trade our lives as dearly as possible. If we can get that pack mule with the howitzer, it's two thousand rounds of ammunition." Just then a hollow, banging thump exploded up the hillside to their left. A projectile whooshed an arc toward the encampment.

"Oh, shit," said Wright.

"God damn the damdest hell!" Gibbon exclaimed. "The Indians will get the damn howitzer and the god damn ammunition!"

*

The soldiers were pinned down by twenty-five sharpshooting braves and were digging shallow holes with trowel bayonets. The chiefs across the way met at the north end of the smoldering camp. Joseph, with his daughter in his arms, said they must lead The People back to get the wounded, bury the dead, and take up what belongings they could gather before nightfall. "The People must get out before One Arm General arrives. We cannot fight a thousand men. You, Looking Glass and Lean Elk, you must hold these soldiers back for one day, with only the few men you have now. White Bird and I will take most of the warriors with The People to protect them if more armies of soldiers are waiting for us ahead."

"Was that my brother?" Ollokot said quietly to Lean Elk as they walked toward the village. They heard a small thump coming from the hill, and in a moment something whistled down, exploding with a flash and zipping fragments in the low ground just before the village. Some weak screams came from the willow thickets and the creek bank, but no one had been struck.

"They have a big gun," Lean Elk said.

Ollokot replied, "I'll send my nephew Yellow Wolf to kill it."

Looking Glass told Joseph, "You must go back to your tipi, Brother," and Joseph simply nodded. He walked back down along the wreckage of the tipis, some still burning like charcoal. The ground was strewn with hides and bedding, dolls and cookware, but mostly women, children, and old people on the ground—two Nimiipuu for every soldier; but Joseph saw a strangely narrow tunnel of daylight, his vision to both sides black and closing in. He faltered, then proceeded to the tipi cut along its canvas sides. Before it lay his dead animal. He pulled the flap and entered. His daughter Sound of Running feet sat rocking her dead sister in her arms, a glassy stare in her eyes. Beside her crying, trembling, little brother Pony looked at the women lying on the ground. Joseph's older wife Springtime lay panting weakly while her sister, Upright Rushes, gently stroked a wet cloth over her bleeding face. It looked as though she had been beaten, and a wound, already wrapped, had torn the ribs along her side. Snows Resting lay still, eyes closed, in her buffalo blanket. Sunlight streaming through a long rent in the canvas bathed her delicate face that looked like something painted in the sky. "She is so beautiful, beautiful," her husband whispered as the last light wandered from his eyes. He felt a hand touch his, knew that Sound of Running Feet had reached up toward him, felt the almost lifeless hand close around his. He watched a long time, standing motionless, promising the Spirit on the Mountains everything if he would bring Snows Resting happy to her dreaming place beyond the summer sky.

*

"Few of us will forget," wrote Gibbon later, "the wail of mingled grief, rage, and horror coming from the camp five hundred yards away when the Indians returned and recognized their slaughtered warriors, women, and children."

*

The People came back to their village like a ragged wave breaking from an ocean's grief. They walked, ran, stumbled on the trampled, bloody, littered ground. Wounded old men, women, and children moaned and cried for water, bleeding from their gunshot wounds out under the sun. Some children charred in blankets lay in their tipis' ashes. No family escaped, and everywhere beloved bodies lay with bullet holes, burned flesh, beaten heads and faces. Some had fallen onto burning camas ovens.

When Morning Sun's mother found her grown child's body, someone had already wrapped it in a blanket and lain it on a buffalo robe. The mother pressed Half Man Half Woman's battered face to hers, then held the marble body across her lap in two strong arms until the old medicine man—the one who had spoken his lack of power in the bloody stream, lifted the body from her, carried it and laid it down beside the bodies of the warrior Wallitze, Shore Crossing, and his wife, the beautiful White Necklace.

When Five Wounds, Pahkatos Owyeen, came upon the laid out body of his brother-friend the warrior Rainbow, bullet through his heart, he cried long, stood with face uncovered weeping, then began to chant his death song. When he finished, Five Wounds said to his friends who stood with him beside Rainbow's body, "This sun, this sun, I, Pahkatos Owyeen, am going to die. My brother is killed, and I shall go with him."

The young man Yellow Wolf wanted to say, "No! You must help us fight!" but understood the promise the friend-brothers had made to each other and their fathers, that both would die the same day. So Five Wounds took his rifle and walked toward the soldiers on the hillside in the trees. Their first shots missed him; he walked on with his gaze above them chanting now again his song of death. The next shots plunged through the warrior's broken heart.

> Pahkatos! dying not for The People but for loyalty;
> the dying People have no heart for blame.

Three times a group of seven warriors tried to bring the body down, away from white men who might desecrate and mock the corpse of a Nez Perce warrior, cut the scalp and stab the body, steal the medicine bag lying on the bloody chest. Two men fell wounded, one of them, called Tipyahlah-nah Kapskaps, or Strong Eagle, with a bullet through the ribs—but on the third attempt one man ran while the others covered him with fire and pulled the body back, a strong man called Bighorn Bow, a man who killed big bull bison with one arrow from a bow so stout only Rainbow, hunter-warrior, and his brother Five Wounds could draw an arrow on it full.

> And so The People buried Rainbow and Five Wounds, mightiest of warriors.
> Broken were their spirits, broken the old war strength of The People,
> who would fight on now as the wounded buffalo fights:
> hopeless, smelling its own ebbing blood on the grass.

The People found two beautiful young women on the ground, shot and beaten by white men. One, the eighteen year old White Feather, lay with a bullet through her shoulder, and face pounded by a man who had rammed his metal-plated rifle butt into her mouth, gashing her lips and breaking out an upper tooth. Her only relative was Gray Hawk, her father, who lay bleeding only steps away: the bullets in his stomach would kill him in the evening of the next day. White Feather, grown weaker each mile of the long retreat, would be left with steely-eyed Lakota—was married to a white man, and then two years after Big Hole died a murder victim of the Blackfeet.

And Halpawinmi, Dawn, twenty years old, tall, strong, and beautiful in form and face and spirit, favorite of all The People, saw her brother shot before her eyes. She walked among the dead and stricken, through the running People, screams, and smoke—to bend over the suffering with water for their thirst, swabbing wounds and wrapping bleeding limbs with what cloth she could find and tear in strips—until a soldier shot her down. She coughed up blood for two days and then was buried where the Nez Perce horses passing trampled the dusty earth and made safe her lost and unmarked small grave.

> So died The People's strength and beauty,
> leaving knowledge and despair to walk with them
> the thousand miles ahead, hand in hand, with painful steps and slow.

When Joseph left his lodge at last, Lean Elk and Looking Glass awaited him outside. "The People must be hurried," Lean Elk said. "You must take charge of them."

"The People must be given time to bury all our dead. Hear me, my chiefs. I will bury my wife and son. I will bury them under the willows by the water. Then The People will begin the long march to Sitting Bull across the border. We have no country now."

*

"You damn fool idiot!" the sergeant yelled at Corporal Sales as soon as he had pulled the lanyard on the howitzer. "You didn't fuse the shell!" The projectile sailed over the village in the distance down below and disappeared into the meadow like a dud.

"The damn thing don't explode if you don't screw a fuse into the shell and set the bastard!" Frederick added. "You, Goale, Mack, go fetch another shell and this time I will set the fuse!"

The men returned and rammed the shell, fused, down the cannon's tube just as the other sergeant, Daly, coming up the slope below said, "Indians. Better pull it now, and out of here with us. God—" A bullet shattered his left shoulder just as Sales pulled; the cannon flashed a red tongue of flame and belched a bursting ball of smoke—the shell exploding harmlessly before reaching the village—and another bullet clipped the Irish sergeant's hat as he went down.

Two mounted Indians rode toward them through the trees and four more were running up the hillside. "Another Custer massacre!" the man from Glasgow, Mack MacGregor, shouted and without turning around to look, both he and Private Goale ran from the piece back down the trail, passing Jewell Washington who rode a small horse with the mule in tow. The two recruits did not stop running until they had put a hundred miles behind them, MacGregor going on from there to Britain, where he told his tall tales of the Wild West for years afterward.

The corporal rode on toward the howitzer, saw Daly on the ground and Sales receive a bullet in the brain. Then Frederick fell down dead, shot in the back. The warriors, all six of them, continued moving toward the gun, shooting now at Washington, whose mount took a hit, skittered for its footing and then toppled sideways, pinning the man by both legs. Old Yellow Wolf, the young brave's uncle, Yellow Wolf, Sun Tied, the man named Dropping From A Cliff, Calf of Leg, and Stripes Turned Down, all reached the crewless cannon and while four men took apart the carriage Sun Tied and Stripes Turned Down ran to the pack mule and downed mount. They stopped when they saw the Black man lying under the horse, and when he saw them he began to chant, "All my trials, all my trials, soon be over."

Sun Tied said, "Don't shoot the buffalo-hair soldier. He sings his death song."

The two braves watched the Black man as he sang softly and drew a knife to prod the horse up off his legs. He rolled aside, and getting to all fours he looked up at the warriors.

"Why does he work for white men?" Stripes Turned Down asked in Nez Perce. "I think they use him like a mule." The soldier raised a hand as if in peace, got to his feet, and stood looking at the two young men.

"You ain't gon kill me? You ain't gon shoot this ole sojer down?" Then he began to sing, "Glory, glory hallelujah, His truth is marching on."

"Maybe he's craftier than the white soldiers," said Stripes Turned Down.

"He's our coyote cousin." Sun Tied pointed down the trail and said "Go!" Then he seized the mule's lead rein.

Seeing the soldier hobbling down the trail, Yellow Wolf took aim, but then, lowering his rifle, he walked to Sun Tied and Stripes Turned Down. He opened the two boxes of rifle ammunition and, as he said later, all the men piled after those two thousand cartridges.

When Lean Elk came up, they lifted out the cannon tube and rolled it down the hillside, hiding it, and then disposed of handspike, rammer, all the implements and ammunition; and spread out moving down the hill. The soldiers, one hundred of them digging frantically with trowel bayonets and butcher knives, were making holes and trenches, determined to make a last stand like General Custer.

Gibbon watched his men dig in, standing up against a tree to get his weight off that punctured and tight-bandaged leg. Lieutenant English said to him, "You know that so-called Captain Catlin can't be trusted to stay here with his volunteers. I heard the man ask 'Who the hell ordered a halt here?' When I said you had, he said he didn't give a damn who ordered it."

"He should know better; he was in the War," said Gibbon. "We've got no other place to go. I'll tell the bastard that myself. Will!"

The Lieutenant jerked upright, then crumpled with his legs turned under him. "Don't tend him, Colonel!" Woodruff shouted, jumping up and holding Gibbon back from bending over the Lieutenant. "Wait 'til we pick the bastard off!"

Lieutenant English lay face up, panting, looking at the Colonel. He straightened out his legs and with a steady, measured voice said, "John. I think. They've done me this time. I'm killed this time."

A soldier called, "He's in that big tree yonder. About four hundred yards."

"Those sons of bitches sure can shoot," said Woodruff angrily. "We can't touch him."

"The hell we can't," said Gibbon, then shouted, "All you men that have a clear view of that tree take aim. Set your sights at four hundred yards. Ready! Fire!" A clap of twenty rifles exploded from the soldiers' holes, sending smoke forward through the trees. "Take aim!" the Colonel shouted as the men worked their chambers. "Ready! Fire!" Another sheet of fire and smoke burst from the twenty rifles, and then someone yelled, "We got him, Colonel!"

An Indian leaped from the tree carrying a rifle in one hand. His other arm hung straight down, plainly broken. Gibbon bent over English and the Lieutenant fixed him with a steady look. "My wife's in Missoula, John."

"She'll nurse you back to health."

"Oh. Not this time." Lieutenant English closed his eyes. "I want to live until I see her once more, John. I want to say goodbye to her, John."

"You will. I'll see to it. I promise you."

*

Red Elk, a Nez Perce who survived the war, years later told in few words what happened as the soldiers waited to be slaughtered. "About sunrise the soldiers dug their hiding places. The fighting stopped awhile when all The People came back to the ruined camp. They all cried when they saw what had been done. Boys, girls, women, children, men who had no guns lay among dead soldiers, burned tipis, and bedding."

The volunteer Bunch Sherrill remembered that day differently. "Several of us young fellows had butcher knives. We had ground them sharp enough to raise some scalps. While on the way we'd take them out and run our thumbs across the edge. Well, the first work I used my scalping knife for was to dig a hole to get into. The next morning, the thing looked like a saw blade."

His brother Tom wrote, "I had picked a trowel bayonet up on the battlefield thinking it might just come in handy. Up on that hillside I got busy, say—and busy's the right word, digging in plain sight of the Indians—which made for dangerous work; I tell you that I hurried some—just what a fellow does who's unsure if he's right with his Maker and don't exactly want close acquaintance with the keeper of the Pit. Bullets struck all around so I laid flat. There wasn't much to do and time passed slow. Finally I crawled a little up the hill, shoving my gun ahead, to George's hole. 'Well, George,' I said, 'seems nothing's doing here. There's not an Indian in sight.' 'Oh, they are out there all right,' he said and when I crawled out to get back to my hole his parting shot was, 'You'll see.' Just then the Indians got funny, tried to pick me off, so I made good time to my hole. Short time later comes this soldier, plunks himself down in my hole and scrootches just as low as he could get. 'Say,' I says, 'can't you see that this hole's just big enough for one if a fellow tries to use his gun?' 'Can't help it,' he says; 'don't try to shoot.' 'Well, what did you come for?' I ask him. 'Aren't you here to shoot Indians?' 'Yes but let the other fellows fight. Lay still.' And then he fell asleep with his mouth wide open snoring. So then a bullet hits a stone which plows a load of gravel, sand, and dirt into his mouth. Say, if ever anyone coughed and snorted right, he did. Once in a while someone would say, 'Another Custer massacre.' Darned talk like that did not make a fellow feel happy you can well believe, especially not in that close place. Later in the morning I went up to visit George again. The soldier says, 'No, you damn fool, no, lie down.' This time I ran instead of crawled but way up the hill an Indian blazed away and cut a trail right through my hair—just missed the piece of ivory in which I had been carrying my brains around for twenty years instead of leaving them home where they'd have been safer than out here in a fight with fellows such as Joseph had at the battle of the Big Hole."

Catlin, captain of the volunteers, wrote that "We lay there all day in the hot sun with no water, and not a mouthful of food except Lieutenant Woodruff's horse, with Indians pelting us from every side, until eleven that night."

Tom Sherrill "noticed from my hole that in Joseph's camp the squaws and papooses were busy gathering the camp outfit—buffalo robes, blankets, and packing up and saddling their horses. They tied their wounded to them and put other wounded on travois and as fast as they could get an Indian strapped onto a pony they would turn it loose. I saw they were badly crippled up with all the wounded they tied to the horses. The squaws were very busy." About Asleep, a boy of fourteen then, said women packed the camp "while some men buried the dead. I saw little babies lying dead. Lots of women killed, lots of children killed, many bad wounded lying all around. What a shame was this! What a shame was this!"

"That evening," Sherrill wrote, "we got anxious for the pack mule's extra ammunition. All that we had was what was in our belts. You bet we tried to make every shot count."

*

The cries of mourning in the village drew the young brave Yellow Wolf back down to look for the dead, while friends of his and Ollokot held the soldiers to their holes. Yellow Wolf found a dead soldier and bent to take the rifle lying next to him. The soldier was not dead, pretended death—and slashed his knife at the brave's face. The warrior leapt away, then swinging his war club cracked the soldier's skull. The young brave took the soldier's gun and ammunition—now a chief, for he had won weapons enough from enemies whom he had killed by hand. But Yellow Wolf had no heart any more for being called a chief, and to his last days he declined the title, either from whites or his own people. His vision of war and of a warrior's life died at Big Hole. "I would not want to hear, I would not want to see again," the men and women crying for their newly dead; wounded children screaming out in pain; and bodies, some warriors lying face to face with soldiers, killed hand to hand.

Two warriors brought a white man out from the willows, a citizen from Bitterroot, a volunteer. He'd thrown away his rifle, trying to pretend he was a non-combatant, but the braves had seen him earlier and found his rifle now. All knew the man—a Stevensville store keeper who had sold them ammunition, whisky, anything they wanted; had smiled, had shown the women calico and sold them flour, some of which blew now scattering like dust. "Kill him," someone shouted, but another man said, "No! He might know something about the One Arm General."

But Otskai, Wild Oats, a cousin of Yellow Wolf, shouted, "Don't waste time—kill him." Rattle on Blanket held the prisoner by his arm but Otskai shot the white man in his grasp. The enraged warrior shouted, "I wouldn't shoot a woman! Had he been a woman I'd have let him go! Women are not to be killed in war. But look around! You see our women lying dead. You see our young girls! Were they warriors, these young women and these girls? These babies you see dead—these old men and these boys—were they warriors? These soldiers, brave soldiers, came upon us when we slept, and then when a few of us began to shoot at them they ran like coyotes! These citizen soldiers! Good friends in the Bitterroot Valley. Traded with us for our gold. Their good words were lies. This citizen was here for our women, to take our scalps, to steal our horses. Why not kill him? Why waste time on him?"

"We knew that he was right," said Yellow Wolf.

Not far away a soldier, wounded, sat up talking to three warriors when a woman crying ran to him and slapped him across the face. The soldier lifted up his booted foot and kicked her with a savage grimace, whereupon one of the warriors shot him instantly. The woman, sobbing, stumbled back to her dead children killed together in their blankets.

Shot through both legs, bugler Michael Gallagher lay near the creek bank when another woman, burying her infant, saw him, took the wide butcher knife she had been using, ran to him and stabbed him three times through the throat.

No heart to go farther through the village, Yellow Wolf turned and walked back toward the hillside. On his way he came across two warriors wrapping up a brave in a wool blanket. The body was Sarpsis Ilppilp, Red Moccasin Tops.

The soldiers thought the sun stood still, so much they wanted darkness so the riflemen surrounding them could not see well enough to shoot. And sometime in the afternoon they caught the first alarming whiff of smoke, the Nez Perce having lit the grass upwind of them to burn them out. But wind itself turned on the warriors and the thin fire died. As evening came, soldiers, some of them still damp from pushing twice in woolen clothes through creek and swale, began to shiver huddled in their holes. Their blankets, food, and medical supplies were parked three miles away back down the trail, well-guarded, hidden, and as good as back at Fort Shaw.

Warriors said they heard the soldiers crying, some of them, the badly wounded raving, calling out to someone only they knew to be there. William English, restless, wanted his boots off; a soldier cut the leather, pulled them off, but English said, "It's no use, no use. I'm done for this time."

Out in the trees now only twenty braves watched silently, heard everything in that high country silence. The chiefs Looking Glass and Ollokot drew them back from the woods and hillside quietly as dawn approached, making a thin line across the creek, up along the far slope.

Joseph and White Bird had moved The People out the afternoon before, and now the rear guard warriors watched as this second dawn began to show them the wreckage of The People's camp below—trampled blankets, charred lodge hides and canvas, broken toys and dolls, smoking pits of baking camas root, dead horses, pots and kettles. A broken line of blackened lodge poles stood like dead crows hanging from a barbed wire fence. The sun rose on their children's belongings.

*

The warriors left a scattering of shots behind them as they slipped away. The soldiers, still hunkered down awaiting an attack by overwhelming numbers and resources, did not stir from their holes for two more hours. And when they did, they saw a dozen mounted Indians come riding loose and easy down the grassy valley. They were not Nez Perce; they wore white cloth strips on their heads and arms: they were the first of Howard's Bannock Indian scouts. They rode into the ruined village and without hesitating went for the fresh graves, disinterring women, stripping off their clothing, cutting the flesh, and slicing off pieces of scalps. Knowing better than to touch the soldiers lying bloated above ground—all left undisturbed except stripped of clothing by The People, not a scalp peeled back and not one body mutilated—the Bannocks looked for Nez Perce warriors.

At last they found the body of the greatest, Wahchumyus, called Rainbow. They laid the body out, admiring it. Not one of the dozen Bannock scouts failed to stab the body with a bayonet or knife. "Where is your strength now, Wahchumyus? Why don't you lift the arm that slew Cheyennes and Lakota like buffalo, strong Wahchumyus?"

They took his scalp, then one of them fastened the ankles with a rope meaning to drag the naked body through the camp, but Gibbon, limping, cursing, bellowing, revolver drawn, ordered the Bannocks to desist. Behind Gibbon several dozen famished, unslept, urine-sodden soldiers stood with rifles ready.

About an hour later, Howard arrived with twenty cavalry, riding ahead of his small army. Reporting that he'd ridden fifty-six miles—it was really twenty-five—to relieve Gibbon, he omitted saying that three days ago, on getting Gibbon's dispatch previous to his attack, he hadn't sent cavalry ahead to help him but had gathered up his army, camped, and started out the next morning. He later claimed he'd rescued Gibbon from destruction. As for John Gibbon, he claimed victory at Big Hole, on grounds that he had driven Joseph from the field. So might the man in Jesus' parable—beaten, robbed, and left for dead—claim to have defeated fair and square the men who robbed him. And Howard, here the Good Samaritan, might claim his terrifying presence drove the thieves in panic back to Jericho.

General Howard found Gibbon's soldiers bathing, catching up on sleep, burying their comrades, and poking through the village for trinkets. "I'm glad to see you, General," Gibbon said. "I hope you have surgeons with you, and some food for my poor men."

"I have—behind me a full day. We've tasted no food ourselves since morning yesterday."

"We'll feed you, then," said Gibbon cheerfully. "Hardtack and coffee, like old times, soon as my train comes up."

"Thank you, Colonel. That will be sufficient, I am sure."

"Well, good enough for a soldier."

After they had eaten their lunch, the two commanders rode through the village. Gibbon made a verbal report and at its conclusion Howard said, "Aceldama." He smiled and added, "Field of blood. Aceldama means field of blood. Like many we have seen before."

"Like none I've seen before, all due respect. At no time in the War did I expect myself and my command to be exterminated by the enemy."

"Well, Colonel, you deserve a rest, and time to mend, God willing. Leave Joseph to me. You and the Seventh Infantry shall go back to Fort Shaw immediately with your wounded, leaving me your cavalry to augment my force."

Gibbon wrote a narrative in verse, a small epic called *A Vision of Big Hole*, meticulously rhymed and measured. Did Homer ever mourn a battle, sail a god-forsaken sea; did Virgil ever fall in hopeless love with loss, or do his duty until it killed his soul; did Milton lose a paradise: never had they put it down to words unless God's silence grieved within them like the death song of the human race itself, perishing of its own nature, and of its own will.

Not all the volunteers from Bitterroot had stayed the night, some slipping off in darkness bringing tales of slaughter, massacre, and personal hardship; but Tom and brother Bunch Sherrill stayed, and Tom stayed much longer, supervising the new park at Big Hole. For most of them it turned out satisfactorily.

That afternoon the General and his son rode over the battlefield, and Howard said, "Guy, let this be a lesson to you. Colonel Gibbon was the best commander, the finest soldier of his grade, in all the Army of the Potomac, perhaps in any army during the late War. If there is any glory in a war, he earned that glory, Son. But here he spent that glory, squandered it. And once you lose your honor and your reputation, you can never get it back. I tell you this—in strictest confidence, of course—Gibbon ordered an attack on sleeping people, children, women, sick and old alike. And he will never live such an action down."

"I mean no disrespect in asking, Sir; but how would you have done it differently? If he had fought them in the open like the Civil War, he would be dead—he and his men."

"Son, I would do exactly what I have been doing all along. The papers accuse me, jeer at me, deride me, for my slowness and my waiting to gather to myself a quantity of men. He attacked his enemy asleep because he had few men. I bring many men. I shall not have to strike a sleeping enemy at dawn. I shall pursue Joseph, surround him with superior numbers, and fight him openly if he so chooses. However, I know the man. He is intelligent. Surrounded, he will know the game is up. He will surrender to me; I shall save the lives of Indians as well as spare the blood of my own men. I shall prevail at length; my critics' mouths shall be stopped and my enemies confounded, please God."

The soldier wounded were brought off in wagons, most of them to Deer Lodge, where civilians prepared to house and nurse them. Lieutenant English and his wife had married only four months ago; she was with child; and Kate rode out to meet his wagon when she heard the wounded from Big Hole were coming in. She climbed into the wagon, smiled at him, and said, "How are you, Willie?" She stayed with him in the wagon all the way to town. Ten days later William English died. His body lies in Indiana next to his faithful Kate, who never remarried.

Two days after Big Hole, Ollokot stood by a shallow grave, the only time this man cried, and said goodbye to Fair Land.

IX

Canyon Creek

The father of the first warrior to die far back in Idaho—Rider's father, Buffalo Song, received no funeral. Shot in the armpit and hip by soldiers at Big Hole, the man could go no farther on his rough, dragging travois. He would not allow The People to delay. His wife, called Healing Tree, had died of gunshot wounds before the sun came up at the Big Hole and now her body lay beneath loose soil under the creek's caved-in bank, perhaps dug up by Howard's Bannock scouts. "Leave me here, my friends. Save my son's wife and their children. I want to walk the Spirit Path tonight." They left him on the trail beside a stunted mountain ash with water and some dry food, and that is where the scouts discovered him. The way they killed him was to stab his throat and watch him bleed to death in pain. They scalped his head and left him in the sun for other scavengers: a circling wheel of ravens showed coyotes and the long-toothed rodents where to find the violated corpse.

A woman died a few days after trying to defend her sister inside their lodge against a volunteer. Her thigh bone broken by a bullet and her skull fractured by an Enfield musket's metal-plated stock, Arrowhead, who had saved Bird Alighting in Idaho, died from her wounds. Her sister and her mother buried her, and The People ran horses across her grave.

Two other women died within a week from illness, but The People could not stop. They crawled under some bushes and died together. A day or two later, a white boy found them lying there. Two squaws, he said, the shock of finding whom put back his growth a year: two dead squaws.

Marking every day with still more mourning and with the bodies of their old and sick, and with their infant children orphaned dry, and with a new hopeless rage, The People kept going—now southward for a hundred miles, trying to reach another resting place, this one called Camas Meadows. Two brothers, Ollokot and Thunder in the Mountains, sang their wives' names on the rising, falling high plains wind.

*

The correspondent Thomas Sutherland recorded in his diary that Howard, by what the General called "my extraordinary marches," had closed the gap to just one day. The infantry had caught up now, and all of Howard's army camped at Camas Meadows, where "Joseph's savages" had camped the night before.

"The General thinks we will engage the hostiles in a day or two. The few remaining Bannock scouts report the Nez Perce seem to drop a couple dead per day. Those dirty scouts of Howard's slash and trample Nez Perce bodies maniacally, like fiends from hell—and then desert us when they tire of taking orders. Wish Joseph would turn on them and settle up." As he was writing, an old acquaintance quietly entered and cleared his throat with mock politeness.

"Why, Trimble! What in the hell are you doing here?"

"I am a reporter, Thomas. I had hoped you would remember."

"I mean, how did you get here?"

"I told you I'd take the road to Missoula and come down from there by horseback. It's no real trick to catch your Christian Soldier. He don't like to march on Sunday, and I expect he thinks every other day is Sunday."

"That's not quite fair, Trimble. Horses are half used up."

"I know. It's wearing on horseflesh to chase women, children, and old men. Even when half of them been shot up by some other army."

"The Indians are driving a big herd of remounts, Trimble."

"I know. How has Howard managed to catch up to them?"

"He took the inside track. He guessed Joseph would hook southwest to follow the river. He guessed right."

"So for the first time in his undistinguished, mediocre life, Otis accomplished something by intelligence. That is like a mule discovering gold."

"You are not fair to Howard. You are still fighting the War."

"If all the Yank generals had been Howards, Tom, I would be reporting on the Congress of the Confederate States of America. But Otis will move. Sherman will make him move."

"What's shummin?"

"My, how Yankees presume upon Southern civility. You know your god damned General Sherman ain't but a hundred miles from here."

"He is?"

"He's touring the new park called Yellowstone, right now as we are talking."

"The Nez Perce are headed for the Yellowstone."

"Sherman ain't afraid. He says the Indians are superstitious. Won't go into the park. Geysers, bubbling mud, steam shooting up out of the ground—all kinds of things to scare Indians."

"He doesn't know the Nez Perce."

"No he does not. He's sent another little army to cut them off somewhere northeast of Yellowstone. A few hundred men under Colonel Samuel D. Sturgis, another damnyankee. Should be enough cavalry to round up your squaws and children."

"That's why Howard gambled."

"Of course that's why. Otis don't want someone else, Sherman's man, to get in on the barbecue first."

"Well, we'll catch them before they get anywhere near Sturgis or the Yellowstone."

"That's not the point. The point is will you let me share your tent? I've got whisky in my saddlebags."

"Southern whisky?"

"No, not real Southern sour mash. But good enough for you, Yank."

"I expect it is."

"Say, Tom, y'all got any of those Bannock scouts around? Ummone buy me a Nez Perce scalp off one of them. Maybe you got one for sale?"

"You are one insulting Rebel, Trimble."

"It's just that I know a lost cause when I see one. I am all for these poor Nez Perce, Tom—as are the people back East, even ones who read your stories praising Howard in his war on these 'savages.' Funny, isn't it, how the more you praise old Otis, the more folks go for Joseph." Sutherland said nothing. Trimble added, "Wonder if you know that, Tom. Wonder if you've somehow figured out a way to please old Otis and stay good with him, while letting people know what's what."

"Yankees are clever, aren't they, Trimble? I will decline to comment and only observe that great poets have it both ways."

"Poets? Your prose, all due respect, is prose, all flat."

"But it will translate well. Think of Virgil. He had it both ways, pleased the Emperor."

"I have read Virgil. He does not translate well."

"I know. All the sadness washes out in English."

"When you build a Rome, you lose your soul."

"It isn't simple."

"Nothing simple about it. Virgil has sadness, you have sarcasm."

"Sarcasm's American. Every story is two stories."

"For you Yanks, maybe. I just tell it straight. Howard's a damnyankee Christian fool. We're all fools."

"I do make an exception in my case."

"I wouldn't be that generous, Thomas. Have you talked to Major Wood?"

"A little."

*

When Yellow Wolf returned to camp he told Chief Ollokot that only Bannock scouts were close. "I want to kill soldiers," the chief said quietly. "Look at us. See what has happened to us."

The People now lay on buffalo and blanket robes; no lodges stood with smoke drifting up from open vent flaps. Few men and women talked, and children lay so listless that the families seemed ill.

Next morning Yellow Wolf, twenty braves, and three chiefs rode out to find white supplies. What they found was a plodding wagon train—eight teams and drivers with a few men riding off to the sides. There was no chase, no hopeless hurtling and careening as drivers, shouting, lashed their whips over the horses' heads and stung the tall mules with rawhide. No: the chiefs rode to the first wagon and stopped the train, then talked to the gathered white men. "I don't think they meant to kill us," said one survivor later. "Not until the braves got into all the whisky we carried."

The chiefs said they would take supplies; they needed everything that they could get. Yellow Wolf had ridden farther back to scout, but when he heard gunshots he galloped forward, finding five dead men, all white, and a dozen drunk young warriors—and then another shot, this one behind a wagon heavy with whisky barrels. "I shot him!" shouted Five Snows, lurching out and grabbing for a horse's harness—but the horses were not there, had been cut loose and picketed. He fell, and kneeling, shouted, "I shot Stripes Turned Down! He wouldn't let me have his whisky! There is plenty of whisky!"

Ollokot grasped his war shirt and pulled him up.

"What have you done? Answer!"

"He has murdered Ketalkpoosmin!" shouted Red Elk, who had run behind the wagon.

"What?" cried Ollokot, both hands holding up the staggering brave. The chief struck him across the face and threw him on the ground. "We are killing each other now? I would kill you too, Five Snows! I would kill you now, except we need every warrior!"

The chief turned to Yellow Wolf. "We chiefs and Ketalkpoosmin were trying to pour out their whisky. Now we shoot and stab each other. Coyote Flints has tried to murder Bear Walking with a knife!"

"I will finish Ketalkpoosmin's work," said Yellow Wolf. "I and my cousin Otskai!"

"Otskai is drunk," said Ollokot.

Two Chinese men sat in a wagon box crying. "What are we going to do with them?"

"We will let them go back to their grandmothers." He turned a grim smile toward Yellow Wolf. "They are not white men."

*

The night that The People camped at Camas Meadows, Black Hair, awake in pain from gunshot wounds still festering from Big Hole, had a vision. He saw warriors riding back to Camas Meadows when the soldiers camped there. He saw warriors in the darkness rounding up the sleeping soldiers' horses, driving them away. Said Hair Combed Over Eyes, "So when our scouts brought word that One Arm General had stopped at Camas Meadows, our old camp, the chiefs considered what Black Hair saw. We would ride back at night, attack the soldiers' camp and take their horses and pack mules, just as the vision foretold."

The One Arm General had caught up fast; The People now were traveling with wounded, so they must find a way to slow the soldiers, make them walk and carry all they have. Peopeo Tholekt—Bird Alighting—rode with Bull Bait and Rattle Blanket back to where the soldiers marched, saw them pitch camp, and Bird Alighting sent the other two to tell the chiefs. When Bird Alighting finally rode up the trail The People made, he found only warriors. The families had left, had gone ahead led by Joseph and White Bird. All the younger warriors stayed to fight. They now sat smoking, bringing their minds to calm and battle, praying their Wayakin to help them kill and stay alive, to help them do what they must do. "They were quiet," Peopeo Tholekt said. "Smoking silently, not singing war songs. 'What is the news?' they asked."

Looking Glass and Two Moons listened to the scout's report. "We'll strike them tonight," said Looking Glass. "We'll be all right. All we want is horses."

The Warriors, led by Looking Glass, Lean Elk, Two Moons, Red Elk, and Ollokot, rode back toward Camas Meadows quietly. The chiefs prohibited the lighting of pipes, loud talk, and especially the firing of guns. The night was clear and in the starry dim light the Nez Perce chiefs and braves—riding straight and easy with their rifles laid across their tough ponies' withers, ghostly spotted Appaloosas with half-dark faces—one last time returned, a short ride back along The People's trail, riding for the last time to the attack, warriors raising rifles high, the high coyote cry terrifying enemies again, war cries cutting night like arrows, cutting the cool late August night. But now, faces grim and blank, no warrior wore war paint; the ponies were not streaked with black and red across their chests, their eyes not circled. One more time to the attack.

*

"My Dearest Wife," wrote John Fitzgerald.

How far we are from one another now! Hundreds of miles stretch out between us now! But soon it will be over, rest assured. We know the Nez Perce camp to be a short day's march ahead. The poor, exhausted Indians have slowed to nurse their wounded from the Big Hole fight, and General Howard told me just an hour ago, 'The hostiles are about played out. They leave their dead and wounded on the trail. There's no fight in them any more.' I now see wisdom in his methods. I think that we shall round them up like sheep tomorrow or the next day, God willing. But for now, I am well, am fit and trim on government repasts of stringy beef and hardtack laid up for a rainy day when North and South were disagreeing back East. Rest well, my Dear. I know that I shall."

*

Close to the sleeping soldiers' camp, Otskai, cousin of the warrior Yellow Wolf, kicked his horse and galloped forward. "Looking Glass!"

"Hold your voice down!" Ollokot whispered fiercely. The young brave, quieter but urgently, said, "I will take my friends and ride to One Arm General's tent. I, Otskai, will kill him!"

"How will you know which tent is his?" asked Two Moons.

"Biggest one!"

"No, you fool!" said Looking Glass. "We need all our men alive! The soldiers will kill you and your friends!"

"Ha!" said Otskai.

"Wild Oats, put down your rifle and think," said Ollokot. "The whites will only find another general. They might replace him with a soldier."

"Young fool," repeated Looking Glass. "Go back and do as you are told!"

The enraged brave turned his horse and trotted back to Yellow Wolf and Red Spy, saying to them, "They will see what I will do!"

Looking Glass and Ollokot held the warriors now, awaiting word from scouts whom they had sent ahead. "The soldiers sleep," reported Blanket Rattle. "Their guards sleep, too."

"The poor soldiers," said Looking Glass. "They must be tired."

"The whites think we will not strike them."

"They think we are weak," said Two Moons.

"We are," said Looking Glass. "But we will strike them."

The chiefs divided, each of them taking a company of warriors. Ollokot told Yellow Wolf and his other fighting men, "The scouts saw two herds, one on this side of their camp, one on the other. We go for the farther herd." He looked at the men's faces. "Be careful. We must all return."

"Why are we doing this if we cannot kill soldiers?" Otskai asked.

"If we kill some of them, the rest will follow us. If we take their mules and horses they will all stop."

But as the soldiers' camp came into sight, a little lake of pup tents pale under the stars, a half dozen larger wall tents here and there like mother hens, and two dark masses of animals, Otskai became excited. Four companies of quiet warriors trotted toward the two sleeping herds, and Otskai said, "I will shoot into that big tent. Maybe I will kill Howard!" He fired from horseback and the shot, a startling crash, woke horses, sleeping sentries, and men lying in tents and in the open.

"Who fired that shot?" said Bird Alighting, Red Elk, and twenty chiefs and warriors all at once. But Ollokot and Two Moons instantly raised up their rifles, fired, and lifted war cries, howling, yipping, kicking up their ponies, and all the warriors charged the closer herd, firing and galloping, singing out the terrifying cries.

The soldiers woke, some going for their rifles, some hugging earth, some running toward the tents of officers. The sentries ran for cover or the tents, and Bird Alighting said he heard some soldiers crying like babies. Officers emerged from tents lifting suspenders, shouting, cursing, firing their revolvers, and the men around them dashed here and there, fired rifles, shouted orders of their own.

Ollokot and Two Moons stopped their companies and began to shoot at firing soldiers as the other chiefs and warriors got the near herd milling. Riding hard and shouting, now the warriors formed a line behind the herd and on two sides, driving the reluctant beasts forward up the trail The People had made the day before.

"Come on! Come on!" Looking Glass shouted, riding up beside Ollokot. "Let's go! We must get out of here! Let's go!"

Howard's thousand infantry, artillery, cavalry, and scouts were now awake and on their feet. Back toward the coming dawn the warriors drove the noisy, stumbling animals, impatient now to get them moving faster ahead of them. And then, some distance up the trail as the first faint light began to raise a gray ribbon in the east, the warriors saw what they were driving: mules.

"Just mules!" said Yellow Wolf. "Only mules!"—disgust still present in his voice decades later.

That morning Howard got cavalry to horse and sent three companies to chase the hostiles. They stopped and thought about it when the warriors turned on them; they sounded recall and pounded back to Howard. That did it for the General: he couldn't pack his stuff. The wagons had no mules, the packs lay on the ground. The General went to his tent and wrote a note to Sherman, offering to block the Nez Perce rear, suggesting that Sturgis on the Yellowstone take up the chase, his fresh cavalry being better suited for pursuit.

The General of the Army, William Tecumseh Sherman, got the note two days later, grimaced, crumpled it like dry leaves. "Like hell! Like hell I'll let that coward quit the chase." The General of the Army's message reached the One Arm General late the next day as Sutherland conferred with Major Wood outside the major's tent. They saw Howard reach for the message from the currier, thank him, then read the note.

His face turned dark and agitated and as Sutherland had seen before when Howard became angry, the General's features seemed to converge, making his face smaller. Sherman's message read in part, "If you are tired, then give command to some young energetic man." The Christian Soldier stalked into his tent and wrote a message back: "I never flag. It was the command"—just as at Chancellorsville it was the General's men who were at fault when Stonewall Jackson's charge shattered the corps whose sentries had sent repeated warnings to Howard at headquarters. "It was the command, including the most energetic young officers, that were worn out and wearied by a most extraordinary march. You need not fear for the campaign. You cannot doubt my pluck and energy."

Then Howard made a shopping trip, riding up to Virginia City and buying the town out of clothing, food, wagons and mules and charging it to Uncle Sam. It seems the Congress of the United States of America had failed to allocate a single dollar that year for the Army out West. Therefore all of Howard's men were marching not only for free, but were doing it in their old duds and sleeping under last year's fashion as far as ratty blankets were concerned. The Nez Perce War was fought and won on credit—a tradition as old as men at war. The Duke of Normandy once pawned his land to England's king to finance a crusade, and for a hundred years both countries paid the interest with a war that was ended only by a dreamer maiden's sacrifice. The crusade came to nothing in the end, an outcome guaranteed since Cain saluted Abel with a stone.

> Dream Catcher, sift true dreams from false,
> and have mercy on the dreamers who awake in history's sacrificial fire.
> Sing Joseph alive, and the Nimiipuu, bearing
> through the waning summer into chill autumn
> the closing of their paradise, wandering toward winter and night.
> Sing of the first Americans
> carrying their children back into snow.

Sherman knew no sounder principle than death, telling Howard now to dog the Nez Perce to the end and execute their leaders. Meanwhile he ordered Colonel Sturgis and his companies of Custer's Seventh Cavalry to move above the Yellowstone and cut the Nez Perce off as they rode to the north of the Park's boundary. They will avoid the Park itself. "Their superstitious minds," he wrote, "fill with all hell's terror at hot springs and geysers."

That day the Nez Perce entered the Park, a hundred twenty families and two thousand horses, together with all their cattle, dogs, and superstitions—driving straight for Old Faithful and the high country beyond.

"The sum of Howard's strategy," wrote Major Shaw years later, "was troops, more troops, and troops." But Sturgis had three hundred sixty veterans. It was enough. He moved his column north: no matter how the Nez Perce got past Yellowstone, they'd have to meet him on the other side.

*

A group of tourists from Montana went to see the geysers at the Park— a married couple and some friends and family camping for a week and looking at the bubbling mud, the deep-cut little canyons, rising steam, and wonders of the animal world: the grazing buffalo, huge-footed moose, the noble-headed elk, and graceful deer.

George Cowan said to Emma, "What do you think now of this great country, hah? We made the right decision coming West after all. You do agree."

"I think I do, but I still miss society a little. The scenery is grand."

"Prosperity is beautiful, remember that. Back East I'd still be clerking in a store, but here I own the store. It's everybody's dream except for—Jesus Christ!"

A cavalcade of twenty mounted warriors, some painted for war, rode out into the wide meadow where the tourist party had set out their tents and gear.

"Wild Indians!" Emma exclaimed, and held both hands over her mouth.

"I'll handle this," said Andrew Arnold. "If you don't show fear, they will respect you and leave you be."

The group of young warriors led by Yellow Wolf and Otskai slowed to a walk and talked it over. "Let us ride to them and take what food they have," said Otskai. "I can smell their bacon cooking."

"Let's kill them," Yellow Wolf said. "All whites are at war against us now. Murderers."

"No," said Barefooted Calf. "We take them to the chiefs and what the chiefs say is what we do with them."

"We'll talk to them and then kill them all. I have had enough."

No more was said until as they drew closer Otskai said, "Two women. We can't kill them all."

"We'll let the women go," said Yellow Wolf. "Or else we would be no better than whites."

They rode up to the two campfires, dismounted, and immediately Arnold walked to Yellow Wolf and offered him his hand. The warrior shook it, saying later, "Now I couldn't kill him—took his hand and looked him in the eye. I saw that he was just like other men."

"What can we do for you?" asked Arnold. "Are you men hungry? You're welcome to have breakfast with us—bacon, flapjacks, coffee, buttermilk."

"We will eat," said Otskai.

"You are welcome to eat all the food you want."

"Do you have flour?" asked Otskai, whose English was the best of all the group.

"You bet we have," said Arnold. "Take some back to your camp."

"We'll take it all."

"Of course. What else do you folks need?"

Trying not to blink, Otskai said, "Sugar, salt."

"And butter?"

"No butter."

"Well help yourselves, and have a bite to eat."

"If we eat together, we are friends," said Yellow Wolf in his language. "I won't eat."

"This is different," Otskai said. "This isn't eating; it is stealing."

"What are you saying?" Arnold asked. "You may have everything you want. All you have to do is ask."

"We will help ourselves," said Otskai.

Here Emma Cowan and her sister Ida moved together and held hands. Several warriors walked up to the wagons and started lifting out the bags of sugar, salt, and flour.

"See here!" Cowan said to Arnold. "We need all the supplies we have to get us back to Helena and Radersburg."

"Now George," said Arnold, clearing his throat for meaning, "it's the Christian thing to do. Share." He looked at Yellow Wolf and Otskai, making sure they understood.

"With other Christians maybe. I didn't bring all this to share it with a bunch of Indians!"

"Understand, George. We can buy more supplies on the way."

But Cowan boldly walked to his wagon and pulled his rifle from the bed. Behind him a young brave began to lift a sack of flour. Cowan, both hands on his rifle like a staff, pushed the Indian away from the wagon. A warrior named Bunched Lightning spoke quietly to Otskai, saying, "Don't shoot him down. We'll bring them and their wagons to the chiefs."

"Break camp!" said Cowan loudly, at which command the tourists tried to act as though no trouble were at hand. The warriors nonchalantly joined the campers, carrying their items to and from the wagons.

Emma later wrote, "We didn't much appreciate the Indians enjoying confiscated property. One young chap laughing dashed past us with several yards of pink swansdown wrapped turban-like around his head. Another tied a piece of good mosquito netting on his horse's tail."

Meanwhile Andrew Arnold handed bags of salt and sugar to any warrior who would take them.

"Stop that!" Cowan ordered angrily but Arnold waved him off and said, "Don't be a fool, George. Look behind you."

A line of thirty Nez Perce warriors walked their horses out from the tree line. All of them were watching with their rifles held resting slanted, stocks against the thigh, hands gripped upon the trigger. Lean Elk quietly dismounted, as did several others.

Both Cowan and Arnold turned to him but George spoke first. "See here! You have authority over these bucks. Tell them to let us leave in peace and leave our property alone."

Arnold shook his head. Lean Elk first looked at Arnold, then addressing Cowan said, "These men do not do what I tell them. Each one does what he thinks best."

"Bah!" Cowan barked. "You are a chief. A chief's a chief. Don't lie to me."

"Shut mouth!" said Yellow Wolf.

"And who the hell are you?"

"He is my brother!" Otskai said, his rifle shaking in his hand.

All of them stood silently, looking at each other, until Arnold broke in: "You men are welcome to anything you need. Take whatever you want. What is ours"—he held his hands to his chest and then opened them outward toward Lean Elk—"is yours."

Already several warriors had resumed inspection of the campers' goods. Disgusted, Cowan spat at Arnold's feet.

Beside him Emma took her husband's arm and said, "I don't want you killed on our anniversary. Let them have it all; it doesn't matter." He looked at her and held his peace.

After a few minutes Lean Elk walked to Arnold. He pointed back to where a large grey horse stood tethered and said, "That is a good horse. Go and get him." Arnold went and Lean Elk followed him. When they got to the big horse Lean Elk put his hand upon the saddle horn and pulled as if to test its seating. His other hand he laid on Arnold's shoulder saying, "You get into the woods. Stay there." He shook Arnold's hand and said, "Go quick," giving him a push.

Arnold scuttled crouching toward the woods and when he got there knelt behind a tree and watched. The Indians rounded up the travelers, ordered both women, Cowan, and Frank Carpenter to mount, then pointed all the other men to drive wagons. As Arnold watched, another man crept backwards toward the woods while the warriors, preoccupied, got the tense cavalcade into motion. The two tourists, walking through the nights to keep from freezing, went three days on pond water and crickets, reaching Howard's cavalry encamped near Henry's Lake.

Meanwhile, the rest of the tourists were escorted toward the Nez Perce camp. Emma rode beside her thirteen year old sister close behind George, observing that what were to her the worst looking Indians were riding nearest them. Years later Yellow Wolf recalled that both the full grown and the small women were good-looking.

Ida recalled that when they reached the Nez Perce village, squaws took the women from the rest, gave them both supper—bread, and bitter tea made from the bark of willows—insisting kindly—very kindly, Ida said—that both eat well and get rest. They laid out buffalo robes and then the squaws lay down around them, guarding them, watching through the night. But neither girl had eaten—could not eat—because of what had happened on the way to the village.

Two young braves had come galloping up beside them—one raised his rifle and shot Cowan from his horse; the other shot a man named Oldham, who dropped to the ground shot through the left shoulder. Emma leapt from her horse and ran to Cowan, bending over him and lifting up his head. Immediately dismounting warriors surrounded the two, and teen-aged Ida vaulted from her horse but found, as if dreaming, that terror petrified her legs. She struggled, pushing, forcing forward, a pasty froth exuding from her mouth.

Emma stammered, "Ge-George! Where are you h-hit, Ge-George?" The man groaned that his leg was all shattered, and Emma bent across him with her arms around his neck. A warrior grabbed her hand and jerked her up from him just as another put a pistol to Cowan's forehead and pulled the trigger, blowing bone and bits of bloody scalp into the air.

Emma passed out, falling on her husband; Ida screamed and tried to run out from the circle of the crowding warriors. One turned, ran after her and caught her by the throat. He held her, choking her, and as he loosed his grip she ground her teeth into his hand—getting, she said, some satisfaction in exchange for two weeks' bruising on her throat. A brave named Red Scout pushed the other braves away—said later that he had no heart to see women abused, no matter what the soldiers did at Big Hole.

A moment later Lean Elk jumped down into the crowd and got the braves to back away from the bodies and the women, whom he put into a wagon. They rode sobbing, leaving the two men lying on the ground behind them, thinking they were dead. The cavalcade, flanked both sides by warriors eating flapjacks, bacon, and corn bread, pushed for the Indian camp.

Both wounded men recovered consciousness, and spent the next three days and nights surviving until Howard's scouts found them. Twenty-four years later, George and Emma returned to their old campsite and had a couple of photographs taken.

> So is History a photograph of what we do today:
> we meet ourselves, and do what we have always done.

The first white people on record to meet Native Americans, the Norse who landed on the coast around the year one thousand, called the red ones *skraelings,* meaning wretches, and immediately drove them away, brandishing their battle axes, metal rimmed shields, and waving their bright short swords. The future Indians were shocked to see a stout and warlike woman lift her arm, bare one fat breast, and slap it with the flat of her sword. The little arrows the red men shot were nothing on the Vikings' shields and steel helmets. A saga testifies to this, a heart-worn memory and mirror of a cold and restless North Atlantic dream, prophetic like the Nez Perce War itself of what the autumn world can become.

*

John Redington, a scout for Howard, saw a Nez Perce woman lying by the trail the Indians had worn in eastern Yellowstone: she lay half-propped by blankets on a large buffalo robe. Beside her lay an empty water bottle; its glass in the high sun was what had caught the scout's attention first. "I came to her," he later wrote, "dismounted, and she closed her eyes, expecting, I guess, that I would put a bullet through her head. Instead I emptied my canteen of water into her bottle, handed it to her. You should have seen the look of unbelief that crossed her face. She nodded thanks a little, drank some water best she could but was so weak she couldn't get much down. I took it from her hand and placed the bottle standing up next to her. She must have told those people just to leave her and go on. I expect she had no family but you can't tell with Indians. A few hours later I was with General Howard making my report when a couple of his Bannock scouts came by on horseback. One of them laughing held up a scalp to show another Indian— it had fresh blood and long white hair. I told Howard about the woman and he got so irritated by it that he called those Bannocks over and in no uncertain terms he let them have it verbally. Then he issued orders that no more prisoners were to be killed but brought to him. All those Bannocks took French leave, a few at a time, and all of them were gone before we left Yellowstone Park."

A fellow scout named Fisher also had enough of voluntary service with the cavalry. "U. S. too slow for business," he observed. After these departures Howard found new volunteers: Lakota and some Cheyenne—Nez Perce enemies who wanted in on the kill.

*

"We did not want to kill those women," Yellow Wolf remembered later. Lean Elk approached Emma Cowan when he heard her weeping. "I don't cry," he told her, lifting up his war shirt and showing her his wound. In front he showed an entry hole, then turned. In back, she wrote, there was an "ugly, ragged" exit wound. "How he escaped blood-poisoning, I cannot say. The bullet had gone through his lung, had not healed yet, and still," she said, "his voice could be heard half a mile. How he could harangue the camp with such a wound was a wonder to us."

The harangue that she heard was a meeting among the chiefs. When it was over, Lean Elk came to the tourists. Emma's brother called him Poker Joe: "Joe came to us, saying, 'Send home now. Send'm sisters home. You too. Your sisters ride, you walk.' I assented," wrote Frank Carpenter.

The Nez Perce chose two slow horses so that the tourists would not reach Howard too soon with information, and that is why Frank was made to walk, said Yellow Wolf.

Lean Elk started them away with speed, however. "Joe now led his horse," Frank wrote, "and taking his gun bade us get on behind him. We started for the river, and reaching Mud Spring, Joe asked me if I had matches. He gave me some when I dismounted, saying, 'Now my friends, good-bye. You go down river, way down. No stop. Go all night. No stop. You go three days, get'm Bozeman. You go all night. You no get'm Bozeman, Injun catch'm you. Me want you tell'm people in Bozeman me no fight no more now. Me no want fight Montana citizens. Me no want fight Montana soldiers. Me want peace. Me no want fight no more now. You tell'm Bozeman people."

The next day the three tourists found out why Injun tell'm go all night, no stop. A company of cavalry from Bozeman found the three and made a military supper for them. As they were packing up, a man came running toward them up the trail. He was from Helena, a tourist like the Carpenters, but with a larger group. At noon that day, these ten white men had been attacked and two men killed. One of the white men had escaped and later in the day found an abandoned house. As he stood in its doorway, six warriors rode up and stopped a pistol shot away. They sat their horses until Barefoot Bull told Yellow Wolf, "I do not like that man. My three young brothers were not warriors. They and my sister all were killed at Big Hole. It was men just like this one who did that killing of my family. He is nothing but a killer, to become a soldier sometime. We will kill him now. I am a man! I am going to shoot him! When I fire you shoot after me." He fired and clipped the white man's arm; another warrior, Shooting Thunder, fired a bullet through the white man's heart and he fell down dead.

*

Colonel Sturgis had been waiting farther up the river at Clark's Fork Canyon, where he thought the Nez Perce must come through because the Absaroka Mountains to the north, impassable even in summer, blocked the northeast corner of the Park. After a week of quiet lonesomeness the Colonel, shot through with agitated inspiration, realized, or so he thought, that the Nez Perce had come out of the park still farther south, so he rushed his whole command southeast toward the Shoshone River. In his absence all The People, with their horses, cattle, dogs, and everything, went into, through, and out of Clark's Fork Canyon quietly and headed north into Montana.

Sturgis, now with time to think things through again, woke up to the fact that too much time had passed—the Indians had fooled him somehow, done something uncanny, because the only other things they could have done aside from going through him were to double back into Howard or go through the mountains. Howard had sent no report of battle; of course the mountains were impassable. The People had gone through the mountains.

The Absarokas were a small version of the Bitterroots: it had not been easy. Even Emma Cowan, with Howard's column now, noticed when the tourists crossed the Nez Perce trail that here and there trees were smeared with horses' blood. The trail was narrow, and before The People got to Clark's Fork Canyon they had clambered down a path so steep that horses slid on their haunches.

Sturgis rushed back toward the park. What he found was not only the Nez Perce trail but Howard's tracks as well. Sturgis was now behind everybody.

His hard-working cavalry mounts were pretty well used up; fortunately not much energy was needed to catch Howard. This time he'd slowed his pace to let his supplies from Helena arrive. Lucullus Jones, whose companies of cavalry led Howard's column, rode side by side with Howard along the fork of Yellowstone that led toward the canyon Sturgis should be blocking. The officers had been discussing Sturgis, how his lone force might even now be standing off charges made by Nez Perce warriors desperate to open a way through. "We haven't heard a thing," Howard observed. "I find that strange and unaccountable."

"He might have sent out couriers, General. The Nez Perce are between Sturgis and us. Couriers might not have gotten through."

"Colonel, I choose not to take so dark a view."

"General, it's Seventh Cavalry again."

"I know. I understand your anxiety."

"Do you think it might be prudent, General, to accelerate our pace somewhat?"

"My scouts would bring word if there were fighting up ahead. I am confident that Sturgis at this very moment is athwart Joseph's path and he is halted. Knowing Joseph, I expect he's scouting for some route around the Canyon. We will strike him from behind tomorrow. I think we'll hear from Sturgis to that or similar effect."

Not long after, a messenger came pounding up the column. "Sergeant Louis Abbot, Sir," the trooper said, saluting. "Seventh Cavalry."

"Seventh!" Howard exclaimed. "Have you encountered difficulty finding us?"

"Colonel Sturgis sends his compliments—requests permission to ride forward and—"

"Forward!" Howard cried. "Where is he?"

"Behind your column roughly two miles, Sir."

"Behind!"

"Yes, Sir. Colonel Sturgis requests permission to ride forward and confer."

Howard looked at Jones and then back at the adjutant. "Tell Colonel Sturgis I will see him now!"

"Yes, Sir!" The adjutant saluted, wheeled his horse, and pounded wearily back down the lengthy column.

"You may feel free, Sir, to make some impolite ejaculation."

"I never use profanity, Colonel."

"This would be occasion for exception, General. My ears are quite attuned."

"No, Sir. I never use profanity."

"Sir, consistency is the mind's hobgoblin."

"I know my Emerson, Colonel, and you have misquoted him. 'A foolish'—note that—'*foolish* consistency is the hobgoblin of little minds.' To refrain from swearing always is not a foolish consistency. 'Swear not at all,' the Scripture saith. 'Let your answer be simply yea or nay.'"

"Well General, please feel free to say yea or nay at the top of your voice."

"No!" cried Howard, pointing back behind them. "What is Sturgis doing behind us?"

"I'll drop back when he arrives, Sir."

"Colonel. Colonel. I wish you to be present. Perhaps your presence will assist me in controlling emotion."

"Yes, Sir." Jones produced a slender metal flask. "Care for a drink, Sir? Always calms me."

Howard did not answer, riding stiffly looking straight ahead. Jones replaced the flask.

*

"My Dear Wife," John Fitzgerald wrote.

"I trust that all is well in our dear home away from home. I have some news, my darling. I have been transferred to the command of Colonel Sturgis and his Seventh Cavalry. They lack a surgeon and tomorrow we will separate from Howard. The officers in Howard's little army are almost one and all disgusted with following Indians to no purpose other than to grandify a general's reputation. But this evening some Cheyenne scouts reported that the Nez Perce are only about one and a half day's ride ahead, and Sturgis has orders to go forward at all speed and bring Joseph to battle. I almost wish the Indians would get away, but it looks as though there will be bloody work. September now, its second week. The trees are yellow; the year ends so early here. A thousand miles away on beans and hay. . . ."

*

Sturgis was a round-faced man with curly gray hair and a Van Dyke beard and moustache. At fifty-five, the man was sensitive about his age; added to that was his chagrin over Indians outwitting him: therefore he took the Seventh Cavalry with all speed forward, glad that Howard added fifty cavalry of his and two mountain howitzers like Gibbon brought to Big Hole.

The Colonel's reputation had had its ups and downs over his long career. A West Point graduate, he went to Mexico with Scott as a lieutenant, got captured, and sat the war out. In the 1850's he fought a lot of Indians—Comanches, Kiowas, Apaches—and then brought that experience into the Civil War. A general of volunteers, he led his brigade at Antietam, and that December endured the worst debacle Mr. Lincoln's army ever suffered: Fredericksburg. But then at Brice's Crossroads he got routed and was obliged to spend the balance of the War on leave. Embarrassed through five years of tedium, he got another chance, put in command of the new Seventh Cavalry, though that chance brought an aggravation: his second in command was George A. Custer. And then George Custer got half of the command annihilated on the Greasy Grass and James G. Sturgis, the commander's son, was found among the mutilated dead.

So Samuel Sturgis was no soft touch when it came to Indians. He had been fooled by these Nez Perce, but when it came to fighting he had it in him to kill like any man. His own department head, not Howard but the cool, efficient Nelson A. Miles stationed at Fort Lincoln in east Montana, had told the Colonel not to ask the Nez Perce to surrender but to strike them hard—"a severe blow"—and that is what the Colonel intended. The odds were two to one, his soldiers over warriors.

He left Howard two days back, writing the fateful message to his rival, Colonel Miles, requesting him to take the field and cut the Nez Perce off before they crossed Montana and reached the Canadian border. Sturgis meanwhile, the night of twelfth September, camped along the main branch of the Yellowstone. Not knowing how well he'd done, the Colonel got moving early the next day, and at noon arrived at a ford of the Yellowstone near Canyon Creek. But he was tired and his men were tired. Convinced by silence that the Nez Perce once more had eluded him, he rested his command, prepared to write to Miles confessing his failure, and rued the fact that Howard's cavalry and artillery had worn out early in the morning, those fifty troopers and the two guns at the mercy of their used-up horses' feet. Sturgis sent his Crow scouts out to try to find the Nez Perce trail, and after his three hundred fifty men crossed through the ford he sat them all down.

Perhaps it was while he was asking powers and principalities why he, Sturgis, of all men, must be cursed, that a Crow scout came galloping—said the Nez Perce were coming, all of them. He'd passed within about three miles of them in the evening dark. And now a mile of Nez Perce families and all they had were coming straight at them. Maybe the powers and principalities were letting him have one more chance. Perhaps the Christian Soldier Howard would consider this a miracle, for Sturgis certainly had not known until now that he stood square athwart the hostiles' route to Canada, and best of all they didn't know it either.

*

For days a scattered group of warriors rode along the valley of the Yellowstone. Otskai, his cousin Yellow Wolf, Bunched Lightning, Hawk Heart, and Lying in Water scouted wide before the families across familiar long plains that used to run with buffalo. One morning Yellow Wolf, alone, unslept the night before—watching and listening—led his horses to a creek and sat down to let them drink. He leaned against a dwarf willow's trunk, warm in the sun though the wind was cold, and in a moment dozed, and slept. Below the bank, his horses crossed the creek and grazed on prairie grass.

The sun rose higher as Yellow Wolf slept; and then the horses pricked up their ears. A voice far off told Yellow Wolf, "Look out—a grizzly!" And then again, as in a dream, "Grizzly close to you!" He opened heavy lids, the voice still in his mind; then when he turned his head at a noise of heavy snuffing, low and near, Yellow Wolf saw him—a big male grizzly, glinting golden, a shaggy hill, enormous head. The warrior pulled the hammer of his rifle as he sprang to his feet. But the bear, standing, roared and raised his claws. Just as the shaggy chest touched the muzzle of the gun the brave pulled the rigger—both the man and golden *hohots* falling backward. The warrior dropped the rifle, pulled his war club, flung himself up against the rolling grizzly, swinging down against the upturned ear. Kneeling down onto the coarse hair, Yellow Wolf raised his club again but the bear exhaling with a gust lay dead. The warrior stood and backed on stiff legs—stood looking at the stretched-out beast. He thought, "I have been close to death! I have been this close." Then he remembered Wayakin telling him no bullet would kill him. And he thought, "I will live through this war."

He looked across the stream where his two horses stood, heads raised, and knowing they would not come near the *hohots* he did not call to them but took up his rifle. Looking one more time at the grizzly, he waded to the other side.

*

That afternoon as Yellow Wolf and Otskai rode together through the ridge country, they saw thin smoke of a campfire snake above a little rise ahead of them. They broke into a run and as they galloped over the ridgeline they saw two white men—and one of them was looking right at them.

"We're going to shoot them!" Otskai said. "All white men here are enemies."

He raised his rifle just as the whites ran for their horses, fired, and one of the two white scouts—prospectors until recruited by the Cavalry—fell crumpled to the ground, his horse shying. The two braves rode down the slope as the other prospector, a tall man all in buckskin, swung up into his saddle and spurred hard.

At dead run following, Otskai shouted to his cousin, "Go on, Brother! My horse is giving out! Grab him by the neck! Jerk him off his horse!"

Yellow Wolf urged his pony, following the buckskin rider across the golden-brown plain. The white man looked back, and when the brave was riding close he jumped down off his horse. Momentum threw him down, but rolling with his rifle he came up on one knee, aimed the rifle just as Yellow Wolf wheeled his pony; both men fired, the brave's shot striking unseen somewhere but the white man's bullet creasing Yellow Wolf across the scalp. The warrior pitched from his horse stunned and bleeding.

Groggy on his hands and knees, the warrior looked up as the white man worked his rifle. "So this is death," thought Yellow Wolf, the muzzle of the white man's gun black and looking bigger than a grizzly's maw. "My Wayakin deceived me! Wayakin was wrong."

The white man, grimacing, tried to force the hammer back and Yellow Wolf, his vision spinning, thought how very slow the white man was, how long death was taking. As everything turned black he heard his cousin's war cry. Otskai, kicking his faltering pony, saw the white man on one knee working at his rifle, saw his cousin topple on his side, fired wildly at the white man, missed him, and then at full gallop struck him with the swung barrel of his gun. He heard and felt the dull crack of the white man's skull, let out a war cry, and leaped to the ground running to his cousin.

He lifted Yellow Wolf's head up—whose face was streaked with bloody streams from the scalp wound—and the brave came around. "Otskai," he said, then said, "Otskai, Brother, why am I alive? Why did the white man not shoot?"

"Strange!" exclaimed Otskai. He lowered Yellow Wolf's head gently and turned, looking at the white man lying face down, rifle beside him. "I think I see," said Otskai. He went to the rifle, picked it up, and brought it to his cousin. "Your bullet bit the white man's rifle." Otskai held the lock mechanism near his cousin's face. "The hammer is bent sideways, Brother!"

The young brave saw it, whispered "Wayakin," then closed his eyes. And then he said, "Never seen so many crows."

"What, Brother?" Otskai cried. "Brother, are you all right?"

Yellow Wolf said softly, "In the sky behind you. Turn around."

Otskai looked, and in the distance seventy or eighty crows were winging in a broken stream across the sky like cavalry strung out at full gallop. Otskai turned back. "I see," he said. "I thought the bullet made you crazy."

"Wayakin said nothing about me being crazy."

*

Two days passed without the warriors seeing soldiers or their scouts; but then, the morning of the day that the Seventh Cavalry forded the Yellowstone, the scouting party discovered a new stagecoach station built that summer on a bank of Canyon Creek. The warriors rode together five abreast, their ponies at the dog trot, watching for the station to discharge its white man out the back, and sure enough, a man dressed in trousers, union suit, and red suspenders scrambled out a window.

The warriors watched the old man run into the brush along the creek, rode to the station, and left their ponies grazing behind the new outhouse beside the building. Walking in, the warriors found a table set for several people, coffee on the stove, a frying pan next to a mixing bowl. "I'm hungry," Hawk Heart said, and Lying in Water told Otskai, "Call the old man back to cook for us."

Going to the open window, Otskai looked out and said, "Come back." He then went to the table and sat down. Yellow Wolf had found a bowler hat and Bunched Lightning lay down on the cot and tipped the derby onto his face.

"I wonder what white people eat," said Yellow Wolf, examining two sacks of flour piled against the cabinet.

"Pigs," said Hawk Heart, pointing at some shelving over Bunched Lightning's bed. Smoked hams and bacon lined the fresh-cut boards.

"Take them," Yellow Wolf told Hawk Heart, who nodded, reaching over the warrior on the bed. "We have nothing to carry with," said Yellow Wolf.

"Here." Bunched Lightning rose from the bed, put on the hat, and jerked the blanket from the bed. He then reached for a bottom corner and pulled off the sheet. "Use this."

"I need a blanket," Hawk Heart said, lifting the blanket from the floor. "It is a good one: three point Hudson Bay."

"Boys, look at this," said Otskai, lifting up an overcoat that had been thrown across a trunk in a corner. He lifted up the lid and took out several shirts, one pair of good wool trousers, and a set of summer underwear.

"Money and ammunition on the bottom," Hawk Heart observed, folding up the blanket while Lying in Water rolled the hams and bacon into the sheet. Otskai handed out the clothing and all five examined it.

"Excuse me," said a voice in English. The old man in the union suit put his face at the window. The braves all stopped and stared at him.

"We're Indians," said Otskai.

"I know," the white man said, "but I was wondering if maybe you could help yourselves and run along."

"What is he saying?" Hawk Heart asked, but Otskai lifted his hand and spoke in English to the man.

"We can kill you."

"Yes, Sir, I know. But see, the stage from Laurel's due at any time." Otskai and the others stared. The man continued, "The passengers, you know—they would be quite frightened."

"What is he saying?" demanded Hawk Heart.

"He's crazy," Otskai answered. Just then the man turned his head.

"Oh, oh," he said. "It's coming now!" With that he tapped a finger on the windowsill, then turned and ran back into the brush.

"Stagecoach is coming," Otskai said, and the warriors filed out the front door to see. The stage immediately stopped and the driver leaping from the box, a dog in flight behind. The stage door opened wide. A lady in a long black ruffled dress inflated with stiff petticoats stepped down, took one brief look, and ran with hem lifted toward the willow bushes, followed by a little yapping dog as black as the dress. Behind, a man came running with a valise. All three took cover in the brush.

"I have always wanted to ride in a stagecoach," Bunched Lightning said.

"I'll drive," said Otskai.

"No," said Yellow Wolf. "Let's talk to the whites first. That box has money in it."

"Let them have it. I want to drive the stagecoach."

"Brother, you may drive, and I will ride inside."

"Me too," said Lying in Water. "Let's go."

"The horses," said Bunched Lightning.

"Tie them behind the stage," said Hawk Heart.

The warriors tied their ponies by the halter ropes and climbed into the coach. Otskai picked up the whip and flourished it, but could not crack it. He threw it away and shook the reins. The horses started out with Otskai yelling and the others looking out the windows.

Back in the bushes things had been unpleasant. The station's manager had gone immediately to the scared passengers. "Edwin Forrest at your service," he whispered. "You'll have to still that dog of yours, Madam."

The lady's small dog wouldn't stop its yapping, no matter how the woman gripped its mouth. Two minutes of that and the driver pulled a Bowie knife and handed it without a word. The lady took it, kissed the little dog, and cut its throat. "I'm sorry," whispered the manager.

"She's been a cutthroat all her life," the other passenger put in. Without a word the lady dropped the knife and slapped the man with her gloved hand.

"Madam," whispered Forrest, "I haven't the pleasure."

She smiled demurely, holding out her hand: "I'm Fanny Clark, the vaudeville entertainer."

"Dance hall girl," the other passenger said.

"A pleasure and an honor," Forrest said and bent his head to kiss her hand.

"Will ye shut up, now!" whispered the stagecoach driver. "Jaysus, Mary, and Joseph, they're stealin' me stage! The bloody redskins are stealin' me stage!"

"Savages," said Miss Clark aloud as the Indians drove off. "What could be more ridiculous than wild Indians driving a stage coach!"

"They could be ridin' in a French barouche, but civilization would never tooch 'em. May God damn the sons o' bitches!"

*

"If there are soldiers anywhere near here," Joseph said to Sound of Running Feet, "they will see that smoke. Our young men act like fools!"

"I think you worry too much, Father. General Two Days Behind will not see." The smoke the two saw came from a barn and haystack two miles ahead.

The People now had brought their herds together for the drive across a canyon that like a funnel narrowed to a pass. Beyond the pass, the country opened wide for several hundred miles north to Canada. Now Thunder in the Mountains and his oldest daughter rode together far behind all the families, watching the men and boys round in the scattered bunches of ponies.

Behind them, clattering and bouncing, came a big stagecoach careening at full speed. By now its passengers had climbed on top, and gripping to the baggage rail they whooped and yipped coyote calls.

"Father," asked Sound of Running Feet, "must I marry a young man?"

The chief, his narrowed eyes averted from the approaching coach, said quietly, "I wonder, Pitty Pat."

Now they saw the driver, Otskai, waving at them and shouting. "That crazy boy, my nephew," Joseph said and then realized that something was wrong.

"Come!" he said to Sound of Running Feet, and struck his heels against his horse's sides. Converging with the coach, Joseph heard Otskai shouting, "Soldiers! Soldiers behind us! Not far!"

"Get on your horses, you men!" Joseph shouted as the coach drew up. "Leave this thing and find Looking Glass, Ollokot, and Lean Elk!"

The five braves jumped down and scrambled for their horses' leads, and in a moment all were riding at full run, spreading out across the dry ground.

A cold wind blew dust from two thousand horses across the wide canyon mouth. On both sides ahead rose bluffs of several hundred feet. Now Joseph saw that braves were riding fast atop them: others had already seen the soldiers. Father and daughter rode at a brisk gallop forward toward The People. The herd was moving slowly, at a walk, while men and boys trotted back and forth outside the herd, cutting in and out, dogs dodging hooves and barking at the ponies' flanks. Lean Elk and the Many Summers Warrior, White Bird, galloped up beside Joseph and Running Feet. "Soldiers!" said Lean Elk. "Horse soldiers."

"I know."

Before Thunder in the Mountains asked, White Bird said, "Maybe three hundred."

Joseph looked up at the bluffs ahead. He said to White Bird, "You and I must get The People going faster."

Lean Elk said, "The boys and women must do it. All the men will be needed to hold back the soldiers."

"Where is my brother?" Joseph asked.

"It's too late!" exclaimed Lean Elk, pointing back to where a column, breaking up and widening like a cloud of smoke, steadily approached, riding at a canter—dark blue U. S. uniforms. And riding hard around from their right flank, a company galloped out and headed toward the canyon's mouth.

"They are riding ahead to cut off the herd!" White Bird wheeled his pony toward the cavalry. "They will get ahead of the herd! They will shoot down the women and children again!"

"Look, Father!" Sound of Running Feet pointed toward the herd. Streaking like an eagle's shadow on his black and white war pony, Ollokot rode furiously toward the charging troopers, his horse's white mane and tail streaming out and flashing in the declining sunlight.

Behind him half a dozen horses' lengths rode forty or fifty warriors or more, strung out shouting, raising their rifles high.

"No!" Thunder in the Mountains cried. "Brother!" He turned to Sound of Running Feet. "Look away! My brother no longer wants to live!"

White Bird reached to grip the halter of Joseph's horse and held it in his strong hand. "Let's go! Let us make sure your brother does not die for nothing!"

Joseph's daughter watched her uncle raise his rifle, riding like the wind.

*

Some fifteen years before this at the battle of Antietam, Sturgis's Division faced the meager remnants of Lee's right flank sniping at him from a little hillside overlooking Burnside's Bridge—as it is called today. The hours it took to take that bridge gave Lee's reinforcements time to reach the field and save the staggering secessionists. If Sturgis could have turned that flank, the Rebel army would have been destroyed. If he had cut behind Lee's army, blocked the only avenue of Lee's retreat, the Civil War might have ended then and there—just like now: if Sturgis could cut off the Nez Perce herd before the hostiles reached the canyon's neck, he'd crush them, end this insurrection. Sturgis ordered line of battle formed and nearly all his troopers to dismount. The walking line of firing men, wide as the canyon's mouth, would force the Indians toward the narrow end, where just one company of mounted troopers—if they had a little speed left in them—could block the exit from the canyon. "Dismount?" repeated one of his lieutenants. "We ought to charge them, Sir!"

"Like hell we will!" retorted Sturgis, who had once remarked, not long before Antietam, that he didn't give "a pinch of owl dung" for his commanding general's orders.

Sturgis didn't do it by the book. He ordered Captain Benteen to take his company and ride like hell beside the Indians and race them to the far end of the canyon. Benteen's veterans had seen enough of their own blood and Custer's blood to be determined men.

The captain trotted his company to the flank of the walking line of battle, then barked the order and with a jolt the horsemen broke into a gallop toward the distant boulders at the far end of the canyon. The troopers, hat brims blowing up flat in front, rode with carbines held in one hand while the other tightly grasped the reins, working with them back and forth like the iron rod along a locomotive's wheels, the horses' big necks plunging. Pointing pistols toward the sky, the officers yelled, "Ride 'em, troopers! Ride, Seventh Cavalry! Let's give 'em hell for General George Custer!"

They pounded past an overturned stagecoach and rode toward the looming rocky bluff, canteens and tin cups clattering and horses blowing hot breath through wide nostrils. They passed the pony herd, sweeping around young boys and women terrified and whipping horses—Benteen shouting, cursing, waving with his Colt revolver. Then out from the boulders, so it seemed, appeared a single warrior, rifle raised—and then behind him twos and threes of yipping braves riding streaking spotted horses coming straight at them at a run, wild like stampeding mustangs, and now out from the Indian horse herd another crowd of warriors—all of them riding without reins, firing from their horses' backs, bullets suddenly in the air like ragged wasps.

*

"Looking Glass!" Joseph's daughter shouts, both seeing now the second group of warriors charging the cavalry, which have begun to halt and
mill. The two warrior companies flash past the cavalry shooting, herding,
riding in toward the whites and swinging shining rifles like coup sticks. The
soldiers fire back from their saddles; men are knocked off their horses by
the warriors' bullets. Now the long knives are raised and slash through the
air, but in the time it takes a hawk to strike from the sky, soldiers turn and
gallop back toward where they had started, one by one and pair by pair until
they all are galloping, and Joseph's brother Ollokot pulls up his horse with
Looking Glass beside him. Both chiefs, seeing Joseph, raise their rifles, and
Thunder in the Mountains lifts his arm to them, lifts it toward the sky.

*

The line of walking soldiers spread from bluff to bluff across the canyon, narrowing with every step. The families and horses pressed toward the
narrow pass at the upper end, and warriors took posts among the rocks and
boulders on the faces of the cliffs, with many settling down behind cover
along the crests. The range was long, but even at four hundred yards a Nez
Perce brave aiming a good Sharps rifle could be certain. Only one man,
called Bare Legs, waited at the canyon floor, set behind a clutter of rocks,
firing steadily, deliberately, at the Long Knives now only two hundred yards
away. The two right companies of troopers slowed their walk and finally
came to a halt to take the unseen Indian under fire. Ranging far behind The
Peoples' rear, Yellow Wolf rode back to where the hidden brave crouched
firing from the rocks.

"My boy, run back from here!" the older warrior called. "Look how
close the soldiers are! They might kill you! You shouldn't stay here with your
horse!"

Yellow Wolf saw that a company of soldiers were taking aim at him. He
turned his pony and kicked its sides, but as the horse leapt forward Yellow
Wolf knew that the saddle, taken from a white man's farm that morning, was
not cinched tight. He pulled up, leapt down, but as he grasped the cinch under the pony's belly, he heard a thunderclap around his head. The company
of soldiers had fired their rifles all at once, some fifty weapons barking at a
stroke. The wind of bullets stormed past the young warrior, who pulled the
cinch tight, mounted, and not looking back kicked up his pony into a run.
"I was not scared," he said in his old age. "My Wayakin had promised that I
would not be killed by bullets."

All along the bluffs on both sides of the canyon, marksmen warriors fired down at the soldiers. The general who had led thousands of men across Antietam Creek too late to win the Civil War now watched his soldiers falter, then run for cover, while farther up the canyon The People rode the river of their ponies through the shadowed pass, vanishing like the summer sun.

X

Forever

The Colonel tried another day and then gave up. His broken-down horses and walking men strung out ten miles behind him, Sturgis tore off
his campaign hat and looked as though he'd throw it in the fire. But he put
it on again and said with quiet evenness, "Fitzgerald, you can understand
how much it galls me, can't you? You have spent three months with Howard.
Now I have to halt and let that pious hypocrite catch up, and put myself back
under his command. And talk to him."

"I find him quite the gentleman."

"'The Prince of Darkness is a gentleman.' That's Shakespeare. Do you
read Shakespeare, Doctor?"

"Not when something better comes to hand, like Correspondent
Sutherland's dispatches."

"I haven't read them."

"He writes what Howard wants him to write."

"A journalistic camp follower—a whore, in plain English. He'd have to
be."

"A woman with a lovely ankle lifts her hem a little extra for a puddle.
A lady with a lovely figure wears dresses cinched about the waist. A doctor with a lovely wife and lovely children earns promotion and Army pay
by hounding to their deaths the poor Nez Perce." Fitzgerald coughed and
pulled his blanket in around his summer Army coat, shivered as he sat in
one of Sturgis's camp chairs. "What have you got against Howard, Colonel,
if I may ask?"

Sturgis stood and squared himself against the fire, warming his hands. "You know that Howard got a medal for his work at Gettysburg."

"He's mentioned it."

"I'm sure he has. My old friend Abner Doubleday commanded the First Corps on July first—stood hours, outnumbered, holding back near twice as many Rebels. Howard's corps collapsed in half an hour, exposing Abner's right flank. Howard put the blame on Doubleday in his report. Wrecked a good man's career." Sturgis sat back down, reaching into his coat for a cigar. "Howard doesn't smoke, though. He's more virtuous than I am." He struck a match along the elbow of his chair. "But you don't seem to mind the man."

"I do in theory; not in practice."

"That's too deep for me."

"The General is a lonely man."

"He's got his son."

Fitzgerald kept his silence. Sturgis resumed, "I'm told he's a professor in uniform."

"I don't know. He'd make a worse professor than a soldier, pedantic beyond all tolerance." Fitzgerald coughed. "He has a mind and curiosity. Some nights up there in the Bitterroot Range he'd lie on his back and look at the stars. The Milky Way was like a flood of sandy light. He'd lie there for a half hour, silent. I wondered what he thought about."

"Said his prayers, probably. 'Now I lay me down to—'"

"I think he wondered if he was right. I mean—" Fitzgerald turned to Sturgis "—wouldn't you if you were he?"

"That's one man whose place I can't imagine myself in."

"Isn't that what mercy's all about?"

"Damn his eyes."

Fitzgerald looked back at the fire. "I think he doubted all that nonsense he believes, like Adam in the Garden, Noah's flood, the parting of a sea for Israelites. If anyone deserved the parting of a sea, it would be Joseph and his suffering people."

"They don't need our sympathy. It's just too bad, that's all."

"The Indians call the Milky Way the Spirit Path. You look up at night long enough, I swear you begin to think like an Indian. Do you suppose that's Howard's problem? What do you think: perhaps deep down General Howard is a Dreamer."

"If Howard is a Dreamer, then I am a Comanche."

"I would wager Howard will give up the chase and let those people go."

"He can afford to take it slow. Hell, he can afford to give up." Fitzgerald turned attentively. Sturgis chuckled. "He's ordered Nelson Miles to head them off up north of here. Miles will do it, too—that is, if the Nez Perce slow up a little. Colonel Miles is on a line to intercept them just this side of Canada. If we slow up—not that we have a choice—the Nez Perce will slow up too, without us pushing them. You saw those half a dozen old and sick along their trail today. I wish to hell that I could get fresh horses and some food. Those Indians must be as bad off or worse than us. They've had no time to hunt. They must be bone-tired, after three months. Bet nothing like this has been done in the whole history of the world. I don't know how they do it. But Miles will catch the bastards sure as hell."

Fitzgerald nodded, looking at the stars and shivering. "'Physician, heal thyself,'" the Colonel said, and puffed his strong cigar.

*

The morning after Sturgis called a halt, a hundred fifty Crow warriors arrived, painted and stripped for battle. A chief called Island Crow told Sturgis that his braves were out for Nez Perce blood, which Sturgis knew meant they were after Nez Perce horses. So now spotted ponies were as deadly to the hostiles as killed or captured men. With the benediction, "Give 'em hell!" the Colonel sent them on their way.

First Lieutenant Charlie Benson couldn't help remarking, "Now there's a tribe of loyal friends for you."

The Colonel grunted. "Can't trust the Crows, I know. But our friends up ahead must nearly be done up. The Crows will skin them good, at very least delay them." He looked at Benson, whose desperado face was grizzled with a two-week beard. "Save work for us."

Benson shook his head. "It's a double double cross. We hunt them down like animals, so they come here and expect their old Crow friends to help them."

"War is hell, Lieutenant."

"I know it is and I've seen plenty of it too, but you and I know the Nez Perce are good people. It's the pinheads in our government that brought this on; and certain military officers—not you, Sir. All those people want is to be left alone."

"You're tired, Lieutenant."

"You know nearly all the men agree with me."

"I know it and I half agree with you myself. But I've got orders, as you know."

"I will hate like hell to be in on the kill."

"Lieutenant—Charlie—our wounded should be taken away from here. I'll detail you and twenty men to take them back to the river and then escort them via steamboat." Lieutenant Benson stiffened and regarded Sturgis carefully.

"Lieutenant, I am not dismissing you."

"I never shirk my duty, Sir."

"That's right. And as of now your duty is to save our wounded men. I am commending you in my report for steadiness and courage under fire. In any case you'll rejoin this command as soon as possible." Sturgis saluted and First Lieutenant Benson smartly touched his hat brim in return.

Two days later Benson halted his slow-moving column of footsore cavalry and springless wagons. A figure dressed in baggy pantaloons, fringed deerskin vest, calico shirt, big hat flapped up in front, and circled by a wide double holster belt resplendent with two shining pearl-handled Colt revolvers came riding down a hillside, hallooing with a war whoop and waving. "Sergeant, what in hell is that?"

"Beats me, Lieutenant. By damn, it looks like a woman!"

Sure enough, her ringlets bobbing as she trotted toward them, she shouted "Martha Jane Canary at your service, Colonel." She lifted off her hat, "Whoo-ee!"

As Benson sat with open mouth, Sergeant Thomas, adjutant, said "I'll be damned. Are you called Calamity Jane?"

"I am, you five-striped polecat! I am the Friday's daughter of a desert sidewinder named Pecos Bill and a Comanche woman white as new-blown snow! My grand-daddy was Big Mike Fink and my great grandpaw was Dan'l Boone hisself sure as I am here; and I can lick my weight in rattlesnakes and Indians and ten times that in grizzly bears!"

Lieutenant Benson interrupted, "Madam—"

"And I ain't seen a man that you could call a man in months. Whoo-ee!"

"O God, Madam," Benson exclaimed, and fell silent—then said as if startled, "See here, we've got four wagon loads of wounded soldiers here!"

"Whoo-ee! Wagon loads?"

"Madam—"

"Aww, Colonel, I ain't interested in men that way unless they're washed or rich. I just need someone to talk to me polite. I'll come along with you and nurse your men real good, as good as any of them Eastern ladies with their garter belts and stockins! Haw! I'll be useful to you, Colonel!"

"Madam, I could use a nurse but not a—"

"Prostitute, you say? I ain't no prostitute, Your Honor; I'm a prospector! I mean it, I will nurse your men professional and there will be no untoward behavior on my part—or theirs, I do guarantee!" With that she drew both pistols and with blazing blue eyes discharged them in the air. Horses jumped and all four wagons lurched; the troopers pulled their reins.

"God damn it, lady," Sergeant Thomas said, "we've just been fighting Indians!"

She smiled and smoothly slipped the Colts back in. "Apologies profound and absolute. A little jumpy, ain't you?"

"Madam, why are you here?" Lieutenant Benson asked. "Where do you live?"

"Aww, just in a dugout yonder, over hill and dale, temporarily. I'm on my way to the Upper Yellowstone to pan for gold. Hell, I done everything else; might as well try prospecting. Tell you what: you just go on, and I'll ride back and pack up my other bronco with some whisky, water, bacon—"

"Now you're talking!" Sergeant Thomas broke in.

She looked at him and laughed. "Ain't never met a soldier boy who wasn't hungry—thirsty too. You know what I mean. Hungry for the Word of the Lord! Whoo-ee!" She wheeled her horse and flailed its flank, cantering back up the hillside.

"I'll be damned!" Sergeant Thomas said. "I thought she was some legend—tall tale—a dime novel heroine. She's real—real as a bright twenty dollar gold piece! Whoo-ee! Now I've seen everything! Wild West! Say, now ain't she a dream, Lieutenant?"

*

October was the fourth month of the long retreat, and now stands of aspen in the valleys glowed luminescent yellow when the sun rode low in mid-afternoon. Once again The People tried to hurry, although many of the horses limped with hoof disease. The footsore walking families were tired, as the wounded bear is tired in late fall—the den is too far, the cave a lost memory. Dogs trotted aimlessly as cold wind ruffled their now long fur. The warriors halted. Again the women, old men, boys and older girls drove the slow pony herds; here the braves waited, a hundred fifty, all ages, while at their center all the chiefs sat their horses, the ponies' heads almost touching.

"All Lean Elk knows," said Looking Glass, "is how to run. The People can run no more."

"You were wrong enough," Lean Elk retorted. "And now you thought those Crow braves were our friends. They have stolen four hundred ponies! With fewer horses, we must go slower still. Let us keep moving. We can't fight both the soldiers and as many Crows as we have warriors."

"We have to fight the Crows."

"We have so little ammunition!"

Joseph now spoke. "It doesn't matter who was right and who was wrong. Looking Glass, decide how to fight this battle. All others will do as you say. You must hurt the Crows enough to send them to their homes. White Bird and I will keep The People moving."

"We will use our last ammunition on the Crows," Lean Elk said.

"Maybe Looking Glass knows a way to scare them all home without shooting them." Joseph backed his pony from the circle, leaving the war chiefs to deal with the Crows.

Passing through the quiet crowd of warriors, he raised his hand in thanks and benediction. Unpainted, grim, some nodded back and some lifted their rifles.

Catching up with the rear of the herd, Joseph rode to Sound of Running Feet, the very last of all The People. She sat her pony watching the boys and older girls round in the fraying edges of the moving mass of animals, urging up the hesitant by crowding them and shouting. "My daughter, you are a chief!"

"Even the boys do what I say, as if your Sound of Running Feet were you."

"They should obey you; you are smarter than the rest of us. I obey you, too."

"If you obeyed me you would rest more. You are thin and tired."

"Some of our young men stole dried buffalo from a Crow camp this morning. We will eat well tonight, unless—." Joseph left it there.

"You are not yourself."

The father nodded, looking at his daughter. So intelligent and calm her eyes, cheerful as sunrise home along the river, patient as the summer moon: she suffers gracefully. "Since the fighting in the canyon, I am sick in my stomach for your brave uncle, Ollokot. He cares for nothing anymore."

"And my father must cheer him."

Joseph smiled sadly. "My brother lived from his heart. If you don't live from your heart, you don't live."

The two rode at a walk watching the herd, listening for rifle fire behind them. "Do you think my little sister and Snows Resting can see us, Father, from the Spirit Path?"

Joseph lowered his head, and he wept. When he opened his eyes again, he said, "I see them always, Pitty Pat. They must see us, too." Joseph sighed deeply. "We have to show The People how to live, no matter how we grieve."

"I know. I am the daughter of a chief."

He reached to take her hand a moment. "You are my sunrise, Sound of Running Feet; you always have been. You always will be. I can do anything because you are my daughter." He brought his hand back to his horse's mane and picked up to the steady, familiar trot. Together, the two rode north behind the tired herd.

*

At first the two chiefs Ollokot and Looking Glass argued, but as the other chiefs spoke up a plan developed that the two agreed upon. The circle broke, and each man rode back to his warriors.

Led by Looking Glass, the hundred fifty Nez Perce men galloped down The People's back trail to a half-mile stand of spruce and aspen. The stretch of trees stood at right angles to the wide trail where, coming east, it bent sharply to the north. The angled light of morning would have backlit anything among the trees, but now late afternoon, a hundred fifty warriors waited in deep shadow. Looking Glass's company of braves were in the center, their chief sitting his horse out in the trail, late sun blazing from the mirror on his breast.

That was the first thing that the Crows saw as they cantered in strung out bands and groups up the trail—the glinting glass of the man who helped them fight the Lakota not long ago. The painted braves slowed to a trot, all crowding forward to a close-packed front. Looking Glass sat unmoving. The hundred fifty Crow braves rode close enough to recognize the chief, and he raised his rifle.

Out from the trees a hundred fifty Nez Perce warriors rode in a perfect line, straight and even as the fire from a Gatling gun, each man in his place. The Crows were not cowards but this was something they had never seen. Slowing to a walk, the wary braves began talking to each other.

Behind Looking Glass, old White Bird now sat his horse—recognized by the older Crow warriors: the man who used to watch the Long Knife soldiers drill. And now out from both far ends of the walking line of Nez Perce warriors, two companies split off and trotted at an angle, still precise and careful but as easy as a practiced hunter dresses out a fresh antelope. The Crow braves saw that the line ahead would stand its ground; the two wings on the flanks would funnel and encircle them. In any, case the strange silence and precision ahead unnerved the young Crow braves.

A few older men shouted to each other; some braves raised their rifles, whooping war cries; the Crow chiefs galloped toward each other but the confused and milling mass of braves prevented them—and then the eerie Nez Perce line began to walk forward and in a moment broke into a trot, and as the flanking lines began to canter, all the Crows decided as one man to run for it—their crowding clumps at first jarring each other like a jam of logs on a forested river, then clearing with a rush as every warrior's pony found its hooves. The streaming raiders galloped miles toward the setting sun, stopping only as each party reached its village, now satisfied with having captured two or three good Appaloosa ponies and returning with their lives.

The Nez Perce chiefs, Looking Glass and Ollokot, Two Moons, White Bird, Lean Elk, Toohoolhoolzote, Red Elk—their warriors now recalled and joking—led the weary way back up the trampled trail where their wives, children, parents, and grandparents plodded forward for their lives. What these chiefs and braves had done had not been seen among the native nations of this continent—and though the tactic was familiar among the warlike killers of what History calls civilization—Hannibal had closed the steel circle at Cannae, and Robert Bruce had destroyed the English flanks at Bannockburn—no one had done it better and for better reason and with less loss; and no defeated army in the world had employed better sense or executed their retreat with more skill than those Crows who had known what war is for.

*

"As likely to quote Shakespeare as to shoot buffalo," someone said of Yellowstone Kelly, and General Nelson Miles in later years recalled Kelly was as "gentle as he was brave, as kind and generous as he was forceful . . . an expert rifleman." Born Luther Kelly in New York, he lied about his age to join the U. S. Army in the Civil War, and then went West and fell in love with a grand and glorious beauty, the Valley of the Yellowstone; and when he died full fifty years after the autumn of the Nez Perce war, his bones were laid by his request on top of Kelly Mountain, where the valley spreads like realms of gold below.

He wore moustaches swept to handlebars, a fur collared coat; and this September in the cold and early snow he wore a beaver cap without a visor or a brim—austerity and luxury, like the bracing air that blew through stands of aspens, cottonwoods, and lodgepole pines from the Bighorn Mountains to the bending Missouri River farther north.

Along this river lay an Army depot, where north-south Cow Creek flowed into the longest river system in America. Cow Island was the place where laden steamboats had to stop for shallow water, lay up their cargo, and go back down the Missouri. Bull trains hauled the tons of bacon, sugar, boots, and clothing up into the wide Northwest for buffalo hides, silver, and piled bales of skins and pelts. Pots and pans, a hundred cast iron stoves, canned groceries, sacks of flour, coffee, beans, chewing tobacco, all lay stacked and orderly against a little bluff, down slope from which a two-foot drainage ditch surrounded several tents and military gear—packs, saddles, rifles, ammunition. A dozen men were lounging out their duty when the famous scout from General Miles rode up and told their captain that a couple hundred Nez Perce warriors, their families and pony herds, were headed right this way.

The men set to with shovels, deepening the trench and throwing up dirt in front—and sure enough, that afternoon a line of Indians appeared across the river. The long procession crossed upstream in shallow water—at least two hours' worth of women, children, dogs and horses—bypassing this entrenched depot; but as The People passed, a group of warriors trotted down the bank. "I'll meet them," Kelly said, but Captain Penwick said, "You'd better not."

"A horse!" called Kelly to a sergeant. "'My kingdom for a horse!'"

He mounted up and walked his horse to where the warriors waited silently. After talking for several minutes he came trotting back. "They want the officer in charge, Captain. Not doing business with the likes of me."

"Will you come with me as interpreter?"

"I'll come along but you won't need my mouth: their English is as good as any man's. And leave your carbine, Captain; these are Nez Perce."

The two rode out and several of the warriors—one who wore a mirror, one named Poker Joe, an adolescent, and a wild-eyed brave—listed in turn the things they wanted: flour, sugar, ammunition, beef, bacon. But the Captain said these were government supplies and he had orders to protect them. The warriors looked surprised, sat silent, so the captain turned away and Kelly, with a raised hand and a headshake, followed.

"Captain," he said, catching up, "these Nez Perce are baffled by your answer."

"They are? What the hell did they expect?"

"To them the rules of hospitality require that you share with them that little mountain of supplies." He pointed at the goods along the bluff.

"And if I don't?"

"We'll see, I guess. 'Discretion is the better part of valor,' Captain."

"You think they'll actually attack?"

"We'll see."

As soon as they dismounted, they saw two of the Nez Perce approaching on foot. Going around the ditch again, the captain and the scout walked out to meet them. Poker Joe was one of them; the other was the boy, who spoke immediately. "Sir, we have money and will pay for what we take. Our families are hungry and there is no food."

"I'm sorry," said the Captain.

"I have orders to safeguard the stores in my care." Again the Captain turned away, again the scout regarded the Nez Perce a moment and then followed.

"Captain, you know they will take what they want, don't you?"

"Over my dead body."

"Indeed. Wouldn't it be better to have a roll of greenbacks to show for your supplies than twelve dead bodies?"

"If you are afraid, Kelly, you may leave at once. I put my country first."

"It's my country, you son of a bitch—" Kelly intended to elaborate, but they heard the boy running up behind them.

"Please, Sir, we are all starving. Please let us buy some food to feed our children and our old people!"

Captain Penwick hesitated, then replied, "Wait here."

He stalked back around the trench and called, "Sergeant, bring that sack of wormy hardtack!"

Kelly shook his head. "Captain, you're a piece of work."

The officer, ignoring Kelly, ordered, "Sergeant drop a side of bacon into that sack, and take it out to that Indian." Then he turned to Kelly. "You've been out here quite a while but so have I. You've got to show the rifle to these reds."

The sergeant walked out to the young Nez Perce and handed him the sack. Within an hour the sergeant hollered, "Captain, look at that," while pointing at a brave in breechclout sitting his horse motionless four hundred yards down river. "Naked means fight, Captain."

"I do believe that it does, Sergeant. Don't those Indians know it's cold?"

The Captain waved his men behind the earthen breastworks, and for ten hours all of them, including Kelly, traded shots with several dozen Nez Perce sharpshooters—none being killed or hit on either side—while Yellow Wolf, Otskai, Bird Alighting, and a team of warriors behind the pile of freight removed what they could use, and then, as Yellow Wolf put it, some "bad boys" burned the rest. For miles around, the pillar of fire and the column of smoke attested to the halted exodus of the Nez Perce. The price of the supplies they captured was prohibitively high: they lost one day.

The officer that Kelly scouted for was angling toward The People's wide trail with upwards of five hundred men, all arms: artillery—a Hotchkiss gun and one Napoleon—one company of walking infantry and five other companies mounted on Indian ponies; three companies of Second Cavalry; three companies of Seventh Cavalry, including one that had fought with

Benteen at the Little Bighorn; and thirty Lakota and Cheyenne scouts. Pack horses, ambulances, and thirty six-mule teams pulling wagons had left their garrison September eighteenth. Each soldier carried fifty rounds of ammunition, with another hundred fifty lumbering behind in wagons loaded with provisions for the soldiers, forage for the mules and horses, and winter coats.

Meanwhile up ahead at Cow Island Landing, Captain Penwick and his men inspected their great heap of smoldering materiel. The Nez Perce hadn't seen much use for cast iron stoves, and now the furnaced objects lay about distorted, warped "artistically" one soldier said, by the bonfire inferno that had immolated the stockpile like an offering to an industrial idol.

As Kelly mounted up to return to Miles's column, Captain Penwick said, "A man like you perplexes me. You don't prospect, don't farm, don't want to join the Army. What keeps you out here?"

"The Yellowstone, Captain. I wouldn't leave her for your weight in gold dust."

"One river is like any other to me. Why the Yellowstone?"

"'Age cannot wither her,'" the scout replied, "'nor custom stale her infinite variety.'" He touched his hat respectfully, or so it might have appeared, then nudged his horse's ribs and cantered southeastward toward the marching troopers of Nelson Miles.

*

It snowed in late September on the high and treeless plains of north Montana—several inches through the night on canvas shelters covering the families. This morning, two days short of October, fog thicker than steam surrounded the Nez Perce. Their spotted horses, grazing herd by herd, loomed up with bony faces deathly gray when Thunder in the Mountains, Sound of Running Feet, and Young Joseph walked in among them carrying halter ropes.

Mounting up, the three with quiet voices urged their herd forward. The ponies, then father, daughter, and son, moved northward, disappearing ghostlike as if drawn into folding hands of cloud. But back among The People packing up their canvas pieces, precious food, blankets, robes, and utensils, the voices of two chiefs, unnaturally loud, broke the muffled stillness of the dawn.

"You are no chief, Poker Joe!" said Looking Glass. "Look at these old ones trying to get up, stiff and sick and tired! A chief takes care of his People! But look—how many of our grandmothers you have left to die along the trail while we have hurried on! Our horses barely walk, their hooves dis-eased. People and animals are worn out! We need to rest! I will lead again! I will act like a chief and take care of The People!"

"I am taking care of them by hurrying. We must do our best to cross into Canada before the soldiers catch up. The People want to hurry!"

"A leader doesn't listen to frightened people; he leads!"

"All right, Looking Glass, you can lead! Take command! I think we will be caught and killed."

"Good, Lean Elk. When we reach Snake Creek this afternoon, we rest three days to graze our horses, hunt buffalo, and make ourselves strong to meet the Lakota in Old Woman Country. May I be killed if I am wrong!"

*

Five days' walk south, Howard's column plodded north. The General had seen enough of snow. He and the other officers wore overcoats; the men had none. Troopers led their walking horses by extended reins, the infantry pushed on like drunkards, almost staggering, stumping worn-thin shoes on covered roots and stones. Up front Howard led the long column, pulled in tight inside his overcoat, his eyes a dark study of his horse's shaggy black mane. Beside him rode Lucullus Jones, a colonel with years of service in the West. He cleared his throat, addressing Howard quietly:

"General, do you want them to get away?"

The general regarded him the way a sailor looks into a spitting wind. "How dare you, Sir," was all he said.

The colonel took his hat into one hand, the other circling tighter on the reins. His matted, steel-gray hair lay painted across a thin face half-gilded by the sun, and for an instant in the dim sunrise, the sweat band of his hat having left a wide white belt across his weathered, high forehead, Jones looked like an old Lakota brave—but only down to the U.S. Army brass button cinching closed the top of his overcoat. He worked his chaw, which he knew Howard hated, but he didn't spit. He pulled the hat back on and briskly brought his hand to the brim, then twitched his mount aside and slowly shambled back along the plodding column of slumping, saddle-sore men who did not look at him.

"*Colonel.*" Howard had followed him and pulled up a couple of feet ahead. "Colonel."

"Yes, Sir. General."

Howard moved his horse around until the stump of his arm almost touched Jones's elbow, looked away and said, "Remind me of where your service took place during the late war, Colonel."

"Fort Phil Kearny. Sir. Out here, keeping these red Indians from murdering and scalping our—"

"—Colonel," Howard interrupted calmly. The line of gawking men was passing in profound silence. "Let us dismount, Colonel."

"I won't fistfight a one-armed man, Sir."

"Dismount, Sir."

Jones backed his horse and slowly tilted off, while Howard gripped the reins between his teeth and promptly swung down. His orderly took both horses' reins. "Let us step away from the men."

"As you wish, General." The two paced stiffly several rods.

"My apologies, Colonel."

Jones abruptly halted, his glare fixed on the distant mountains. "A general need not apologize. Sir."

"A Christian does."

"General, I am indifferent whether you are a Christian or not."

"It matters to me. I apologize for pointing to your inadequate war record, Jones." The colonel turned his face away.

"That is an apology, in your Bible?"

Howard chewed his lower lip. "Again, Colonel, my apologies. Want of self-control, not want of courage, precluded your service in the Eastern armies."

Jones eyed Howard: "Drunkenness and cowardice are the same thing in your estimation, are they not?"

"They used to be. They are no longer, Jones. You are my mainstay here."

"Thank you, General."

"We shall have no more pique expressed between us, Colonel."

"As you wish, General."

Howard grunted. "In expression or in spirit."

"Yes, Sir."

"I shall speak plainly to you, Sir."

Jones remained at virtual attention. "Colonel, you must never accuse a superior officer of conscious disobedience of orders. Is that understood?"

"Completely, General."

"Colonel Jones, last week some companies of the Seventh Cavalry and Second Cavalry, mounted infantry, supported by more infantry and two field pieces, together with scouts, left Tongue River marching northwest. Fresher men and better men than I have. Under the command of General Miles."

Jones's face began to smoothen. "I see."

"Colonel Jones, I am not solicitous for my reputation. Despite what you might have been told about my past service."

"Sir."

"The Seventh Cavalry will catch them."

"Yes, Sir."

"When the time comes, I shall ride forward to ensure that the hostiles get decent treatment. I shall leave you in command here."

"Yes, Sir. Thank you, General. I wish you the best of luck."

"Let us give these men the rest they deserve."

Howard mounted, remarking to his aide, "Thus did Herod and Pilate become friends."

*

"Well, hallelujah!" Sutherland exclaimed. "Bless your squirrelly moustache, Major Wood!"

The Major eyed him cautiously. "You won't reveal your source, I trust."

"Major, this is personal and privileged information. And it won't matter a pot of beans who first told me Howard's giving up, because it will all be long over when I finally release the story to the outside world. But I knew it, Major. I took Howard's measure right away; I knew he didn't have it in him as a soldier or a man to bring Joseph to bay."

"Hell you did," observed correspondent Trimble, who rose from his camp chair while dashing his coffee into the fire. "You wrote him up like Napoleon and Buffalo Bill Cody rolled into one. You lied like a whore."

"Thank you, Trimble; so I did. I wasn't fooled. I was a sell-out, but not a fool."

"A sell-out is a fool, I'd say. What say you, Major?"

The Major, his face darkening, said, "Some of us have little choice, Trimble. Listen, you two literary men, I have been talking to you all along only to see to it that the truth is told. I hope you won't kill my career, but Howard will no doubt do that without help from you. I want the real story to be told. I want some justice done in history. I want those poor Nez Perce to get their due—the very least that they deserve." He turned and walked back toward Howard's headquarters tent.

He hadn't said a word, but John Fitzgerald, sitting shivering in one of Howard's Army coats, raised up his tin coffee cup. Seeing the gesture, Trimble resumed his seat beside the doctor.

"I take it you were never one of Howard's worshippers, Doctor."

"He has his virtues," Fitzgerald whispered hoarsely. "But I am happier with Sturgis. He has virtues, like Howard, but they aren't advertised." He coughed weakly.

"You better roll yourself in blankets and cheap whisky, Doctor," Sutherland suggested.

"'Physician, heal thyself,'" the doctor said.

"Home to wife and cozy fireside?" asked Trimble.

"Home to wife and all that's good. Soon!" The doctor raised his cup again.

But next day, after Howard issued orders for the infantry, artillery, and all the cavalry whose horses were unfit for service in the field to return south to the Yellowstone, a hard-riding aide from Nelson Miles reported that the Colonel's force had struck the Nez Perce trail. Chief Joseph and his hostiles had been caught at Bear's Paw, just under forty miles from Canada. Howard ordered out twenty cavalry who still had decent mounts, and with his son rode north in haste to get in on the finish.

*

The country of the Bear Paw Mountains changes color in the fall from flowing grassland green to dun. Beside the little mountain range, the land along Snake Creek looks like the moon—or like the No Man's Land of World War One: an undulating bleak plain pocked with coulees, ravines, small draws, and sunken craters hollowed by dried creeks. Look at the dreary waste dismounted and you see a level table, but walk across it and you stumble into drops, depressions, cups separated by scrub-rough wrinkles hardly large enough to be called ridges. Picture an ancient giant's graveyard where the lids have fallen in long centuries ago. The swales along Snake Creek were thick with brush and stunted cottonwood.

In these low places tired People could find respite from the frigid wind. The creek's water was enough for all The People camping now along it, burning shrubs and dry buffalo dung, cooking fresh meat hunted by the warriors—Joseph's band of Wallowa People southernmost, banked by a long ridge that runs from east to west, and Husis Kute's Palouses; north several hundred yards along the tight winding stream camped Looking Glass's Alpowai People; up farther, makeshift canvas lodges covered White Bird's Lamtamas; and northernmost lay Toohoolhoolzote and fifteen families of Pikunan People. The People tried either to rest or to dry the buffalo brought down by the young men. Their ponies grazed on long brown grass west of Snake Creek, hungry past what one day's grazing could assuage, limping with the same disease of hoof that Howard's cavalry, and Sturgis's, were halted by.

The People had been seen. Miles's Lakota and Cheyenne scouts were out, and ranging far ahead of the horse soldiers they had seen a squad of warriors running buffalo to kill. Close enough to perceive the men's striped blankets worn against the needling sleet, and knowing only Nez Perce brought such blankets out here on the plains, the scouts withdrew, reporting what they saw to the white colonel.

That day The People's scouts had seen the dark crawl of moving figures miles away, but thought they must be plains people because they knew that General Day After Tomorrow was far behind. But it was the horses, marching men, wagons, and artillery of Nelson Miles.

Hair Combed Over Eyes had seen them, too; but he had seen them in a dream. The early night of thirtieth September had fallen dark and bitter cold with a steady snow that in the morning lay five inches deep. Hair Combed Over Eyes had been out scouting and had come to camp when all light was gone. Directed to his people's shelter, he wrapped himself in blankets and slept the hungry sleep of long riders. In his dream, he saw the undulating coulee land that he had been visible in the night; and he saw the waters of Snake Creek run red with blood. The smoke of battle, dark and low, had settled on The People. The man awoke, put on his moccasins, and walked out where The People slept in early dawn. He saw the pocked landscape of his dream—the level meadows, creek, and washed-out gullies, even the surrounding bluffs and Bear Paw Mountains in the still-dim distance, he said later.

"I go back to my poor, torn canvas shelter and sleep. The same dream-vision came, the mingled blood on running water, smoke-darkened air; but with it all came falling leaves, withering flowers." And then he saw the same with springtime grass; instead of smoke, the blooming springtime flowers, "sunshine, peace. These signs I understood, and knew we would be very soon attacked."

Getting up again and putting on his blanket, moccasins, and leggings, the warrior walked the narrow camp. "I called out everywhere, My People, listen to my words! Listen to my dream! Last night I dreamed of someplace where we camped, and when I woke this morning and came out, I saw that this ground was the very ground I dreamed, this place the place of my vision! I saw the smoke of battle! In the stream we drink from now will run the blood of soldiers, Indians together. My vision tells me very soon we'll be attacked! I lay back down and went to sleep again. I saw the same vision! I heard my power's voice saying to me, 'My boy, do not worry any more about this war—it will be finished soon. Open your eyes!' I opened them and saw frost-yellowed leaves falling, mingling with withered flowers and grass, and I knew that this will be the end. Those leaves were dead, the flowers dead. Soon we will be attacked for the last time. Our guns will be laid down!"

From inside Looking Glass's shelter came a wrathful voice still dense with sleep. "Shut up out there and let The People rest. Go back to sleep, Wottolen!"

About that time some miles southeast, a man named Owen Hale, a veteran captain in command of three companies of Seventh Cavalry, said suddenly to his lieutenant, "My God! Now I am to be killed this beautiful morning?"

*

At eight-thirty Nelson Miles—the large commander dressed in buck-skin jacket, bow tie, black-striped uniform trousers, pale slouch hat—gave the order to advance. His troopers in their heavy line of battle commenced to trot, and then increased to full gallop—exhilarating to the soldiers and, wrote Miles years afterward, the culmination of their march and "beautiful." On each flank companies of Lakota and Cheyenne warriors stripped for battle, painted, wearing feather war bonnets, raised their war cries.

A Nez Perce scout a mile away saw them coming, rode to the ridge overlooking The People's camp, and waved his blanket: "Enemies right on us!"

Looking Glass called out, "Go slow, don't hurry. Let the children eat their fill. Plenty of time!" But everywhere The People ran to fetch their food and blankets.

Joseph leapt out from his tent and shouted louder than the confused din, "Horses! Horses! Save the horses!" His daughter ran to him; together they ran through the snow with many women and young warriors to the grazing ponies. Now all could hear a rumble, heavy rumbling like thunder coming down from mountains—four hundred troopers riding down the ridge with guerdons snapping, buglers sounding charge as Colonel Miles shouted, "Charge them, damn them!"—four hundred men in streaming capes and greatcoats, each armed with pistol, Springfield carbine or Long Tom rifle, and a hundred bullets gleaming in their ammunition belts and bulging from leather pouches.

The running braves went for their horses or jumped into sink holes and depressions, singling out the charging officers as the blue tide came down the ridge. Now soldiers rode among the canvas scraps of Joseph's Wallowas, troopers sheathing their carbines to draw pistols, shooting down the running boys and women, pulling up and taking aim at old men standing with their bows and arrows—riding down squaws stubborn with old rifles—saddles emptying as warriors fired point blank from shelters in the sunken ground. Now again the voice of Toohoolhoolzote bellowing as if we were a wounded buffalo: "My warriors, take your rifles! Shoot these white men down!"

In front of Joseph's shelter stood his brother Ollokot, carbine raised against his shoulder. Calmly, carefully, he took his aim and fired, again, again, head on at a squad of troopers leveling their pistols; and the third blue soldier flung his arms and pitched back off his saddle in a tumbling jumble of overcoat and cape. The others rode toward the brave chief's face and pulled their triggers, riding past where he had stood—the chief with seven bullets in his chest and face lay dead a few yards from the rough tent where Joseph's Sit Beside Me Wife crouched huddled over two small children and Young Joseph.

When she raised her head and looked through the open flap she cried out, sobbing—then as quickly as she cried she gripped her young son by the shoulders: "Take your sister and your brother out of here! Run behind the soldiers to the mountains!" She pressed them quickly to her breast then sobbed out, "Go!" and cupped her hands over her face. She rose a moment later and seized Joseph's rifle from where it leaned against the short center pole.

Across Snake Creek nearly a hundred of The People streamed across the trampled snow to catch horses. "Daughter!" Joseph cried and lifted Sound of Running Feet up onto a stepping pony. "My daughter, Pitty Pat— ride out of here! Ride north out of here to sitting Bull!"

"Daddy!" she sobbed, leaning down to embrace him.

"Go, my Sunshine!" he gasped, face broken by sobs.

"I love you, Daddy!"

He looked at her, tears streaming, then struck her pony's flank. "I love you, Pitty Pat! Pitty Pat!" The pony ran and the girl hugged its neck.

Cheyenne rode among them now and Joseph saw two women shot through their backs and tumble from their horses. "Great Spirit!" Joseph cried. "Save Sound of Running Feet! Save her! Save my daughter!"

Bullets cut through both of Joseph's sleeves; another tore along the loose back of his woolen shirt. Running sobbing toward the creek, Joseph saw the soldiers fire and gallop on; he saw his oldest son with the two little ones run out from the low ground where their shelter lay.

He splashed across the creek, again felt snatches and stings across his clothing—and then he saw his brother's body lying bloody on its back. He ran to it and lifted it against his chest, and looking up he cried, "Great Spirit, why have you abandoned us?" He held his brother's shattered head against his face.

Behind him Springtime shouted, "Joseph! Joseph!" He turned to look: she stood before the tent flap with his rifle held out. "Take your rifle and fight!" He laid his brother down and stood up, and with no words took the rifle and the leather bag of bullets from her hands. Breathing heavily, with one last look down at Ollokot, Joseph started walking up beside the creek.

Gunpowder smoke hung layered in the air; soldiers rode back past him now, not stopping to fire, shots cracking behind them. Up ahead, Looking Glass stood up and waved his arm at Joseph. "Here! Run here! We are driving them off! Come!" But Joseph turned, and as calmly as his brother had, he carefully took aim at soldiers galloping from all directions.

Smoke drifted everywhere and Joseph couldn't see what strikes he might have made. At his feet an officer lay grimacing, shot twice—through neck and stomach. Joseph went to one knee next to him, the man with wide eyes stared up at him—then gasping, he expired, blood ceasing to stream from his neck. Joseph could not know the man was Captain Owen Hale, who two hours earlier had known that he would die this sunny early winter day. Joseph unbuttoned the white man's greatcoat and turned him out of it. He brought it back and laid it over his brother Ollokot.

*

"Charge them, damn them!" Miles ranged the battlefield ordering his mounted men to spread two wings, enveloping the Indians' camp.

"The Nez Perce stopped our first charge cold," a trooper later wrote.

"I saw a line of covered bodies laid out behind the line," recalled Yellowstone Kelly.

But on the Nez Perce side the losses were as bad among the men, and worse among the women and children.

"In God's name, who are you?" A Nez Perce voice called out in English. "We don't want to fight!"

The women and other noncombatants gathered in a long coulee at the camp of Toohoolhoolzote and dug with knives, pans, and trowel bayonets captured at Big Hole a colony of dugouts, trenches, and traverses, some connected underground by tunnels. Astounded visitors, awed fifty years later, compared the earthen works to the Western Front of the First World War, that brought an old world to dust.

The Army brought a brass Napoleon to Bear's Paw and before the first day ended shelled The People in the coulee—but not the warriors, all in rifle pits between the noncombatants and the soldiers—one shell burying six people in a bursting avalanche of soil. A girl of twelve years, Atsipeeten, and her grandmother, named Intetah, were killed outright; three women and a boy were saved from suffocation by the frantic digging of relatives. But underneath the loamy sod, the bones of Intetah and Atsipeeten remain. At Verdun today a visitor can see a dozen bayonets protruding from the earth where twelve young men stood ready in a deep trench when a German shell exploded, caving their apocalypse upon them like a lid.

A scout for Colonel Miles helped nurse the wounded soldiers. "Fourteen men killed and thirty wounded, horses shot and crippled everywhere. Men dug one long trench and placed the dead in side by side and shoveled back the dirt. Some of the men were literally shot to pieces, but no time was taken for their sakes to clean or fix them up in any way; they laid the bodies in with spurs and everything still just the way they died. An officer who had a service book read words over them and a shot was fired over their graves. I had been anxious to get in the fight, but what I witnessed there, the dead and wounded, took the notion out of me. One cannot realize the feeling that such carnage puts into a person if you haven't been in battle. Warfare is a horrible and gruesome sight."

Lean Elk was shot dead with a bullet through his skull by a brave who thought the lonely chief so far forward must be a Cheyenne or a Lakota. He died among his enemies, as he had lived—but a Nez Perce, and "Poker Joe" no more.

Nelson Miles wrote later that the Nez Perce were the best soldiers and the best marksmen he had ever faced. All day the warriors pinned his soldiers down behind their ditches, ripples, and high ground, although the Nez Perce encampment on the creek lay lower than the land around it on three sides. For years the Army men talked about how when a man lay wounded, these red people didn't scalp or mutilate them—pulled them to their holes and gave them water, food, whatever little help they could. But neither did they attack, for all the Nez Perce ponies had been driven off or captured.

"The only question's time," the Colonel told his captains that evening. The man knew prisoners when he saw them: he had been commandant of the prison where Jefferson Davis had been held after the War. "We've got them. All we have to do is wait for them to realize it. How long depends on blankets, food, and ammunition. Looks like snow again tonight. Keep up the fire."

And snow it did, another several inches, while the wounded in the No Man's Land between the lines lay freezing with no man to help.

*

Six hundred People lay under the sleet and snow without warm food, and warriors stripped for battle in the forward rifle pits lay shivering in agony. "I did not eat for five days," a warrior said. Not many slept, for fear of attack or from the intermittent cracking reports of Miles's Hotchkiss Gun, a miniature Napoleon trained on The People huddled in the gully. No fires in the Nez Perce camp, and none except behind the long line of soldiers, relieved the blowing cold or the intense dark.

Kelly had observed Nez Perce marksmanship that day: he saw a man behind a rock with nimble fingers place a little stone on top—it didn't last ten seconds. Nor had Kelly's Army friend, a corporal, John Haddo, who died the instant that a warrior's bullet blew a tunnel through his heart. Bleeding soldiers lay too close to Indian rifle pits. "Come take our hair," the braves would call, then later belly crawl up to the troopers, take their ammunition, guns, and money, reassure them that they would not be murdered, sometimes leaving water or a handful of smoke-dried buffalo.

*

The best account we have of the Nimiipuu's last days and hours at Bear Paw (also called Bear's Paw) Mountain, was told by Yellow Wolf (also called White Thunder or White Lightning) to a trusted white man named Lucullus Virgil McWhorter bit by bit from 1908 to 1935; that is, thirty to sixty years after the events. As Yellow Wolf spoke very little English, a series of Native American translators rendered the old warrior's sentences to McWhorter. One of the best of these translators, some of whom were inadequately versed in old Nez Perce culture, said of the "hard words" in Nimiipuu, "I will make them nearest I can." Anyone with experience in more than one culture knows that translations cannot be literal; those who have survived the trauma of battle know that "the real war will never get in the books." Through the reflecting and dimming glass of memory, across eras and cultures, through the filters of translators, and by means of the compassionate but human heart of Lucullus Virgil McWhorter, comes an account of the battle still sharp with dismay, a Virgilian sadness perceptible in nearly every phrase. "Tragedy was written in every lineament of his face," wrote McWhorter. It is the death chant of Joseph's People.

Yellow Wolf's account begins with Wounded Head, Husis Owyeen, who had received his painful name at Big Hole. Now this "brave warrior" fell a second time, a bullet creasing his head. Fighting together in the traditional Nez Perce way, Yellow Wolf and his brother Otskai faced the cavalry "on foot until the charging horse soldiers turned and ran." Soldiers were shot from their saddles while "many Indians were killed." A Nez Perce warrior called Grizzly Bear Lying Down spoke in hasty sign language with a Cheyenne chief fighting for the Army: *You must be crazy! You are fighting your friends! We are Indians. We are humans!* Shortly afterwards, Yellow Wolf saw Grizzly killed by soldiers, then saw the Cheyenne catch a woman's bridle and shoot her with his pistol.

Husis Kute, said Yellow Wolf, made a "bad mistake." Seeing four warriors far ahead of the ragged Nez Perce line and assuming them to be Cheyenne and Lakota fighting for the Army, the sharpshooting Husis Kute shot each of them. One of them was Lean Elk. "Four of our best warriors," lamented Yellow Wolf, "killed by friends by mistake!"

The killing went on and on. "Women were dead. Children were dead. Some even then tried to bury their dead. A young warrior wounded lay on a buffalo robe, dying without complaint. Children were crying with the cold. . . Everywhere crying; everywhere the death wail."

In the morning the battle continued. "Wild and stormy, the cold wind blew thick with snow. . . The soldiers' big gun threw bursting shells. The sun rose hidden. I felt the coming end." Then, like the soldier in *All Quiet on the Western Front*, the twenty-one year old warrior thought of another world. "Tipis along the bending river. Blue, clear lake. Wide meadows with horse and cattle herds. Down from the mountain forests, voices seemed to call. I felt that I was dreaming, and not my living self. The noise of shooting deepened and I raised to look around." Yellow Wolf stood up and aimed at the soldiers in fearless abandon. Bullets singed the air around him and shells from the soldiers' cannon burst again and again, striking not the warriors but "The People in the camp."

The soldiers broke off and ate lunch. The Nimiipuu warriors had no food, fighting on empty stomachs throughout the day. "With darkness came a stronger cold and thicker snow . . . We had no warm food that night. Then came the third sun of the battle. Chief Looking Glass was killed. The dark dawn rose and someone saw a mounted Indian. Looking Glass rose up to look, saying 'See! The Sioux of Sitting Bull have come just as I told you!' He always thought that things were better than they were. A shot from a white sharpshooter hit his left forehead, and he fell backward. Chief Looking Glass was dead."

That afternoon the soldiers sent down a white flag, asking to talk to Chief Joseph. He went forward with three warriors and talked, but as they turned back Colonel Miles called to Joseph to wait. "I could see it all from where Otskai and I lay in our rifle pits," said Yellow Wolf. "Miles arrested our chief. It was a trick! Under a flag of truce, they took him. I saw Chief Joseph led to the soldier camp a prisoner. The white flag was a lie!"

Shortly thereafter an officer was captured by the warriors. The Nez Perce "took good care of the prisoner. They gave him water and our best food, plenty of blankets, let him sleep on a buffalo robe; let him walk around." The officer penciled a note to Colonel Miles telling him that he was being treated as if he were at home, and urged Miles to treat Joseph the same way. "But our Chief Joseph was not treated well. No good food. Rolled in two blankets. Before the letter came to Miles, Chief Joseph had been hobbled hands and feet!" Later that day Miles traded Joseph for that officer.

The People's horses had been run off. One of the men suggested to Joseph that everyone who could walk should slip away on foot during the night. "But Joseph said 'No. We will not leave our old, our sick, our wounded. No wounded Indian ever left with soldiers recovered his life!'" Then Chief White Bird said they should attack the soldiers, fight it out to the death. Again Joseph said No. "'If we are killed, we leave our women, old people, and our children to the soldiers." Yellow Wolf said the sky was so darkened that they did not see the sun set. "It grew still colder and it snowed again." Dawn came as it had the days before: "dark, with heavy wind and snow, and children cried again for hunger, damp, and cold." The slow day passed, and Yellow Wolf learned that many of his friends had been killed: Going Alone, Two Moons, Peopeo Tholekt, and others. Word was passed that Toohoolhoolzote, shot the first day of the fighting, had died. And then Tom Hill, a young Nez Perce who had spent time in a white school and spoke English well, heard the soldiers talking. He slipped to Joseph and told him that One Arm General had arrived.

With Howard and his contingent of cavalry were two old Nez Perce who had daughters among The People shivering in the holes. They said Howard wanted to stop the fighting. He and Miles were promising to return The People's horses and let them go back to Lapwai Reservation. Joseph asked the two men, "Do the soldiers think that Sitting Bull is on his way to help us?" The men answered that the white soldiers were afraid of Sitting Bull. "It would be good to quit," Joseph said. "Then we can go back to Idaho. No more killing, no more dead." Chief White Bird objected: "Joseph, you do not know the white men's hearts! Never, never will the Americans keep a promise made to Indians. If you quit this war, I will take my people north on foot!" The remaining chiefs had been gathering around. Joseph asked them what they wanted to do. "Husis Kute said, 'The only air we can breathe is air that white men give us.' I saw Joseph's face. It was brave and full of sorrow. He told Tom Hill, the chiefs, and all of us,

"'*Tell General Howard I know his heart. What he told me I remember. I am tired of fighting. Our chiefs are killed. Looking Glass is dead. Toohoolhoolzote is dead. The old men are all dead. Now it is the young men who say yes or no. But he who led the young men is dead. It is cold and we have no blankets. The little children are freezing to death. Some of my people have run to the hills and have no blankets, no food. No one knows where they are—perhaps freezing to death. I want to have time to look for my children, and see how many I can find. Maybe I shall find them among the dead. Hear me, my chiefs. I am tired. My heart is sick and sad. From where the sun now stands I will fight no more, forever."'*

"The young generation behind us," said Yellow Wolf years later; "for them I tell the story. It is for them! I want the next generation of whites to know and treat the Indians as themselves."

Resuming his narrative, the aging warrior said, "Then Tom Hill and the old men went to talk to the white generals. I left the dugout and went back to the rifle pit where my brother Otskai watched to shoot at Cheyenne scouts and soldiers. I told him, 'Our uncle will surrender to the whites tomorrow.' He said nothing. I said, 'White Bird will take his people north tonight.' My brother said, 'I will not go with White Bird. He and his young fools started this war. But Brother, I will not surrender.' I said, 'Tonight you and I will walk north.'"

*

A little after that a soldier shouted, "We are going to charge you all to hell!" Otskai shouted back, "Charge us, hell, you god damn sons of bitches! You ain't fighting Sioux!" Otskai smiled at Yellow Wolf. "English is a good language for bad talk."

"What language do white people in Canada speak?" asked Yellow Wolf.

"I think all whites speak the same language."

*

That night two hundred thirty-three People departed from the camp with Chief White Bird, among them dead Chief Ollokot's other wife: "We left that night before Chief Joseph gave his gun to General Miles. We walked away from many of our friends. Some were too bad wounded to go. Only forty unwounded men stayed with Joseph, and many women and children. The night grew colder as we walked. It was slow going; we had children along. We took some blankets, but not enough for camping in the snow. It was lonesome, the leaving. Husband dead. Friends buried, or prisoners. I felt that I was leaving all I had, but I did not cry. You know how you feel when you lose friends and kindred through sickness. You do not care if you die. With us it was worse. Strong men, healthy women, little children, killed and buried. They had done no wrong to be so killed. We had only asked to be left in our own homes, the homes of our ancestors. If we surrendered, we would be put in bondage. Our going was with heavy hearts, broken spirits. All lost, we walked silently into the winter night. But we would be free."

White Bird later said he and his people left the last encampment "with women's hearts breaking, children weeping, and men silent, wanderers on the prairie. For what? For white man's greed. The white man wanted what we had, and got it through destruction of our people. We who yesterday were rich are beggars today, made so by orders of a Christian white chief. We have no country, no people, no home. We do not desire longer life, and we pray day and night that the Great Spirit will remove us."

Two months later, in December, Miles wrote: "All these people have been hitherto loyal to the Government and friends of the white race from the time their country was explored, and in their skillful campaigns have spared hundreds of lives and thousands of dollars worth of property that they might have destroyed, and as they have, in my opinion, been grossly wronged in years past, have lost most of their warriors, their homes, property and everything except a small amount of clothing; I have the honor to recommend that ample provision be made for their civilization . . . . They are sufficiently intelligent to appreciate the consideration which in my opinion is just due them from the Government . . . . Chief Joseph is a man of more sagacity and intelligence than any Indian I have ever met."

*

"I envy the good doctor," Trimble said to Sutherland. "He'll be on his way back to his wife when we're through here, and we will go on to the next war, wherever that decides to start. Arizona, maybe. South Dakota. Why not the Philippines?"

"I wouldn't envy him; he's a sick man. He's coughing blood. He'll be dead in two years."

"Everyone's a sick man, Sutherland. That is why there's prayer, and alcohol."

"Yes, and correspondents. Nothing really happens without witnesses."

"You mean, nothing matters without witnesses."

"We witnessed this war. It just happened, that's all. Nothing mattered. Like your war."

"Like my war? I thought it mattered."

"Because we freed the slaves?"

"Because we fought. When fight is all you can do, it matters."

*

Morning came, a dusty glow rising over the Bear Paws, cold light spreading down across the rumpled prairie coulees where bodies clothed in wool and buckskin lay half-covered with snow. Families huddled close in dugouts; soldiers shivered in greatcoats; and Joseph rose, standing in his sunken shelter, the boy Tom Hill beside him raising a white flag, a washing towel of Springtime's, Joseph's Sit Beside Me Wife. The tall man held his rifle in both hands for the last time, and walked up and forward toward the soldier line.

The boy beside him tried to match his plodding strides, hurrying more than he wanted to. Three soldiers rose ahead of them, one lifting a white flag, one in high boots pointing with gloved hand, motioning the Nez Perce chief to walk down behind the row of rifle pits and ready soldiers. Some thirty officers and men stood or sat in camp chairs around cook fires where orderlies hung coffee pots and stirred cast iron skillets full of corn and bacon mush. Joseph knew the bearded, one-armed man, and Colonel Miles, who sat beside him looking steadily at the two Nez Perce.

Tom Hill said quietly, "The One Arm General has an honest-looking face."

Joseph said, "Look twice at a two-faced man."

Then Thunder in the Mountains walked to the two white men and held his rifle forward. Without standing, Howard reached up for the gun. But Joseph pulled it back. "I do not give my rifle to you, General Howard. It was not your soldiers who defeated us. You followed us like a frightened squaw. At any time I could have whipped you with a hundred men. I give my gun to Miles." He held it out and Miles reached up to take it with both hands.

*

The terms of surrender were the terms that Miles and Howard learned from U. S. Grant during the Civil War: unconditional—but with the understanding given Joseph by both commanding officers that all the Nez Perce people would be taken back to Idaho, to the reservation according to Howard's original orders and intent. Though not free to leave their narrow boundaries, nor free to hunt buffalo across the mountains or to go along the rivers in Spring to fish for salmon, The People would be home, among the forests, streams, and hills they knew—to mourn like caged birds. Such was Howard's promise and intent; such were Miles's; and Joseph knew both men's hearts, and so surrendered in faith and confidence.

But General Sherman felt himself impaired by Howard's promises, no sooner reading them by telegraph than countermanding them. His order was "to send the Nez Perces where they will never disturb the people of Oregon or Idaho again." They would be transported two thousand miles south to Oklahoma Territory—hot as an inferno to The People of Oregon and Idaho, barren and malarially humid in some places. More than two hundred surrendered survivors would die during several years in The Hot Place, among them old *Halahtookit*, son of William Clark, whose name rendered in English reads like an image of his People: Daytime Smoke.

When the families, having been marched by the Seventh Cavalry to a railhead, saw the boxcars waiting, wails of helpless grief rose from The People, their cries riding the high plains wind like ashes. On their way, The People would be de-trained at Bismarck, North Dakota, marched to camp, and surrounded by a cordon of troops.

All across the nation, newspapers had been printing stories by Sutherland and others. On that day when the Nez Perce were brought in, the citizens of Bismarck went out to their camp by ones and twos, dozens, then by the score and hundred, bearing baskets full of cooked food—halves of ham, pots of beef, baked and roasted chicken, bread, vegetables, fruit, biscuits, pies, and cakes: mothers, waitresses, fathers with their children—beating back troops lined shoulder to shoulder, distributing the endless loaves and fishes of their hearts to hungry, wondering Nez Perce families. The officers said nothing until all the food was given out.

Ten thousand people, it was said, came to see Chief Joseph before his People were entrained again. Six children died in boxcars on that leg of exile on the way to Leavenworth, the fort in Kansas where The People camped through summer, 1878, until arrangements had been made in Oklahoma Territory. Mosquito season took young children and the weakened elderly: cholera, malaria, and yellow fever.

Joseph said, "I cannot tell how much my heart suffered for my people while at Leavenworth. The Great Spirit who rules above seemed to be looking some other way, and did not see what was being done to my people."

From Leavenworth through seven years in Oklahoma Territory, not one child born to a Nez Perce woman survived its infancy. While in exile Joseph and his people, wrote a white man, took on the melancholy that you see on Nez Perce faces in the photographs. The cries of Joseph's people reached the ears of General Howard, who at his expense brought Joseph east to Washington by train to tell the U. S. Congress of their sorrow and to plead for the survivors, that they be released and sent back to the Northwest.

The grieving chief whose people lay in narrow graves from Montana and Idaho to Oklahoma spoke a plea for people everywhere, a creed for the free and a lament of the oppressed:

I have heard talk and talk but nothing is done. Good words do not last unless they amount to something. Words do not pay for my dead people. Words to not protect my father's grave. Good words will not give me back my children. Good words will not give my people good health and stop their dying. Good words will not get my people a home. Some of you think we are like wild animals. We only ask to be recognized as men and women. We only ask an even chance to live as others live, and to be treated as you want to be treated yourselves. We ask that the same law shall work alike on all people. Let me be free—free to travel, free to stop, free to work, free to trade where I choose, free to choose my own teachers, free to follow the religion of my fathers, free to think and talk and act for myself. When you treat us as you would treat yourselves, we shall be all alike, children of one father and one mother, with one sky over us, one land around us, one government for all. Then the Great Spirit who rules above will smile upon this land, and send rain to wash away the blood stains made by brothers' hands upon the face of earth. I hope that no more groans of wounded men and women rise to the ear of the Great Spirit. I hope that all people will be one people.

While Joseph was in Oklahoma, Sound of Running Feet and many others returned to Idaho. The daughter of the chief was not permitted to go south to join her father and the exiles, but someone brought a photograph of the young woman to *Hinmatooyalahtqit*. He never knew that while he was in *Eeikish Pah*, the Hot Place, his Sound of Running Feet among the captives up in Idaho, sickened, and turned her face toward the Ghost Road. No one brought word or those who knew kept silent, and the lonely chief through all his sad drawn days, through all the long seasons of the years whose snows made white the braided hair of Joseph, Thunder in the Mountains—never knew that the Sunshine of his life was gone. They let The People go, but not their chief: Joseph was sent to Colville Reservation, State of Washington, a semi-arid stretch of colorless low hills and bare winds. One hundred eighteen People chose to leave, but all the rest, a hundred forty-nine, stayed with their chief. From May until December, 1885, eight years after the war, the remnant camped at Fort Spokane, waiting again, waiting this time to be marched off to the little town of Nespelem and the reservation, to become "but words in some poor child of Longfellow's pen."

The *Spokane Evening Review* wrote, "The government has done a cruel and unwise thing," to whites of Washington by bringing in these Indians. In his years at Colville Reservation, Joseph was The People's Chief, reciting prayers at mealtime, laying hands on the sick, presiding over traditional ceremonies, conducting funerals. He never joined a Christian church, and while he wore the white man's flannel shirt, he always wore the leggings, breech cloth, moccasins, and jewelry of a Nez Perce warrior and chief. The People came to him the way the Israelites sought Moses, asking for his blessings, judgments, consolations. "A stubborn savage," wrote the Colville agent, citing his refusal to live inside a house of brick or clapboard, choosing instead to shelter in a tipi or long lodge, summer and winter.

As the years wore on, Joseph, dignified and grave, sat outside his lodge. In his hands he held tenderly the photograph of Sound of Running Feet. Kapkap Ponmi, my Sunshine, my light of the dawning sun, the peace of the resting snow. . .

> *Spirit, give the dying man a dream, the eagle flight*
> *of a dream higher than thunder rising to mountain heights,*
> *a dream more sacred than land where fathers died, a dream of freedom*
> *and of love as happy as the sound of running feet*
> *and sacred as snow resting,*
> *a dream of the promised land beyond the Ghost Road,*
> *a dream from the Great Spirit's own heart,*
> *that the dying man may awake to find it true—*
> *Hinmatooyalahtqit, and all The People.*

On the first day of autumn in the year 1904, the last great chief of the Nez Perce people, the man called Joseph, *Hinmatooyalahtqit*, Thunder Rising to Greater Mountain Heights, closed his eyes. The agency's physician wrote, "Today Chief Joseph died of a broken heart."

> *Looking Glass is dead.*
> *Toohoolhoolzote is dead.*
> *All the old men are dead.*
> *The little children are freezing to death.*
> *Some of my people have run away to the hills, and have no blankets, no food.*
> *No one knows where they are.*
> *Maybe I shall find them among the dead.*
> *Hear me, my chiefs.*
> *I am tired.*
> *My heart is sick and sad.*
> *I want to have time to look for my children.*

*

The young interpreter Tom Hill was ordered to go out on the plains among the Sioux and round up all the Nez Perce who had escaped. "I obeyed the order and left for good," he wrote. Years later he returned to Lapwai and asked for baptism. His heart was changed, he said; he wished to be at peace with all people.

When Yellow Wolf left Canada, the government of the United States gave him a choice. The Nez Perce interpreter phrased it this way to the erstwhile warrior: "Where do you want to go? Lapwai and be Christian, or Colville and just be yourself?"

*

A fenced-in plot of high plains desert in Washington on Colville Reservation contains the graves of Joseph, Yellow Wolf, and others of The People who stayed, and their descendants.

The day before he died, the old man Yellow Wolf said, "I am going in the morning, when the new sun pauses on horizon's edge. I will leave you then, my children, son and daughters. You were lent to me by Ahkunkenekoo, our God. You are my brothers and my sisters. I will go with the new sun." In the morning, though he could not see it, when the sun emerged on the long horizon Yellow Wolf said, "I am going now! My old friends have come for me! There stand Going Alone, Red Spy, Otskai! Warriors, mothers, fathers, children. My friends! My People! Do you not see them?"

So died the chief who would not call himself a chief,
The young man grown old with memory of the Long-Travel War,
Whose Wayakin *foretold the deaths of his People—*
His bones with Joseph, Dreamer with the broken heart.
So died White Necklace, Looking Glass, and Sound of Running Feet;
So died The People's laughter and The People's dreams
Beneath the shadow that a dark-winged future cast;
So died a past that has not ever passed.

Still stand the Bitterroot Mountains, but far away from their shadow,
Side by side in their narrow graves, The People are sleeping.
Inside the chain link fence of the little Nez Perce graveyard
In the high northern desert they lie, unknown and unnoticed.
Daily the traffic still passes—American life and its shadow—
Millions on millions in cities with concrete canyons and proud tower mountains,
Far from the valley of the shadowy pines and the swift salmon streams.
Still flows the Bitterroot River, but far away from its current
The children of Joseph are buried with the man who once loved them.
Descendants still walk the high desert, and memory haunts the still moon.
Does the Ghost Road high above them—the changeless and far-blinking stars—
Still lead to the Beautiful Place, and the meadows of the broken of heart?